Turn to the back for a preview
of Ruth Ware's third novel

THE LYING GAME

Available now.

THE
WOMAN
IN
CABIN
10

RUTH WARE

PUBLISHED BY SIMON & SCHUSTER
New York   London   Toronto   Sydney   New Delhi

SIMON &
SCHUSTER
CANADA

Simon & Schuster Canada
A Division of Simon & Schuster, Inc.
166 King Street East, Suite 300
Toronto, Ontario M5A 1J3

This Simon & Schuster Canada edition May 2018

SIMON & SCHUSTER CANADA and colophon are trademarks of Simon & Schuster, Inc.

For information about special discounts for bulk purchases, please contact Simon & Schuster Special Sales at 1-800-268-3216 or CustomerService@simonandschuster.ca.

Interior design by Jaime Putorti

Manufactured in the United States of America

10 9 8 7 6 5 4 3 2 1

Library and Archives Canada Cataloguing in Publication

Ware, Ruth, author
    The woman in cabin 10 / Ruth Ware. — New edition.
Previously published: 2017.
ISBN 978-1-5011-5178-1 (softcover)
    I. Title. II. Title: Woman in cabin ten.
PS6123.A745W66 2018   823'.92   C2017-906238-7

ISBN 978-1-5011-5178-1
ISBN 978-1-5011-5177-4 (pbk)
ISBN 978-1-5011-5179-8 (ebook)

To Eleanor, with love

In my dream, the girl was drifting, far, far below the crashing waves and the cries of the gulls in the cold, sunless depths of the North Sea. Her laughing eyes were white and bloated with salt water; her pale skin was wrinkled; her clothes ripped by jagged rocks and disintegrating into rags.

Only her long black hair remained, floating through the water like fronds of dark seaweed, tangling in shells and fishing nets, washing up on the shore in hanks like frayed rope, where it lay, limp, the roar of the crashing waves against the shingle filling my ears.

I woke, heavy with dread. It took me a while to remember where I was, and still longer to realize that the roar in my ears was not part of the dream but real.

The room was dark, with the same damp mist I'd felt in my dream, and as I pulled myself to sitting I felt a cool breeze on my cheek. It sounded like the noise was coming from the bathroom.

I climbed off the bed, shivering slightly. The door was shut, but as I walked across to it, I could hear the roar building, the pitch of my heart rising alongside. Taking my courage in both hands, I flung open the door. The noise of the shower filled the small room as I groped for the switch. Light flooded the bathroom—and that's when I saw it.

Written across the steamy mirror, in letters maybe six inches high, were the words STOP DIGGING.

PART ONE

- CHAPTER 1 -

The first inkling that something was wrong was waking in darkness to find the cat pawing at my face. I must have forgotten to shut the kitchen door last night. Punishment for coming home drunk.

"Go away," I groaned. Delilah mewed and butted me with her head. I tried to bury my face in the pillow but she continued rubbing herself against my ear, and eventually I rolled over and heartlessly pushed her off the bed.

She thumped to the floor with an indignant little *meep* and I pulled the duvet over my head, but even through the covers I could hear her scratching at the bottom of the door, rattling it in its frame.

The door was closed.

I sat up, my heart suddenly thumping, and Delilah leaped onto my bed with a glad little chirrup, but I snatched her to my chest, stilling her movements, listening.

I might well have forgotten to shut the kitchen door, or I could even have knocked it to without closing it properly. But my bedroom door opened outward—a quirk of the weird layout of my flat. There was no way Delilah could have shut herself inside. *Someone* must have closed it.

I sat, frozen, holding Delilah's warm, panting body against my chest and trying to listen.

Nothing.

And then, with a gush of relief, it occurred to me—she'd probably been hiding under my bed and I'd shut her inside with me when I came home. I didn't remember closing my bedroom door, but I might have swung it absently shut behind me when I came in. To be honest, everything from the tube station onwards was a bit of a blur. The headache had started to set in on the journey home, and now that my panic was wearing off, I could feel it starting up again in the base of my skull. I *really* needed to stop drinking midweek. It had been okay in my twenties, but I just couldn't shake off the hangovers like I used to.

Delilah began squirming uneasily in my arms, digging her claws into my forearm, and I let her go while I reached for my dressing gown and belted it around myself. Then I scooped her up, ready to sling her out into the kitchen.

But when I opened the bedroom door, there was a man standing there.

There's no point in wondering what he looked like, because, believe me, I went over it about twenty-five times with the police. "Not even a bit of skin around his wrists?" they kept saying. No, no, and no. He had a hoodie on, and a bandanna around his nose and mouth, and everything else was in shadow. Except for his hands.

On these he was wearing latex gloves. It was that detail that scared the shit out of me. Those gloves said, "I know what I'm doing." They said, "I've come prepared." They said, "I might be after more than your money."

We stood there for a long second, facing each other, his shining eyes locked on to mine.

About a thousand thoughts raced through my mind: Where the hell is my phone? Why did I drink so much last night? I would have heard him come in if I'd been sober. Oh Christ, I wish Judah was here.

And most of all—those gloves. Oh my God, those gloves. They were so professional. So *clinical.*

I didn't speak. I didn't move. I just stood there, my ratty dressing gown gaping, and I shook. Delilah wriggled out of my unresisting hands and shot away up the hallway to the kitchen, and I just stood there, shaking.

Please, I thought. Please don't hurt me.

Oh God, where was my phone?

Then I saw something in the man's hands. My handbag—my new Burberry handbag, although that detail seemed monumentally unimportant. There was only one thing that mattered about that bag. My mobile was inside.

His eyes crinkled in a way that made me think he might be smiling beneath the bandanna, and I felt the blood drain from my head and my fingers, pooling in the core of my body, ready to fight or flee, whichever it had to be.

He took a step forwards.

"No . . ." I said. I wanted it to sound like a command, but it came out like a plea—my voice small and squeaky and quavering pathetically with fear. "N—"

But I didn't even get to finish. He slammed the bedroom door in my face, hitting my cheek.

For a long moment I stood, frozen, holding my hand to my face, speechless with the shock and pain. My fingers felt ice-cold, but there was something warm and wet on my face, and it took a moment for me to realize it was blood, that the molding on the door had cut my cheek.

I wanted to run back to bed, to shove my head under the pillows and cry and cry. But a small, ugly voice in my skull kept saying, *He's still out there. What if he comes back? What if he comes back for you?*

There was a sound from out in the hall, something falling, and I felt a rush of fear that should have galvanized me but instead paralyzed me. *Don't come back. Don't come back.* I realized I was holding my breath, and I made myself exhale, long and shuddering, and then slowly, slowly, I forced my hand out towards the door.

There was another crash in the hallway outside, breaking glass, and with a rush I grabbed the knob and braced myself, my bare toes dug into the old, gappy floorboards, ready to hold the door closed as long as I could. I crouched there, against the door, hunched over with my knees to my chest, and I tried to muffle my sobs with my dressing gown while I listened to him ransacking the flat and hoped to God that Delilah had run out into the garden, out of harm's way.

At last, after a long time, I heard the front door open and shut, and I sat there, crying into my knees and unable to believe he'd really gone. That he wasn't coming back to hurt me. My hands felt numb and painfully stiff, but I didn't dare let go of the handle.

I saw again those strong hands in the pale latex gloves.

I don't know what would have happened next. Maybe I would have stayed there all night, unable to move. But then I heard Delilah outside, mewing and scratching at the other side of the door.

"Delilah," I said hoarsely. My voice was trembling so much I hardly sounded like myself. "Oh, Delilah."

Through the door I heard her purr, the familiar, deep, chainsaw rasp, and it was like a spell had been broken.

I let my cramped fingers loosen from the doorknob, flexing them painfully, and then stood up, trying to steady my trembling legs, and turned the door handle.

It turned. In fact it turned too easily, twisting without resistance under my hand, without moving the latch an inch. He'd removed the spindle from the other side.

Fuck.

Fuck, fuck, fuck.

I was trapped.

- CHAPTER 2 -

It took me two hours to prize my way out of my bedroom. I didn't have a landline, so I had no way of calling for help, and the window was covered by security bars. I broke my best nail file, hammering away at the latch, but at last I got the door open and I ventured out into the narrow hallway. There are only four rooms in my flat—kitchen, living room, bedroom, and tiny bathroom—and you can pretty much see the full extent of it from outside my bedroom, but I couldn't stop myself from peering into each doorway, even checking the cupboard in the hallway where I keep my hoover. Making sure he was really gone.

My head was pounding and my hands were shaking as I made my way outside and up the steps to my neighbor's front door, and I found myself looking over my shoulder into the dark street as I waited for her to answer. It was around four a.m., I guessed, and it took a long time and a lot of banging to wake her up. I heard grumbling, over the sound of Mrs. Johnson's feet clumping down her stairs, and her face when she cracked open the door was a mixture of bleary confusion and fright, but when she saw me huddled on the doorstep in my dressing gown, with blood on my face and on my hands, her expression changed in an instant and she took off the chain.

"Oh my days! Whatever's happened?"

"I got burgled." It was hard to talk. I don't know if it was the chilly autumn air, or the shock, but I had started shivering convulsively and my teeth chattered so hard I had a momentary horrible image of them shattering in my head. I pushed the thought away.

"You're bleedin'!" Her face was full of distress. "Oh, bless my soul, come in, come in!"

She led the way into the paisley-carpeted entrance to her maisonette, which was small and dark and grimly overheated, but right now felt like a sanctuary.

"Sit down, sit down." She pointed to a red plush sofa and then went creakily to her knees and began to fiddle with the gas fire. The gas popped and flared, and I felt the heat rise a degree as she got painfully to her feet again. "I'll make you some hot tea."

"I'm fine, honestly, Mrs. Johnson. Do you think—"

But she was shaking her head sternly.

"There's nothin' to beat hot sweet tea when you've had a shock."

So I sat, my shaky hands clasped around my knees, while she rattled around in the tiny kitchen and then came back with two mugs on a tray. I reached out for the closest and took a sip, wincing at the heat against the cut on my hand. It was so sweet I could barely taste the dissolving blood in my mouth, which I supposed was a blessing.

Mrs. Johnson didn't drink but just watched me, her forehead wrinkled in distress.

"Did he . . ." Her voice faltered. "Did he *hurt* you?"

I knew what she meant. I shook my head, but I

took another scalding sip before I could trust myself to speak.

"No. He didn't touch me. He slammed a door in my face—that's the cut on my cheek. And then I cut my hand trying to get out of the bedroom. He'd locked me in."

I had a jolting flash of myself battering at the lock with a nail file and a pair of scissors. Judah was always teasing about using the proper tools for the job—you know, not undoing a screw with the tip of a dinner knife, or prizing off a bike tire using a garden trowel. Only last weekend he'd laughed at my attempt to fix my showerhead with duct tape, and spent a whole afternoon painstakingly mending it with epoxy resin. He was away in Ukraine and I couldn't think about him right now. If I did, I'd cry, and if I cried now, I might never stop.

"Oh, you poor love."

I swallowed.

"Mrs. Johnson, thank you for the tea—but I really came to ask, can I use your phone? He took my mobile, so I've got no way of calling the police."

"Of course, of course. Drink your tea, and then it's over there." She indicated a doily-covered side table, with what was probably the last turn-dial phone in London outside an Islington vintage-retro boutique. Obediently I finished my tea and then I picked up the phone. For a moment my finger hovered over the nine, but then I sighed. He was gone. What could they reasonably do now? It was no longer an emergency, after all.

Instead, I dialed 101 for nonemergency response and waited to be put through.

And I sat and thought about the insurance I didn't have, and the reinforced lock I hadn't installed, and the mess tonight had become.

I was still thinking about that, hours later, as I watched the emergency locksmith replace the crappy bolt-on latch of my front door with a proper deadlock, and listened to his lecture on home security and the joke that was my back door.

"That panel's nuffing but MDF, love. It'd take one kick to bash it in. Want me to show you?"

"No," I said hastily. "No, thanks. I'll get it fixed. You don't do doors, do you?"

"Nah, but I got a mate who does. I'll give you his number before I go. Meantime, you get your hubby to whack a good piece of eighteen-mil plywood over that panel. You don't want a repeat of last night."

"No," I agreed. Understatement of the century.

"Mate in the police says a quarter of all burglaries are repeats. Same guys come back for more."

"Great," I said thinly. Just what I needed to hear.

"Eighteen-mil. Want me to write it down for your husband?"

"No, thanks. I'm not married." And even in spite of my ovaries, I *can* remember a simple two-digit number.

"Aaaah, right, gotcha. Well, there you go, then," he said, as if that proved something. "This doorframe ain't nothing to write home about, neither. You want one of them London bars to reinforce it. Otherwise you can have the best lock in the business, but if they kick it out the frame you're back in the same place as before. I got one in the van that might fit. Do you know them things I'm talking about?"

"I know what they are," I said wearily. "A piece of metal that goes over the lock, right?" I suspected he was milking me for all the business he could get, but I didn't care at this point.

"Tell you what"—he stood up, shoving his chisel in his back pocket—"I'll do the London bar, and I'll chuck in a piece of ply over the back door for free. I got a bit in the van about the right size. Chin up, love. He ain't getting back in *this* way, at any rate."

For some reason the words weren't reassuring.

After he'd gone, I made myself a tea and paced the flat. I felt like Delilah after a tomcat broke in through the cat flap and pissed in the hallway—she had prowled every room for hours, rubbing herself up against bits of furniture, peeing into corners, reclaiming her space.

I didn't go as far as peeing on the bed, but I felt the same sense of space invaded, a need to reclaim what had been violated. *Violated?* said a sarcastic little voice in my head. *Puh-lease, you drama queen.*

But I did feel violated. My little flat felt ruined—soiled and unsafe. Even describing it to the police had felt like an ordeal—yes, I saw the intruder; no, I can't describe him. What was in the bag? Oh, just, you know, my life: money, mobile phone, driver's license, medication, pretty much everything of use from my mascara right through to my travel card.

The brisk impersonal tone of the police operator's voice still echoed in my head.

"What kind of phone?"

"Nothing valuable," I said wearily. "Just an old iPhone. I can't remember the model, but I can find out."

"Thanks. Anything you can remember in terms of the exact make and serial number might help. And you mentioned medication—what kind, if you don't mind me asking?"

I was instantly on the defensive.

"What's my medical history got to do with this?"

"Nothing." The operator was patient, irritatingly so. "It's just some pills have got a street value."

I knew the anger that flooded through me at his questions was unreasonable—he was only doing his job. But the burglar was the person who'd committed the crime. So why did I feel like I was the one being interrogated?

I was halfway to the living room with my tea when there was a banging at the door—so loud in the silent, echoing flat that I tripped and then froze, half standing, half crouching in the doorway.

I had a horrible jarring flash of a hooded face, of hands in latex gloves.

It was only when the door thudded again that I looked down and realized that my cup of tea was now lying smashed on the hallway tiles and that my feet were soaked in rapidly cooling liquid.

The door banged again.

"Just a minute!" I yelled, suddenly furious and close to tears. "I'm coming! Will you stop banging the bloody door!"

"Sorry, miss," the policeman said when I finally opened the door. "Wasn't sure if you'd heard." And then, seeing the puddle of tea and the smashed shards of my cup: "Crikey, what's been going on here then? Another break-in? Ha-ha!"

It was the afternoon by the time the policeman finished taking his report, and when he left, I opened up my laptop. It had been in the bedroom with me, and it was the only bit of tech the burglar hadn't taken. Aside from my work, which was mostly not backed up, it had all my passwords on it, including— and I cringed as I thought about it—a file helpfully named "Banking stuff." I didn't actually have my pin numbers listed. But pretty much everything else was there.

As the usual deluge of e-mails dropped into my in-box, I caught sight of one headed "Planning on showing up today ;)?" and I realized with a jolt that I'd completely forgotten to contact *Velocity*.

I thought about e-mailing, but in the end, I fetched out the twenty-pound note I kept in the tea caddy for emergency cab money and walked to the dodgy phone shop at the tube station. It took some haggling, but eventually the guy sold me a cheap pay-as-you-go plus SIM card for fifteen pounds and I sat in the café opposite and phoned the assistant features editor, Jenn, who has the desk opposite mine.

I told her what happened, making it sound funnier and more farcical than it really had been. I dwelled heavily on the image of me chipping away at the lock with a nail file and didn't tell her about the gloves, or the general sense of powerless terror, or the horribly vivid flashbacks that kept ambushing me just as I was rummaging for change, or stirring tea, or thinking of something else completely.

"Shit." Her voice at the end of the crackly line was full of horror. "Are you okay?"

"Yeah, more or less. But I won't be in today, I've got to clear up the flat." Although, in actual fact, it wasn't that bad. He'd been commendably neat. For, you know, a criminal.

"God, Lo, you poor thing. Listen, do you want me to get someone else to cover you on this northern lights thing?"

For a minute I had no idea what she was talking about—then I remembered. The *Aurora*. A boutique super-luxury cruise liner traveling around the Norwegian fjords, and somehow, I still wasn't quite sure how, I had been lucky enough to snag one of the handful of press passes on its maiden voyage.

It was a huge perk—in spite of working for a travel magazine, my normal beat was cutting and pasting press releases and finding images for articles sent back from luxury destinations by my boss, Rowan. It was Rowan who had been supposed to go, but unfortunately, after saying yes she had discovered that pregnancy didn't agree with her—hyperemesis, apparently—and the cruise had landed in my lap like a big present, fraught with responsibility and possibilities. It was a vote of confidence from her, giving it to me when there were more senior people she could have buttered up, and I knew if I played my cards right on this trip, it would be a big point in my favor when it came to jockeying for Rowan's maternity cover and maybe—just maybe—getting that promotion she'd been promising for the last few years.

It was also this weekend. Sunday, in fact. I'd be leaving in two days.

"*No*," I said, surprising myself with the firmness in my voice. "No, I definitely don't want to pull out. I'm fine."

"Are you sure? What about your passport?"

"It was in my bedroom; he didn't find it." Thank God.

"Are you *absolutely* sure?" she said again, and I could hear the concern in her voice. "This is a big deal—not just for you, for the mag I mean. If you don't feel up to it, Rowan wouldn't want you—"

"I am up to it," I said, cutting her off. There was no way I was letting this opportunity slip through my fingers. If I did, it might be the last one I had. "I promise. I really want to do this, Jenn."

"Okay . . ." she said, almost reluctantly. "Well, in that case, full steam ahead, eh? They sent through a press pack this morning, so I'll courier that across along with your train tickets. I've got Rowan's notes somewhere; I think the main thing is to do a really nice puff piece on the boat, because she's hoping to get them on board as advertisers, but there should be some interesting people among the other guests, so if you can get anything else done in the way of profiles, so much the better."

"Sure." I grabbed a pen from the counter of the café and began taking notes on a paper napkin. "And remind me what time it leaves?"

"You're catching the ten thirty train from King's Cross—but I'll put it all in the press pack."

"That's fine. And thanks, Jenn."

"No worries," she said. Her voice was a little wist-

ful, and I wondered if she'd been planning to step
into the breach herself. "Take care, Lo. And 'bye."

It was still just about light as I trudged slowly home.
My feet hurt, my cheek ached, and I wanted to go
home and sink into a long, hot bath.

The door of my basement flat was bathed in
shadow as it always was, and I thought once again
that I must get a security light, if only so that I could
see my own keys in my handbag, but even in the
dimness I could see the splintered wood where he'd
forced the lock. The miracle was that I hadn't heard
him. *Well, what do you expect, you were drunk, after
all*, said the nasty little voice in my head.

But the new deadlock felt reassuringly solid as
it clunked back, and inside I locked it shut again,
kicked off my shoes, and walked wearily down the
hall to the bathroom, stifling a yawn as I set the taps
running and slumped onto the toilet to pull off my
tights. Next I began to unbutton my top . . . but then
I stopped.

Normally I leave the bathroom door open—it's
only me and Delilah, and the walls are prone to
damp, being under ground level. I'm also not great
with enclosed spaces, and the room feels very small
when the window blinds are down.

The front door was locked, and the new London
bar was in place, but I still checked the window and
closed and locked the bathroom door before I finished peeling off my clothes. I was tired—God, I was
so tired. I had an image of falling asleep in the tub,
slipping below the water, Judah finding my naked

bloated body a week later . . . I shook myself. I needed
to stop being so bloody dramatic. The tub was barely
four feet long. I had trouble contorting myself so I
could rinse my hair, let alone drown.

The bath was hot enough to make the cut on my
cheek sting, and I shut my eyes and tried to imagine
myself somewhere else, somewhere quite different
from this chilly, claustrophobic little space, far away
from sordid, crime-ridden London. Walking on a
cool Nordic shore, perhaps, in my ears the soothing
sound of the . . . er . . . would it be the Baltic? For a
travel journalist I'm worryingly bad at geography.

But unwanted images kept intruding. The locksmith saying "a quarter of all burglaries are repeats."
Me, cowering in my own bedroom, feet braced
against the floorboards. The sight of strong hands
encased in pale latex, the black hairs just showing
through . . .

Shit. *Shit.*

I opened my eyes, but for once the reality check
didn't help. Instead, I saw the damp bathroom walls
looming over me, shutting me in. . . .

You're losing it again, my internal voice sniped.
You can feel it, can't you?

Shut up. Shut up, shut up, shut up. I squeezed my
eyes closed again and began to count, deliberately,
trying to force the pictures out of my head. *One. Two.
Three. Breathe in. Four. Five. Six. Breathe out. One.
Two. Three. Breathe in. Four. Five. Six. Breathe out.*

At last the pictures receded, but the bath was
spoiled, and the need to get out of the airless little
room was suddenly overwhelming. I got up, wrapped
a towel around myself and another around my hair,

and went into the bedroom, where my laptop was still lying on the bed from earlier.

I opened it, fired up Google, and typed: *What % burglars return.*

A page of links came up and I clicked on one at random and scanned down it until I came to a paragraph that read:

WHEN BURGLARS RETURN . . .

A nationwide survey indicated that, over a twelve-month period, approximately 25 to 50 percent of burglaries are repeat incidents; and between 25 and 35 percent of victims are repeat victims. Figures gathered by UK police forces suggest that 28 to 51 percent of repeat burglaries occur within one month, 11 to 25 percent within a week.

Great. So it seemed like my friendly doom-and-gloom merchant, the locksmith, had actually been *under*stating the problem, not winding me up. Although the maths involved in up to 50 percent repeat offenses but only 35 percent repeat victims made my head hurt. Either way, I didn't relish the idea of being among their number.

I had promised myself I wouldn't drink tonight, so after I had checked the front door, back door, window locks, and front door for the second—or maybe even the third—time, and put the pay-as-you-go phone on to charge beside my bed, I made myself a cup of chamomile tea.

I took it back through to the bedroom with my laptop, the press file for the trip, and a packet of chocolate cookies. It was only eight o'clock and I hadn't had any supper, but I was suddenly exhausted—too exhausted to cook, too exhausted even to phone for takeaway. I opened up the Nordic cruise press pack and huddled down into my duvet, and waited for sleep to claim me.

Except it didn't. I dunked my way through the whole packet of cookies and read page after page of facts and figures on the *Aurora*—just ten luxuriously appointed cabins . . . maximum of twenty passengers at any one time . . . handpicked staff from the world's top hotels and restaurants . . . Even the technical specifications of the boat's draft and tonnage weren't enough to lull me to sleep. I stayed awake, shattered yet somehow, at the same time, wired.

As I lay there in my cocoon I tried not to think about the burglar. I thought, very deliberately, about work, about all the practicalities I had to sort out before Sunday. Pick up my new bank cards. I had to pack and do my research for the trip. Would I see Jude before I left? He'd be trying my old phone.

I put down the press pack and pulled up my e-mails.

"Hi, love," I typed, and then I paused and bit the side of my nail. What to say? No point in telling him about the burglary, not yet. He'd just feel bad about not being here when I needed him. "I've lost my phone," I wrote instead. "Long story, I'll explain when you get back. But if you need me, e-mail, don't text. What's your ETA on Sunday? I'm off to Hull early, for this Nordic thing. Hope we can see each other before I leave—otherwise, see you next week? Lo x"

I pressed send, hoping he didn't wonder what I

was doing up and e-mailing at 12:45 a.m., and then shut down the computer, picked up my book, and tried to read myself to sleep.

It didn't work.

At 3:35 a.m. I staggered through to the kitchen, picked up the bottle of gin, and poured myself the stiffest gin and tonic I could bring myself to drink. I gulped it down like medicine, shuddering at the harsh taste, and then poured a second and drank that, too, more slowly this time. I stood for a moment, feeling the alcohol tingling through my veins, relaxing my muscles, damping down my jangled nerves.

I poured the dregs of the gin into the glass and took it back to the bedroom, where I lay down, stiff and anxious, my eyes on the glowing face of the clock, and waited for the alcohol to take effect.

One. Two. Three. Breathe in. Four. . . . Five. . . . Fi . . .

I don't remember falling asleep, but I must have. One minute I was looking at the clock with bleary, headachy eyes, waiting for it to click over onto 4:44, the next minute I was blinking into Delilah's furry face as she butted her whiskery nose against mine and tried to tell me it was time for breakfast. I groaned. My head ached worse than yesterday— although I wasn't sure if it was my cheek or another hangover. The last gin and tonic was half full on my bedside table, beside the clock. I sniffed it and almost choked. It must have been two-thirds gin. What had I been thinking?

The clock said 6:04 and I calculated that meant I'd had less than an hour and a half's sleep, but I was awake now, no point in trying to fight it. Instead, I got up, pulled back the curtain, and peered into the gray dawn and the thin fingers of sun that trickled into my basement window. The day felt cold and sour, and I shoved my feet into my slippers and shivered as I made my way down the hall to the thermostat, ready to override the automatic timer and start the heating for the day.

It was Saturday, so I didn't have to work, but somehow the work involved in getting my mobile number assigned to a new phone and my bank cards reissued took up most of the day, and by the evening I was drunk with tiredness.

It felt as bad as the time I'd flown back from Thailand via LA—a series of red-eyes that left me wild with sleep deprivation and hopelessly disoriented. Somewhere over the Atlantic, I realized that I had gone beyond sleep, that I might as well give up. Back home, I fell into bed like falling into a well, plunging headlong into oblivion, and I slept for twenty-two hours, coming up groggy and stiff-limbed to find Judah banging at my door with the Sunday papers. But this time, my bed was no longer a refuge.

I *had* to get myself together before I left for this trip. It was an unmissable, unrepeatable opportunity to prove myself after ten years at the coalface of boring cut-and-paste journalism. This was my chance to show I could hack it—that I, like Rowan, could network and schmooze and get *Velocity*'s name in there with the high fliers. And Lord Bullmer, the owner of the *Aurora Borealis*, was a very high flier indeed, from what I'd gathered. Even 1 percent of his advertising budget could keep *Velocity* afloat for months, not to mention all the well-known names in travel and photography who would doubtless have been invited along on this maiden voyage, and whose bylines on our cover would look very nice indeed.

I wasn't about to start hard selling Bullmer over dinner—nothing as crude and commercial as that. But if I could get his number on my contacts list and ensure that when I phoned him up, he took my call . . . well, it would go a long way to finally getting me that promotion.

As I ate supper, mechanically forking frozen pizza into my face until I felt too full to continue, I picked up where I'd left off with the press pack, but the words and pictures swam in front of my eyes, the adjectives blurring into one another: *boutique . . . glittering . . . luxury . . . handcrafted . . . artisan . . .*

I let the page drop with a yawn, then looked at my watch and realized it was past nine. I could go to bed, thank God. As I checked and rechecked the doors and locks, I reflected that the one silver lining to being so shattered was that it couldn't possibly be a repeat of last night.

I was so tired that even if a burglar *did* come, I'd probably sleep right through it.

At 10:47, I realized I was wrong.

At 11:23, I started to cry, weakly and stupidly.

Was this it, then? Was I never going to sleep again?

I had to sleep. I *had* to. I'd had . . . I counted on my fingers, unable to do the maths in my head. What . . . less than four hours of sleep in the last three days.

I could *taste* sleep. I could *feel* it, just out of my reach. I had to sleep. I had to. I was going to go crazy if I didn't sleep.

The tears were coming again—I didn't even know what they were. Tears of frustration? Rage, at myself, at the burglar? Or just exhaustion?

I only knew that I couldn't sleep—that it was dangling like an unkept promise just inches away from me. I felt like I was running towards a mirage that kept receding, slipping away faster and faster the more desperately I ran. Or that it was like a fish in water, something I had to catch and hold, that kept slipping through my fingers.

Oh God, I want to sleep. . . .

Delilah turned her head towards me, startled. Had I really said it aloud? I couldn't even tell anymore. Christ, I was losing it.

A flash of a face—gleaming liquid eyes in the darkness.

I sat up, my heart pounding so hard that I could feel it in the back of my skull.

I had to get away from here.

I got up, stumbling, trancelike with exhaustion, and pushed my feet into my shoes, and my sleeves into my coat, over the top of my pajamas. Then I picked up my bag. If I couldn't sleep, I'd walk. Somewhere. Anywhere. I'd try to exhaust myself into sleeping.

If sleep wouldn't come to me, then I'd damn well hunt it down myself.

- CHAPTER 3 -

The streets at midnight weren't empty, but they weren't the same ones I trod every day on my way to work, either.

Between the sulfur-yellow pools of streetlight, they were gray and shadowed, and a cold wind blew discarded papers against my legs, leaves and rubbish gusting in the gutters. I should have felt afraid—a thirty-two-year-old woman, clearly wearing pajamas, wandering the streets in the small hours. But I felt safer out here than I did in my flat. Out here, someone would hear you cry.

I had no plan, no route beyond walking the streets until I was too tired to stand. Somewhere around Highbury and Islington I realized that it had begun to rain, that it must have started some time back because I was wet through. I stood in my soggy shoes, my exhausted punch-drunk brain trying to formulate a plan, and almost by themselves my feet began to walk again, not homewards, but south, towards Angel.

I didn't realize where I was going until I was there. Until I was standing beneath the porch of his building, frowning dazedly at the bell panel, where his name was written in his own small, neat handwriting. LEWIS.

He wasn't here. He was away in Ukraine, not due back until tomorrow. But I had his spare keys in my coat pocket, and I couldn't face the walk back to my flat. *You could get a cab*, carped the small, snide voice in the back of my head. *It's not the walk you can't face. Coward.*

I shook my head, sending raindrops spattering across the stainless-steel bell panel, and I sorted through the bunch of keys until I found the one for the outside door and slipped inside, into the oppressive warmth of the communal hallway.

Up on the second floor, I let myself cautiously into the flat.

It was completely dark. All the doors were closed, and the entrance hall had no windows.

"Judah?" I called. I was certain he wasn't home, but it wasn't impossible that he'd let a mate crash there, and I didn't want to give anyone a middle-of-the-night heart attack. I knew, all too well, what that felt like. "Jude, it's just me, Lo."

But there was no answer. The flat was silent—completely and utterly silent. I opened the door to the left of me, the door to the eat-in kitchen, and tiptoed inside. I didn't switch on the light. I just peeled off my wet clothes—coat, pajamas, and all—and dumped them in the sink.

Then I walked, naked, through to the bedroom, where Judah's wide double bed lay empty in a shaft of moonlight, the gray sheets tumbled as if he'd just that moment got up. I crawled on my hands and knees into the middle of the bed, feeling the lived-in softness of the sheets, and smelling the scent of him, of sweat and aftershave and just—*him*.

I shut my eyes.

One. Two. . . .

Sleep crashed over me, claiming me like a wave.

I woke to the sound of a woman screaming, and the feeling of someone on top of me, holding me down, someone grappling with my hands even as I fought.

A hand grabbed at my wrist, the grip far stronger than mine. Blind, mad with panic, I groped in the pitch black with my free hand, searching for something, anything, to use as a weapon, and my hand closed over the bedside lamp.

The man's hand was over my mouth now, smothering me, the weight of him choking me, and with all my strength, I lifted up the heavy lamp and brought it crashing down.

There was a shout of pain, and through the fog of terror I heard a voice, the words slurred and broken.

"Lo, it's me. It's me for Christ's sake, stop!"

What?

Oh God.

My hands were shaking so much that when I tried to find the light, all I did was knock something over.

From beside me I could hear Judah, gasping, alongside a bubbling sound that terrified me. Where the hell was the lamp? Then I realized—the lamp was gone. I'd smashed it into Judah's face.

I stumbled out of bed, my legs shaking, and found the switch by the door, and the room was instantly flooded with the unforgivingly bright glare of a dozen halogen spots, each illuminating every detail of the horror show in front of me.

Judah was crouched on the bed, holding his face, with blood soaking his beard and his chest.

"Oh my God, Jude!" I scrambled across to him, my hands still trembling, and began to grab tissues from the box by the bed. He pressed them to his face. "Oh God, what happened? Who was screaming?"

"You!" he groaned. The paper was already sodden and red.

"What?" I was still flooded with adrenaline. I looked confusedly around the room for the woman and the attacker. "What do you mean?"

"I came home," he said painfully, his Brooklyn accent blurred through the paper. "You started screaming, half-asleep. So I tried to wake you up and—this."

"Oh, fuck." I put my hands to my mouth. "I'm so sorry."

That screaming—it had been so real. Was it really just me?

He took his hands cautiously away from his mouth. There was something in the wad of scarlet paper, something small and white. It was only when I looked at his face that I realized—one of his teeth was missing.

"Oh Jesus."

He looked at me, blood still dripping slowly from his mouth and his nose.

"What a welcome home," was all he said.

"I'm sorry." I felt tears prick at the back of my throat but I refused to cry in front of the taxi driver. Instead, I swallowed against the hard ache. "Judah?"

Judah said nothing; he just looked out of the window at the gray dawn that was starting to break over London. It had taken two hours at UCH accident and emergency, and then all they'd done was stitch Judah's lip and refer him to an emergency dentist who shoved the tooth back in place and told him, more or less, to cross his fingers. Apparently the tooth might be saved if it reimplanted. If not, it would be either a bridge or a dental implant. He shut his eyes wearily, and I felt my gut twist with remorse.

"I'm sorry," I said again, more desperately this time. "I don't know what else to say."

"No, I'm sorry," he said wearily. The word came out as *shorry,* like a drunken Sean Connery impression, the local anesthetic in his lip making it hard to talk.

"You? What are you sorry for?"

"I don't know. Fucking up. Not being there for you."

"The burglar, you mean?"

He nodded.

"That. But any time, really. I wish I wasn't away so much."

I leaned across and he put his arm around me. I rested my head on his shoulder and listened to the slow, steady thud of his heart, reassuringly unhurried in comparison to my own panicky drumming pulse. Beneath his jacket he was wearing a blood-spattered T-shirt, the fabric soft and worn beneath my cheek. When I breathed in, a long, shaky breath, it smelled of his sweat, and I felt my pulse slow in time with his.

"You couldn't have done anything," I said into his chest. He shook his head.

"I still should have been there."

It was growing light as we paid off the taxi driver and climbed wearily up the two flights of stairs to his flat, and when I looked at my watch I saw that it was nearly six. Shit. I had to be on a train to Hull in a few hours.

Inside, Judah stripped off his clothes and we fell into bed, skin against skin. He pulled me against him, inhaling the scent of my hair as he closed his eyes. I was so tired I could hardly think straight, but instead of lying back and letting sleep claim me, I found myself climbing on top of him, kissing his throat, his belly, the dark stripe of hair that arrowed to his groin.

"Lo . . ." He groaned, and he tried to pull me up towards him, to kiss me, but I shook my head.

"Don't, your mouth. Just lie back."

He let his head fall back, his throat arching in the pale strip of dawn that penetrated the curtains.

It was eight days since I'd last seen him. Now it would be another week until I saw him again. If we didn't do this now . . .

Afterwards, I lay in his arms, waiting for my breathing and heart to steady, and I felt his cheek against mine crinkle in a smile.

"That's more like it," he said.

"More like what?"

"More like the homecoming I was expecting."

I flinched and he touched my face.

"Lo, honey, it was a joke."

"I know."

We were both quiet for a long time. I thought he was slipping into sleep, and I shut my own eyes and let the tiredness wash over me, but then I felt his chest lift, and the muscles in his arm tense as he took a deep breath.

"Lo, I'm not going to ask again, but . . ."

He didn't finish, but he didn't have to. I could feel what he wanted to say. It was what he'd said on New Year's Eve—he wanted us to move forward. Move in together.

"Let me think about it," I said at last, in a voice that didn't seem to be mine, a voice that was unusually subdued.

"That's what you said months ago."

"I'm still thinking."

"Well, I've made up my mind." He touched my chin, pulling my face gently towards his. What I saw there made my heart flip-flop. I reached out for him, but he caught my hand and held it. "Lo, stop trying to make this go away. I've been really patient, you know I have, but I'm starting to feel like we're not on the same page."

I felt my insides flutter with a familiar panic—something between hope and terror.

"Not on the same page?" My smile felt forced. "Have you been watching *Oprah* again?"

He let go of my hand at that, and something in his face had closed off as he turned away. I bit my lip.

"Jude—"

"No," he said. "Just—no. I wanted to talk about this but you clearly don't, so— Look, I'm tired. It's nearly morning. Let's go to sleep."

"Jude," I said again, pleadingly this time, hating myself for being such a bitch, hating *him* for pushing me into this.

"I said no," he said wearily, into the pillow. I thought he was talking about our conversation, but then he continued. "To a job. Back in New York. I turned it down. For you."

Fuck.

- CHAPTER 4 -

I was sleeping a deep, stupefied sleep, as if I'd been drugged, when the alarm dragged me to consciousness a few hours later.

I didn't know how long it had been going off, but I suspected a long, long time. My head ached, and I lay for a long moment trying to orientate myself before I managed to reach out and silence the clock in case it woke Judah.

I rubbed the sleep out of my eyes and stretched, trying to work the kinks from my neck and shoulders, and then levered myself painfully up to vertical, climbed out of bed, and made my way through to Judah's kitchen. While the coffee percolated, I took my pills, and then hunted in the bathroom for painkillers. I found ibuprofen and paracetamol, as well as something in a brown plastic bottle that I vaguely remembered Judah being prescribed when he twisted his knee in a football match. I opened the childproof lid and inspected the pills inside. They were huge, half-red and half-white, and looked impressive.

In the end I chickened out of taking them, and instead pressed two ibuprofen and a fast-acting paracetamol into my palm from the assorted blister packs on the bathroom shelf. I gulped them down with a cup of coffee—black, there was no milk in the empty fridge—and then sipped the rest of the cup more slowly as I thought about last night, about my stupid actions, about Judah's announcement. . . .

I was surprised. No, more than surprised—I was shocked. We'd never really discussed his plans long-term, but I knew he missed his friends in the US, and his mum and younger brother—neither of whom I'd met. What he'd done . . . had he done it for himself? Or for us?

There was half a cup of coffee left in the jug, and I poured it into a second mug and carried it carefully through to the bedroom.

Judah was lying sprawled across the mattress as if he'd fallen there. People in films always look peaceful in sleep, but Judah didn't. His battered mouth was hidden beneath his upflung arm, but with his angular nose and furrowed brow he looked like an angry hawk, shot down by a gamekeeper midflight and still pissed off about it.

I set the coffee cup very gently on his bedside table and, putting my face close on the pillow next to him, I kissed the back of his neck. It was warm, and surprisingly soft.

He stirred in his sleep, putting out one long tanned arm to loop over my shoulders, and his eyes opened, looking three shades darker than their usual hazel brown.

"Hey," I said softly.

"Hey." He scrunched up his face and yawned, and then pulled me down beside him. For a moment I resisted, thinking of the boat and the train and the car waiting for me at Hull. Then my limbs seemed to melt like plastic and I let myself fold into him, into his warmth. We lay there staring into each other's eyes, and I reached out and tentatively touched the Steri-Strip across his lip.

"Think it'll re-root?"

"I don't know," he said. "I hope so, I've got to go to Moscow tomorrow, and I don't want to be messing around with dentists while I'm out there."

I said nothing. He closed his eyes and stretched, and I heard his joints click as he did. Then he rolled onto his side and put his cupped hand gently over my bare breast.

"Judah . . ." I said. I could hear the mix of exasperation and longing in my voice.

"What?"

"I can't. I've got to go."

"So go."

"Don't. Stop that."

"Don't, stop? Or don't stop?" He gave a slow lopsided smile.

"Both. You know which one I mean." I pulled myself upright and shook my head. It hurt, and I regretted the movement instantly.

"Your cheek okay?" Judah asked.

"Yeah." I put a hand up to it. It was swollen, but not as much as before.

His face was troubled, and he put out a finger to stroke the bruise, but I flinched away in spite of myself.

"I should have been there," he said.

"Well, you weren't," I said snappishly, more snappishly than I'd meant to. "You never are."

He blinked and pulled himself up on his elbows to look at me, his face still soft with sleep, crumpled with marks from his pillow.

"What the . . . ?"

"You heard me." I knew I was being unreasonable, but the words came tumbling out. "What's the future, Jude? Even if I move in here—what's the plan? Do I sit here weaving my shroud like Penelope and keeping the home fires burning while you drink Scotch in some bar in Russia with the other foreign correspondents?"

"Where'd this come from?"

I just shook my head and swung my legs out of bed. I began pulling on the pile of spare clothes I'd left on the floor after the trip to A&E.

"I'm just tired, Jude." *Tired* was an understatement. I hadn't slept longer than two hours in the last three nights. "And I can't see where this is heading. It's hard enough now when it's just the two of us. I don't want to be your wife-in-every-port stuck at home with a kid and a raging case of postnatal depression while you're getting shot at in every hellhole this side of the equator."

"Recent events kind of imply I'm in more danger in my own apartment," Judah said, and then winced as he saw my face. "Sorry, that was an asshole thing to say. It was an accident, I know that."

I swung my still-damp coat round my shoulders and picked up my bag.

"'Bye, Judah."

"'Bye? What do you mean, 'bye?"

"Whatever you want."

"What I *want* is for you to stop acting like a goddamn drama queen and move into my flat. I love you, Lo!"

The words hit me like a slap. I stopped in the doorway, feeling the weight of my tiredness like something physical around my neck, pulling me down.

Hands in pale latex, the sound of a laugh . . .

"Lo?" Judah said uncertainly.

"I can't do this," I said, my face to the hallway. I was not sure what I was talking about—I can't leave; I can't stay; I can't have this conversation, this life, this everything. "I just— I have to go."

"So that job," he said, the beginnings of anger in his voice. "The one I turned down. Are you saying I was wrong?"

"I never asked you to do that," I said. My voice was shaking. "I never asked you. So don't you put that on me." I hoisted my bag up onto my shoulder and turned to the door.

He didn't say anything. He didn't try to stop me. I walked out of the flat reeling like I was half-drunk. It was only when I got on the tube that the reality of what had just happened hit me.

- CHAPTER 5 -

I love ports. I love the smell of tar and sea air, and the scream of the gulls. Maybe it's years of taking the ferry to France for summer holidays, but a harbor gives me a feeling of freedom in a way that an airport never does. Airports say *work* and *security checks* and *delays*. Ports say . . . I don't know. Something completely different. *Escape*, maybe.

I had spent the train journey avoiding thoughts of Judah and trying to distract myself with research on the trip ahead. Richard Bullmer was only a few years older than me, but his CV was enough to make me feel hopelessly inadequate—a list of businesses and directorships that made my eyes water, each a stepping-stone to an even higher level of money and influence.

When I brought up *Wikipedia* on my phone, it showed a bronzed, handsome man with very black hair, arm in arm with a stunningly beautiful blonde in her late twenties. *Richard Bullmer with his wife, the heiress Anne Lyngstad, at their wedding in Stavanger,* read the caption.

Given his title, I'd assumed that his wealth had been handed to him on a plate, but it looked, from *Wikipedia* at least, as if I'd been unfair. The early part of the picture was cushy enough—prep school, Eton and Balliol. However, in his first year at university his father had died—his mother seemed already to be out of the picture, it wasn't entirely clear—and the family estate had been swallowed up in death duty and debts, leaving him, at nineteen years of age, homeless and alone.

Under those circumstances, the fact that he got through Oxford with a degree would have been achievement enough, but he had also created a dot-com start-up in his third year. Its stock market flotation in 2003 was the first in his string of successes, culminating with this boutique ten-cabin cruise liner conceived as a super-luxury retreat for hopping the Scandinavian coastline.

Available for the wedding of your dreams, a dazzling corporate event to woo your clients with the "wow" factor, or simply for an exclusive holiday you and your family will never forget, I read from the press pack as the train hurtled north, before turning to a floor plan of the cabin deck. There were four large suites in the nose of the boat—the prow, I supposed you'd call it, and a separate section with six smaller cabins arranged in a horseshoe shape at the back. Each cabin was numbered, odd and even on either side of a central corridor, with cabin 1 right in the tip of the prow, and cabins 9 and 10 adjoining each other in the curved stern of the boat. I guessed I'd be in one of the smaller cabins—presumably the suites were reserved for VIPs. There were no measurements on the floor plan and I frowned, remembering some of the cross-channel ferries I'd been on, the claustrophobic, windowless little rooms. The thought of spending five days in one of those wasn't a comfortable one, but surely on a boat like this, we'd be talking something considerably more spacious?

I turned the page again, hoping to find a photo of one of the cabins to reassure myself, but instead I was confronted with a shot of a dazzling array of Scandinavian delicacies spread out on a white cloth. The chef on the *Aurora* had trained at Noma and elBulli, apparently. I yawned and pressed my hands into my eyes, feeling the grit of tiredness and the weight of everything from last night pressing down on me once again.

Judah's face as I'd left him, stitched up with the blow from the night before, came into my head and I flinched. I wasn't even sure what had happened. Had Judah and I broken up? Had I dumped him? Every time I tried to reconstruct the conversation, my exhausted brain took over, adding in stuff I hadn't said, the responses I wished I'd made, making Judah more clueless and more insulting, to justify my own position, or alternatively more unconditionally loving, to try to convince myself this was all going to be okay. I hadn't *asked* him to turn down the job. So why was I suddenly expected to be grateful for it?

I dozed off for about thirty painful minutes in the car from the station to the port, and when the car driver's cheerful announcement broke into my sleep it was like a splash of cold water to the face. I stumbled out of the car into the searing sunshine and the salt-sting of the breeze, feeling bleary and dazed.

The driver had dropped me off almost at the end

of the gangway, but as I looked across the steel bridge to the boat, I couldn't quite believe we were in the right place. The pictures from the brochure were familiar—huge glass windows reflecting the sun without a single fingerprint or speck of salt water, and gleaming white paint so fresh that it could have been finished that morning. But what had been missing from the brochure photos was a sense of scale. The *Aurora* was so *small*—more like a large yacht than a small cruise liner. *Boutique* had been the phrase in the press pack—and now I saw what they meant. I'd seen bigger boats hopping around the Greek islands. It seemed impossible that everything mentioned in the brochure—library, sunroom, spa, sauna, cocktail lounge, and all the other things apparently indispensable to the *Aurora*'s pampered passengers—could fit into this miniature vessel. Its size, along with the perfection of its paintwork, gave it a curiously toylike quality, and as I stepped onto the narrow steel gangway I had a sudden disorienting image of the *Aurora* as a ship imprisoned in a bottle—tiny, perfect, isolated, and unreal—and of myself, shrinking down to match it with every step I took towards the boat. It was a strange feeling, as if I were looking down the wrong end of a telescope, and it gave me a dizzying sensation almost like vertigo.

The gangway shifted beneath my feet, the oily, inky waters of the harbor swirling and sucking beneath, and I had a momentary illusion that I was falling, the steel beneath my feet giving way. I shut my eyes and gripped the cold metal rail.

Then I heard a woman's voice from up ahead.

"It's a wonderful smell, isn't it!"

I blinked. A stewardess was standing in the entrance to the ship. She was bright, almost white blond, with tanned walnut-brown skin, and beaming as if I were her rich, long-lost relative from Australia. I took a breath, trying to steady myself, and then made my way across the rest of the gangway and onto the *Aurora Borealis*.

"Welcome, Miss Blacklock," the stewardess said as I entered. Her accent was slightly clipped in a way I couldn't place, and her words somehow managed to convey the impression that encountering me was a life experience on a par winning the lottery. "I am so *very* pleased to welcome you on board. Can one of our porters take your case?"

I looked around me, trying to work out how she knew who I was. My bag was gone before I could protest.

"Can I offer you a glass of champagne?"

"Um," I said, distinguishing myself with witty repartee. The stewardess took that for yes and I found myself accepting the dewy flute she put into my hand. "Uh, thanks."

The interior of the *Aurora* was gobsmacking. The boat might be small, but they had crammed in enough bling for a vessel ten times the size. The gangway doors opened up onto the landing of a long, curving staircase and literally every surface that could be French polished, encased in marble, or draped with raw silk had been so. The whole flight was illuminated by an eye-watering chandelier, suffusing the place with tiny splashes of light that reminded me of nothing so much as the sun glinting off the sea on a summer's day. It was slightly nauseating—not in a social-conscience sort of way, although if you thought about it too hard, that too. But more the disorientation—the way the crystals acted like a prism on every drop of light, dazzling you, throwing you off-balance with a sensation like peering into a child's kaleidoscope. The effect, combined with lack of sleep, was not completely pleasant.

The stewardess must have seen me gawping, because she gave a proud smile.

"The Great Stairway is really something, isn't it?" she said. "That one chandelier has more than two thousand Swarovski crystals."

"Gosh," I said faintly. My head throbbed and I tried to remember if I'd packed the ibuprofen. It was hard not to blink.

"We are *very* proud of the *Aurora*," the stewardess continued warmly. "My name is Camilla Lidman and I am in charge of hospitality on the vessel. My office is on the lower deck, and if there is *anything* I can do to make your stay with us more enjoyable *please* do not hesitate to ask. My colleague Josef"—she indicated a smiling blond man to her right—"will show you to your cabin and give you a tour of the facilities. Dinner is at eight, but we would invite you to join us at seven p.m. in the Lindgren Lounge for a presentation on the boat's facilities and the wonders you can expect to enjoy on this cruise of the famous Norwegian fjords and the Swedish archipelago islands. Ah! Mr. Lederer."

A tall dark man in his forties was coming up the gangway behind us, followed by a porter struggling with a huge suitcase.

"Please be careful," he said, wincing visibly as the

porter bumped the trolley over a joint in the gangway. "That case has some very delicate equipment
in it."

"Mr. Lederer," Camilla Lidman said, with the exact
same amount of near-delirious enthusiasm she had
injected into her welcome to me. I had to hand it to
her; I was impressed at her acting skills, though in
the case of Mr. Lederer it probably took less effort
since he was kind of easy on the eye. "Let me welcome you aboard the *Aurora*. Can I offer you a glass
of champagne? And Mrs. Lederer?"

"Mrs. Lederer won't be coming," Mr. Lederer said.
He ran a hand through his hair and glanced up at the
Swarovski chandelier with an air of slight bemuse-
ment.

"Oh, I am so sorry." Camilla Lidman's flawless
brow puckered in a frown of concern. "I hope nothing is wrong."

"Well, she's in fine health," Mr. Lederer said. "In
fact, she's fucking my best friend." He smiled and
took the champagne.

Camilla blinked and then said smoothly, almost
without pause, "Josef, please do take Miss Blacklock
to her cabin."

Josef gave a little half bow and extended a hand
towards the downward sweep of the staircase.

"This way, please?" he said.

I nodded dumbly and allowed myself to be ush-
ered away, still clutching my glass of champagne.
Over my shoulder I could hear Camilla telling Mr.
Lederer about her office on the lower deck.

"You are in cabin nine, the Linnaeus Suite," Josef
told me as I followed him down into the beige dim-

nose of a thickly carpeted, windowless corridor. "All the cabins are named after notable Scandinavian scientists."

"Who gets the Nobel?" I cracked nervously. The corridor was giving me a strange, stifled feeling, a heavy weight of claustrophobia on the back of my neck. It wasn't just the size but the soporifically low lamps and lack of natural light.

Josef answered seriously.

"On this particular voyage, the Nobel Suite will be occupied by Lord and Lady Bullmer. Lord Bullmer is director of the Northern Lights Company, which owns the vessel. There are ten cabins," he told me as we descended a set of stairs. "Four forward and six aft, all on the middle deck. Each cabin consists of a suite of up to three rooms, with its own bathroom, featuring full-sized bath and separate shower, full-sized double bed, and private veranda. The Nobel Suite has a private hot tub."

Veranda? Somehow the idea of having a veranda on a cruise ship seemed completely wrong, but I supposed, thinking about it, it wasn't any weirder than having any other open-deck area. Hot tub—well, least said about that the better.

"Every cabin has a named steward to assist you, day or night. Your stewards will be myself and my colleague Karla, who you will be meeting later this evening. We will be delighted to help you in any way we can during your stay on the *Aurora*."

"So this is the middle deck, right?" I asked. Josef nodded.

"Yes, this deck is solely passenger suites. Upstairs you will find the dining room, spa, lounge, library,

sundeck, and other public areas. All are named after
Scandinavian writers—the Lindgren Lounge, the
Jansson Dining Room, and so on."

"Jansson?"

"Tove," he supplied.

"Oh, of course. Moomins," I said stupidly. God my
head was aching.

We had reached a paneled wooden door with a
discreet plaque reading 9. LINNAEUS. Josef threw open
the door and stood back to allow me to step inside.

The place was, by no stretch of exaggeration, about
seven or eight times nicer than my flat at home, and
not a great deal smaller, either. Mirrored wardrobes
stretched away to my right, and in the center, flanked
by a sofa to one side and a dressing table to the other,
was a huge double bed, the white linen expanse invitingly smooth and crisp.

But the thing that made the biggest impression
on me was not the space—which was impressive—
but the light. Coming out of the narrow, artificially
lit corridor, the light streaming in from the huge
veranda doors opposite was blinding. Sheer white
curtains waved in the breeze and I saw that the sliding door was open. I felt an instant sense of relief, as
if a tightness in my chest had lifted.

"The doors can be latched back," Josef explained
from behind me, "but the catch will automatically
disengage in the event of adverse weather conditions."

"Oh, great," I said vaguely, but all I could think of
was how much I wanted Josef to *go,* so I could flop
down on the bed and sink into oblivion.

Instead, I stood awkwardly, suppressing my yawns, while Josef told me unnecessarily about the functions of the bathroom (yes, I had used one before, thank you), the fridge and minibar (all complimentary— unfortunately for my liver), and explained that the ice would be refreshed twice a day and I could ring for him or Karla at *any* time.

At last my drooping yawns were no longer ignorable, and he gave a little half bow and excused himself, leaving me to take in the cabin.

There's no point in pretending I wasn't impressed. I was. Mainly by the bed, which was practically shrieking an invitation to throw myself down and sleep for maybe thirty to forty hours.

I looked at the pristine white duvet and the gold and white scatter cushions, and longing washed through me like a physical substance in my veins, sending prickles from the nape of my neck to the tips of my fingers and toes. I *needed* sleep. I was beginning to crave it, like a drug addict, counting the hours until my next fix. The thirty uncomfortable minutes in the taxi had only made it worse. But I couldn't sleep now. If I did, I might not wake up, and I could not afford to miss dinner.

I might be able to skip some of the functions later in the week, but I absolutely *had* to go to tonight's dinner and presentation. It was the first night on board—everyone would be making contacts and networking furiously. If I missed that, it would be a huge black mark against me, and I would never catch up.

Forcing down a yawn, I went out to the balcony,

hoping the fresh air would help me wake from the creeping fog of exhaustion that seemed to encroach every time I stopped moving or talking.

The veranda was as delightful as one would imagine a private balcony on a luxury cruise ship to be. The barrier was made of glass so that sitting inside the suite you could almost imagine there was nothing between you and the ocean at all, and there were two deck chairs and a tiny table so that one could sit there on an evening and enjoy the midnight sun or northern lights, depending on which cruise one had booked.

I spent a long, long time watching the little ships toiling in and out of Hull harbor and feeling the salty wind in my hair, and then suddenly something about the feel of the ship changed. For a minute I couldn't think what it was—and then I realized. The engine, which had been purring discreetly for the last half hour or so, had gone up a notch, and something about the boat had shifted. With a grinding roar, we began to inch round, away from the quayside, to point out towards the sea.

As I stood and watched, the boat edged out of the harbor, past the green and red lights showing the mouth of the safe passage, and I felt the change in its movement as we left the shelter of the harbor wall and entered the North Sea, the smooth lapping waves giving way to the great, rolling swells of the deep ocean.

Slowly, the shoreline slipped away, and the buildings of Hull dwindled into ridges on the horizon, and then into a dark line that could have been anywhere. As I watched it disappear, I thought of Judah, and everything I'd left undone. My phone was heavy in my pocket, and I took it out, hoping for something from him before we left the range of the UK transmitters. *Good-bye. Good luck. Bon voyage.*

But there was nothing. The signal dipped by one bar, and then another, and the phone in my hand was silent. As the coast of England disappeared from view, the only noise was the crashing of the waves.

From: Judah Lewis
To: Laura Blacklock
Sent: Tuesday, 22 September
Subject: Are you ok?

Hey honey, I haven't heard from you since your e-mail on Sunday. Not sure if our messages are crossing. Did you get my reply, or the text I sent you yesterday?

Getting kind of worried, and hoping you don't think I'm off somewhere being an asshole and nursing my wounds. I'm not. I love you, I miss you, and I'm thinking about you.

Don't worry about what happened back home—and the tooth is okay. I think it'll re-root like the doc said. I'm self-medicating with vodka anyway.

Let me know how the cruise is going—or if you're busy, just drop me a line to say you're okay.

Love you, J

From: Rowan Lonsdale
To: Laura Blacklock
CC: Jennifer West
Sent: Wednesday, 23 September
Subject: Update?

Lo, could you please reply to my e-mail sent two days ago requesting an update on the cruise? Jenn tells me you've filed nothing, and we were hoping for some kind of copy by tomorrow—a sidebar piece at the least.

Please let Jenn know ASAP where you're at with this, and cc me to your reply.

Rowan

PART TWO

- CHAPTER 6 -

Even rich people's showers were better.

The jets buffeted and massaged from every angle, numbing in their ferocity, so after a while it was hard to tell where the water started and my body ended.

I soaped my hair, then shaved my legs, and finally I just stood underneath the stream, watching the sea and the sky and the circling gulls. I'd left the bathroom door open and I could see across the bed and out to the veranda and the sea beyond. And the effect was just . . . well, I'm not going to lie, it was pretty nice. I guess you had to get something for the eight grand or whatever it was they were charging for this place.

The amount was slightly obscene, in comparison to my salary—or even Rowan's salary. I had spent years drooling over the reports she sent back from a villa in the Bahamas or a yacht in the Maldives and waiting for the day when I, too, would be senior enough to get those kinds of perks, but now I was actually getting a taste of it, I wondered—how did she stand it, these regular glimpses into a life no regular person would ever be able to afford?

I was idly trying to work out how many months I'd have to work to pay for a week on the *Aurora* as a passenger, when I heard something—an indistinct little noise—beneath the roar of the water, that I couldn't place, but it definitely sounded like it came from my room. My heart quickened a little, but I kept my breathing firm and steady as I opened my eyes to turn off the shower.

Instead, I saw the bathroom door swinging towards me, as though someone had shoved it with a swift, sure hand.

It banged shut, the solid, firm clunk of a heavy door that was made of the very best-quality material, and I was left in the hot, wet dark with the water pounding on the top of my skull and my heart beating hard enough to register on the boat's sonar.

I couldn't hear anything above the hiss of blood in my ears and the roar of the shower. And I couldn't see anything, apart from the red gleam of the digital controls to the shower. Fuck. *Fuck*. Why hadn't I double-locked the cabin door?

I felt the walls of the bathroom closing in on me, the blackness seeming to swallow me whole.

Stop. Panicking, I told myself. No one's hurt you. No one's broken in. Chances are it's just a maid come to turn down the bed, or the door shutting by itself. *Stop. Panicking.*

I forced myself to feel for the controls. The water went freezing, then agonizingly hot so that I yelped and staggered back, cracking my ankle against the wall, but then finally I found the right button, the stream stopped, and I groped my way to the lights.

They came on, flooding the little room with

an unforgiving glare, and I stared at myself in the mirror—bone white, with wet hair plastered to my skull like the girl from *The Ring*.

Shit.

Was this going to be what it was like? Was I turning into someone who had panic attacks about walking home from the tube or staying the night alone in the house without their boyfriend?

No, fuck that. I would *not* be that person.

There was a bathrobe on the back of the bathroom door, and I swathed it hastily around myself and then took a deep, shaking breath.

I would not be that person.

I opened the bathroom door, my heart beating so hard and fast that I was seeing stars in my vision.

Do not panic, I thought fiercely.

The room was empty. Completely empty. And the door *was* double-locked, even the chain was across. There was no way anyone had got in. Maybe I'd just heard someone in the corridor. Either way, it was obviously just the tilting movement of the ship that had caused the door to swing shut, impelled by its own weight.

I checked the chain again, feeling the thick weight of it heavy in the palm of my hand, reassuringly solid, and then, on weak legs, I made my way to the bed and lay down, my heart still pounding with suppressed adrenaline, and waited for my pulse to return to something approaching normal.

I imagined burying my face in Judah's shoulder and for a second I nearly burst into tears, but I clenched my teeth and swallowed them back down.

Judah was not the answer to all this. The problem was me and my weak-ass panic attacks.

Nothing happened. Nothing happened.

I repeated it in time with my rapid breaths, until I felt myself begin to calm down.

Nothing happened. Not now. Not then. Nobody hurt you.

Nothing happened.

Okay.

God, I needed a drink.

Inside the minibar was tonic, ice, and half a dozen miniatures of gin, whiskey, and vodka. I shook ice into a tumbler and then emptied in a couple of the miniature bottles, pouring with a hand that still shook slightly. I topped up with a splash of tonic water and gulped it down.

The gin was so strong it made me choke, but I felt the warmth of the alcohol spreading through my cells and blood vessels and felt instantly better.

When the glass was empty, I stood up, feeling the lightness in my head and limbs, and pulled my phone out of my bag. No reception, so clearly we were out of range of the UK transmitters, but there was Wi-Fi.

I clicked on mail and downloaded my e-mails, chewing my nails as they popped one by one into the in-box. It wasn't quite as bad as I'd been fearing—it was a Sunday after all—but as I scanned down the list, I realized I was tense as an elastic band about to snap, and at the same time, I understood what I was looking for, and why. There was nothing from Judah. I felt my shoulders slump.

I answered the few that were urgent, marked the

others unread, and then pressed compose to start a new e-mail.

Dear Judah, I wrote, but the rest of the words wouldn't come. I wondered what he was doing right now. Was he packing his bag? Crammed onto some economy flight? Or was he lying on his bed in his room, tweeting, texting, thinking of me . . .

I relived again the moment I'd smashed the heavy metal lamp into his face. What had I been *thinking*?

You weren't thinking, I told myself. You were half-asleep. It's not your fault. It was an accident.

Freud says there are no accidents, said the voice in the back of my head. *Maybe it's you. . . .*

I shook my head, refusing to listen.

Dear Judah, I love you.
   I miss you.
   I'm sorry.

I deleted the one to Judah and started a new one.

To: Pamela Crew
From: Laura Blacklock
Sent: Sunday, 20 September
Subject: Safe and sound

Hi, Mum, safe on board the boat, which is seriously swanky. You'd love it! Just a quick reminder to pick up Delilah tonight. I've left her cat basket on the table, and the food is under the sink. I had to change the locks—Mrs. Johnson upstairs has the new key.
   Lots of love and THANKS!
   Lo xx

I pressed send, then pulled up Facebook and messaged my best friend, Lissie.

This place is insanely nice. There are UNLIMITED
free drinks in the minibar in my cabin—sorry, I
mean fucking enormous SUITE—which doesn't
bode well for my professionalism, or my liver. See
you on the other side, if I'm still standing. Lo xx

I poured myself another gin and then I went back to the Judah e-mail.

I had to write something. I couldn't leave things the way they were when I walked out.

Dear J. I'm sorry I was such a bitch before I left. What I
said—it was incredibly unfair. I love you so much.

I had to stop at that, because tears were blurring the screen. I paused and took a couple of shaking breaths. Then I scrubbed crossly at my eyes and finished.

Text me when you get to Moscow. Safe journey.
    Lo xxx

I refreshed my in-box, less hopefully this time, but nothing new downloaded. Instead, I sighed and drained my second gin. The clock by the bed read 6:30, which meant it was time for ball gown number one.

Rowan, after she'd informed me that the dress code for dining on board was "formal" (translation: insane), had recommended that I rent at least seven evening dresses, so that I wouldn't have to wear the same dress twice; but since she wasn't proposing to shell out the cost. I had rented three, which was three more than I'd have done if left to my own devices.

My favorite in the shop had been the most over-the-top one—a long silvery-white sheath studded with crystals that, the shop assistant had claimed without a glimmer of sarcasm, made me look like Liv Tyler in *The Lord of the Rings*. I'm not sure I kept my face sufficiently straight when she said that, because she kept shooting me suspicious looks as I tried on the others.

But I wasn't feeling quite brave enough to kick off with crystal studs, given there might well be people there wearing jeans, for all I knew, so I picked out the most modest choice—a long, narrow slip in dark gray satin. There was a little spritz of sequined leaves across the right shoulder because you didn't seem to be able to get away with none. Apparently the majority of ball gowns were designed by five-year-old girls armed with glitter guns, but at least this one didn't look entirely like an explosion in a Barbie factory.

I wriggled into it and zipped it up the side, then I shook out the full array of ammo from my makeup bag. It was going to take more than a swipe of lip gloss to get me looking even halfway human tonight. I was just smudging concealer across the cut on my cheekbone when I realized my mascara wasn't among the clutter.

I hunted through my handbag in the vain hope that it might be there, trying to remember where I'd last seen it. Then I realized. It had been in my handbag— pinched along with everything else. I don't always wear it, but without dark lashes, my smoky-eye makeup looked strange and out of proportion—like

I'd given up halfway through. I thought briefly and ridiculously about improvising with liquid eyeliner, but instead I tried one last, vain hunt in my bag—tipping everything out onto the bed, just in case I'd misremembered, or had a spare one stuck in the lining. In my heart, though, I knew it wasn't there, and I was replacing everything back into the bag when I heard a noise from the cabin next door—the roar of the pressurized toilet flushing, recognizable even above the muted hum of the engine.

Taking my room key in my hand, I went out barefoot into the corridor.

The ash wood door to my right had a little plaque that read 10. PALMGREN, which made me think that the supply of eminent Scandinavian scientists must have worn a little thin by the time they finished fitting out this boat. I knocked, slightly hesitantly.

There was no answer. I waited. Maybe the occupant was in the shower.

I knocked again, three sharp knocks, and then, as an afterthought, a final loud whack in case they were hard of hearing.

The door flew open, as if the occupant had been standing on the other side.

"What?" she demanded, almost before the door had opened. "Is everything okay?" And then her face changed. "Shit. Who are you?"

"I'm your neighbor," I said. She was young and pretty with long dark hair, and she was wearing a ratty Pink Floyd T-shirt with holes, which somehow made me like her quite a lot. "Laura Blacklock. Lo. Sorry, I know this sounds really weird, but I wondered if I could borrow some mascara?"

There was a scatter of tubes and creams visible on the dressing table behind her, and she was wearing quite a bit of it herself, which made me fairly sure I was on safe ground.

"Oh." She looked flustered. "Right. Hang on."

She disappeared, closing the door behind her, and then came back with a tube of Maybelline and stuck it into my hand.

"Hey, thanks," I said. "I'll bring it right back."

"Keep it," she said. I protested, automatically, but she waved my words away. "Seriously, I don't want it back."

"I'll wash the brush," I offered, but she shook her head impatiently.

"I told you, I don't want it."

"Okay," I said, slightly puzzled. "Thanks."

"You're welcome." She shut the door in my face.

I went back to my cabin wondering about the odd little encounter. I felt out of place enough on this trip, but she looked even more of a fish out of water. Someone's daughter, maybe? I wondered if I'd see her at dinner.

I'd just finished applying the borrowed mascara when there was a knock at the door. Maybe she'd changed her mind.

"Hey," I said, opening the door, holding it out. But it was a different girl outside, one wearing a steward-ess's uniform. Her eyebrows had been rather savagely overplucked, giving her an expression of permanent surprise.

"Hello," she said, with a singsong Scandinavian

inflection. "My name is Karla and I'm your suite attendant along with Josef. This is just a courtesy call to remind you of the presentation at—"

"I remember," I said, rather more brusquely than I'd intended. "Seven p.m. in the Pippi Longstocking Room or whatever it's called."

"Ah, I see you know your Scandinavian writers!" She beamed.

"I'm not so hot on the scientists," I admitted. "I'll be right up."

"Wonderful. Lord Bullmer is looking forward to welcoming you all on board."

After she'd gone I rummaged in my case for the wrap that had come with the dress—a sort of gray silk shawl that made me feel like a long-lost Brontë sister—and draped it round my shoulders.

I locked the door behind me and dropped the key inside my bra, and then I made my way along the corridor, up to the Lindgren Lounge.

- CHAPTER 7 -

White. *White.*

Everything was white. The pale wood floor. The white velvet sofas. The long raw-silk curtains. The flawless walls. It was spectacularly impractical for a public vessel—deliberately so, I had to assume.

Another Swarovski chandelier hung from the ceiling and I couldn't help but pause in the doorway, more than a little dazed. It wasn't just the light, the way it glinted and refracted from the crystals on the ceiling, it was something about the scale. The room was like a perfect replica of a drawing room in a five-star hotel, or a reception room on the *QE2*, but it was *small*. There could not have been more than twelve or fifteen people in the room, and yet they filled the space, and even the chandelier was scaled down to fit. It gave the strangest impression—a little like looking in through the doorway of a doll's house, where everything is miniaturized and yet slightly off-kilter, the replica cushions a little too large and stiff for the tiny chairs, the wineglasses the same size as the fake champagne bottle.

I was scanning the room, looking for the girl in the Pink Floyd T-shirt, when a low, amused voice came from the corridor behind me.

"Blinding, isn't it?"

I turned to see the mysterious Mr. Lederer standing there.

"Just a touch," I said. He held out his hand.

"Cole Lederer."

The name was faintly familiar but I couldn't put my finger on it.

"Laura Blacklock." We shook, and I took him in. Even in jeans and a T-shirt struggling up the gangway, he was what Lissie would have called "eye candy." Now he was wearing a dinner jacket in a way that made me remember Lissie's rule of thumb: a dinner jacket added 33 percent to a man's attractiveness.

"So," he said, taking a glass off a tray proffered by yet another smiling Scandinavian stewardess. "What brings you to the *Aurora*, Miss Blacklock?"

"Oh, call me Lo. I'm a journalist, I work for *Velocity*."

"Well, very happy to meet you, Lo. Can I offer you a drink?"

He picked up a second flute and held it out with a smile. The empty miniatures in the cabin floated up before my eyes, and I wavered for a moment, knowing I was on the cusp of drinking too much so early in the evening but not wanting to seem rude. My stomach was very, very empty and the gin hadn't quite worn off, but surely one more glass couldn't hurt?

"Thanks," I said at last. He handed it over, his fingers brushing mine in a way I wasn't sure was accidental, and I took a gulp, trying to drown my nerves. "How about you? What's your role here?"

"I'm a photographer," he said, and I suddenly realized where I'd heard the name before.

"Cole Lederer!" I exclaimed. I was ready to kick myself. Rowan would have been all over him, right from the gangway. "Of course—you did that amazing shoot for the *Guardian* of the melting ice caps."

"That's right." He grinned, unashamedly pleased at being recognized, though you would have thought the thrill would have worn off for him by now. The guy was only a couple of steps down from David Bailey. "I've been invited to cover this lot, you know, moody shots of the fjords and stuff."

"It's not usually your thing, is it?" I said doubtfully.

"No," he agreed. "I tend to do mainly endangered species or at-risk environments these days, and I don't think you could say this lot were at any particular risk of extinction. They all look particularly well-fed."

We gazed around the room together.

I had to agree with him when it came to the men. There was a little knot in the far corner who looked like they could survive for several weeks off their fat reserves, if we were ever shipwrecked. The women were a different story, though. They all had that lean, polished look that spoke of hot Bikram yoga and a macrobiotic diet, and they didn't look like they'd survive long if the ship went down. Maybe they could eat one of the men.

I recognized a few faces from other press shindigs—there was Tina West, whippet-thin and wearing jewelry weighing more than she did, who edited the *Vernean Times* (motto: *Eighty days is just the start*); the travel journalist Alexander Belhomme, who wrote features and foodie articles for a number of cross-channel and in-flight magazines and was sleek and rotund as a walrus; and Archer Fenlan, who was a well-known expert on "extreme travel."

Archer, who was maybe forty but looked older with his perma-tanned weathered face, was shifting from foot to foot, looking distinctly uncomfortable in his tie and dinner jacket. I couldn't quite imagine what he was doing here—his normal beat was eating witchetty grubs up the Amazon, but maybe he was having a bit of time off.

I couldn't see the girl from the next-door cabin anywhere.

"Boo!" said a voice from behind me.

I whipped round.

Ben Howard. What the hell was he doing here? He was grinning at me through a thick hipster beard that was new since I'd last seen him.

"Ben," I said thinly, trying to suppress my shock. "How are you? Have you met Cole Lederer? Ben and I used to be at *Velocity* together. Now he writes for the . . . what is it at the moment? *Indie*? *Times*?"

"Me and Cole know each other," Ben said easily. "We covered that Greenpeace thing together. How's it going, man?"

"All right," Cole said. They did that sort of manly half-hug thing, where you're too metrosexual for a handshake and not hip enough for a fist bump.

"Lookin' good, Blacklock," Ben said, turning to me and giving me the once-over in a way that made me want to knee him in the balls, except that the sodding dress was too tight. "Although . . . have you, er, been cage fighting again?"

For a minute I couldn't work out what he was on about. Then I realized: the bruise on my cheek. Obviously my expertise with the concealer wasn't as good as I'd thought.

The flashing memory of the door slamming into my cheek and the man in my flat—about Ben's height, with the same liquid dark eyes—was so vivid that my heart had begun thumping and my chest felt tight, and for a long moment I couldn't find the words to reply. I just stared at him, not trying to keep the ice out of my expression.

"Sorry, sorry." He held up a hand. "My own beeswax, I know. Christ, this collar's tight." He yanked at his bow tie. "How did you land this gig, then? Going up in the world?"

"Rowan's ill," I said shortly.

"Cole!" A voice broke into the awkward pause and we all turned to look. It was Tina, sashaying smoothly across the pristine white-oak floor, her silver dress rustling like snakeskin. She gave Lederer a lingering kiss on both cheeks, ignoring me and Ben. "Sweetie, it's been *far* too long." Her voice was throaty with emotion. "And *when* are you going to do that shoot you promised for the *Vernean*?"

"Hi, Tina," Cole said, with just a touch of weariness in his tone.

"Let me introduce you to Richard and Lars," she purred, and, slipping her arm through his, she bore him off to the knot of men I'd noticed at the beginning. He allowed himself to be carried away, with just a little rueful smile over his shoulder as he went. Ben watched him go and then turned back to me, cocking an eyebrow with such perfect comic timing that I let out a snort.

"I think we know who the belle of the ball is,

right?" he said dryly, and I had to nod. "So how are you, anyway?" he continued. "Still with the Yank?"

What could I say? I don't know? There's a strong possibility I might have screwed things up enough to have lost him?

"Still very much unavailable," I said at last, sourly.

"Shame. But you know, what happens in the fjords stays in the fjords. . . ."

"Oh, piss off, Howard," I snapped. He put up his hands.

"Can't blame a guy for trying."

Yes, I can, I thought, but I didn't say it. Instead, I grabbed another glass from a passing waitress and looked round for something to change the subject.

"Who are the others, then?" I asked. "I've got you, me, Cole, Tina, and Archer ticked off. Oh, and Alexander Belhomme. What about that crowd over there?" I nodded at the little group Tina was chatting to. There were three men and two women, one of them about my age but about fifty thousand pounds better dressed, and the other . . . well, the other was sort of a surprise.

"That's Lord Bullmer and his cronies. You know, he's the owner of the boat and the . . . I guess you'd call it the company figurehead?"

I stared at the little knot in the corner, trying to make out Lord Bullmer from the snap on *Wikipedia*. At first I couldn't work out which one he was, and then one of the men gave a full-throated laugh, throwing back his head, and I knew at once it was him. He was tall, wirily slim, and dressed in a suit so well cut that I was certain it must be tailored. He was fiercely tanned, as if he spent a lot of time outdoors, his bright blue eyes narrowed into slits as he laughed, and there was a streak of premature gray at each temple, but it was the grayness that comes sometimes with extremely black hair, not old age.

"He's so young," I said wonderingly. "Seems kind of weird for someone our age to be a peer, don't you think?"

"He's Viscount Something as well, I think. The money's mainly down to his wife, of course. She's the Lyngstad heiress, her family owned that huge car manufacturer. You know the ones I mean?"

I nodded. My business knowledge might be shaky, and the family might be famously private, but even I'd heard of the Lyngstad Foundation. Every time I saw footage of an international disaster zone, their logo was on the trucks and aid parcels. I had a sudden memory of a shot I'd seen all over the papers last year—it might even have been one of Cole's—of a Syrian mother standing in front of a Lyngstad-branded truck with a baby in her arms, holding the child up towards the driver like a talisman to make the vehicle stop.

"And is that her?" I nodded at the willowy white-blonde with her back to me, who was laughing at something one of the other men had said. She was dressed in a devastatingly simple gown of rose-colored wild silk that made me feel like I'd cobbled mine together from my childhood dressing-up box. Ben shook his head.

"No, she's Chloe Jenssen. Ex-model and married to that chap with the blond hair, Lars Jenssen. He's a big noise in finance, head of a Swedish investment group. I imagine Bullmer's got him here as a potential investor. No, that's Bullmer's wife, next to him, in the headscarf."

Oh . . . She was the surprise. In contrast to the other women in the group, the woman in the head-scarf looked . . . well, she looked ill. She was wearing a kind of shapeless gray silk kimono wrap that matched her eyes, and looked halfway between an evening dress and a dressing gown, but even from here I could see she was wearing a silk scarf wound around her scalp, and her skin was waxily pale. Her gray pallor stood out in sharp contrast to the rest of the group, who looked almost obscenely healthy in contrast. I realized I was staring and dropped my eyes.

"She's been ill," Ben said unnecessarily. "Breast cancer. I think it was pretty serious."

"How old is she?"

"Barely thirty, I think. Younger than him, anyway."

As Ben drained his glass and turned to look for a waiter to fill up, I found my gaze drawn back. I would never in a million years have recognized her from the photograph I'd seen on *Wikipedia*. Perhaps it was the gray skin, or the loose-fitting silks, but she seemed years older, and with that glorious mane of golden hair gone, she looked like a completely different woman.

Why was she here and not at home lying on a sofa? But then again, why *shouldn't* she be here? Maybe she didn't have long to live. Maybe she was trying to make the most of her time. Or maybe—here was a thought—just maybe, she wished that the woman in the gray dress would stop staring at her with pitying eyes and leave her alone.

I looked away again and cast around for someone less vulnerable to speculate about. There was only one person left in the group unaccounted for, a tall older man with a neatly clipped graying beard and a gut that could only be the product of a lot of long lunches.

"Who's the Donald Sutherland look-alike?" I said to Ben. He turned back round.

"Who? Oh, that's Owen White. UK investor. Richard Branson type—just on a slightly smaller scale."

"Jesus, Ben. How do you *know* all this? Have you got an encyclopedic knowledge of high society or something?"

"Er, no." Ben looked at me, a touch of disbelief in his expression. "I rang up the press office for a list of guests and then googled them. It's not exactly Sherlock Holmes stuff."

Fuck. *Fuck*. Why hadn't I done that? It was what any good reporter would have done—and I'd not even thought of it. But then, Ben probably hadn't spent the last few days in a haze of sleep deprivation and PTSD.

"How about—"

But whatever Ben had been about to say, it was drowned out by the *ting ting ting!* of metal against champagne flute, and Lord Bullmer moved into the center of the room. Camilla Lidman put down the flute and teaspoon she was holding and made as if to step forward and introduce him, but he waved a hand and she melted into the background with a self-effacing smile.

The room fell into a respectful, faintly anticipatory silence, and Lord Bullmer began to speak.

"Thank you, everyone, for coming to join us here on the *Aurora* on this, its maiden voyage," he began. His voice was warm, and had that curiously class-less tone that people from public school seemed to strive for, and his blue eyes had a kind of magnetic quality that was hard to look away from. "My name is Richard Bullmer, and my wife, Anne, and I would like to welcome you aboard the *Aurora*. What we have sought to do with this ship is make it nothing less than a home away from home."

"Home away from home?" Ben whispered. "Maybe his home has a sea-view balcony and a free minibar. Mine sure as hell doesn't."

"We do not believe that travel has to mean compro-mise," Richard Bullmer continued. "On the *Aurora*, everything should be as you would wish, and if it's not, my staff and I want to hear." He paused and gave a little wink at Camilla, including her in the remark as an acknowledgment that she would likely be on the sharp end of any complaints.

"Those of you who know me will know of my passion for Scandinavia—for the warmth of its peo-ple"—he shot a quick smile at Lars and Anne—"for the excellence of its food"—he nodded at the tray of dill and prawn canapés traveling past—"and the spectacular glory of the region itself: from the roll-ing forests of Finland, to the scattered islands of the Swedish archipelago, to the majesty of the fjords in my wife's native Norway. But I think that, for me, the defining quality of the Scandinavian landscape is—perhaps paradoxically—not the land at all, but the skies—wide, and almost preternaturally clear. And it is those skies that provide what for many is the crowning glory of the Scandinavian winter experience—the northern lights, the aurora borealis. With nature nothing is certain, but I very much hope to share the spectacular majesty of the northern lights with you on this trip. The aurora borealis is something that everyone should see before they die. And now, please raise your glasses, ladies and gentlemen, to the maiden voyage of the *Aurora Borealis*—and may the beauty of her namesake never fade."

"To the *Aurora Borealis*," we chorused obediently, and downed our glasses. I felt the alcohol trickle through me, taking the edge off everything, even my still-aching cheek.

"Come on, Blacklock," Ben said, setting down his empty glass. "Let's go do our bit and schmooze."

I felt a twinge of reluctance to approach the group with him. The thought of being taken for a couple was awkward, given our past, but I wasn't about to let Ben start making connections while I hung back. As we started across the room, I saw Anne Bullmer touch her husband's arm and whisper something in his ear. He nodded, and she gathered up her wrap and the two of them began to make their way towards the doorway, Richard holding Anne's arm solicitously. We passed in the center of the room, and she smiled, a sweet smile that illuminated her drawn, fine-boned face with a shadow of what must have been her former beauty, and I saw that she had no eyebrows at all. The lack of them, together with her jutting cheekbones, gave her face a curious, skull-like appearance.

"You'll excuse me, I'm sure," she said. Her voice was pure BBC English, no trace of accent that I could detect. "I'm very tired—I'm afraid I'm ducking out of dinner tonight. But I look forward to meeting you tomorrow."

"Of course," I said awkwardly, and then tried to smile. "I—I look forward to it, too."

"I'm just going to see my wife to her cabin," Richard Bullmer said. "I'll be back before dinner is served."

I looked at them as they walked slowly away and then said to Ben, "Her English is amazing. You'd never know she was Norwegian."

"I don't think she actually lived there much when she was younger. She spent most of her childhood at boarding schools in Switzerland, as far as I know. Right, cover me, Blacklock, I'm going in."

He strode across the room, scooping up a handful of canapés as he went, and inserted himself into the little group with the practiced ease of a born journalist.

"Belhomme," I heard him say, his tone full of a sort of Old Etonian faux bonhomie, which I knew to be completely out of keeping with his actual background, growing up on an Essex council estate. "Great to see you again. And you must be Lars Jenssen, sir, I read that profile of you in the *FT*. I very much admire your stance on the environment—mixing principles with business isn't as easy as you make it look."

Ugh, look at him, networking like a bastard. No wonder he was working at the *Times* doing proper investigative stuff, while I was stuck in Rowan's shadow at *Velocity*. I should get over there. I should inveigle myself into conversation with them just as Ben had. This was my chance and I knew it. So why was I standing here, holding my glass with cold fingers, unable to make myself move?

The waitress came past with a bottle of champagne and, slightly against my better judgment, I let her fill up my glass. As she moved away, I took a reckless gulp.

"Penny?" said a low voice in my ear, and I whipped round to see Cole Lederer standing behind me.

"Sorry, Penny who?" I managed, though my palms were prickling with sweat. I had *got* to get over this.

He grinned, and I realized my mistake.

"Oh, of course, for my thoughts," I said, cross with myself, and with him for being so coy.

"Sorry," he said, still smiling. "Stupid cliché. I don't know why I said it. You just looked particularly pensive standing there, biting your lip like that."

I was biting my lip? Well, hell, why not trail the tips of my Mary Janes in the dirt as well and maybe flutter my eyelashes?

I tried to remember what I had been thinking about, other than Ben and my lack of networking skills. The only thing that came to mind was the bastard who broke into my flat, but I was damned if I'd bring that up here. I wanted Cole Lederer to respect me as a journalist, not feel sorry for me.

"Oh . . . uh . . . politics?" I brought out, at last. The champagne and the tiredness were starting to hit. My brain didn't seem to be working properly, and my head was starting to ache. I realized that I was halfway to being drunk, and not the good kind of drunk, either.

Cole looked at me skeptically.

"Well, what were *you* thinking, then?" I said crossly. There's a reason why we keep thoughts inside our heads for the most part—they're not safe to be let out in public.

"Other than looking at your lips, you mean?"

I resisted the urge to roll my eyes and tried to channel my inner Rowan, who would have flirted with him until she got his business card.

"If you must know," Cole continued, propping himself against the wall as the ship heaved over a wave and the ice in the champagne buckets rattled, "I was thinking about my soon-to-be ex-wife."

"Oh. Sorry," I said. He was drunk, too, I saw, just hiding it well.

"She's screwing my best man, from our wedding. I was thinking how much I'd like to return the favor."

"Screw her bridesmaid?"

"Or just . . . anyone, really."

Huh. As propositions went, it was certainly direct. He grinned again, somehow managing to make the line sound fairly charming, like he was trying his luck, rather than acting like a sleazy pickup artist.

"Well, I think you shouldn't have too much trouble," I said lightly. "I'm pretty sure Tina would oblige."

Cole gave a snort of laughter, and I felt a sudden twinge of guilt, thinking about how I would feel if Ben and Tina were over on the other side of the room making jokes about me throwing myself at Cole for the sake of my career. So Tina had turned on the charm. Big deal. It was hardly the crime of the century.

"Sorry," I said, wishing I could take back the remark. "That was a pretty cheap dig."

"But accurate," Cole said dryly. "Tina would skin her own grandmother for the sake of a story. My only worry"—he took another slug of champagne and grinned—"would be coming out of the encounter alive."

"Ladies and gentlemen . . ." A steward's voice broke into our conversations. "If you would like to make your way through to the Jansson room, dinner will shortly be served."

As we started to file through, I felt someone's eyes on my back, and I turned to see who it was. The person standing behind me was Tina, and she was looking at me very speculatively indeed.

- CHAPTER 8 -

It took a surprisingly long time for the staff to usher us through into the miniature dining room next door. Somehow I'd been expecting something practical, like the ferries I had been on with rows of tables and a long lunch counter. Of course, the reality was quite different—a room about the size of a private dining room in a restaurant. We could have been in someone's home, if I knew anyone whose home had raw-silk curtains and cut-glass goblets.

By the time we sat down, my head was throbbing painfully, and I was desperate for some food—or better still some coffee, though I presumed I'd have to wait until dessert for that. It felt like a long way off.

The guests had been arranged into two tables of six each, but there was an empty place at each. Was one where the girl in cabin 10 had been supposed to sit? I did a quick head count under my breath.

Table one had Richard Bullmer, Tina, Alexander, Owen, and Ben. The spare place was opposite Richard Bullmer.

Table two had me, Lars and Chloe, Archer, Cole, and a spare place beside Cole.

"You can clear this," Cole said to the waitress who arrived with a bottle of wine. He waved a hand at the unused setting. "My wife wasn't able to attend the trip."

"Oh, my apologies, sir." She gave a little half bow, said something to her colleague, and the place setting was whisked away. Well that explained that. The empty place at the first table remained, though.

"Chablis?" the waitress asked.

"Yes, please." He held out his glass. As he did, Chloe Jenssen leaned across the table with her hand extended towards me.

"I don't think we've been introduced." She had a low, husky voice, quite unexpected for her tiny frame, and the hint of an Essex accent. "I'm Chloe—Chloe Jenssen, although my professional name's Wylde."

Of course. Now that she'd said it, I recognized her, the famous wide cheekbones and slightly Slavic tilt to her eyes, the white-blond hair. Even without stagy makeup and lighting, she looked slightly otherworldly, like she'd been plucked from a tiny Icelandic fishing village, or a Siberian dacha. Her looks made the story of her being discovered by a modeling scout in an out-of-town supermarket all the more incongruous.

"Pleased to meet you," I said, and took her hand. Her fingers were cold, and her grip was almost painfully strong, made more so by the chunky rings she wore, which cut into my knuckles. Up close she was even more stunning, the austere beauty of her dress so obviously outclassing mine, I felt like we might as well have come from different planets. I resisted the urge to tug at the neckline. "I'm Lo Blacklock."

"Lo Blacklock!" She gave a gurgling laugh. "I like it. Sounds like a fifties film star, the sort with a wasp waist and tits up to her chin."

"I wish." In spite of the growing ache in my head, I grinned. There was something about her amusement that was infectious. "And this must be your husband . . . ?"

"This is Lars, yes." She looked across at him, ready to bring him into the conversation and introduce him, but he was deep in conversation with Cole and Archer, and she just rolled her eyes and turned back to me.

"Have they got someone else joining them?" I nodded at the spare place at the first table. Chloe shook her head.

"I think that was for Anne—you know, Richard's wife? She's not well. Decided to have supper in her cabin, I think."

"Of course." I should have thought of that. "Do you know her well?" I asked. Chloe shook her head.

"No, I know Richard quite well, via Lars, but Anne doesn't often leave Norway." She lowered her voice and spoke confidentially. "She's supposed to be kind of a recluse, actually, so I was surprised to find she was on board—but I'd imagine that having cancer might make you—"

But whatever she had been about to say was interrupted by the arrival of five dark square plates, scattered across with small rainbow-colored squares and clumps of foam arranged on what looked like grass clippings. I realized I had no idea what I was about to eat.

"Beet-pickled razor clam," announced the head server, "with a bison grass foam and air-dried samphire shards."

The waiters retreated and Archer picked up his

fork and poked at the most neon-colored of the squares.

"Razor clam?" he said dubiously. His Yorkshire accent was somehow stronger than it sounded on TV. "Never been that keen on raw shellfish, somehow. It gives me the willies."

"Really?" Chloe said. She gave a curving, catlike smile that indicated something between flirting and disbelief. "I thought bush tucker was your thing— you know, bugs and lizards and stuff."

"If you got paid to eat droppings for your day job, maybe you'd fancy a nice steak on your day off, too," he said, and grinned. He turned to me and stuck out his hand. "Archer Fenland. Not sure if we've been introduced."

"Lo Blacklock," I said through a mouthful of something that I was *hoping* was not cuckoo spit, though it was hard to be sure. "We've met, actually, but you won't remember. I work for *Velocity*."

"Oh, aye. Do you work for Rowan Lonsdale, then?"

"That's right."

"She like that piece I did for her?"

"Yes, it was very popular. Got a lot of tweets."

Twelve Surprisingly Delicious Foods You Didn't Know Were Edible, or something along those lines. It had been illustrated with a picture of Archer roasting something unspeakable over a fire and grinning up at the camera.

"Aren't you going to eat it?" Chloe said, nodding at Archer's plate. Her own plate was nearly clear and she swiped her finger across a slick of foam and licked it up.

Archer hesitated and then pushed his plate away.

"I think I'll sit this one out," he said. "Wait for the next course."

"Fair play," Chloe said. She gave another slow, curving smile. A movement in her lap caught my eye and I saw that beneath the level of the table, not quite hidden by the cloth, she and Lars were holding hands, his thumb rhythmically stroking across her knuckles. The sight was somehow so intimate, yet so public, that I felt a little shock run over me. Maybe her flirtatious persona wasn't all it seemed?

I realized Archer was talking to me, and I turned my attention back to the table and focused on him with an effort.

"I'm sorry," I said. "I was somewhere else. What did you say?"

"I said, can I refill you? Your glass is empty."

I looked down at it. The Chablis had gone—though I barely remembered drinking it.

"Yes, please," I said. As he poured, I stared into the glass, trying to work out how much I had drunk already. I took a sip. As I did, Chloe leaned over and said quietly, "I hope you don't mind me asking, but what happened to your cheek?"

Maybe my surprise showed in my face, because she flapped a hand in a *forget about it* gesture.

"Sorry, ignore me, none of my business. I just . . . well, I've been in bad relationships, that's all."

"Oh, no . . ." For some reason the misunderstanding made me feel ashamed, like it was my fault or I'd been criticizing Judah behind his back, although neither was true. "No, it's nothing like that. I got burgled."

"Really?" She looked shocked. "While you were in?"

"Yup. Getting more common, apparently, or so the police said."

"And he attacked you? Jesus."

"Not quite." I felt an odd reluctance to go into details, not just because talking about it brought back unpleasant flashes of what had happened but also out of a kind of pride. I wanted to sit at this table as a professional, the smooth, capable journalist able to take on all comers. I didn't relish the portrait of myself as a frightened victim, cowering in my own bedroom.

But the story was out now—at least 90 percent of it was—and not explaining felt like getting sympathy under false pretenses.

"It—it was an accident really. He slammed a door in my face; it hit my cheek. I don't think he meant to hurt me."

I should have just stayed in my room, head beneath the duvet, was the truth. Stupid Lo, sticking your neck out.

"You should learn self-defense," Archer said. "That's how I started, you know. Royal Marines. It's not about size, even a girl like you can overpower a man if you get the leverage right. Look, I'll show you." He pushed back his chair. "Stand up."

I stood, feeling slightly awkward, and with extraordinary swiftness he grabbed my arm and twisted it up behind my back, tilting me off-balance. I grabbed for the table with my free hand, but the twisting motion in my shoulder continued, pulling me backwards, the muscles screaming in protest.

I made a noise, half of pain and half of fright, and out of the corner of my eye I saw Chloe's shocked face.

"Archer," she said, and then more urgently, "Archer—you're scaring her!"

He let go, and I sank back into my chair, my legs trembling, trying not to show how much my shoulder was protesting.

"Sorry," Archer said with a grin as he pulled his chair back to the table. "Hope I didn't hurt you. Don't know my own strength. But you see what I mean—very tricky to get out of, even if your attacker's bigger than you. Anytime you want a lesson . . ."

I tried for a laugh, but it came out sounding fake and shaky.

"You look like you need a drink," Chloe said bluntly, and she topped up my glass. Then, as Archer turned away to speak to a waiter, she added in a lower voice, "Ignore Archer. I'm starting to believe the rumors about his first wife were true. And look, if you want something to cover up that bruise, come over to my cabin sometime. I've got a whole array of stuff and I'm a pretty mean makeup artist. You need it in the trade."

"I'll do that," I said, and attempted a smile. It felt false and strained and I picked up my glass and took a sip to hide it. "Thanks."

After the first course, the places switched around and I found myself, somewhat to my relief, at the other table from Archer, sitting between Tina and Alexander, who were having a very knowledgeable conversation about foods of the world over the top of my head.

"Of course the one type of sashimi you really *must* try is fugu," Alexander said expansively, smoothing his napkin across his straining cummerbund. "It's simply the most exquisite taste."

"Fugu?" I said, trying to insert myself into the conversation. "Isn't that the horribly poisonous one?"

"Absolutely, and that's what *makes* the experience. I've never been a drug taker—I know my own weaknesses, and I am very aware of being one of life's lotus-eaters, so I've never trusted myself to dabble in that sort of thing—but I can only assume that the high one experiences after eating fugu triggers a similar neuron response. The diner has diced with death, and won."

"Don't they say," Tina drawled, sipping at her wine, "that the art of the really superlative chef is to slice as closely as possible to the poisonous parts of the fish and leave just a sliver of the toxins on the flesh to heighten the experience?"

"I have heard that," Alexander conceded. "It is supposed to act as a stimulant in very small quantities, although that particular slicing technique may be more to do with the expense of the fish and the chef's disinclination to waste even a morsel."

"So how poisonous is it?" I asked. "In terms of quantity, I mean? How much would you have to eat?"

"*Well*, that's the question, isn't it?" Alexander said. He leaned across the table, a rather unpleasant gleam in his eye as he warmed to his topic. "Different parts of the fish have a different toxic load, but in terms of the most poisonous parts—which is to say, the liver, the eyes, and the ovaries—we're talking very,

very little. Grams, if that. They say it's around a thousand times more deadly than cyanide." He pushed a forkful of fish carpaccio into his mouth and spoke through the delicate flesh. "It must be a quite horrible way to die—the chef who prepared it for us in Tokyo took great delight in describing the process of the poison—it paralyzes the muscles, you know, but the mind of the victim is quite unaffected, and they stay fully conscious throughout the experience as their muscles atrophy and they become unable to breathe." He swallowed, licked his moist lips, and smiled. "Eventually they quite simply suffocate."

I looked down at the slivers of raw fish on my own plate, and whether it was the wine, or Alexander's vivid description, or whether the sea had picked up, I felt rather less hungry than I had before dinner. I put a piece reluctantly in my mouth and chewed.

"Tell us about yourself, darling," Tina said suddenly, surprising me by flicking her attention abruptly from Alexander to me. "You work with Rowan, I hear?"

Tina had started at *Velocity* in the late eighties and had briefly crossed paths with Rowan, who still talked about her and her legendary ferocity.

"That's right." I swallowed my mouthful with uncomfortable haste. "I've been there about ten years."

"She must think very highly of you to send you on a trip like this. Quite the coup, I would have thought."

I shifted in my chair. What could I say in answer to that? *Actually, I don't think there's any way she would have trusted me with this if she weren't on a hospital drip?*

"I'm very lucky," I said at last. "It's a real privilege to be here, and Rowan knows how keen I am to prove myself."

"Well, enjoy it is my advice." Tina patted my arm, her rings cool against my skin. "You only live once. Isn't that what they say?"

- CHAPTER 9 -

We swapped seats twice more, but somehow I never found myself next to Bullmer, and it was not until the coffee was served, and we were free to leave our seats and return to the Lindgren Lounge, that I had the chance to accost him. I was just walking across the room, a cup of coffee in my hand, balancing myself precariously against the shifting of the boat, when a flash went off in my face, and I stumbled, narrowly avoiding drenching myself in coffee. As it was, a few drops spattered the hem of the rented gown and the white sofa next to me.

"Smile," said a voice in my ear, and I realized the photographer was Cole.

"Shit, you *idiot*," I said crossly, and then instantly wanted to kick myself. The last thing I wanted was him reporting my rudeness back to Rowan. I must be drunker than I thought. "Not you," I said awkwardly, trying to cover my slip. "Me, I meant. The sofa."

He saw my discomfort and laughed.

"Nice recovery. Don't worry, I'm not going to tell tales on you to your boss. My ego's not that fragile."

"I didn't . . ." I floundered, but it was so uncannily close to what I *had* been thinking that I couldn't think how to finish. "I just—"

"Forget about it. Where were you off to in such a hurry anyway? You were striding across the room like a marksman hunting down a lame antelope."

"I . . ." It felt slightly pathetic to admit it, but my head was throbbing with a mix of tiredness and alcohol, and somehow it seemed easier to tell the truth. "I was hoping to talk to Richard Bullmer. I've been trying to speak to him all evening, I just never had the chance."

"And you were making your move when I wrecked it," Cole said with a gleam in his eye. He smiled again, and I realized it was his incisors that gave him a slightly wolfish, predatory air. "Well, I can sort that out anyway. Bullmer!"

I cringed as Richard Bullmer turned from his conversation with Lars and looked across.

"Did I hear my name?"

"You did indeed," Cole said. "Come and speak to this nice girl, make amends for my ambushing her."

Bullmer laughed, picked up his cup from the arm of the chair next to him, and strolled across. He moved easily, in spite of the slight roll of the ship, and I had the impression of someone who was very physically fit, and probably hard as nails beneath the well-cut suit.

"Richard," Cole said with a wave of his hand, "this is Lo—Lo, Richard. I surprised her with a candid shot as she was making her move on you, and she spilled her coffee."

My cheeks flamed red, but Bullmer was shaking his head at Cole.

"You know what I said about being discreet with that thing." He nodded at the heavy camera slung around Cole's neck. "Not everyone wants paparazzi shots of themselves at inopportune moments."

"Ah, they love it," Cole said easily, showing his teeth in a wide grin. "Gives 'em the proper celebrity experience along with the swanky venue."

"I mean it," Richard said, and although he was smiling, his voice no longer sounded amused. "Anne, especially." He lowered his voice. "You know she's self-conscious since . . ."

Cole nodded, the laugh dying out of his face.

"Yeah, sure, man. That's different. But Lo here doesn't mind, do you, Lo?" He slung an arm around my shoulders, crushing me into him so that my shoulder crunched against his camera, and I tried to smile.

"No," I said awkwardly. "No, of course not."

"That's the spirit," Bullmer said, and he gave a little wink. It was an odd gesture—the same one I'd noticed before when he spoke to Camilla Lidman— not avuncular, as it might have been, but more as if he were trying to level what he knew to be an intimidatingly uneven playing field. *Don't think of me as an international millionaire*, that wink said. *I'm just an ordinary approachable guy*.

I was just trying to think how to reply, when Owen White tapped him on the shoulder and he turned.

"What can I do for you, Owen?" he said, and before I had a chance to open my mouth, the opportunity was gone.

"I—" I managed as he turned away, and he looked back over his shoulder at me.

"Hey, look, it's always hard to talk at these things.

Why don't you swing past my cabin tomorrow after the planned activities, and we can chat properly?"

"Thanks," I said, trying not to sound too pathetically grateful.

"Great. It's number one. Looking forward to it."

"Sorry," Cole said in a low voice, his breath tickling the hair tucked behind my ear. "Did my best. What can I say? He's a wanted man. How can I make it up to you?"

"Never mind," I said awkwardly. He was standing uncomfortably close and I wanted to take a step back, but Rowan's voice was nagging in the back of my head: *Network, Lo!* "Tell me . . . tell me something about yourself instead. What made you come? You said it's not your usual thing."

"Richard's kind of an old friend," Cole said. He grabbed a coffee from a passing stewardess's tray and took a gulp. "We were at Balliol together. So when he asked me to come, I felt I couldn't say no."

"Are you close?"

"I wouldn't say close. We don't really move in the same circles—it's hard when one of you is a struggling photographer and the other one's married to one of the wealthiest women in Europe." He gave a grin. "But he's a good guy. He might look like he was born with a silver spoon in his mouth, but that's not the full picture. He's had some tough times and I guess that's what makes him hold on all the harder to . . . well, all this." He waved a hand at our surroundings—at the silk and crystals and burnished fittings. "He knows what it's like to lose things. And people."

I thought of Anne Bullmer, and the way Richard had walked her to her cabin in spite of the roomful of guests waiting to talk to him. And I thought perhaps I knew what Cole meant.

It was around eleven that I finally made my way back to my room. I was drunk. Very, very drunk. Although it was hard to tell exactly *how* drunk, as we were now midocean, and the shifting movement of the sea mixed queasily with the champagne . . . and the wine . . . oh, and the frozen shots of aquavit. Christ. What had I been thinking?

There was a moment of clarity when I got to my door and stood for a moment, steadying myself on the frame. I knew why I'd got drunk. I knew exactly why. Because if I was drunk enough, I would sleep the sleep of the dead. I couldn't cope with another broken night—not here.

But I pushed the thought away and began the task of retrieving my room key from where I'd stashed it inside my bra.

"Need a hand, Blacklock?" slurred a voice behind me, and Ben Howard's shadow fell across the door-frame.

"I'm fine," I said, turning my back so that he couldn't see me struggling. A wave hit the boat and I lurched and staggered. *Go away, Ben.*

"Sure?" He leaned over me, deliberately peering over my shoulder.

"Yes"—my teeth were gritted with fury—"I'm sure."

"Because I could help." He gave a lascivious grin and nodded towards the top of my dress, which I was gripping with one hand to stop it from peeling down. "You look like you could use an extra hand. Or two."

"Fuck *off*," I said shortly. There was something wedged beneath my left shoulder blade, something warm and hard that felt a lot like a key. If I could only get my fingers far enough round . . .

He moved closer, and before I'd realized what he was about to do, he shoved his hand roughly down the front of my dress. I felt a streak of pain as his cuff links dragged over my skin, and then his fingers closed over my bare breast and squeezed, hard, in a way that was presumably meant to be erotic.

It wasn't.

I didn't even think about it. There was a ripping noise like a snarling cat, and my knee connected with his groin so hard that he didn't even cry out, he just toppled slowly to the floor, making a kind of weak, gasping whimper.

And I burst into tears.

Some twenty minutes later I was sitting on the bed in my cabin, still sobbing and wiping borrowed mascara off my cheeks, and Ben was crouched next to me, one arm around my shoulders and the other holding a tumbler of ice against his crotch.

"I'm sorry," he said again, his voice still croaky with suppressed pain. "Please, Lo, please, stop crying. I'm really sorry. I was a dick, a complete arsehole. I deserved it."

"It's not you," I sobbed, though I wasn't sure he could understand the words. "I can't cope anymore,

Ben, ever since the burglar I've just been— I think I'm going mad."

"What burglar?"

I told him—between sobs. Everything I hadn't told Jude. What it had been like, waking up, realizing there was someone in my flat, realizing that no one would hear if I cried out, realizing that I had no way of getting help, no chance of fighting the intruder off, that I was vulnerable in a way I'd never thought I was before that night.

"I'm sorry," Ben kept repeating, like a mantra. He rubbed my back with his free hand. "I'm so sorry."

His awkward sympathy only made me sob harder.

"Look, sweetheart—"

Oh no.

"Don't call me that." I sat up, shaking my hair away from my face, and pulled out of his hold.

"Sorry, it just— It slipped out."

"I don't care, you can't say that anymore, Ben."

"I know," he said distractedly. "But, Lo, if I'm honest, I never—"

"Don't," I said urgently.

"Lo, what I did, I was a shit, I know I was—"

"I said *don't*. It's over."

He shook his head, but his words, somehow, had stopped my crying. Maybe it was the sight of him, stricken, hunched, and so very miserable.

"But, Lo." He looked up at me, his brown eyes puppy-dog soft in the soft bedside light. "Lo, I—"

"No!" It came out harsher and louder than I meant, but I had to shut him up. I wasn't sure what he was about to say, but whatever it was, I was certain I couldn't afford for him to say it. I was stuck on this boat with Ben for the next five days. I couldn't let him embarrass himself more than he already had done, or this trip would become unendurable when we had to rub shoulders in the cold light of day. "Ben, no," I said more gently. "It was over a long time ago. Anyway, *you* were the one who wanted out, remember?"

"I know," he said wretchedly. "I know. I was a twat."

"You weren't," I said. And then, feeling dishonest: "Okay, you were. But I know I wasn't the easiest— Look, that's not the point now. We're friends, right?" That was overstating it, but he nodded. "Okay, then don't screw this up."

"All right," he said. He stood up painfully and swiped at his face with the arm of his dinner jacket, then looked at it ruefully. "Hope they've got an onboard dry cleaner."

"Hope they've got an onboard dress mender." I nodded at the rip all the way up the side of the gray silk dress.

"Will you be all right?" Ben said. "I could stay. I don't mean that in a sleazy way. I could sleep on the couch."

"You totally could," I agreed, looking at the length of it, and then shook my head as I realized how my words sounded. "No, you couldn't. It's big enough, but you can't; I don't need you to. Go back to your cabin. For Christ's sake, we're on board a ship in the middle of the ocean—it's about the safest place I could possibly be."

"All right." He walked, hobbling slightly, to the door and half opened it, but he didn't actually go. "I—I'm sorry. I mean it."

I knew what he was waiting for, hoping for. Not just forgiveness, but something more, something that would tell him that squeeze wasn't completely unwanted.

I was damned if I'd give it to him.

"Go to bed, Ben," I said, very weary, and very sober. He stood in the doorway a moment longer, just a millisecond *too* long, long enough for me to wonder, with a shift in my stomach that echoed the shifting sea, what I would do if he didn't go. What I'd do if he shut the door and turned around and came back into the room. But then he turned and went, and I locked the door after him and then collapsed onto the sofa with my head in my hands.

At long last, I don't know how much later, I got up, poured myself a whiskey from the minibar, and drank it down in three long gulps like medicine. I shuddered, wiped my mouth, and peeled off my dress, leaving it coiled on the floor like a sloughed-off skin.

I stripped off my bra, stepped out of the sad little pile of clothes, and then fell into bed and into a sleep so deep, it felt like drowning.

I don't know what woke me up—only that I shot into consciousness as if someone had stabbed me in the heart with a syringe of adrenaline. I lay there rigid with fear, my heart thumping at about two hundred beats per minute, and I scrabbled for the soothing phrases I'd repeated to Ben just a few hours before.

You're fine, I told myself. *You're completely safe.*

We're on a boat in the middle of the ocean—no one can get in or away. It's about the safest place you could possibly be.

I was clutching the sheets with a rigor mortis–like grip, and I forced my stiff fingers to relax and flexed them slowly, feeling the pain in my knuckles subside. I concentrated on breathing in . . . and out. In . . . and out. Slow and steady, until at last my heart followed suit, and I could no longer feel its frantic pounding in my chest.

The drumming in my ears subsided. Apart from the rhythmic shush of the waves, and the low engine hum that permeated every part of the vessel, I couldn't hear anything.

Shit. *Shit.* I had to get a grip.

I couldn't self-medicate with booze every night for the rest of this trip, not without sabotaging my career and flushing any chance of advancement at *Velocity* down the drain. So that left—what? Sleeping pills? Meditation? None of that seemed much better.

I rolled over and switched on the light and checked my phone: 3:04 a.m. Then I refreshed my e-mail. There was nothing from Judah, but I was too wide-awake now to go back to sleep. I sighed and picked up my book instead, lying splayed like a broken-backed bird on the bedside table, and opened it to the last page I'd read.

But although I tried to concentrate on the words, something niggled at the corner of my mind. It wasn't just paranoia. *Something* had woken me up. Something that left me jumpy and strung out as a meth addict. Why did I keep thinking of a scream?

I was turning the page when I heard something

else, something that barely registered above the sound of the engine and the slap of the waves, a sound so soft that the scrape of paper against paper almost drowned it out.

It was the noise of the veranda door in the next cabin sliding gently open.

I held my breath, straining to hear.

And then there was a splash.

Not a small splash.

No, this was a big splash.

The kind of splash made by a body hitting water.

JUDAH LEWI3
24 September at 8.50am
Hey, guys, bit concerned about Lo. She hasn't
checked in for a few days since she left on a
press trip. Anyone heard from her? Getting kinda
worried. Cheers.
Like   Comment   Share

LISSIE WIGHT Hi Jude! She messaged me on
Sunday—20th I guess it must have been? Said the
boat was amazing!
Like · Reply   24 September at 9.02am

JUDAH LEWIS Yeah, I heard from her then, too,
but she didn't reply to my e-mail or my text on
Monday. And she hasn't updated facebook or
twitter, either.
Like · Reply   24 September at 9.03am

JUDAH LEWIS Anyone? Pamela Crew? Jennifer
West? Carl Fox? Emma Stanton? Sorry if I'm tag-
ging random people, I'm just—this is kind of out of
character to be honest.
Like · Reply   24 September at 10.44am

PAMELA CREW She emailed me on Sunday, Jude
love. Said the boat was lovely. Do you want me to
ask her dad?
Like · Reply   24 September at 11.13am

JUDAH LEWIS Yes, please, Pam. I don't want to
worry you both, but I feel like she'd have made
contact by now, normally. But I'm stuck here in

Moscow, so I don't know if she's been trying to
phone and not getting through.
Like · Reply   24 September at 11.21am

JUDAH LEWIS Pam, did she tell you the name of
the boat? I can't find it.
Like · Reply   24 September at 11.33am

PAMELA CREW Hi, Judah, sorry, I was on the
phone to her dad. He's not heard anything, either.
The boat was the Aurora, apparently. Let me know
if you hear anything. Bye love.
Like · Reply   24 September at 11.48am

JUDAH LEWIS Thanks, Pam. I'll try the boat. But if
anyone hears anything, please message me.
Like · Reply   24 September at 11.49am

JUDAH LEWIS Anything?
Like · Reply   24 September at 3.47pm

JUDAH LEWIS Please, guys, anything?
Like · Reply   24 September at 6.09pm

PART THREE

- CHAPTER 10 -

I didn't even think about what to do next.

I ran to the veranda, threw open the French windows, and hung out over the rail, desperately searching for a glimpse of something—or someone—in the shifting waves. The dark surface was spattered with bright refracted light from the ship's windows, making it almost impossible to make out the shape of anything in the swell, but I thought I saw something beneath the crest of a black wave—a swirling white shape that trailed beneath the surface as it sank, like a woman's hand.

Then I turned to look at the balcony next to mine.

There was a privacy screen between the two cabins, so I couldn't see very much, but as I peered over, I saw two things.

The first was that there was a smear on the glass safety barrier of the next-door veranda. A smear of something dark and oily. A smear that looked a lot like blood.

The second was a realization, and one that made my stomach clench and shift. Whoever had been standing there—whoever had thrown that body overboard—could not have missed my stupid, headlong dash to the balcony. In all likelihood they'd been standing on the next-door veranda as I dashed onto mine. They would have heard my door crash back. They would probably even have seen my face.

I darted back into the room, slamming the French windows behind me, and checked the cabin door was double-locked. Then I put the chain across. My heart was thumping in my chest, but I felt calm, calmer than I had in ages.

This was it. This was real danger, and I was coping.

With the cabin door secure, I ran back and checked the veranda windows. There was no deadlock on this—just the normal latch—but it was as secure as I could make it.

Then I picked up the bedside phone with fingers that shook only slightly and dialed 0 for the operator.

"Hello?" said a singsong voice. "How can I help you, Miss Blacklock?"

For a minute I was so disconcerted that she knew it was me that I completely lost my train of thought. Then I realized—my room number would probably come up on the desk phone. Of course it would be me. Who else would be phoning from my room in the middle of the night?

"H-hello!" I managed. In spite of the tremor, my voice sounded surprisingly calm. "Hello. Who is this, please?"

"It's your cabin stewardess, Karla, Miss Blacklock. Can I help you?" Beneath her perky phone manner a touch of concern had crept in. "Are you all right?"

"No, no, I'm not all right. I—" I stopped, aware how ridiculous this might sound.

"Miss Blacklock?"

"I think—" I swallowed. "I think I've just seen a murder."

"Oh my goodness." Karla's voice was shocked, and she said something in a language I didn't understand—Swedish perhaps, or maybe Danish. Then she seemed to control herself and spoke in English again. "Are you safe, Miss Blacklock?"

Was I safe? I looked across at the cabin door. It was double-locked and with the chain across, I was as certain as I could be that no one could get in.

"Yes, yes, I think I am. It was in the next-door cabin—number ten. Palmgren. I—I think someone threw a body overboard."

My voice cracked as I said it, and I suddenly felt like laughing—or maybe crying. I took a deep breath and pinched the bridge of my nose, trying to get ahold of myself.

"I will send someone right away, Miss Blacklock. Don't move. I will call you when they are at the door so you know who it is. Hold on, please, and I will call you right back."

There was a click, and she hung up.

I was still holding the receiver, and I put it gently back on the cradle, feeling oddly dissociated, almost like I was having an out-of-body experience. My head was throbbing, and I realized I needed to get dressed before they arrived.

I picked up the bathrobe from where it hung on the back of the bathroom door—and did a double take. When I went down to dinner I had left it on the floor, along with the clothes I'd worn on the train. I remembered looking back over my shoulder at the bomb site I'd made in the bathroom—clothes on the floor, makeup scattered across the counter, lipstick-smeared tissues in the sink—and thinking, *I'll deal with that later.*

It was all gone. The bathrobe had been hung up, my dirty clothes and underwear had disappeared, whisked off to God knows where.

On the vanity counter, my cosmetics had been neatly set out in rows, along with my toothbrush and toothpaste. Only my tampons and pills were left inside my toiletry bag, a weirdly coy touch that was somehow worse than everything being out in the open, and made me shudder. Someone had been inside my room. Of course they had. That was what maid service *meant*, for heaven's sake. But someone had been inside my room, messing with my things, touching my wrinkled tights and my half-used eyeliner pencil.

Why did the thought make me want to cry?

I was sitting on the bed, head in my hands and thinking about the contents of the minibar, when the phone rang, and a couple of seconds later, as I crawled across the duvet to pick up the receiver, there was a knock on the door.

I picked up the phone.

"Hello?"

"Hello, Miss Blacklock?" It was Karla.

"Yes. There's someone at the door. Should I answer it?"

"Yes, yes, please do. It is our head of security, Johann Nilsson. I will leave you now with him, Miss Blacklock, but please do call me at any time if you need any further assistance."

There was a click and the line went dead, and the knock on the door came again. I belted my bathrobe more securely and went to open it.

Outside was a man I hadn't seen before, dressed in some kind of uniform. I don't know what I was expecting—something pseudo-policeman-like. This was more like a nautical uniform—closer to a purser or something. He was about forty or thereabouts, and tall enough to have to stoop as he took a step forward into the doorway, with rumpled hair that looked like he'd only just got out of bed, and eyes so startlingly blue that it looked almost as if he were wearing colored contacts. I was staring at them when I realized, suddenly, that he was holding out a hand.

"Hello, you must be Miss Blacklock, I presume?" His English was very, very good. Just a faint trace of a Scandinavian accent, so slight he might almost have been Scottish or Canadian. "My name is Johann Nilsson. I am head of security on the *Aurora*. I understand you've seen something that disturbed you."

"Yes," I said firmly, suddenly painfully aware of the fact that I was in a dressing gown with my mascara halfway down my cheeks while he was fully and professionally dressed. I tightened the belt again, nervously this time. "Yes. I saw—heard—something thrown overboard. I—I think it was, it must have been . . . a body."

"You saw, or heard?" Nilsson said, cocking his head to one side.

"I heard a splash—a very loud splash. It was quite clearly something very big falling overboard—or being pushed. And then I ran to the balcony and I saw something—a body, it looked like—disappearing under the waves." Nilsson's expression was grave but guarded, and as I spoke his frown deepened. "And there was blood on the glass wall of the balcony," I added.

His lips tightened at that, and he gave a short nod towards the veranda door.

"Your balcony?"

"The blood? No. Next door."

"Can you show me?"

I nodded, pulled the belt again, and watched as he undid the latch of the veranda door. Outside, the wind had picked up, and it was very cold. I led the way to the narrow space, which felt painfully small now with Nilsson's bulk beside me. He seemed to take up all the room there was and more, but part of me was very glad he was there. I didn't think I could have brought myself to go out there on my own.

"There." I pointed over the privacy barrier that separated my veranda from that of cabin 10. "Look over there. You'll see what I mean."

Nilsson peered over the barrier and then looked back at me, frowning slightly.

"I don't see where you mean. Could you show me?"

"What do you mean? It was a big smear all down the glass."

He edged backwards, extending a hand towards the barrier by way of invitation, and I pushed past him to peer over. My heart was pounding in spite of myself. I didn't expect to see the murderer still there, or to get a fist in my face, or feel a bullet fly past my ear. But it felt horribly vulnerable to peer over the wall not knowing what I might find on the other side.

But what I found was . . . nothing.

No murderer, crouched to spring. No smear of blood. The glass barrier shone in the moonlight, clean, innocent of so much as a fingerprint.

I turned back to Nilsson, knowing that my face must be stiff with shock. I shook my head, tried to find the words. He watched me, something sympathetic in his blue eyes.

It was the sympathy that stung more than anything else.

"It was there," I said angrily. "He's obviously wiped it off."

"He?"

"The murderer! The fucking murderer, of course!"

"There's no need to swear, Miss Blacklock," he said mildly, and went back inside the cabin. I followed him, and he carefully shut and latched the door behind me and then stood, his hands by his sides, as if waiting for me to say something. I could smell his cologne—not an unpleasant smell, faintly woody. But suddenly the spacious room felt oppressively small.

"What?" I said at last, trying and failing not to make the word sound aggressive. "I told you what I saw. Are you saying I'm lying?"

"Let's go next door," he said diplomatically.

I yanked the bathrobe belt tighter still, so tight now I could feel it digging into my stomach, and followed him, barefoot, into the corridor. He gave one short knock at the door of cabin 10, and then, when there was no answer, produced a passkey from his pocket and opened the door.

We stood in the doorway. Nilsson said nothing, but I could feel his presence at my back as I gazed, openmouthed, at the room.

It was utterly empty. Not just of people—but of everything. There were no suitcases. No clothes. No cosmetics in the bathroom. Even the bed was stripped back to the mattress.

"There was a girl," I said at last, my voice unsteady. I shoved my hands in the pockets of the bathrobe so that he wouldn't see how my fingers were clenched into fists. "There was a girl. In this room. I *talked* to her. I spoke to her. She was here!"

Nilsson said nothing. He walked through the silent moonlit suite and opened the door of the veranda, then looked outside, inspecting the glass barrier with almost insulting conscientiousness. But I could see from here there was nothing. The glass gleamed in the moonlight, misted faintly with ocean spray but otherwise quite untouched.

"She was here!" I repeated, hearing and hating the edge of hysteria in my voice. "Why won't you believe me?"

"I didn't say that I didn't believe you." Nilsson came back into the room and latched the veranda window. Then he walked me to the cabin door, and closed and locked it behind us.

"You don't have to," I said bitterly. My own door was still open and he escorted me inside. "But I tell you, she was there. She lent me— Oh!" Something suddenly struck me, and I ran to the bathroom. "She lent me a mascara. God damn it, where is it?"

I was rummaging through the carefully set-out cosmetics, but it wasn't there. Where had it gone?

"It's here," I said desperately. "I know it is." I looked around wildly, and something caught my eye, a flash of shocking pink behind the retractable shaving mirror at the side of the basin, I pulled it out—and there it was—an innocent little pink tube with a green cap.

"There!" I brandished it triumphantly at him, like a weapon. Nilsson took a step back, and then took the mascara gently from my hand.

"I see," he said, "but with respect, Miss Blacklock, I'm not sure what this proves, apart from the fact that you borrowed a mascara from someone today—"

"What does it prove? It proves she was really there! It proves she existed!"

"It proves you saw a girl, yes, but—"

"What do you *want*?" I interrupted, desperately. "What more do you want from me? I've told you what I heard—what I saw. I've told you there was a girl in that cabin, and now she's gone. Look on the manifest—there's a guest missing. Why aren't you more concerned?"

"That cabin is empty," he said gently.

"I know!" I shouted, and then, seeing Nilsson's face, I made a huge, concentrated effort to get myself under control. "I know—that's what I've been trying to tell you, for God's sake."

"No," he said, still with that same quiet gentleness, the gentleness of a big man with nothing to prove. "This is what I'm trying to explain, Miss Blacklock. It has *always* been empty. There was no guest in that cabin. There never has been."

- CHAPTER 11 -

I stared at him, openmouthed.

"What do you mean?" I managed at last. "What do you mean, no guest?"

"The cabin is empty," he said. "It was reserved for another guest, an investor named Ernst Solberg. But he pulled out at the last minute—personal reasons, I understand."

"So the girl I saw—she wasn't supposed to be there?"

"Perhaps she was a member of the staff, or a cleaner."

"She *wasn't*. She was getting dressed. She was *staying* there."

He said nothing. He didn't have to—the question was obvious. If she was staying there, where was all her stuff?

"Someone could have taken it out," I said weakly. "Between seeing me and your coming."

"Really?" Nilsson's voice was quiet, his question not skeptical, not mocking, just . . . uncomprehending. He sat down on the sofa, the springs squeaking beneath his bulk, and I sank onto the bed and put my face in my hands.

Because he was right. There was no way someone could have cleared the room. I didn't know exactly how much time had elapsed between me calling Karla and Nilsson appearing at my door, but there was no way it was more than a few minutes. Five, seven at the outside. Probably not even that.

Whoever was in there *might* have had time to wipe the blood off the glass, but that was it. There was no way they could have emptied the entire cabin. What could they have done with the stuff? I would have heard if they had tipped it over the side. And there simply hadn't been time for them to pack it up and take it down the corridor.

"Shit," I said at last, into my hands. *"Shit."*

"Miss Blacklock," Nilsson said slowly, and I had a sudden premonition that I was not going to like his next question. "Miss Blacklock, how much did you have to drink last night?"

I looked up, letting him see my ravaged makeup and the fury in my sleep-bleared eyes.

"I *beg* your pardon?"

"I simply asked—"

There was no point in denying it. There were enough people who'd seen me at the dinner last night, knocking back champagne, then wine, then after-dinner shots, to blow a hole a mile wide in any claim that I was completely sober.

"Yes, I was drinking," I said nastily. "But if you think that half a glass of wine turns me into some hysterical drunk who can't tell reality from fantasy, you've got another think coming."

He said nothing to that, but his gaze traveled to the bin beside the minibar, where a number of whiskey and gin miniatures and a considerably smaller quantity of tonic cans were stacked up.

There was a silence. Nilsson didn't ram home his point, but he didn't need to. Bastard room cleaners.

"I may have been drinking," I said through clenched teeth, "but I *wasn't* drunk. Not like that. I know what I saw. Why would I make it up?"

He seemed to accept that and nodded wearily.

"Very well, Miss Blacklock." He rubbed a hand over his face, and I heard his blond stubble rasp against his palm. He was tired, and I noticed, suddenly and incongruously, that his uniform jacket was buttoned up askew, with an orphan buttonhole at the bottom. "Look, it is late, you are tired."

"*You're* tired," I shot back with more than a touch of malice, but he only nodded, without rancor.

"Yes, I am tired. I think there is nothing we can do now until the morning."

"A woman has been thrown—"

"There is no proof!" he said louder, his voice cutting over mine, and for the first time there was exasperation in his tone. "I'm sorry, Miss Blacklock," he said more quietly. "I should not have contradicted you. But I don't feel there is sufficient evidence to wake the other passengers at this point. Let us both get some sleep"—*and you can sober up* was the unspoken translation—"and we will try to resolve this in the morning. Perhaps if I take you to meet the ship's staff we can track down this girl that you saw in the cabin. It is evident that she was not a passenger, correct?"

"She wasn't at the dinner last night," I admitted. "But what if she was a staff member? What if someone's missing, and we're wasting time in raising the alarm?"

"I'll speak to the captain and the purser now, let them know the situation. But there are no staff members unaccounted for that I am aware of; if there were, someone would have noticed. This is a very small ship with a tight-knit crew. It would be hard for someone to go missing undetected, even for a few hours."

"I just think—" I began, but he cut me off, politely and firmly this time.

"Miss Blacklock, I will not wake up sleeping staff and passengers for no good reason. I'm sorry. I will inform the captain and the purser and they will take whatever action they see fit. In the meantime, perhaps you could give me a description of the girl you saw, and I can double-check the passenger manifest and arrange that all the off-duty staff members who match the description are in the staff restaurant for you to meet tomorrow after breakfast."

"All right," I said sulkily. I was beaten. I *knew* what I had seen, what I'd heard, but Nilsson was not budging, that much was plain. And what could I do, out here in the middle of the ocean?

"So," he prompted. "She was how old, how tall? Was she Caucasian, Asian, black . . . ?"

"Late twenties," I said. "About my height. White—very pale skin, in fact. She spoke English."

"With an accent?" Nilsson put in. I shook my head.

"No, she was English—or if she wasn't, she was completely bilingual. She had long, dark hair . . . I can't remember what color eyes. Dark brown, I think. I'm not certain. Slimmish build . . . she was just—pretty. That's all I remember."

"Pretty?"

"Yes, pretty. You know? Nice features. Clear skin. She was wearing makeup. Lots of eye makeup. Oh— and she was wearing a Pink Floyd T-shirt."

Nilsson wrote it all down solemnly and then rose, the springs squeaking in protest, or perhaps relief.

"Thank you, Miss Blacklock. And now I think we should both get some sleep." He rubbed his face, looking for all the world like a big blond bear dragged out of hibernation.

"What time should I expect you tomorrow?"

"What time would suit you? Ten? Ten thirty?"

"Earlier," I said. "I won't sleep, not now." I was buzzing, and I knew I would never get back to sleep.

"Well, my shift starts at eight. Is that too early?"

"That's perfect," I said firmly. He walked to the door, suppressing a yawn as he did, and I watched as he lumbered off along the corridor towards the stairs. Then I shut and double-locked the door, and went and lay on the bed, staring at the sea. The waves were dark and slick in the moonlight, heaving themselves up like the backs of whales, and then slipping back down, and I lay and felt the boat rise and fall with the swell.

I would never sleep. I knew that. Not with my blood ringing in my ears, and my heart beating in angry staccato thumps in my chest, I would never relax.

I was furious—but I was not sure why. Because a woman's body was even now floating down into the black darkness of the North Sea, probably never to be found? Or was part of it something smaller, baser—the fact that Nilsson had not believed me?

Maybe he's right, the nasty little voice in my

head whispered. Pictures flitted across my mind's eye—me, cowering in the shower because of a door blowing shut in the wind. Defending myself against a nonexistent intruder by attacking Judah. *Are you completely sure? You're not exactly the most reliable witness. And at the end of the day, what did you actually* see?

I saw the blood, I told myself firmly. And a girl is missing. Explain that.

I switched the light out and drew the cover across myself, but I didn't sleep. Instead, I lay on my side watching the sea, rising and falling with strange hypnotic silence outside the thick, stormproof panes. And I thought, *There is a murderer on this boat. And no one knows but me.*

- CHAPTER 12 -

"Miss Blacklock!" The knock came again, and I heard a passkey in the door, and the bang as the door itself opened a centimeter and the security chain pulled taut.

"Miss Blacklock, it's Johann Nilsson. Are you okay? It's eight o'clock. You asked me to call you?"

What? I struggled up onto my elbows, my head pounding with the effort. Why the hell had I asked to be called at eight o'clock?

"One sec!" I managed. My mouth was dry, as if I'd swallowed ashes, and I reached for the glass of water by my bed and choked some down. As I did, the memory of last night came flooding back.

The noise that had woken me in the night.

The blood on the veranda glass.

The body.

The splash . . .

I swung my legs out of bed and felt the boat shift and lurch beneath me, and I felt suddenly and violently nauseous.

I ran to the bathroom and just managed to get myself positioned over the bowl in time for the retching heave of last night's dinner against clean white porcelain.

"Miss Blacklock?"

Go. Away.

The words didn't make it out of my mouth, but maybe the sound of splashing vomit conveyed the sentiment, because the door shut, very quietly, and I was able to stand up and examine myself without an audience.

I looked awful. The dregs of my eye makeup were smudged across my cheeks, and I had vomit in my hair, and my eyes were bloodshot and red-rimmed. The bruise on my cheek just added to the whole impression.

The boat heaved itself up onto a wave and down the other side, and everything around the sink shifted and clinked. I pulled my dressing gown around myself and went back into the cabin, where I pulled the door open the tiniest, tiniest crack—barely enough to see through.

"I've got to take a shower," I said tersely. "Do you mind waiting?" And then I shut the door.

Inside the bathroom I flushed the toilet and wiped around the rim, trying to destroy all traces of my vomit. But when I straightened, it was not my own pale, ravaged face that caught my eye, but the tube of Maybelline, standing sentinel by the sink. As I stood, clutching the vanity table, my breath coming short and sharp, the ship gave another roll, and everything on the countertop shifted and wobbled, and the tube fell, with a tiny crack, and rolled into the bin. I reached in bare-handed and pulled it out, holding it in my fist.

It was the only tangible evidence that that girl *had* existed, that I wasn't going mad.

Ten minutes later I was dressed in jeans and a crisp white shirt, pressed by whoever unpacked my case, and my face was pale but clean. I pulled back the security chain and opened the door to find Nilsson waiting patiently in the corridor, talking on a radio. He looked up when he saw me and shut it off.

"I'm very sorry, Miss Blacklock," he said. "Perhaps I should not have woken you, but you were so insistent last night . . ."

"It's fine," I said through gritted teeth. I didn't mean to sound quite so curt, but if I opened my mouth too much I might be sick again. Thank God the movement of the boat provided an alibi for my queasy stomach. Being a bad sailor was not exactly chic, but it was less unprofessional than being considered an alcoholic.

"I have spoken to the staff," Nilsson said. "No one has been reported missing, but I suggest you come down to the staff quarters and you can see if the woman you spoke to is there. It may put your mind at rest."

I was about to protest that she *wasn't* staff, not unless the cleaners valeted rooms wearing Pink Floyd T-shirts and not much else. But then I shut my mouth. I wanted to see below decks for myself.

I followed him along the lurching corridor to a small service door by the stairwell. It was fitted with a keypad lock, into which he tapped a quick six-digit code, and the door swung outwards. From the outside I would have assumed the door hid a cleaning cupboard, but in fact there was a small, dimly lit landing and a flight of narrow stairs led down into the depths of the ship. As we descended I realized, unsettlingly, that we must now be below the waterline, or very near it.

We emerged into a cramped corridor that had a completely different feel to the passenger part of the ship. Everything was different—the ceiling was lower, the air was several degrees hotter, and the walls were closer together and painted a dingy shade of beige, but it was the lights that made me feel instantly claustrophobic—dim and fluorescent, with a strange high-frequency flicker that made your eyes tire almost at once.

Doors opened off to the left and the right, eight or ten cabins crammed into the same space as two above. We passed one door that was ajar and I saw a windowless shared bunk room lit by the same graying fluorescent light, and an Asian woman sitting on a bunk inside, pulling on her tights, her head and shoulders cramped in the narrow space beneath the bunk above. She looked nervously up as Nilsson passed, and then at the sight of me her face froze, like a panicked rabbit in the headlights. For a moment she just sat, motionless, and then with a convulsive start she reached out with her foot and kicked the door shut, the sound as loud as a gunshot in the confined space.

I felt myself blush like a Peeping Tom caught in the act, and hurried after Nilsson's retreating back.

"This way," Nilsson said over his shoulder, and we turned into a door marked STAFF MESS.

This room was larger at least, and I felt the growing sense of claustrophobia lift slightly. The ceiling was still low, and there were still no windows, but the room opened out into a small dining room, a lot like a miniature version of a hospital canteen. There were only three tables, each seating maybe half a dozen people, but the Formica surfaces, the steel grab rails, and the powerful smell of institutional cooking all combined to underline the difference between this deck and the one above.

Camilla Lidman was seated alone at one of the tables, drinking coffee and going through some kind of spreadsheet on a laptop, and across the room, five girls were sitting around another, eating breakfast pastries. They looked up as Nilsson entered.

"*Hej*, Johann," one of them said, and followed with something in singsong Swedish, or maybe Danish, I wasn't sure.

"Let's speak in English, please," Nilsson said, "as we have a guest present. Miss Blacklock is trying to trace a woman she saw in the next-door cabin—number ten, Palmgren. The woman she saw was white, with long dark hair, in her late twenties or early thirties, and she spoke good English."

"Well, there's me and Birgitta," said one of the girls with a smile, nodding at her friend opposite. "My name is Hanni. But I don't think I've been in Palmgren. I work behind the bar mainly. Birgitta?"

But I was shaking my head. Hanni and Birgitta both had pale skin and dark hair but neither was the girl from the cabin, and even though Hanni's English was excellent, she had a noticeable Scandinavian accent.

"I'm Karla, Miss Blacklock," said one of the two blond girls. "We met yesterday, if you recall. And we spoke on the phone last night."

"Of course," I said absently, but I was too busy scanning the faces of the other girls to pay proper attention. Karla and the fourth girl at the table were both blond, and the fifth had Mediterranean coloring and very short hair, almost a pixie cut. More important, none of them looked like my memory of that vivid, impatient face.

"It's not any of you," I said. "Is there anyone else who fits the description? What about the cleaners? Or the sailing crew?"

Birgitta frowned and said something to Hanni in Swedish. Hanni shook her head and spoke in English.

"The crew are mainly men. There's one woman, but she's redheaded and perhaps forty or fifty, I think. But Iwona, one of the cleaners, has dark hair. She's Polish, I'm not sure how old she is."

"I'll get her," Karla said. She got up with a smile and squeezed out from behind the table.

"There's Eva," Nilsson said thoughtfully, as Karla left the room in search of the absent Iwona. "She's one of the spa therapists," he added to me.

"She's up in the spa, I think," said Hanni. "Setting up for the day. But she's in her late thirties at least, maybe forties."

"We'll go and speak to her after this," Nilsson said.

"Don't forget Ulla." The pixie-haired girl spoke up for the first time.

"Ah, yes," Nilsson said. "Is she on duty? Ulla is one of the stewardesses for the forward cabins and the Nobel Suite," he added to me.

The girl nodded.

"Yes, but I think she'll be coming off shortly."

"Miss Blacklock," said a voice from behind me, and I turned to see Karla presenting a colleague, a small, dumpy woman in her forties with dyed-black hair showing threads of gray at the roots. "This is Iwona."

"I can to help?" Iwona said, in a heavy Polish accent. "There is a problem?"

I shook my head.

"I'm so sorry." I wasn't sure whether to address the answer to Iwona, Nilsson, or Karla. "She's— You're not the woman I saw. But I just want to say: there's no question of this woman being in trouble. It's not that she's stolen anything or anything like that. I'm worried about her—I heard a scream."

"A scream?" Hanni's narrow eyebrows nearly disappeared into her fringe, and she exchanged a look with Karla, who opened her mouth to say something, but behind us, Camilla Lidman rose, and spoke for the first time.

"I am sure none of the crew is the woman you're looking for, Miss Blacklock." She came across the room to stand by the table, putting her hand on Hanni's shoulder. "They would have said if they had any cause for alarm. We are a very—what's the expression—very tightly knitted."

"Very close," Karla said. Her gaze flickered to Camilla Lidman and back to me, and she smiled, although her raised, overplucked brows gave the expression an oddly unconvincing, anxious air. "We are a very happy crew."

"Never mind," I said. I could see I wasn't going to get anything out of these girls. The mention of the scream had been a mistake; they had closed ranks now. And maybe speaking to them with Camilla and Nilsson present had been an error, too. "Don't worry. I'll go and speak to . . . Eva, was it? And Ulla. Thank you for talking to me. But if you hear anything, anything at all—I'm in cabin nine, Linnaeus. Please do come and see me, anytime."

"We heard nothing," said Hanni firmly. "But of

course we will let you know if that changes. Have a wonderful day, Miss Blacklock."

"Thanks," I said. As I turned, the ship lurched, making the girls at the table give little laughing shrieks of alarm, and clutch hold of their coffees. I stumbled, and would have fallen if Nilsson hadn't grabbed my arm.

"Are you all right, Miss Blacklock?"

I nodded, but actually his grip had hurt, leaving my arm aching. The shock of the movement had sent a stabbing pain through my head and I wished I'd taken an aspirin before heading out.

"I enjoy that the *Aurora* is a smaller ship, not one of these Caribbean monsters, but it does mean that you can feel the impact of a big wave more than you might on a larger vessel. Are you sure you're okay?"

"I'm fine," I said shortly, rubbing my arm. "Let's go and speak to Eva."

"First, let us take a detour via the kitchen," Nilsson said. "Then we can head up to the spa to speak to Eva, and finally we can finish in the breakfast room." He had a list of staff in his hand and was crossing off names. "That should be everyone apart perhaps from two members of the sailing crew, and a few cabin stewards we can find at the end."

"Fine," I said tersely. In truth I wanted to get out— out from the narrow, claustrophobic walls and the airless corridors, away from the gray lighting and the feeling of being hemmed in, trapped below the waterline. I had a brief, horrible image of the ship striking something, water flooding the confined space, mouths gasping for the fleeing scraps of air.

But I could not give up now. To do that would

be to admit defeat, to admit that Nilsson was right. Instead, pushing the thoughts away, back into my subconscious, I followed him down a corridor towards the nose of the ship, feeling the floor shift and lurch beneath me, while the smell of cooking became stronger. There was bacon and hot fat, and the distinctive buttery tang of baking croissants, but also boiled fish, and gravy, and something sweet. The combination brought a rush of saliva to my mouth, not in a good way, and I gritted my teeth again and grabbed hold of the rail as the ship heaved up another wave and dropped into the trough, leaving my stomach behind.

I was just wondering whether it was too late to turn back and ask Nilsson if we could do this another time, when he stopped at a steel door with two small glass windows and pushed it open. White-hatted heads turned, their faces registering polite surprise as they saw me standing behind Nilsson.

"*Hej, alla!*" Nilsson said, followed by something else in Swedish. He turned to me. "I'm sorry, all of the deck and hospitality staff speak English but not all the cooks do. I'm just explaining why we're here."

There were smiles and nods from the staff, and one of the chefs came forward, his hand stuck out.

"Hello, Miss Blacklock," he said, in excellent English. "My name is Otto Jansson. Any of my staff will be pleased to help, although they do not all speak good English. I can translate. What do you need to know?"

But I couldn't speak. I could only gulp, staring down at his outstretched hand, in the pale latex catering glove, while the blood hissed in my ears.

I looked up, into his friendly blue eyes, and then back down at the latex glove, with dark hairs showing through, pressed against the rubber, and thought, *I must not scream. I must not scream.*

Please God, don't let me scream.

Jansson looked down at his hand, as if to see what I was gaping at, and then laughed, and pulled the glove off with his other hand.

"So sorry, I forget I am wearing these. They are for catering, you know?"

He threw the pale flaccid glove into the bin and then shook my limp, unresisting hand; his grip was firm, his fingers warm and slightly dusty from the latex coating.

"I'm looking for a girl," I said, knowing I was being abrupt, but too shaken to be more polite. "Dark-haired, about my age or a bit younger. Pretty, with pale skin. She didn't have an accent—she was either English or completely bilingual."

"I'm sorry," Jansson said regretfully, and he did look sorry. "I don't think any of my staff fit that description, though you are welcome to take a walk around and see if any of them are the girl you are looking for. I have only two female staff members and neither speak very good English. Jameela is over by the serving hatch, and Ingrid is on salads, behind the grill station there. But neither of them fit your description. Perhaps one of the stewards or waiting staff?"

I craned my head to see the two women he indicated, and saw that he was right. Neither was remotely like the girl I'd seen. Although she had her head bowed and her body hunched away from me,

I was certain that Jameela was the Asian woman I'd seen in the cabin as we came down. She was Pakistani or Bangladeshi, I thought—and absolutely tiny, probably not even five feet tall. Ingrid, on the other hand, was Scandinavian and at least two hundred pounds, plus she had a good six inches on me. As I looked at her she put her hands on her hips, squaring up to me almost aggressively, although I knew it was unfair to think that—it was her height that made the gesture seem threatening.

"Never mind," I said. "Sorry for disturbing you."

"*Tack*, Otto," Nilsson said, and then made a joke in Swedish that set Otto laughing. He patted Nilsson on the back and said something that made Nilsson guffaw in return, a great belly laugh that set his stomach shaking. He raised his hand to the rest of the crew. "*Hejdå!*" he called, and then ushered me out into the corridor.

"I'm sorry about that," he said over his shoulder, as he led the way towards the stairs. "The official language of the boat is English and it's policy that we don't speak other languages in front of our English guests, but I thought under the circumstances . . ." He trailed off and I nodded.

"It's fine. Better that everyone was comfortable and understood what they were being asked properly."

We were passing the crew's cabins again, and as we passed the few open doors I glanced in, shocked afresh at the dinginess of the cramped quarters. I couldn't imagine spending week after week, month after month, in the windowless confines. Perhaps Nilsson felt my silence at his back, for he spoke again.

"They're a little small, aren't they? But there's only

a dozen or so staff on the boat, excluding the sailing crew, so we don't need much space. And I can tell you, they are better than much of the accommodation on rival ships."

I didn't say what I was thinking, which was not that it was the space itself that shocked but the contrast with the light, airy rooms above. In truth the rooms were no worse than plenty of cross-channel ferries I'd traveled on; in fact they were more spacious than some. But it was the graphic illustration of the gap between the haves and have-nots that was upsetting, a modern upstairs-downstairs in action.

"Does everyone share?" I asked, as we passed a darkened cabin where someone was getting dressed with the door ajar, while their bunkmate snored. Nilsson shook his head.

"The junior staff share cabins, the cleaners and the younger stewards and so on, but all the senior staff have their own."

We had reached the staircase that led to the upper deck and I made my way slowly up, following Nilsson's wide back, and holding on to the grab rails as the ship heaved and tipped. Nilsson opened the dividing door that separated the guest part of the ship from the workers and then turned to me, as he shut the door behind us both.

"I'm sorry that did not work out so well," he said. "I had hoped that one of the girls would be the woman you saw, and put your mind at rest."

"Look . . ." I rubbed my face, feeling the roughness of the healing scar on my cheek, and the pressure headache that was beginning to build. "Look, I'm not sure—"

"Let's press on and speak to Eva," Nilsson said firmly. And he turned and led the way along the corridor towards yet another set of stairs.

The ship heaved itself up another crest, and down in the trough, and I swallowed against the gush of spit in my mouth and felt the cold clamminess of sweat on my spine, beneath my shirt. For a moment I almost considered ducking back to my cabin. It wasn't only my head—I had work to do—I still had to finish reading the press pack, and I needed to make a start on the piece Rowan would be expecting when I got back. I was horribly conscious that Ben, Tina, Alexander, and all the others were probably already making notes, filing pieces, googling Bullmer, and sorting out press shots.

But then I steeled myself. If I wanted Nilsson to take me seriously I had to go through with this. And as much as I wanted to climb the ladder at *Velocity*, some things were more important.

We found Eva in the spa reception, which was a beautiful, tranquil room on the upper deck, almost all glass, with long curtains that floated in the cool breeze from the open door. The glass walls looked out onto the deck, the light almost searingly bright after the beige warren of dimly lit rooms below decks.

A striking dark-haired woman in her forties with wide gold hoops in her ears looked up as Nilsson and I entered.

"Johann!" she said pleasantly. "What can I do for you? And this must be . . . ?"

"Lo Blacklock," I said, holding out my hand. I felt

instantly better out of the claustrophobic confines of the staff quarters, the clammy nausea retreating in the sea breeze.

"Good morning, Ms. Blacklock," she said, smiling. I shook her hand, her grip firm, her fingers bony but strong. Her English was astonishingly good—almost as good as the girl in the cabin's had been, but it wasn't her. She was much too old, her carefully moisturized skin still betraying that slight weathering of a complexion that had seen a little too much sun. "What can I do for you?"

"I'm sorry," I said. "I was looking for someone, and the girls below decks suggested it might be you, but it's not."

"Miss Blacklock saw a woman last night," Nilsson put in. "In the cabin next to hers. She was in her twenties, with long dark hair and pale skin. Miss Blacklock heard some noises that made her concerned, and we were trying to ascertain if it was a member of staff."

"I'm afraid it wasn't me," Eva said, but quite kindly. There was no trace of the slightly tribal defensiveness the girls downstairs had betrayed. She gave a little laugh. "If I'm being honest, it's a long time since I was in my twenties. Have you spoken to the stewardesses? Hanni and Birgitta both have dark hair and are around that age. And so does Ulla."

"Yes, we've spoken to them," Nilsson said. "And we're on our way to see Ulla now."

"She's not in any trouble," I said. "The woman, I mean. I'm worried for her. If you can think of anyone it might be . . ."

"I'm sorry not to be able to help," Eva said. She

spoke directly to me, and she did look sorry, the most genuinely concerned of any of the people I had spoken to so far. There was a little frown between her beautifully plucked brows. "I really am. If I hear anything . . ."

"Thank you," I said.

"Thanks, Eva," Nilsson repeated, and turned to go.

"You're welcome," Eva said. She walked us to the door. "I look forward to seeing you later, Ms. Black-lock."

"Later?"

"At eleven a.m. It is the ladies' spa experience—in your press schedule?"

"Thanks," I said. "See you then." And as I turned to leave I thought, guiltily, of the unread pages of the press pack back in my cabin, and wondered what else I might have missed.

We left the spa via the exit to the deck, and as the door swung back, it was wrenched out of my hand by the strong breeze, banging sharply against a rubber stand put there for the purpose. Nilsson closed it behind me, and I moved to the ship's rail, shivering in the wind.

"Are you cold?" Nilsson shouted, above the roar of the wind and the noise of the engines. I shook my head.

"No, I mean, yes, I am, but I need the fresh air."

"Are you still feeling unwell?"

"Not out here. But my head's aching."

I stood, holding on to the cold painted iron of the railing, and leaned out, looking down, past the glass walled balconies of the cabins aft, down at the creaming waves at the ship's wake, and the great dark expanse farther out, unimaginably deep and cold. I thought of the fathoms and fathoms of swirling blackness beneath us, of the darkness and silence below, and how something—someone—might fall for days through those black depths, to rest at last on a lightless seabed.

I thought of the girl the night before, how easy it would be for someone—Nilsson, Eva, anyone—to just walk up behind me, give me a gentle push . . .

I shuddered.

What *had* happened? I couldn't have imagined it. The scream, and the splash maybe. But not the blood. I couldn't have imagined that.

I took a huge lungful of the clean North Sea air, turned around, and smiled determinedly at Nilsson, shaking my hair back, where the wind had whipped it across my face.

"So whereabouts are we?"

"International waters," Nilsson said. "On our way to Trondheim, I believe."

"Trondheim?" I tried to think back to the bits of the press pack I'd actually read. "I thought we were going to Bergen first."

"A change of plan, perhaps. I know that Lord Bullmer is very much hoping that you will all get a glimpse of the northern lights. Perhaps there are particularly good conditions tonight so he wanted to hasten north. Or it might have been a suggestion of the captain; there may be climatic reasons why it's better to do the trip that way round. We have no fixed itinerary. We are very much able to cater to the whims of our passengers. It may be that someone at dinner last night was particularly anxious to see Trondheim."

"What's in Trondheim?"

"Trondheim itself? Well, there is a famous cathedral. And parts of the city are very attractive. But it's mainly the fjords. That and the fact that the city is of course much farther north than Bergen, so there's a better chance of seeing the aurora. But it might be that we have to go farther north still, to Bodø or even Tromsø. At this time of year, it's still uncertain."

"I see." For some reason his words unsettled me. It was one thing to feel yourself part of an organized, itinerized trip. It was quite another to realize you were a helpless passenger with someone else at the wheel.

"Miss Blacklock—"

"Call me Lo," I interrupted. "Please."

"Lo, then." Nilsson's broad, comfortable face looked pained, something troubled in his teddy-bear expression. "I don't want you to think that I don't believe you, Lo, but in the cold light of day—"

"Am I still sure?" I finished. He nodded. I sighed, a little unhappily, thinking back to my doubts of the night before and the way Nilsson's unspoken question echoed the unpleasant little nagging voice at the back of my skull. I twisted my fingers in the cloth of my top before I spoke. "The truth is, I don't know. It was late, and you're right, I had been drinking—I could have been mistaken about the scream and the splash. Even the blood—I guess it *could* have been a trick of the light, although I'm pretty sure of what I saw. But the woman in the cabin—there's no way I could have imagined her. I just couldn't. I *saw* her, I *spoke* to her. If she's not here—not on the ship, I mean—then where is she?"

There was a long silence.

"Well, we haven't spoken to Ulla," he said at last. "From your description, I'm not sure it's her, but we should rule it out at least." He drew out his staff radio and began tapping at the buttons. "I don't know about you, but I could do with a coffee, so perhaps we could ask her to meet us in the passenger dining room."

The breakfast room was the same room we had eaten dinner in last night, but the two large tables had been broken up into half a dozen smaller ones, and when Nilsson pushed open the door, no one was there apart from a young waiter with corn-colored hair swept into a side parting. He came forward to greet me with a smile.

"Miss Blacklock? Are you ready for breakfast?"

"Yes, please," I said vaguely, looking around the room. "Where should I sit?"

"Anywhere you like." He waved a hand at the empty tables. "Most of the other guests have chosen to breakfast in their cabins. Perhaps by the window? Can I bring you tea, coffee?"

"Coffee, please," I said. "Milk, no sugar."

"And a cup for me, please, Bjorn," Nilsson said. And then, over Bjorn's shoulder, "Ah, hello, Ulla."

I turned to see a stunningly beautiful girl with a heavy black bun walking across the dining room to our table.

"Hello, Johann," she said. Her singsong accent clinched the matter, but I was sure, even before she spoke, that she wasn't the girl in the cabin. She was singularly beautiful, her skin against her black hair as white and clear as porcelain. The girl in the cabin had been vividly good-looking, but not that delicate, classical loveliness, like a Renaissance painting. Also Ulla must have been nearly six feet. The girl in the cabin had been around my height, nowhere near Ulla's. Nilsson gave me a questioning look, but I shook my head.

Bjorn returned with two cups on a tray and a menu for me, and Nilsson cleared his throat.

"Won't you have a cup with us, Ulla?"

"Thank you," she said, shaking her head so that her heavy bun swayed at the nape of her neck. "I've had breakfast already today, but I'll sit for a moment."

She slipped onto a chair opposite and looked at us both, smiling expectantly. Nilsson coughed again.

"Miss Blacklock, this is Ulla. She's the stewardess for the forward cabins, so the Bullmers, the Jenssens, Cole Lederer, and Owen White. Ulla, Miss Blacklock is looking for a girl who she saw yesterday and is anxious to trace. She's not on the passenger list, so we are thinking she may be a member of staff, but we have had no luck in finding her. Miss Blacklock, do you want to describe the girl you saw?"

"She had long dark hair," I said. "She was about your age—late twenties, maybe—really pretty, and she spoke English like someone born in Britain. She was about my height. Can you think of anyone"—I was aware my voice had started to sound pleading— "*anyone* who would fit that description?"

"Well, I have dark hair, obviously," Ulla said with a laugh. "But it was not me, so after that I am not so sure. There is Hanni, she has dark hair, and Birgitta—"

"I've met them," I interrupted. "It's not them. Anyone else? Cleaners? Sailing crew?"

"N-no . . . there's no one on the sailing crew who could fit that description," Ulla said slowly. "On the staff there is also Eva, but she is too old. Have you spoken to the kitchen staff?"

"Never mind." I was beginning to despair. This was starting to feel like a recurring nightmare, interviewing person after person after person, while all the while the memory of the dark-haired girl began to dissolve and shimmer, slipping through my fingers like water. The more faces I saw, each corresponding slightly but not completely to my memory, the harder I was finding it to hold on to the image in my head.

And yet, there was something defining about that girl, something I was sure I'd recognize if I saw her again. It wasn't the features—they were pretty, but ordinary enough. It wasn't the hair, or the Pink Floyd T-shirt. It was something about *her*, the sheer liveliness and vivacity of her expression as she peered sharply out into the corridor, her surprise as she had seen my face.

Was it really possible she was dead?

But the alternative was not much better. Because if she wasn't, the only other possibility—and suddenly I wasn't sure if it was better or worse—was that I was going mad.

- CHAPTER 13 -

Ulla and Nilsson both excused themselves when my breakfast arrived, leaving me to stare out the window as I ate. Up here, with a view of the sea and the deck, I didn't feel quite so sick, and I managed a respectable amount of breakfast, feeling the energy come back into my limbs and the nagging nausea abate. It struck me that at least half the reason I had been feeling so crappy was probably low blood sugar. I always get strange and shaky on an empty stomach.

But though the food and the sight of the ocean made me feel physically better, I could not stop running over last night's events in my head, replaying the conversation with the girl, the surprise on her face, the touch of irritation as she shoved the mascara into my hand. Something had been going on—I was sure of it. It felt like coming into a film halfway through, struggling to work out who the characters were. I had interrupted the girl *doing* something. But what?

Whatever it was, it was probably linked to her disappearance. And whatever Nilsson thought, I could not believe she had been cleaning the room. No one cleaned a room in a thigh-skimming Pink Floyd T-shirt. And besides—she just hadn't *looked* like a cleaner. You didn't get hair and nails like that on a

cleaner's wage. The gloss on that thick dark mane had
spoken of years of conditioning wraps and expensive
low lights. Industrial espionage? A stowaway? An
affair? I remembered the cold glint in Cole's eyes as
he spoke about his ex-wife, and Camilla Lidman's
bland reassurances downstairs. I thought of Nilsson's lumbering strength, of Alexander unpleasantly
dwelling on the topic of poison and unnatural death
last night at dinner—but each possibility seemed
more unlikely than the last.

It was her face that troubled me. The more I struggled to remember it, the more it blurred. The concrete bits—her height, the color of her hair, the state
of her nails—all that I could picture clearly. But her
features . . . a neat nose . . . narrow dark brows carefully plucked. That was about it. I could say what she
was *not*: plump, old, acne-spotted. Saying what she
was was far harder. Her nose had been . . . normal.
Her mouth . . . normal. Not wide, not rosebud, not
pouting, not bee-stung. Just . . . normal. There was
nothing distinctive that I could put my finger on.

She could have been me.

I knew what Nilsson wanted. He wanted me to
forget what I'd heard, the scream, the stealthy slide
of the screen door, and that horrible, huge slithering
splash.

He wanted me to start doubting my own account
of things. He was taking me seriously, only to make
me start undermining myself. He was letting me
ask all the questions I wanted—enough to convince
myself of my own fallibility.

And part of me couldn't blame him—this was the
Aurora's maiden voyage, and the boat was stuffed

with journalists and photographers and influential people. There was hardly a worse time for something to go wrong. I could imagine the headlines now: "Voyage to Death—Passenger on Luxury Press Trip Drowned." As head of security, Nilsson's neck would be on the line. He'd lose his job, at the very least, if something went wrong on the *Aurora*, on the very first voyage he was involved in.

But more than that—the kind of publicity that an unexplained death would generate could sink the whole enterprise. Something like this could scupper the *Aurora* before she was even launched, and if that happened, everyone on board could lose their jobs, from the captain down to Iwona, the cleaner.

I knew that.

But I had heard *something*. Something that had made me start from my sleep with my heart pounding two hundred beats per minute, and my palms wet with sweat, and the conviction that somewhere very close by, another woman was in grave trouble. I *knew* what it was like to be that girl—to realize, in an instant, how incredibly fragile your hold on life could be, how paper-thin the walls of security really were.

And whatever Nilsson might say, if nothing had happened to that girl, then where was she? The scream, the blood—all those I could have imagined. But the girl—I definitely hadn't imagined the girl. And she could not have vanished into thin air without help.

I rubbed my eyes, feeling the gritty residue of last night's eye makeup, and I realized—I had just one single thing to prove she had not been a figment of my imagination: that Maybelline mascara.

Wild thoughts tripped through my head, one after the other. I would take it back to England in a plastic bag and get it fingerprinted. No, better yet, I'd get it DNA tested. There was DNA on makeup brushes, wasn't there? On *CSI: Miami* they would have based an entire prosecution case on a trapped eyelash. There must be *something* they could do.

I pushed aside the mental image of myself marching up to Crouch End police station with a mascara in a bag and demanding advanced forensic analysis from a police officer only barely restraining his amused smile. *Someone* would believe me. They had to. And if they didn't I'd—I'd pay to get it done myself.

I pulled out my phone, ready to google "private DNA testing cost," but even before I had unlocked the home screen, I realized how crazy it was. I wasn't going to get police-grade DNA testing from an Internet company specializing in cheating spouses. And what would the results tell me anyway, without anything to compare it to?

Instead, I found myself checking my e-mail. Nothing from Judah. In fact, nothing at all. There was no phone reception, but I seemed to be connected to the boat's Wi-Fi network and I forced a refresh. But nothing happened. The little "updating" icon whirred and whirred, and then NO NETWORK CONNECTION popped up.

With a sigh, I put the phone away in my pocket and surveyed the blueberries on my plate. The pancakes had been delicious, but my appetite was gone. It seemed impossible, surreal: I'd witnessed a murder—or had heard one at least—and yet here I was, trying to force down pancakes and coffee, while all the time there was a murderer walking free and there was nothing I could do.

Did they know they'd been heard and reported? With the noise I'd been making, and the questions I'd been asking all round the boat, if they didn't last night, they did now.

The boat took another wave, broadside on, and I pushed the plate away and stood up.

"Is there anything else, Miss Blacklock?" Bjorn asked, and I jumped violently and swung around. He had appeared as if by magic from a door set into the paneling at the back of the room. It was almost impossible to see unless you knew it was there. Had he been there all that time, watching me? Was there some kind of *spy hole*?

I shook my head and did my best to smile as I walked across the slowly tilting floor.

"No, thank you, Bjorn. Thanks for all your help."

"Have a wonderful morning. Do you have plans? If you haven't tried it, the view from the deck-top hot tub is stunning."

I had a sudden vision of myself, alone in the hot tub, a hand in latex gloves pushing me beneath the water . . .

I shook my head again.

"I'm supposed to be going to the spa, I think. But I might go for a lie-down in my cabin first. I'm very tired. I didn't sleep well last night."

"Of course." He pronounced it like *off course*. "I completely understand. A little ara and ara is prescribed, perhaps!"

"Ara and ara?" I was puzzled.

"Is that not the expression? Ara und ara, rest and relaxion?"

"Oh!" I blushed. "Rest and relaxation. Yes, of course. Sorry—like I said, I'm so tired . . ." I was edging towards the door, my skin suddenly crawling at the thought of the unseen eyes that could be watching our conversation. At least in my cabin I could be sure of being alone.

"Enjoy your rest!"

"I will," I said. I turned to go—and walked slap into a bleary-eyed Ben Howard.

"Blacklock!"

"Howard."

"Last night . . ." he said awkwardly. I shook my head. I wasn't about to have this conversation in front of the softly spoken Bjorn, who was smiling at the opposite side of the room.

"Let's not go there," I said curtly. "We were both drunk. Have you only just woken up?"

"Yeah." He stifled a huge yawn. "After I left your cabin I bumped into Archer and we ended up playing poker with Lars and Richard Bullmer until stupid o'clock."

"Oh." I chewed my lip. "What time did you get to bed?"

"Christ knows. Four-ish, I think."

"Only because . . ." I started. And then stopped. Nilsson did not believe me. I was getting to the point where I barely believed myself. But Ben . . . He would believe me—right?

I thought back to our time together, to how it ended . . . Suddenly I wasn't so sure.

"Never mind," I said shortly. "I'll tell you later. Have your breakfast."

"Are you all right?" he said as I turned to go. "You look terrible."

"Great. Thanks."

"No, I just mean—you look like you've barely slept."

"I didn't." I was trying not to snap, but anxiety and exhaustion were making me more abrupt than I meant. Then, as the boat lurched over another wave, "I'm finding this sea a bit rough."

"Yeah? I'm lucky, I never get seasick." There was an irritating touch of smugness in his voice and I resisted the urge to snap back something short and sharp. "Never mind, we'll be in Trondheim early tomorrow."

"Tomorrow?" My voice must have betrayed my dismay, for he looked at me sharply.

"Yes. Why, what's the matter?"

"I thought—I imagined, today . . ." I trailed off. He shrugged.

"It's a long way, you know."

"Never mind." I needed to get back to my room, think this through—try to work out what I had and hadn't seen. "I'm going to go back to my room—have a lie-down."

"Sure. See you later, Blacklock," Ben said. His tone was light. But his eyes, as he watched me walk away, were worried.

I thought I was heading for the stairs to the lower deck, but I must have taken a wrong turn because I ended up in the library—a tiny paneled version of a country-house library, complete with green-shaded reading lamps and tiered shelving, re-created on a miniature scale.

I sighed, and tried to work out where I'd gone wrong, and if there was a quicker route back than retracing my steps and facing Ben again. It seemed impossible to get lost on such a small boat, but there was something very confusing about the way the rooms were fitted together, like a locking puzzle designed to squeeze out every inch of empty space, and navigating the maze was made more complicated by the way the boat's movement messed with my sense of direction.

It didn't help that, unlike a ferry, there were no floor plans or maps, and minimal signage—I supposed to help the impression that this was a private home that you just happened to share with a load of rich people.

There were two exits, and more or less at random, I opened the door to the deck. At least outside I could be certain which way I was facing, relative to the direction of travel. As I stepped outside, feeling the wind buffet my face, I heard a hoarse, nicotine-soaked voice from behind me.

"Darling, it's a miracle you're standing! How are you this morning?"

I turned. It was Tina, standing beneath a curved glass smoking shelter, a cigarette between her fingers. She took a long drag.

"Little bit the worse for wear?"

I suppressed the urge to turn and flee. I was supposed to be networking. I couldn't let a self-inflicted hangover get in the way of that. I attempted a smile, hoping it was convincing.

"A bit. I shouldn't have drunk so much."

"Well, I was rather impressed by the amount you

put away," she said, with a slightly mocking smile. "As my old boss told me when I started at the *Express* back in the days of the *really* long lunch, if you can outdrink your interviewee, you're on your way to your first scoop."

I looked at her through the haze of smoke. Office gossip was that she had made her way up the corporate ladder by treading on the backs of more young women than you could count, and then, once she was through the glass ceiling, pulling the ladder up behind her. I remembered Rowan once saying, *Tina is one of those women who thinks every bit of estrogen in the boardroom is a threat to her own existence.*

But somehow, I couldn't quite square her remarks with the woman standing in front of me. I knew at least one ex-colleague who said she owed Tina her career, and as I looked at her now, her heavily made-up eyes laughing at me, I thought about what it must have been like to be a female journalist in that generation, clawing your way up through the ranks of the old-boys' network. It was hard enough now. Maybe it wasn't Tina's fault she couldn't take every other woman in the office with her.

"Come here, darling, I'll let you into a little secret," she said, and beckoned me over, her rings chinking on her skeletal fingers. "Hair of the dog, followed by a long, slow screw."

There was only one possible response that didn't start with *eeeeeeww,* and that was a noncommittal silence. Tina gave her throaty, nicotine-soaked laugh again.

"I've shocked you."

"Not really. It's just—you know—we're a little short on candidates."

"I thought you and that sexy little Ben Howard were looking rather friendly last night . . ." she drawled. I repressed a shudder.

"Ben and I were together, years back," I said firmly. "And I've got no desire to go back there."

"Very sensible, darling." She patted my arm, her rings clinking against my skin. "As the Afghans say, a man may never bathe in the same lake twice."

I wasn't sure what to say to this.

"What's your name again?" she said abruptly. "Louise, was it?"

"Lo. It's short for Laura, actually."

"Nice to meet you, Lo. And you're with Rowan at *Velocity*, is that right?"

"Yes, that's right," I said. "I'm a features writer." And then, surprising myself, "But I'm hoping to cover her maternity leave while she's off. It's partly why I got this trip, I think. They wanted to test the waters. See how I did."

Although if this was a test, I was well on my way to failing it. Accusing my hosts of covering up a death was definitely not what *Velocity* had had in mind.

Tina drew on her cigarette again, and then spat out a thread of tobacco and looked at me appraisingly.

"Lot of responsibility, that role. But it's good that you want a step up. And what will you do when she gets back?"

I opened my mouth to reply—and then stopped. What *would* I do? Go back to my old job? I was just wondering how to answer when she spoke.

"Give me a call sometime, when we're back in the

office. I'm always on the lookout for freelancers, particularly savvy little things with a bit of ambition."

"I'm on a staff contract," I said regretfully. I appreciated it was a compliment, and I didn't want to throw it back at her, but I was pretty sure my noncompete clause wouldn't let me moonlight.

"Suit yourself," Tina said with a shrug. The boat lurched as she spoke, and she staggered against the metal rail. "Blast, my ciggie's gone out. You don't have a light, do you, sweetie? I left mine in the lounge."

"I don't smoke," I said.

"Damn it." She flicked the end over the rail and we both watched as it was snatched by the wind and whisked out of sight, gone before it even hit the churning water. I really should have given her my card, or at the very least started subtly pumping her about the *Vernean*'s plans for future issues and how far she'd got in buttering up Lord Bullmer. It was what Rowan would have done. Ben would probably have scored a freelance contract by now, and sod the noncompete stuff.

But right at this moment—with Nilsson probably even now shooting holes in my story to the captain—my career didn't seem as important. If anything, I should be quizzing her, working out her whereabouts last night. After all, Ben had been playing poker with Lars, Archer, and Bullmer, which left a comparatively small pool of people who could have been in the cabin next to mine. Was Tina strong enough to push a woman overboard? I eyed her covertly as she began to hobble across the salt-sprayed deck toward the door, her narrow heels skidding slightly on the painted metal deck. She was greyhound thin, more sinew than muscle, but I could imagine there would be a wiry strength in her arms, and the picture Rowan had painted was of a woman whose ruthlessness more than compensated for her physical size.

"So how about you?" I said as I followed her towards the door. "Did you have a good time last night?"

She stopped abruptly at that, the heavy door held in one hand, her fingers clenched on the metal, the tendons on the back of her hand standing out like iron cables. She turned to stare at me.

"What did you say?" Her neck was thrust forward like a velociraptor's, her eyes boring into me.

"I—" I stopped, taken aback by the ferocity of her response. "I didn't—I was just wondering . . ."

"Well, I suggest you stop wondering, and keep your insinuations to yourself. A clever girl like you knows better than to make enemies in this business."

Then she let go of the door and let it slam shut behind her.

I stood on deck, staring blankly after her retreating back through the salt-misted door, and wondering what on earth had just happened.

I shook my head and pulled myself together. There was no point in trying to figure it out now. I should be back in the cabin, preserving the one bit of evidence I had left.

I had locked the door before I left with Nilsson but I realized, as I made my way carefully down the stairs to the cabin deck and saw the cleaners pulling their vacuums after them, their trolleys piled with towels and linens, that I had forgotten to put out the DO NOT DISTURB sign.

Inside, the suite had been valeted to within an inch of its life. The sink had been polished. The windows cleaned of salt spray. Even my dirty clothes had magically disappeared. The torn evening dress was also gone.

But I wasn't interested in any of it. Instead, I went straight to the bathroom, to the neat ranks of makeup and cleansers on the vanity surface.

Where was it?

I pushed aside the lipstick and gloss, the toothpaste, moisturizer, eye makeup remover, half-used blister pack of pills . . . but it wasn't there. No flash of pink and green leaped out at me. Under the counter, then—in the bin.

I went through to the main bedroom, opening drawers one after another, hunting under chairs. Where was it? Where *was* it?

But I knew the answer, even as I sank to the bed, head in my hands. It was gone. The tube of mascara— my one link to the missing girl—was gone.

Saturday, 26 September

Harringay Echo website

LONDON TOURIST MISSING FROM NORWEGIAN CRUISE VESSEL

Friends and relatives of missing Londoner Laura Blacklock are said to be growing "increasingly concerned" about her safety. Blacklock (32), who resides in West Grove in Harringay, was reported missing by her partner, Judah Lewis (35), during a holiday aboard the exclusive tourist ship the *Aurora Borealis*.

Mr. Lewis, who was not with Miss Blacklock on board, reported that he had become concerned after Miss Blacklock did not return messages on board the cruise liner, and when attempts to contact her failed.

A spokesperson for the *Aurora Borealis*, whose maiden voyage left Hull last Sunday, confirmed that Blacklock had not been seen since a planned trip to Trondheim on Tuesday, 22 September, but the company said that it had been initially assumed that she had decided to curtail her trip. It was only when Miss Blacklock failed to return to the UK on Friday and her partner raised the alarm that they became aware that her departure had not been planned.

Pamela Crew, the missing woman's mother, said that it was extremely out of character for her daughter not to have made contact, and appealed for anyone who might have seen Miss Blacklock, also known as Lo, to come forward.

PART FOUR

- CHAPTER 14 -

I tried not to let the panic overwhelm me.

Someone had been in my room.

Someone who *knew*.

Someone who knew what I'd seen, and what I'd heard, and what I'd said.

The minibar had been restocked, and I longed with a sudden visceral sharpness for a drink, but I shoved the thought aside and began to pace the cabin, which had seemed so large yesterday and now seemed to be closing in on me.

Someone had been in here. But who?

The urge to scream, to run away, to hide under the bed and never come out, was almost overwhelming, but there was no escape—not until we reached Trondheim.

The realization jolted my thoughts out of their rat-run and I stood, my hands on the dressing table, my shoulders bowed, looking at my white, gaunt face in the mirror. It wasn't just the lack of sleep. There were deep circles of exhaustion under my eyes, but it was something in my eyes themselves that made me pause—a look of fear, like an animal run to ground.

A whining roar came from the corridor, and I remembered, with a jolt, the cleaners valeting the rooms. I took a deep breath and stood straighter, shaking my hair back over my shoulder. Then I opened the door and put my head out into the corridor, where the hum of the vacuum cleaner still buzzed. Iwona, the Polish woman I had been introduced to downstairs, was cleaning Ben's cabin just up the corridor, the door wide-open.

"Excuse me!" I called, but she didn't hear. I ventured closer. "Excuse me!"

She jumped and turned around, her hand on her heart.

"Excuse!" she said, breathlessly, putting her foot down on the switch to silence the hoover. She was wearing the dark blue uniform all the rest of the cleaners wore, her heavy features pink with exertion. "I am startle."

"I'm sorry," I said penitently. "I didn't mean to shock you. I wanted to ask—did you clean my room?"

"Yes, I did already. Something is not clean?"

"It's not that. It's very clean—beautiful, in fact. It's just that I wondered—did you see a mascara?"

"Mass—?" She shook her head, but not meaning no, her expression was uncomprehending. "What it is?"

"Mascara. For your eyes—like this." I mimed putting it on, and her face cleared.

"Ah! Yes, I know," she said, and said something that sounded like *toosh do resh*. I had no idea if this was Polish for *mascara* or *I put it in the bin*, but I nodded vigorously.

"Yes, yes, in a pink-and-green tube. Like—" I pulled out my phone, meaning to google Maybelline, but the Wi-Fi still wasn't working. "Oh, damn, never mind. But it's pink and green. Have you seen it?"

"Yes, I see last night when I clean."

Shit.

"But not this morning?"

"No." She shook her head, her face troubled. "Is not in bathroom?"

"No."

"I am sorry. I did not see. I can to ask Karla, stewardess, if possible to, um . . . how say . . . to buy new—"

Her floundering words and worried expression made me realize, suddenly, what this must seem like—a madwoman half-accusing a cleaner of stealing a used mascara. I shook my head, put out my hand to her arm.

"I'm sorry. It doesn't matter. Please don't worry."

"But yes, it matter!"

"No, honestly. It was probably me. I expect I left it in a pocket."

But I knew the truth. The mascara was gone.

Back in the cabin I double-locked the door and put the chain across, then I picked up the phone, pressed 0, and asked to be put through to Nilsson. There was a long piped-music delay, and a woman who sounded like Camilla Lidman came back on the line.

"Miss Blacklock? Thank you for holding. I'll put you through."

There was a click and a crackle, and then a man's deep voice came on the line.

"Hello?" It was Nilsson. "Johann Nilsson speaking. Can I help you?"

"The mascara is gone," I said without preamble. There was a pause; I could feel him sorting through his mental filing cabinet of notes. "The mascara," I said impatiently. "The one I told you about last night—that the woman in cabin ten gave to me. This *proves* my point, can't you see?"

"I don't see—"

"Someone came into my cabin and took it." I spoke slowly, trying to keep ahold of myself. I had the strange feeling that if I didn't speak calmly and clearly, I might start screaming down the phone. "Why would they do that, if they didn't have anything to hide?"

There was a long pause.

"Nilsson?"

"I'll come and see you," he said at last. "Are you in your cabin?"

"Yes."

"I'll be about ten minutes. I'm with the captain, I must finish here, but I will come as soon as possible."

"Good-bye," I said, and banged the phone down, more angry than afraid, though I wasn't sure if it was with myself, or with Nilsson.

I paced the small cabin again, running through the events of last night, the pictures, sounds, fears, crowding my head. The feeling I could not get over was one of violation—someone had been in my *room*. Someone had taken advantage of the fact that I was busy with Nilsson to come and pick through my belongings and pull out the one piece of evidence that supported my story.

But who had access to a key? Iwona? Karla? Josef?

There was a knock at the door and I turned sharply and went to unlock it. Nilsson stood outside, an uneasy mixture of truculent, ursine, and tired. The dark circles under his eyes were not as big as mine, but they were getting there.

"Someone took the mascara," I said.

He nodded.

"May I come in?"

I stood back, and he edged past me into the room.

"Can I sit?"

"Please."

He sat, the sofa protesting gently, and I perched opposite him on the chair from the dressing table. Neither of us spoke. I was waiting for him to begin—perhaps he was doing the same, or simply trying to find the words. He pinched at the bridge of his nose, a delicate gesture that looked oddly comic in such a big man.

"Miss Blacklock—"

"Lo," I said, firmly. He sighed and began again.

"Lo, then. I have spoken to the captain. None of the staff are missing, we are quite certain of that now. We've also spoken to all the staff and none of them saw anything suspicious about that cabin, all of which leads us to the conclusion—"

"Hey," I interrupted hotly, as if somehow preventing him from saying the words would affect the conclusion he and the captain had come to.

"Miss Blacklock—"

"No. No, you don't get to do this."

"Don't get to do what?"

"Call me 'Miss Blacklock' one minute, tell me you respect my concerns and I'm a valued passenger blah blah blah, and then the next minute brush me off like a hysterical female who didn't see what she saw."

"I don't—" he started, but I cut him off, too angry to listen.

"You can't have it both ways. Either you believe me or— Oh, no, wait!" I stopped in my tracks, unable to believe I hadn't thought of it before. "What about CCTV? Don't you have some kind of security system?"

"Miss Blacklock—"

"You could check the tapes of the corridor. The girl will be on there—she must be!"

"Miss Blacklock," he said more loudly, "I have spoken to Mr. Howard."

"What?"

"I have spoken to Mr. Howard," he said, more wearily. "Ben Howard."

"So?" I said, but my heart was thumping fast. "What can Ben possibly know about this?"

"His cabin is on the other side of the empty one. I went to see him, to find out if he could have heard anything, if he could corroborate your account of a splash."

"He wasn't there," I said. "He was playing poker."

"I know that. But he told me . . ." Nilsson trailed off.

Oh, Ben, I thought, and there was a sinking sensation in my stomach. Ben, you traitor. What have you done?

I knew what he'd said. I knew it from Nilsson's face, but I wasn't going to let him off the hook that easily.

"Yes?" I said through gritted teeth. I was going to force him to do this properly. He was going to have to spell this out, one excruciating syllable at a time.

"He told me about the man in your flat. The burglar."

"That has nothing to do with this."

"It, um—" He coughed and folded first his arms, then his legs. The picture of a man his size, perched uncomfortably on a sofa, trying to efface himself into nothing, was almost ludicrously comic. I said nothing. The sensation of watching him squirm was almost exquisite. *You know*, I thought viciously, *you know what a shit you're being.*

"Mr. Howard tells me that you, er, you haven't been sleeping well, since the, er, the break-in," he managed.

I said nothing. I sat there cold and hard with rage against Nilsson, but mostly against Ben Howard. That was the last time I confided in him. Would I never learn?

"And then there is the alcohol," he said. His fair, crumpled face was unhappy. "It, um . . . it doesn't mix well with . . ."

He trailed off. His head turned towards the bathroom door, to the pathetic pile of personal belongings.

"With what?" I said, my voice low and hard and totally unlike my own. Nilsson raised his eyes to the ceiling, his discomfort radiating through the room.

"With . . . antidepressants," he said, his voice almost a whisper, and his gaze flicked again to the crumpled half-used packet of pills beside the sink, and then back to me, every inch of him apologetic.

But the words were said. They could not be unsaid, and we both knew it.

I sat, saying nothing, but my cheeks were burning as if I'd been slapped. So this was it. Ben Howard really had told him everything, the little shit. A few minutes, he'd talked to Nilsson. One conversation, and in that time he'd not only failed to support my story—he'd spilled every detail of my biography that he had at hand, and made me look like an unreliable, chemically imbalanced neurotic in the process.

Yes. Yes, I take antidepressants. So what?

No matter that I've been taking—and drinking on—those pills for years. No matter that I had anxiety attacks, not delusions.

But even if I'd had full-blown psychosis, that didn't detract from the fact that, pills or no pills, *I saw what I saw.*

"So that's it, then," I spoke, finally, the words clipped and flat. "You think, just because of a handful of pills, I'm a paranoid nutjob who can't tell fact from fiction? You do know that there are hundreds of thousands of people on the same medication I take?"

"That is absolutely not what I was trying to say," Nilsson said awkwardly. "But it is a fact that we have no evidence to support your account and, Miss Blacklock, with respect, what you believe happened is very close to your own exper—"

"NO!" I shouted, standing up, towering over his unhappily crouched body, in spite of the fact that he must have half a foot on me ordinarily. "I told you, you do *not* get to do this. You don't get to call me obsequious names and then dismiss what I've told you. Yes, I haven't been sleeping. Yes, I'd been drinking. Yes, someone broke into my flat. It has *nothing to do with what I saw.*"

"But that is the problem, isn't it?" He stood, too, now, nettled, a flush across his broad cheeks. "You didn't *see* anything. You saw a girl, of which there are many on this boat, and then much later you heard a splash. From that you have jumped to conclusions which are very close to the traumatic event you yourself experienced a few nights ago—a case of two and two making five. This does not warrant a murder investigation, Miss Blacklock."

"Get out," I said. The ice around my heart seemed to be melting. I could feel that I was about to give way to something very stupid.

"Miss—"

"*Get. Out!*"

I stalked to the door and wrenched it open. My hands were trembling.

"Get out!" I repeated. "Now. Unless you want me to call the captain and tell him that a lone female traveler asked you repeatedly to leave her cabin and you refused. GET THE FUCK OUT OF MY CABIN."

Nilsson hunched his head into his neck and walked stiffly to the door. He paused in the doorway for a moment, as if he was about to say something, but perhaps it was my face, or something in my eyes, because when he looked up and met my gaze, he seemed to flinch and turn away.

"Good-bye," he said. "Miss—"

But I didn't wait to hear any more. I slammed the door in his face and then flung myself on the bed to sob my heart out.

- CHAPTER 15 -

There's no reason, on paper at least, why I need these pills to get through life. I had a great childhood, loving parents, the whole package. I wasn't beaten, abused, or expected to get nothing but As. I had nothing but love and support, but that wasn't enough somehow.

My friend Erin says we all have demons inside us, voices that whisper we're no good, that if we don't make this promotion or ace that exam we'll reveal to the world exactly what kind of worthless sacks of skin and sinew we really are. Maybe that's true. Maybe mine just have louder voices.

But I don't think it's as simple as that. The depression I fell into after university wasn't about exams and self-worth, it was something stranger, more chemical, something that no talking cure was going to fix.

Cognitive behavioral therapy, counseling, psychotherapy—none of it really worked in the way that the pills did. Lissie says she finds the notion of chemically rebalancing your mood scary, she says it's the idea of taking something that could alter how she really is. But I don't see it that way; for me it's like wearing makeup—not a disguise, but a way of making myself *more* how I really am, less raw. The best me I can be.

Ben has seen me without makeup. And he walked away. I was angry for a long time, but in the end, I realized, I don't blame him. The year I turned twenty-five was pretty bloody awful. If *I* could have walked away from myself, I would have.

But that didn't excuse what he'd done now.

"Open up!"

The sound of laptop keys stopped, and I heard a chair scrape back. Then the cabin door opened cautiously.

"Yes?" Ben's face filled the gap, his expression turning to surprise as he saw me. "Lo! What are you doing here?"

"What do you think?"

He had the grace to look slightly abashed at that. "Oh, that."

"Yes, *that*. You spoke to Nilsson," I said tightly.

"Look—" He put up a hand, placating, but I wasn't to be soothed.

"Don't *look* me. How could you, Ben? How long did it take you to spill all the beans—the breakdown, the meds, the fact that I almost lost my job—did you tell him all that? Did you tell him about the days I couldn't get dressed, couldn't leave the house?"

"No! Of course not. Christ, how could you think that?"

"Just the pills, then? And the fact that I was broken into, and a few other spicy details to give the idea that I'm definitely not to be trusted?"

"No! It wasn't like that!" He walked to the veranda door and then turned to face me, running his hands through his hair so it stood on end. "I just— Shit, it all came out. I don't know how. He's good at his job."

"You're the journalist! What the hell happened to 'No comment'?"

"No comment," he groaned.

"You have no idea what you've done," I said. My hands were clenched into fists, my nails biting into my palms, and I forced myself to unclench them, rubbing my aching palms on my jeans.

"What d'you mean? Look, hang on, I need a coffee. Want one?"

I wanted to tell him to sod off. But the truth was, I did want a coffee. I nodded curtly.

"Milk, no sugar, right?"

"Right."

"Some things haven't changed," he said, as he filled the espresso machine with mineral water and slotted in a foil pod. I shot him a look.

"A hell of a lot has changed, and you know it. How *could* you tell him that stuff?"

"I'm— I don't know." He shoved his hands into his unruly hair again, gripping the roots as if he could somehow grasp an excuse out of his head if he pulled hard enough. "He ran into me on the way back from breakfast, stopped me in the corridor, and started saying he was concerned about you—stuff about noises in the night—I was hungover, I actually couldn't really work out what he was on about. I thought he was talking about the break-in at first. Then he starts on about you being in a fragile state— Jesus, Lo, I'm sorry, it's not like I went and knocked his door down desperate for a chat. What was he on about?"

"It doesn't matter." I took the coffee he held out. It was too hot to drink, and I held it in my lap.

"It does. It's clearly knocked you for six. Did something happen last night?"

About 95 percent of me wanted to tell Ben Howard to piss off, and that he had forfeited the right to my trust by blabbing about my private life and reliability as a witness to Nilsson. Unfortunately the remaining 5 percent seemed to be particularly forceful.

"I . . ." I swallowed against the ache in my throat, and the desire to tell *someone* what had happened. Maybe if I told Ben he could suggest something I'd not thought of? He *was* a reporter, after all. And, though it hurt to admit it, a pretty respected one.

I took a deep breath and then relayed the story I'd told Nilsson the night before, gabbling this time, desperate to make my case convincing.

"And the thing is she *was* there, Ben," I finished. "You have to believe me!"

"Whoa, whoa," Ben said. He blinked. "Of course I believe you."

"You do?" I was so surprised, I put down the cup of coffee with a crack on the glass tabletop. "Really?"

"Of course I do. I've never known you to imagine anything."

"Nilsson doesn't."

"I can see why Nilsson doesn't *want* to believe you," Ben said. "I mean, we all know that crime on cruise ships is a pretty murky area."

I nodded. I knew as well as he did—as well as any travel journalist did—the rumors that abounded about cruise ships. It's not that the owners are any more criminal than any other area of the travel industry, it's just that there's an inherent gray area surrounding crime committed at sea.

The *Aurora* wasn't like some ships I'd written about, which were more like floating cities than boats, but it had the same contradictory legal status in international waters. Even in cases of well-documented disappearances, things get brushed under the carpet. Without a clear police jurisdiction to take control, the investigation is too often left to the onboard security services, who're employed by the cruise liner and can't afford to ruffle feathers, even if they wanted to.

I rubbed my arms, feeling suddenly cold, in spite of the fuggy warmth of the cabin. I'd gone in to Ben to bawl him out with the aim of making myself feel better. The last thing I expected was for him to back up my unease.

"The thing that worries me most . . ." I said slowly, then stopped.

"What?" Ben prompted.

"She . . . she lent me a mascara. That was how I met her—I didn't know the cabin was empty, and I banged on the door to ask if I could borrow one."

"Right . . ." Ben took another gulp of coffee. His face over the top of the cup was puzzled, clearly not seeing where this was leading. "And?"

"And . . . it's gone."

"What—the mascara? What d'you mean, gone?"

"It's gone. It was taken out of my cabin while I was with Nilsson. Everything else I could almost write off—but if there's nothing going on, why take the mascara? It was the only concrete thing I had to show that there *was* someone in that cabin, and now it's gone."

Ben got up and went to the veranda, pulling the gauze curtains shut, although it seemed an odd, unnecessary gesture. I had the strange, fleeting impression that he didn't want to face me and was thinking about what to say.

Then he turned and sat back down on the end of the bed, his expression pure businesslike determination.

"Who else knew about it?"

"About the mascara?" It was a good question, and one, I realized with a touch of chagrin, that I had not thought to ask myself. "Um . . . I guess . . . no one apart from . . . Nilsson."

It was not a reassuring thought. We looked at each other for a long time, Ben's eyes reflecting the uncomfortable questions that were suddenly churning inside me.

"But he was with me," I said at last. "When it was taken."

"The whole time?"

"Well . . . more or less . . . No, wait, there was a gap. I ate breakfast. And I spoke to Tina."

"So he could have taken it."

"Yes," I said slowly. "He could." Had *he* been the one in my cabin? Was *that* how he had known about my medication, and the advice not to mix them with alcohol?

"Look," Ben said at last. "I think you should go and see Richard Bullmer."

"Lord Bullmer?"

"Yes. Like I said, I played poker with him last night

and he seems like a decent bloke. And there's no sense in messing around with Nilsson—Bullmer is where the buck stops. My dad always used to say, if you've got a complaint, go straight to the top."

"This is hardly a customer services issue, Ben."

"Regardless. But this Nilsson guy—it doesn't look good for him, does it? And if there's anyone on this boat who can hold Nilsson accountable, it's Bullmer."

"But will he? Hold him accountable, I mean? He's got as much motive as Nilsson for hushing this up. More, in fact. Like you say, this has got the potential to play out very badly for him, Ben. If this gets out, the *Aurora*'s future will be very shaky. Who the hell wants to pay tens of thousands of pounds for a luxury trip on a boat where a girl died?"

"I bet there's a niche market," Ben said, with a slightly twisted smile. I shuddered. "Look, it can't hurt to go and see him," he persisted. "At least we know where he was all last night, which is more than we can say for Nilsson."

"You're sure none of the people you were with left the cabin?"

"Absolutely sure. We were in the Jenssens' suite—there's only one door and I was sat facing it all night. People got up and went to the loo and stuff, but they all used the bathroom in the cabin suite. Chloe sat and read for a while and then went into the bedroom next door—there's no exit from that except through the main room of the suite. No one left until four at the earliest. You can rule out all four men, plus Chloe."

I frowned, ticking off passengers on my fingers.

"So that's . . . you, Bullmer . . . Archer . . . Lars, and

Chloe. Which leaves Cole, Tina, Alexander, Owen White, and Lady Bullmer. Plus the staff."

"Lady Bullmer?" Ben raised an eyebrow. "I think that's stretching it."

"What?" I said defensively. "Maybe she's not as ill as she looks."

"Yup, that's right, she's faked four years of recurrent cancer and grueling chemo and radiotherapy just to provide an alibi for the murder of a strange girl."

"There's no need to be sarcastic. I was just making the point."

"I think the passengers are a red herring, though," Ben said. "You can't get away from the fact that you and Nilsson were the only people who knew about that mascara. If he didn't take it, he must have told the person who did."

"Well . . ." I said, and then stopped. An uneasy feeling, not unlike guilt, was trickling down the back of my neck.

"What?"

"I—I was trying to think. When Nilsson took me round the staff. I can't absolutely remember . . . I could have mentioned it."

"Jesus, Lo," Ben said. He stared at me. "Did you? Or didn't you? It kind of matters."

"I know that," I said peevishly. The boat heaved up and down a wave, and the feeling of nausea swept over me again, the half-digested pancakes shifting uneasily in my gut. I tried to think back to the conversations below decks, but it was hard to remember, I'd been so hungover, so distracted by the claustrophobic artificial light of those narrow, windowless cabins. I shut my eyes, feeling the sofa lurch and tilt beneath me, and tried to think back to the staff canteen and the pleasant, scrubbed faces of the girls tipped up towards me. What the *hell* had I said?

"I can't remember," I said at last. "I really can't. But I could have mentioned it. I don't *think* I did, but I can't absolutely say that I didn't."

"Bollocks. Well, that widens things out considerably."

I nodded soberly.

"Look," Ben said at last. "Maybe one of the other passengers saw something. Someone going in and out of the empty cabin, or whoever stole the mascara going into yours. Who's in the aft cabins?"

"Um . . ." I counted them out on my fingers. "Well, there's me in nine, you in eight. Alexander is in . . . I think it might be six?"

"Tina's in five," Ben said thoughtfully. "I saw her go in last night. Which means Archer must be in seven. Okay. Want to go and do some door stepping?"

"All right," I said. For some reason, maybe it was the surge of anger, or the feeling of being believed, or maybe just the effect of having a plan, I was feeling better already. But then I caught sight of the clock on Ben's laptop. "Shit, I can't, not now. I've got this bloody ladies' spa thing."

"What time does it finish?" Ben asked.

"No idea. But I shouldn't think it will run over lunchtime. What are the men supposed to be doing?"

Ben stood up and flicked through a brochure on the desk.

"Tour of the bridge. Nice and sexist—blokes get technology, women get aromatherapy. Oh, no, wait, there's a men's spa morning tomorrow. Maybe it's just to do with space." He picked up a pad and pen from the dressing table. "I need to be going, too, but let's see what we can dig up this morning, and then we can rendezvous back here after lunch and door step the remaining passengers. After that we can take the whole lot to Bullmer. Maybe he can get the boat to divert—get the local police on board."

I nodded. Nilsson hadn't taken me seriously, but if we could find out something to corroborate my story—even just someone else who'd heard the splash, it would be a lot harder for Bullmer to ignore.

"I keep thinking about her," I blurted as we reached the door. Ben stopped, his hand on the latch.

"What do you mean?"

"About the girl—the girl in Palmgren. What she must have felt when he went for her—whether she was alive when she went over. I keep thinking what it must have been like, the shock of the cold water, the sight of the boat pulling away . . ."

Had she screamed as the waves closed over her? Had she tried to call out, as the salt water flooded her lungs, her chest laboring as the cold bit harder and the oxygen leached from her blood, and she sank deeper and deeper . . . ?

And her body, drifting through the cold silent blackness of the deep ocean, white as bone, the fishes nibbling at her eyes, her hair floating in the current like a stream of dark smoke . . . All that I was thinking of, too, though I didn't say it.

"Don't," Ben said. "Don't let your imagination run away with you, Lo."

"I know what it's like," I said, as he opened the

door. "Don't you see? I know what she must have felt like, when someone came for her in the middle of the night. That's why I have to find out who did this to her."

And because if I didn't find out, they might come for me next.

- CHAPTER 16 -

Chloe and Tina were waiting in the spa when I arrived. Tina was leaning over the counter, reading something on the laptop Eva had left open behind the desk, and Chloe was ensconced deep in a luxuriously upholstered vintage leather chair, playing on her phone. I was surprised to see that without her makeup on, she looked completely different—the huge smoky eyes and jutting cheekbones of last night looking somehow faded and flat by the light of day.

She caught me looking at her in the mirror and grinned.

"Apparently I'm down for a facial, so I took it off. I told you, I'm quite the makeup artist."

"Oh, I didn't . . ." I trailed off, feeling myself blush.

"Contouring," Chloe said. She swung the chair around to face me and winked. "Honestly, it'll change your life. I could turn you into anyone from Kim Kardashian to Natalie Portman with what I've got in my cabin."

I was just about to make a joking reply, when I caught a movement out of the corner of my eye, and I saw with a shock that one of the full-length mirrors behind the desk was moving, swinging inwards. Another door?

Seriously, how many concealed entrances did this boat have?

Tina's head jerked up from the laptop as Eva came through the gap, smiling politely.

"Can I help you, Miss West?" she asked. "We keep our client lists and confidential information on that computer, so I'm afraid we don't allow guests to use it. If you wish to use a computer, Camilla Lidman will be delighted to arrange one for your cabin."

Tina straightened awkwardly and turned the laptop to face the desk again.

"Sorry, darling." She had the grace to look slightly shamefaced. "I, ah . . . was just looking for the list of treatments."

Since there was a full list in the press pack, it was a slightly lame excuse.

"I would be delighted to give you a printout," Eva said. There was no hint of coolness in her tone, but she looked at Tina rather appraisingly. "We have the usual types of massage and therapies, facials, pedicures, and so on. The manicures and hair treatments take place in this room." She indicated the chair that Chloe was perching on.

I was just wondering where the other treatments took place, as there was only one chair in the spa, and no more room on the upper deck as far as I could make out—the hot tub and the sauna took up most of the rest of the space—when the deck door swung open and, somewhat to my surprise, Anne Bullmer came in. She looked a little better than last night, her skin less sallow, her face somehow slightly less drawn, but her dark eyes were circled with deep shadows as though she hadn't slept.

"I'm sorry," she said, breathlessly, trying to smile. "It takes me so long on the stairs at the moment."

"Here." Chloe stood up hastily and tried to edge out of the way into an unoccupied corner of the room. "Have my seat."

"There's no need," Anne said. Chloe began to insist, but Eva cut across their polite exchange with a smile.

"We're heading to the treatment rooms now, in any case, ladies. Lady Bullmer, if you would like to take a seat here. Miss West, Ms. Blacklock, and Mrs. Jenssen, shall we make our way down?"

Down? Before I could wonder what that meant, she opened the mirrored door behind the desk—a touch at the frame sent it swinging inwards—and we began to descend a set of narrow, dark stairs, one after the other.

The contrast, after the light and air of the reception room, was extreme, and I found myself blinking, my eyes trying to get used to the low light. Small electric tea lights were placed in holders at intervals along the staircase, but the flickering yellow glow they cast merely intensified the darkness around them, and as the boat tilted slightly over a big wave, I had a momentary wash of vertigo. Perhaps it was the staircase disappearing into darkness below us— or perhaps it was the realization that the lightest of touches from Chloe—who was directly behind me—would send me tumbling into the back of Tina and Eva in front. If I broke my neck, there would be no way of knowing that I hadn't simply tripped in the dark.

At last, after what seemed like an interminable

descent, we stopped in a small lobby. There was the sound of water from a small electric water feature in a niche on the wall, the kind that trickled endlessly recycled water over a stone globe into a bowl below. The noise should have been soothing, and probably would have been on dry land, but the effect on a boat was somehow different. I began to think about leaks, and emergency exits. Were we below the waterline here? There were no windows at all.

My chest started to feel tight and I clenched my fists. *Don't panic. Do not, for God's sake, have a panic attack down here.*

One. Two. Three. . . .

I realized that Eva was speaking, and tried to concentrate on her words, not on the low ceiling and cramped airless space. Perhaps when we got into the treatment rooms, and were less crowded, it would be better.

". . . three treatment rooms down here," Eva was saying. "Plus the chair upstairs, so I have taken the liberty of selecting therapies that we can run concurrently."

Please, please, please let mine be an upstairs one. My fingernails were digging into my palms.

"Miss West, I have you down for an aromatherapy session in treatment room one with Hanni," Eva said, consulting her list. "Miss Jenssen, you are having a facial in treatment room two with Klaus. I hope you don't mind a male therapist? Miss Blacklock, I have booked you a mud wrap in room three with Ulla."

I felt my breath quicken.

"What about Lady Bullmer?" Chloe said, looking around. "Where's she?"

"She is having a manicure upstairs."

"Um . . ." I spoke diffidently. "I don't suppose . . . could I have a manicure upstairs, too?"

"I'm sorry," Eva said, and she did sound sorry. "But there's only one chair upstairs. I'd be delighted to book you in for a manicure this afternoon, after your wrap. Or is there another treatment you'd prefer? We can offer Reiki, Swedish massage, Thai massage, reflexology. . . . We also have a flotation tank—if you've never tried one, they're incredibly soothing."

"No!" I said reflexively. Tina and Chloe turned their heads, and I realized suddenly how loudly I'd spoken, and consciously lowered my voice. "No, no, thank you. Flotation's not . . . not really my thing."

Just the thought of lying down here in a sealed plastic coffin full of water . . .

"No problem," Eva said with a smile. "Well, if you're all ready to begin? The treatment rooms are down the corridor. Each has its own en suite shower. Robes and towels are provided."

I nodded, hardly hearing her instructions, and then as she turned to go back upstairs, I followed Chloe and Tina down the corridor, hoping that my growing fear didn't show in my face. I could do this. I could *not* let my phobias get in the way of doing a good job. *Hi, Rowan, no, I didn't try the spa because it was two floors down and had no windows. Sorry.*

No. No way. It would be better once we were out of this narrow corridor and in our own treatment rooms.

I'd been hoping that the spa treatment time would give me a chance to talk to Tina, Anne, and Chloe, and sound them out about their movements last night, but as Chloe disappeared into her treatment room, the door closing behind her, I realized that wasn't going to be the case.

On the other side of the corridor, Tina had stopped at a door marked "Treatment Room 1," and I waited for her to enter so I could pass on down the corridor, but she turned back to face me, her hand on the doorknob.

"Darling," she said awkwardly, "I, um . . . I may have been a little abrupt, when we last spoke."

For a moment I couldn't think what she was talking about, and then it came back—our encounter on the deck, her spitting fury at my questions. Why *had* she been so touchy about her movements last night?

"What can I say . . . hangover . . . lack of cigs. But that's no excuse for snapping at you." Her whole bearing and manner screamed a woman more used to demanding apologies than giving them.

"It's fine," I said stiffly. "I completely understand, I'm not a morning person, either. I— Honestly, consider it forgotten." But I felt my face flush with the lie.

Tina put her hand out and squeezed my arm, with what I assumed was meant to be a friendly gesture of farewell, but her rings were cold against my skin, and as the door swung shut behind her, I let the shudder I had been repressing roll over me.

Then I took a deep breath and tapped at the door of treatment room three.

"Come in, Miss Blacklock!" said a voice from inside, and the door swung open and Ulla was standing there smiling, wearing a white spa uniform. I stepped inside the little room, looking around me. It was small—but not as narrow as the corridor, and with only Ulla and myself, it felt considerably less crowded. I felt the tightness in my chest ease slightly.

The room was lit with the same flickering electric candles as the stairwell, and there was a raised bed in the center, covered with clear plastic film. A white sheet was folded at the foot.

"Welcome to the spa, Miss Blacklock," Ulla said. "Today you will be experiencing a mud wrap. Have you had one before?"

I shook my head, mutely.

"It is very pleasurable and very good for detoxing the skin. The first step is to please remove your clothes and lie upon the bed, covering with the sheet."

"Should I keep my underwear on?" I said, trying to sound as if I went to spas every day.

"No, the mud will stain," Ulla said firmly. My face must have expressed my feelings, because she bent and took what looked like a piece of crumpled hand towel from a cupboard.

"If you prefer, we provide disposable panties. Some of our guests use them, some do not; it is entirely how you feel comfortable. And now I will leave you to undress. The shower, if you wish it, is through here."

She indicated a door to the left of the bed, and then backed out of the room with a smile, closing the door softly, and I began to strip off my clothes layer by layer, feeling more and more uncomfortable. I piled them on the chair along with my shoes and then, when I was completely naked, I stepped into the flimsy paper knickers and climbed onto the bed, my bare skin sticking uncomfortably to the plastic, and pulled the white sheet up to my chin.

Almost as soon as I'd done so—quickly enough to make me wonder queasily whether there was some kind of camera in the room—there was a soft knock on the door and I heard Ulla's voice.

"May I come in, Miss Blacklock?"

"Yes," I said croakily, and she entered, holding a bowl of what looked like, and presumably was, warm mud.

"If you would like to lie on your front," Ulla said softly, and I wriggled around. It was surprisingly difficult, with the sticky film clinging to my skin, and I felt the sheet slip, but Ulla deftly tweaked it back into place. She touched something to the side of the door and the room was filled with soft whale sounds and the crash of waves. I had the unsettling image again of the weight of water just the other side of the thin metal hull . . .

"Could you . . ." I said awkwardly, speaking into the bed. "Is there another track?"

"Of course," Ulla said. She pressed something and the music changed to Tibetan metal bells and wind chimes. "Is that better?"

I nodded, and she said, "Now, if you're quite ready . . . ?"

The treatment was surprisingly soothing, once I had forced myself to relax a little. I even got used to the feeling of having a complete stranger massaging mud into my mostly naked body. Halfway through I realized, with a jolt, that Ulla was speaking to me.

"Sorry," I managed sleepily. "What did you say?"

"If you could turn over," she murmured, and I turned onto my back, the mud slipping and sliding against the plastic. Ulla draped the sheet over my upper body once again and began to massage the fronts of my legs.

She worked her way methodically up my body, and at last smoothed the mud over my forehead, cheeks, and closed eyes, before speaking again, in her low, soothing voice.

"I will wrap you up now, Miss Blacklock, to allow the mud to work, and I will return in about half an hour to help you unwrap and shower. If you need anything, there's a call button to your right." She pressed my hand to a button set into the side of the bed. "Is everything quite all right?"

"Quite all right," I said drowsily. The warmth of the room and the soft chimes of the music were extraordinarily soporific. I was finding it hard to remember everything that had happened the night before. Harder to care. I just wanted to sleep. . . .

I felt the plastic film close around me, and then something heavy and warm on top of that—a towel, I thought. Behind my closed lids, I was aware that the lights of the room had been dimmed.

"I will be just outside," she said, and I heard the soft click of the door. I stopped fighting the tiredness, and I let the warmth and the darkness close over my head.

I dreamed of the girl, drifting miles below us in the cold, sunless depths of the North Sea. I dreamed of her laughing eyes white and bloated with salt water, of her soft skin, wrinkled and sloughing, of her T-shirt ripped by jagged rocks and disintegrating into rags.

Only her long black hair remained, floating

through the water like fronds of dark seaweed, tangling in shells and fishing nets, washing up on the shore in hanks like frayed rope, where it lay, limp, the roar of the crashing waves against the shingle filling my ears.

I woke uneasy and heavy with dread. It took me a while to remember where I was, and still longer to realize that the roar in my ears was not part of the dream but real.

I climbed off the bed, shivering slightly, and wondering how long I'd been lying here. The warm towel had cooled off and the mud on my skin had dried and cracked. The noise sounded like it was coming from the en suite shower room.

My heart was thumping in my chest as I approached the closed door, but taking my courage in both hands, I turned the bathroom door handle and flung open the door, a wave of hot steam engulfing me. I coughed as I fought my way across the misty bathroom to turn off the shower, getting half drenched in the process. Had Ulla come in and turned it on? But why hadn't she woken me?

As the shower trickled and gurgled to a halt, I groped my way back to the door, my dripping hair plastered to my face, and felt for the light, which would activate the extractor fan and clear some of the steam.

I hit the switch and light flooded the shower room—and that's when I saw it.

Written across the steamy mirror, in letters maybe six inches high, were the words *STOP DIGGING*.

Monday, 28 September

BBC News Website
Monday 28th September

MISSING BRITON LAURA BLACK-LOCK: BODY FOUND BY DANISH FISHERMEN

Danish fishermen dredging in the North Sea off the coast of Norway have found the body of a woman.

Scotland Yard have been called in to assist the Norwegian police investigation into the discovery of a body, dredged up in the early hours of Monday morning by Danish fishermen, lending weight to speculation that the deceased may be missing British journalist Laura Blacklock (32), who disappeared last week while holidaying in Norway. A spokesperson for Scotland Yard confirmed that they have been called in to help with the investigation, but declined to comment on possible links to Ms. Blacklock's disappearance.

Norwegian police said that the body was that of a young Caucasian woman, and that the process of confirming the woman's identity was under way.

Laura Blacklock's partner, Judah Lewis, when telephoned at his home in North London, refused to respond to the speculation, except to say that he was and is "devastated by Laura's continued disappearance."

PART FIVE

- CHAPTER 17 -

For a second I couldn't do anything. I just stood, staring at the dripping letters, my heart beating until I thought I would be sick. There was a strange roaring in my ears, and I could hear sobbing sounds, like a frightened animal—it was a horrible noise halfway between terror and pain and an odd, detached part of myself knew that the person making the sounds was me.

Then the room seemed to shift and the walls started to close in, and I realized I was having a panic attack, and was going to pass out unless I got myself somewhere safe. Half crawling, I lurched to the bed, where I lay, curled in the fetal position, trying to slow my breathing. I remembered what my CBT coach used to say: *Calm conscious breathing, Lo, and progressive relaxation—one muscle at a time. Calm breathing . . . conscious relaxation. Calm . . . and conscious. Conscious . . . and . . . calm . . .*

I hated him even then. It barely took the edge off the panic attack at the time, let alone now, when there really was something to panic about.

Calm . . . and conscious . . . I heard his light, smug tenor in my head and somehow the well-remembered fury anchored me, made me strong enough to slow my shallow, panicked breaths and, at last, to sit up, dragging my hands through my damp hair and look about me for a phone.

Sure enough, there was one on the counter, beside an empty pack of spa mud. My hands were shaking, and crusted with dried mud so that I could barely pick up the phone, let alone dial 0, but when I did, and I heard a Scandinavian-accented voice say, "Hallo, may I help you?" I did not speak, I just sat, my finger poised over the dial.

Then I put the phone down with a click.

The message was gone.

I could see the shower-room mirror from where I sat on the bed, and now that the shower was turned off and the extractor fan was running, the steam had all but disappeared. All you could see were a couple of runnels of water where the bottom of the two *I*s in *DIGGING* had been, and that was it.

Nilsson would never believe me.

When I had showered and dressed, I walked back along the corridor. I looked in as I passed the other two rooms, but they were quite empty, their doors open, showing neatly cleared couches ready for the next clients. How long had I been asleep for?

When I made my way up the stairs to the spa reception, it, too, was empty, apart from Eva, who was sitting at the desk and typing something on a laptop. She looked up as I emerged from the concealed door and smiled.

"Ah! Miss Blacklock. Did you enjoy your treatment? Ulla went down to remove the wraps a little while ago but you were deeply asleep; she was planning to return in quarter of an hour. I hope you weren't disorientated to wake up alone."

"It's fine," I said tightly. "When did Chloe and Tina leave?"

"About twenty minutes ago, I think."

I nodded at the door behind me, the one I'd just come through—now closed again and invisible unless you knew the mirror's secret.

"Is this the only entrance to the spa?"

"It depends what you mean by *entrance*," she said slowly, obviously confused by the question. "It is the only entrance but it is not the only exit. There is a fire exit downstairs that leads into the staff quarters, but it is . . . what's the word. Single way? It opens outwards only. Also it is alarmed, so I don't recommend you use it or there will be an evacuation! Why do you ask?"

"No reason."

I had made a mistake in blabbing to Nilsson this morning. I wasn't going to make that mistake again. I was keeping my cards close to my chest this time.

"They are serving lunch in the Lindgren Lounge," Eva said, "but don't worry, you haven't missed anything—it is a buffet lunch, so people are free to come and go. Oh, and I almost forgot," she said as I turned to go. "Did Mr. Howard find you?"

"No." I stopped dead, my hand on the door. "Why?"

"He came here looking for you. I explained that you were undergoing a treatment so he could not speak to you personally, but he went downstairs to leave a message with Ulla. Would you like me to try to find it?"

"No," I said shortly. "I'll find him myself. Did anyone else go down?"

She shook her head.

"No. I have been here the whole time. Miss Blacklock, are you *sure* nothing is wrong?"

I didn't answer. I just turned and left the spa, feeling the chill damp of my skin beneath my clothes, and a cold dread that had spread far deeper.

The Lindgren Lounge was empty except for Cole, who was sitting at a table with his camera in front of him, and Chloe, who was across from him, staring out of the window and forking salad absentmindedly into her mouth. She looked up when I came in and nodded at the chair next to her.

"Hey! Wasn't the spa amazing?"

"I guess," I said as I pulled up a chair, and then, realizing how strange and ungracious I must be sounding, I tried again. "I mean, yes, it was. My treatment was very good. I'm just—I'm not good with enclosed spaces. I'm kind of claustrophobic."

"Oh!" Her face cleared. "I wondered why you looked so tense downstairs. I thought you were hungover."

"Well." I gave a false-sounding laugh. "That too, probably."

Could it have been her, down in the spa? It was definitely possible. But Ben had been so clear about last night—she had never left the room.

What about Tina, then? I thought of her wiry strength, and her fierce reaction to my question about where she had been last night, and I abso-

lutely could believe she would push someone overboard.

Could it have been *Ben*? He had come down into
the spa, and I only had his own word for his alibi last
night, after all.

I wanted to scream. This was sending me mad.

"Listen," I said casually to Chloe, "you were playing poker last night, weren't you?"

"I wasn't playing. But I was there, yes. Poor Lars
got fleeced, but then, he can afford it." She gave a
short, rather heartless laugh, and Cole looked up
from the other table and flashed her a grin.

"This is going to sound like an odd question . . .
but did any of the others leave the cabin?"

"I couldn't honestly say," Chloe said. "I went
through to the bedroom after a while. Poker's the
most boring game to watch. Cole was there for a bit
of it, weren't you, Cole?"

"Only for about half an hour," Cole said. "Like
Chloe says, poker's not really a spectator sport. I do
remember Howard leaving. He went to get his wallet." My mouth was suddenly dry as he continued,
"Why d'you want to know?"

"Doesn't matter." I tried to force a smile, and
changed the subject before he could pin me down
for an answer. "How are the photos?"

"Take a look if you like," he said, tossing the camera across with such casualness that I gasped, and
nearly dropped it. "Press the play button on the back
and you can scroll through them. I'll send you a print
of any you like."

I began to work my way through the pictures,
going back in time through the voyage, past moody

shots of clouds and wheeling gulls, past the poker game last night, pictures of Bullmer laughing and scooping Ben's chips towards him, and Lars groaning as he laid down a pair of twos to Ben's three fives. One, from last night, almost took my breath away. It was a photo of Chloe, taken from very close. Her eyes had just flicked towards the camera. You could see the tiny hairs on her cheek, golden in the lamplight, and the smile that just tugged at the corner of her mouth, and there was something so intimate and so tender about the shot that I felt like an intruder even looking at it. My gaze went to Chloe, almost inadvertently, wondering about her and Cole, and she looked up.

"What is it? Found one of me?"

I shook my head and hastily flicked on to the next picture before she had time to look over my shoulder at the little screen. The next one was of myself, the shot that Cole had taken last night that had caught me unawares and caused me to spill my coffee. He had snapped me as I flung my head up in alarm, and the look in my eyes made me flinch.

I pressed the button to continue.

The others were just more of the ship . . . one of Tina on deck looking piercingly at the camera, her eyes like a raptor's, one of Ben carrying an oversize rucksack up the gangway. I was reminded again of Cole's enormous trunk. What *was* in it? Photographic equipment, he'd said, but all I'd seen him use so far was this one point-and-click.

And then I was past the pictures of the ship and into some society party. I was about to hand the camera back when my heart seemed to stutter in my chest and I froze. The screen was displaying a picture of a man eating a canapé.

"Who's he?" Chloe said over my shoulder. And then, "Wait, isn't that Alexander Belhomme in the background, talking to Archer?"

It was. But it wasn't Alexander or Archer I was looking at.

It was the waitress holding the tray of canapés.

She had her face turned half away from the camera and her dark hair was falling out of its clip, across her cheek.

But I was almost certain—almost completely certain—that she was the woman in cabin 10.

- CHAPTER 18 -

I handed the camera back carefully, my heart thumping, wondering whether to say anything. This was proof—irrefutable proof—that Cole, Archer, and Alexander had been in the same room as the woman I'd seen. Should I ask Cole if he knew her?

I sat in an agony of indecision as he switched off his camera and began packing it away.

Fuck. *Fuck.* Should I say something?

I had no idea what to do. It was possible Cole didn't realize the significance of the picture he'd taken. The girl was half out of the shot, the focus was on some other person completely, a man I'd never met.

If Cole had something to hide, I'd be incredibly foolish to flag what I'd just seen. He'd deny it, and then he'd probably delete the picture.

On the other hand, it was very likely he had no idea who the girl was and might be willing to let me have the image. But if I raised the issue now, in front of Chloe, and with who knew who else possibly listening . . .

I thought of the way Bjorn had appeared from behind the paneling at breakfast and I involuntarily looked over my shoulder. The last thing I wanted was for this picture to go the way of the mascara. I wasn't going to make the same mistake twice. If I did decide to confront Cole, I should do it in private. The photo had been safe on Cole's camera up until now; it would be safe a little longer.

I stood up, my knees suddenly shaky.

"I'm—I'm actually not very hungry," I said to Chloe. "And I'm supposed to be meeting Ben Howard."

"Oh, I forgot," she said casually. "He was in here looking for you. I met him coming up out of the spa. He said he had something important to tell you."

"Did he say where he was going?"

"Back to his cabin to do some work, I think."

"Thanks."

Bjorn appeared again like a genie from behind the concealed screen.

"May I get you a drink, Miss Blacklock?"

I shook my head.

"No, I've remembered I'm supposed to be meeting someone. Could you please send a sandwich to my suite?"

"Certainly." He nodded, and I slipped out of the room with an apologetic nod to Cole and Chloe.

I was hurrying along the corridor that led towards the aft cabins when I rounded a corner and ran slap into Ben himself—literally. We collided with a crash that knocked the breath out of me.

"Lo!" He grabbed my arm. "I've been looking for you everywhere."

"I know. What were you doing down in the spa?"

"Didn't you just hear me? Looking for you."

I stared at him, at his face, the picture of innocence,

his eyes above his dark beard round and full of urgency. Could I trust him? I had absolutely no idea. A few years ago I would have said I knew Ben inside out—right up until the moment he walked out. Now I had learned that I couldn't even totally trust myself, let alone another person.

"Did you come into my treatment room?" I asked abruptly.

"What?" He looked momentarily confused. "No, of course not. They said you were getting a mud wrap. I didn't think you'd want me barging in. I was told to look for some girl called Ulla, but she wasn't there, so I pushed a note under your door and came back up."

"I didn't see any note."

"Well, I left one. What's this about?"

Something in my chest felt like bursting—a mixture of fear and frustration. How could I possibly know if Ben were telling the truth? The note would be a stupid thing to lie about anyway—even if he'd written the message in the steam, why fib about leaving me a note? Perhaps it *had* been there, and I'd just overlooked it in my panic.

"Someone else left me a message," I said at last. "Written in steam on the mirror of the shower next door while I was having the treatment. It said *Stop digging.*"

"*What?*" His pink face went slack with shock, his mouth hanging open. If he was acting, it was the best performance I'd ever seen him give. "Are you serious?"

"One hundred percent."

"But—but didn't you see them go in? Is there another entrance to the bathroom?"

"No. They must have come through the room I . . ." I felt oddly ashamed saying it, but I put my chin up, refusing to be apologetic. "I fell asleep. There's only one entrance to the spa, and Eva says no one went down except for Tina and Chloe . . . and you."

"And the spa staff," Ben reminded me. "Plus, surely there must be a fire exit down there?"

"There's an exit, but it's one-way. It leads into the staff quarters, but you can't open it from the other side. I asked."

Ben looked unconvinced.

"Not that hard for someone to wedge it open, though, right?"

"No, but it's alarmed. There would have been sirens going off all over the place."

"Well, I guess it's possible if you knew enough about the system you could fiddle with the alarm settings. But Eva wasn't there the whole time, you know."

"What do you mean?"

"She wasn't there when I came back up. Anne Bullmer was—she was waiting for her nail varnish to dry. But Eva was gone. So if she says she was there for the whole time, she's not telling the truth."

Oh God. I thought about myself, lying there, half-naked beneath the thin film wraps and towels, and how someone—anyone—could have come in and placed a hand over my mouth, wound a sheet of plastic around my head . . .

"So what did you want to see me about?" I said, trying to sound normal. Ben looked uneasy.

"Oh . . . that. Well, you know we were on a tour of the bridge and so on?"

I nodded.

"Archer was trying to text someone, I think, and he dropped his phone. I picked it up, and it was open on the contacts page."

"And?"

"The name just said *Jess*, but the preview picture was a girl, a lot like the one you described. Late twenties, long dark hair, dark eyes . . . and this is the thing—she was wearing a Pink Floyd T-shirt."

Something cold trickled down my spine. I remembered Archer last night, his laughing face as he twisted my arm up behind my back, Chloe's disapproving *maybe the rumors about his first wife are true.* . . .

"Was she the person he was trying to text?" I asked. Ben shook his head.

"I don't know. He might have pressed a few buttons when he fumbled the phone."

Automatically, I pulled out my own phone, ready to google "Jess Fenlan"—but the search bar whirred fruitlessly. The Internet was still down, and my e-mails were still not loading.

"Is your Internet working?" I asked Ben. He shook his head.

"No, there's some issue with the router, apparently. I suppose teething problems are par for the course with maiden voyages, but it's a right pain. Archer was sounding off about it over lunch; he kicked up quite a stink to poor Hanni. I thought she was about to burst into tears at one point. Anyway, she went and spoke to Camilla Wotserface, and it'll be fixed shortly, apparently. At least, I bloody hope it will be, I've got a piece to file."

I frowned as I pushed the phone back in my pocket.

Could Archer have been the person who wrote the message in the steam? I thought of his strength, the hint of cruelty in his smile last night, and I felt sick at the idea of him tiptoeing past me while I slept.

"We went down to the engine room," Ben said, almost as if reading my thoughts. "It's three decks down, we probably passed fairly close to that exit from the spa you were talking about."

"Would you have noticed if someone had peeled off from the group?" I asked. Ben shook his head.

"I doubt it. The engine deck was very cramped, we were all kind of strung out, slotting in and out of small spaces, the group only got back together when we got upstairs."

I felt suddenly and nauseously claustrophobic, as if the stifling opulence of the boat were closing around me.

"I've got to get out," I said. "Anywhere."

"Lo." Ben put a hand out towards my shoulder, but I pulled myself away from his grasping fingers and staggered towards the deck door, forcing it open against the wind.

On deck, the wind hit me in the face like a punch, and I stumbled to the rail, hanging over it, feeling the pitch of the boat. The dark gray waves stretched out like a desert—mile upon mile, stretching to the horizon, no sign of land of any kind, nor even a ship. I shut my eyes, seeing the fruitless whirling of the Internet search engine icon. There was literally no way of calling for help.

"Are you all right?" I heard over my shoulder, the words snatched by the wind. Ben had followed me. I screwed my eyes shut against the salt spray that smacked the side of the ship and shook my head.

"Lo . . ."

"Don't touch me," I said through gritted teeth, and then the boat went up and over a particularly big wave and I felt my stomach clench and I threw up over the rail, my stomach heaving and heaving until my eyes watered and there was nothing left but acid. I saw, with a kind of vicious pleasure, that my vomit was spattered across the hull and porthole below. *Paintwork not so perfect now*, I thought as I wiped my mouth with my sleeve.

"Are you okay?" Ben said again from behind me, and I clenched my fists on the rail. *Be nice, Lo . . .*

I turned round and forced myself to nod.

"I actually feel a bit better. I've never been a great sailor."

"Oh, Lo." He put an arm around me and squeezed, and I let myself be pulled into his hug, suppressing the urge to pull away. I needed Ben on my side. I needed him to trust me, to think I trusted him. . . .

A whiff of cigarette smoke caught my nostrils and I heard the *tap, tap* of high heels coming along the port side of the boat.

"Oh God." I stood up straighter, moving away from Ben almost as if it were accidental. "It's Tina, can we go in? I can't face her at the moment."

Not now. Not with tears drying on my cheeks and vomit on my sleeve. It was hardly the professional, ambitious image I was trying to project.

"Sure," Ben said solicitously, and he held open the

door as we hurried inside, just as Tina rounded the corner of the deck.

After the roar of the wind the corridor was suddenly quiet, and stiflingly hot, and we watched in silence as Tina strolled to the rail and leaned over, just a few paces upwind of where I had vomited moments before.

"If you want to know the truth," Ben said, looking out through the glass at Tina's unconscious back, "my money would be on her. She's a stone-cold bitch."

I looked at him in shock. Ben had sometimes been hostile about the women he worked with, but I'd never heard such naked dislike in his voice.

"*Excuse* me? Because she's an ambitious woman?"

"Not just that. You haven't worked with her, I have. I've met a few careerists in my time, but she's in another league. I swear she'd kill for a story or a promotion, and it's women she seems to pick on. I can't stand women like that. They're their own worst enemy."

I kept silent. There was something close to misogyny in his words and tone, but at the same time, it was so uncomfortably close to what Rowan had said that I wasn't sure if I could dismiss it as just that.

But Tina *had* been downstairs in the spa with me when the message appeared. And then there was her defensiveness earlier this morning. . . .

"I asked her where she was last night," I said, half reluctantly. "She was really odd. Very aggressive. She said I shouldn't go about making enemies."

"Oh *that*," Ben said. He smiled, but it wasn't a pleasant smile, there was something rather unkind about it. "You won't get her to admit it, but I happen to know she was with Josef."

"*Josef?* As in, cabin attendant Josef? Are you kidding me?"

"Nope. I got it from Alexander during the tour. He saw Josef tiptoeing out of Tina's cabin in the early hours in a state of—let's just say *déshabillé.*"

"Blimey."

"Blimey indeed. Who'd have thought Josef's devotion to passenger comfort would extend so far. He's not really my type, but I wonder if I could persuade Ulla to do the same. . . ."

I didn't laugh. Not with the narrow, sunless rooms just a couple of decks beneath where we were standing right now.

How far might someone go to escape their confines?

But then Tina turned from where she was smoking at the rail and caught sight of me and Ben inside the boat. She flicked her cigarette over the rail and gave me a little wink before making her way back along the deck, and I felt suddenly vile at the thought of all the men chuckling about her little adventure behind her back.

"What about Alexander, then, if it comes to that?" I said accusingly. "His cabin's aft, along with ours. And what was he doing spying on Tina in the middle of the night?"

Ben snorted.

"Are you kidding me? He must be three hundred and fifty pounds. I can't see him lifting an adult woman over a rail."

"He wasn't playing poker, so we've no idea where he was, apart from the fact that he was prowling around in the early hours of the morning." I remembered, too, with a sudden chill, that he had been in the photo on Cole's camera.

"He's the size of a walrus. Plus he's got a heart condition. Have you ever seen him take the stairs? Or, more to the point, heard him? He sounds like a steam train, and you start to worry when he gets to the top that he'll kark it and fall back on you. I can't imagine him overcoming anyone in a struggle."

"She could have been very drunk. Or drugged. I bet anyone could tip an unconscious woman overboard—it would be just a matter of leverage."

"If she was unconscious, then what about the scream?" Ben said, and I felt a sudden pulse of fury run through me.

"God, do you know what, I'm so fed up with everyone picking at and questioning me as if I should have the answers to all this. I don't *know*, Ben. I don't know what to think anymore. All right?"

"All right," he said mildly. "I'm sorry—I didn't mean it like that. I was just thinking aloud. Alexander—"

"Taking my name in vain?" came a voice from up the corridor, and we both swung around. I felt my cheeks go scarlet. How long had Alexander been there? Had he heard my speculations?

"Oh, hello, Belhomme," Ben said smoothly. He didn't seem at all put out. "We were just talking about you."

"So I heard." Alexander drew level with us, panting slightly. Ben was right, I realized. The smallest exertion set him gasping breathlessly. "All good, I hope?"

"Of course," Ben said. "We were just discussing dinner tonight. Lo was saying how knowledgeable you were about food."

For a minute I couldn't think of anything to say, stunned by how good a liar Ben had become since we were together. Or had he always been such a slick deceiver and I'd just never noticed?

Then I realized both Ben and Alexander were waiting for me to speak, and I stammered, "Oh, yes, remember, Alexander? You were telling me about fugu."

"Of course. *Such* a thrill. I do think it's one's responsibility to wring every *ounce* of sensation out of life, don't you? Otherwise, without that, it's just a short, nasty, and brutal interlude until death."

He gave a broad, slightly crocodile-like smile, and hoisted something beneath his arm. It was a book; a volume of Patricia Highsmith, I saw.

"Where are you off to?" Ben asked casually. "We've got a few hours free until dinner now, I think."

"Don't tell anyone," Alexander said confidentially. "But this color isn't *entirely* natural." He touched his— now that he mentioned it—rather walnut-colored cheek. "So I'm off to the spa for a little touch-up. My wife always says I look better with a color."

"I didn't know you were married," I said, hoping my surprise wasn't too evident in my voice. Alexander nodded.

"For my sins. Thirty-eight years this year. You get less for murder, I'm led to believe!"

He gave a slightly grating laugh, and I inwardly cringed. If he hadn't heard what we were saying earlier, it was an odd remark. If he *had* heard, then it was in very poor taste indeed.

"Have a nice time in the spa," I said at last, lamely. He smiled again.

"I will. See you at dinner!"

He was turning to go when I spoke, suddenly, compelled by an impetus I couldn't quite dissect.

"Wait, Alexander—"

He turned, one eyebrow raised. I felt my courage falter, but I carried on.

"I—this is going to sound a little strange, but I heard some noises last night, coming from cabin ten, the one at the end of the ship. It's supposed to be empty but there was a woman in it yesterday—only now we can't track her down. Did you see or hear anything last night? A splash? Any other noise? Ben said you were up."

"I was *indeed* up," Alexander said dryly. "I have trouble sleeping—you do, you know, when you get to my age, and a new bed always makes the matter worse. So I slipped up on deck for a little midnight walkies. And on my way there and back I saw quite a few comings and goings. Our dear friend Tina had a little visit from our *very* attentive cabin crew. And that dishy Mr. Lederer was prowling round here at one stage. I don't know *what* he was doing out of bounds. His cabin is at quite the other end of the ship. I did wonder if he might have been coming to see you . . . ?"

He cocked an eyebrow at me and I blushed furiously.

"No, definitely not. Could he have been going into cabin ten?"

"I didn't see," Alexander said regretfully. "I just caught a glimpse of him rounding the corner. On his way back to his cabin to establish an alibi for his crimes, perhaps?"

"What time did you see all this?" Ben asked. Alexander pursed his lips, thinking.

"Hmm . . . it must have been around four or four thirty, I think."

I exchanged a glance with Ben. I had been woken up at 3:04. That meant that the sighting of Josef at four a.m. probably ruled out Tina—presumably he had been in her cabin all night. But Cole . . . what reason could he possibly have for being down at this end of the ship?

I thought again of his huge case of equipment being bumped up the gangway.

"And who was the woman I saw coming out of *your* cabin?" Alexander said, rather slyly, looking at Ben. Ben blinked.

"Sorry? Are you sure you have the right cabin?"

"Number eight, isn't that right?"

"That's mine"—Ben gave an uneasy laugh—"but I can assure you no one was in my cabin apart from me."

"Is that so?" Alexander raised his eyebrow again, and then chuckled. "Well, if you say so. It *was* dark. Perhaps I mistook the cabin." He hoisted his book under his arm again. "Well, if you have no further questions, my dears?"

"N-no . . ." I said, slightly reluctantly. "At least, not now. May I come and find you if I think of anything else?"

"Of course. In that case, adieu until dinner, when I shall emerge bronzed as a young Adonis, and basted as a Christmas turkey. Toodle pip . . ."

He puffed away, up the corridor. Ben and I watched as he rounded the corner.

"He's the full package, isn't he?" Ben said when he'd disappeared.

"He's—he's just so full-on. Do you think that character is all an act? Or is he really like that twenty-four/seven?"

"I have no idea. I suspect it started out as a bit of a pose, but it's become second nature now."

"And his wife—have you ever met her?"

"No. But apparently she really exists. She's supposedly something of a dragon—daughter of a German count, and apparently quite the beauty in her day. They've got this incredible house in South Kensington, it's full of original artworks—Rubens and Titians, utterly unbelievable stuff. It was featured in *Hello!* a while back and there were all these rumors that they were actually looted Nazi stuff and they got a tap on the shoulder from the IFAR, but I think that's bollocks."

"I can't work out whether he said anything useful." I rubbed my hands over my face, trying to scrub away the weariness that was starting to settle over me like a black cloud. "That stuff about Cole, that was weird, right?"

"Y-yes . . . I guess. But if it was around four, does that really help? And, to be honest, I'm starting to think that he's maybe just making stuff up for effect. That thing about me having a girl in my cabin was pure bollocks. You *do* believe that, right?"

"I—" I felt a lump rise in my throat. I was so tired. I was *so* tired. But I couldn't rest. Jesus, so much for this trip being the making of my career. If I carried on causing trouble like this I could end up with an address book full of enemies, not contacts. "Yes, of course," I managed. Ben looked at me, as if trying to gauge whether I was telling the truth.

"Good," he said at last. "Because, I swear, there was no one in my cabin. Unless someone got in while I was out, of course."

"Do you think he heard us?" I asked, more to change the subject than because I wanted to know. "Before, I mean. The way he came round that corner— you wouldn't think someone so big could creep up on you like that."

Ben shrugged.

"I doubt it. I don't think he's the type to hold a grudge, anyway."

I said nothing, but inwardly I wasn't sure I agreed. Alexander struck me as *exactly* the type to hold a grudge, and enjoy holding it, too.

"What do you want to do now?" Ben asked. "Want me to come with you to find Bullmer?"

I shook my head. I needed to go back to my cabin, get some food inside me. And besides, I wasn't at all sure I wanted Ben to come with me to see Lord Bullmer.

- CHAPTER 19 -

The door to my cabin was locked, but inside an open sandwich was resting on a room service tray on the dressing table, alongside a bottle of mineral water. It had been there some time, judging by the runnels of condensation on the side.

I wasn't hungry, but I'd had nothing since breakfast, and most of that I'd thrown up, so I sat and forced myself to eat it. It was prawn and hard-boiled egg on heavy rye bread, and as I chewed it, I watched the sea rise and fall outside the window, its ceaseless movement echoing the restless thoughts that were running around inside my head.

Cole, Alexander, and Archer had actually been in the same room as that girl—I was almost sure of it. Her face had been turned away from the camera, and it was hard for me to remember the brief flash of features I'd seen through the open cabin door yesterday, but the jolt of recognition I had felt when I saw the picture had been like an electric shock—I *had* to hang on to that certainty.

Archer at least had an alibi—but I was beginning to realize that it was one that rested entirely on Ben's evidence, and that he had his own reasons for wanting that room to be secure. And no matter how you spun it, he had deliberately lied to me. If it hadn't been for Cole's chance remark, I would never have known that Ben himself had left the cabin.

But Ben. *Ben?* Surely not. If I could trust anyone on board this boat it *had* to be him, right?

I wasn't sure anymore.

I swallowed the final crust of bread, wiped my fingers on the napkin, and stood, feeling the rock and sway of the boat beneath me. While I'd eaten, a sea mist had crept in, and the room had become darker, so I switched on the light before checking my phone. There was nothing there—nothing from Judah, either. I refreshed, hoping without hope for an e-mail from someone, anyone. I didn't dare think about Judah—about what his silence meant.

When the CONNECTION FAILED notification came up, I felt a shift in my stomach that was mingled fear and relief. Relief because it meant that perhaps, just perhaps, Judah had been trying to contact me. That his silence didn't mean what I feared it might.

But fear because the longer the Internet was down, the more I was starting to think that someone was deliberately trying to stop me from accessing the Web. And that was starting to make me feel very worried indeed.

The door to suite 1, Nobel, was the same anonymous white wood as the rest of the cabin doors, but you could tell from the fact that it was by itself in the prow of the boat, with a blank expanse of corridor stretching away behind us, that it must be something pretty special.

I knocked, cautiously. I'm not sure what I expected—Richard Bullmer, or perhaps even a maid, neither would have surprised me. But I was thrown completely when the door opened and Anne Bullmer was standing there.

She had clearly been crying, her dark eyes rimmed with red and circled with deep shadows, and there were traces still on her gaunt cheeks.

I blinked, completely losing the thread of the carefully prepared request I'd rehearsed in my head. Phrases skittered through my mind, each more inappropriate and impossible than the other: *Are you okay? What's wrong? Is there anything I can do?*

I said none of them, just gulped.

"Yes?" she said, with a touch of defiance. She brought up a corner of her silk robe and wiped at her eyes, and then put her chin up. "Can I help you?"

I swallowed again, and then said, "I, yes, I hope so. I'm sorry for intruding, you must be tired after the spa morning."

"Not particularly," she said, rather shortly. I bit my lip. Maybe referring to her illness hadn't been tactful.

"I was actually hoping to speak to your husband."

"Richard? He's busy, I'm afraid. Is it something I can help with?"

"I—I don't think so," I said awkwardly, and then wondered whether to make my excuses and leave, or stay and explain. I felt bad disturbing her, but it seemed equally wrong to knock and then leave so abruptly. Part of my discomfort was the tears—pulling me in two directions, to go and leave her to her private grief, to stay and offer comfort. But it was also because I found her gaunt, smooth face so unsettling. She seemed so unassailable in every other way. To see someone like Anne Bullmer, so privileged, with every advantage that money could buy—the latest medicine, the best doctors and treatments available—to see her fighting for her life like this, before our very eyes, was almost unbearable.

I wanted to run away, but that knowledge forced me to stand my ground.

"Well, I'm sorry," she said. "Perhaps it can wait until later? Can I tell him what it's about?"

"I . . ." I twisted my fingers together. What could I possibly say? There was no way I was spilling my suspicions to this frail, haunted-looking woman. "I— He promised me an interview," I said, remembering his throwaway words after dinner. It was kind of half-true, after all. "He told me to come to the cabin this afternoon."

"Oh." Her face cleared. "I am sorry. He must have forgotten. I think he's gone to the hot tub with Lars and a few others. Hopefully you can catch him at dinner."

I had no intention of waiting that long, but I didn't say that, just nodded.

"Am I— Will we see you at dinner?" I asked, and cringed at the way I was stumbling over my words. *For God's sake. She's ill, not a leper.* She nodded.

"I hope so. I'm feeling a little better today. I get very tired, but it seems like a capitulation to let my body win too often."

"Are you still undergoing treatment?" I asked. She shook her head, the soft silk scarf around her skull rustling as she did.

"Not at the moment. I've finished my last round of

chemotherapy, for the moment, anyway. I'll undergo radiotherapy when we get back, and then I suppose we'll see."

"Well, best of luck," I said, and then winced at the way the innocent remark seemed to make her survival into a kind of game of chance. "And, um, thanks," I finished.

"No problem at all."

She shut the door and I turned to walk back towards the stairs to the upper deck, feeling my face burn with a kind of shame.

I had never been to the hot tub, but I knew where it should be—on the top deck above the Lindgren Lounge, just outside the spa. I made my way up the thickly carpeted stairs towards the restaurant deck, expecting that feeling of light and space that I'd had before—but I'd forgotten the sea mist. When I got to the door that opened onto the deck, a wall of gray greeted me behind the glass, blanketing the ship in its folds so you could barely see from one end of the deck to the other, giving a strange, muffled feeling.

The mist had brought a chill to the air, fogging the hairs on my arms with drizzle, and as I stood uncertainly in the lee of the doorway, shivering and trying to get my bearings, I heard the long, mournful boom of a fog horn.

The whiteness made everything seem unfamiliar, and it took me a few minutes to work out where the stairs to the top deck were, but eventually I realized they must be to my right, further up towards the prow of the boat. I couldn't imagine anyone enjoying a Jacuzzi in this weather, and for a moment I wondered if Anne Bullmer had been mistaken. But as I rounded the glassed-in tip of the restaurant I heard laughter and looked up to see lights glowing in the mist above my head, coming from the deck above. Seemingly there were people mad enough to strip down, even in this cold.

I wished I'd brought a coat, but there was no sense going back for one, so I wrapped my arms around myself and climbed the slippery vertiginous steps to the upper deck, following the sound of voices and laughter.

There was a glass screen halfway along the deck, and when I slipped round it, there they were—Lars, Chloe, Richard Bullmer, and Cole, seated around the edge of the most enormous Jacuzzi I'd ever seen. It must have been eight or ten feet across, and they were leaning back against the sides, with just their shoulders and heads showing, the steam rising so densely from the bubbling water that it was hard for a moment to see who was in there.

"Miss Blacklock!" Richard Bullmer called heartily, his voice carrying easily above the roaring of the jets. "Have you recovered from last night?"

He stuck out a tanned, muscular arm, steaming and goose-bumped in the cold air, and I shook his dripping hand and then wrapped my arms back around myself, feeling the warmth of his grip fade immediately and the chill of the wind on my now-damp hands.

"Come for a dip?" Chloe asked with a laugh, waving an inviting hand at the rolling cauldron of bubbles.

"Thanks"—I shook my head, trying not to shudder—"but it's a bit cold."

"It's warmer in here, I can tell you!" Bullmer gave a wink. "Hot Jacuzzi, cold shower"—he indicated an open-sided shower to one side of the Jacuzzi, a vast rainwater shower rose poised above the tray. There was no temperature control, just a steel push button with a blue center, and the sight made me shudder involuntarily—"and then straight into the sauna," he finished, jerking a thumb at a wooden cabin tucked behind the glass screen. Craning my head round I could see a glass door streaming with condensation, and through the trickling runnels, the red glow of a brazier. "Then rinse and repeat as many times as your heart can stand it."

"It's not really my cup of tea," I said awkwardly.

"Don't knock it till you've tried it," Cole said. He grinned, showing his pointed incisors. "I have to say, jumping out of the sauna into the cold shower was a pretty incredible experience. What doesn't kill you makes you stronger, right?"

I flinched.

"Thanks, but I think I won't."

"Suit yourself." Chloe smiled. She stretched out a languorous arm, dripping water onto Cole's camera, which was resting on the floor below, and picked up a frosted glass of champagne from a little table placed alongside the tub.

"Look . . ." I took my courage in both hands and spoke directly to Lord Bullmer, trying to ignore the watching, interested faces of the others. "Lord Bullmer—"

"Call me Richard," he interrupted. I bit my lip and nodded, trying to keep my thoughts in order.

"Richard, I was hoping to talk to you about something, but I'm not sure if now is the right time. Could I come and see you later, in your cabin?"

"Why wait?" Bullmer shrugged. "One thing I've learned in business—now almost always *is* the right time. What feels like prudence is almost invariably cowardice—and someone else gets in there before you."

"Well . . ." I said, and then stopped, unsure what to do. I really didn't want to speak in front of the others. The "someone gets there before you" part certainly wasn't reassuring.

"Have a glass of something," Bullmer said. He pressed a button on the rim of the Jacuzzi and a girl appeared silently out of nowhere. It was Ulla.

"Yes, sir?" she said politely.

"Champagne, for Miss Blacklock."

"Certainly, sir." She melted away.

I took a deep breath. There was no alternative. No one could divert the boat except Bullmer, and if I didn't do this now, I might never get the chance. Better to speak up, even with an audience, than risk . . . I pushed that thought away.

I opened my mouth. *Stop digging* hissed the voice inside my head, but I forced myself to speak.

"Lord Bullmer—"

"Richard."

"Richard, I don't know if you've spoken to your head of security, Johann Nilsson. Have you seen him today?"

"Nilsson? No." Richard Bullmer frowned. "He reports to the captain, not to me. Why do you ask?"

"Well . . ." I began. But I was interrupted by Ulla

appearing at my elbow with a tray, on which was a champagne glass and a bottle in a holder full of ice.

"Um, thanks," I said uncertainly. I wasn't sure I wanted to drink right now—not after Nilsson's biting comments earlier, and on top of the hangover from last night—and it seemed an incongruous accompaniment to what I was about to say. But I felt again the impossibility of my position—I was Bullmer's guest, and *Velocity*'s representative, and I was supposed to be impressing all these people with my professionalism and dazzling them with my charm, and instead I was about to hurl the very worst of all possible accusations at his staff and guests. The least I could do was to accept his champagne with good grace.

I took the glass, sipping tentatively at it as I tried to get my thoughts in order. It was sour and made me shiver, and I almost pulled a face before realizing how rude that would appear to Bullmer.

"I— This is difficult."

"Nilsson," Bullmer prompted. "You were asking if I'd spoken to him."

"Yes. Well, last night I had to phone him. I . . . I heard noises, coming from the cabin next to mine. Number ten," I said, and then stopped.

Richard was listening, but so were the other three, rather avidly in Lars's case. Well, since I didn't have a choice, maybe I could turn that to my advantage. I cast a quick look round the circle of faces, trying to gauge their reactions, check for any trace of guilt or anxiety. Out of the three, Lars's moist red lips were curled in a disbelieving skepticism, and Chloe's green eyes were wide with frank curiosity. Only Cole was looking worried.

"Palmgren, yes," Bullmer said. He was frowning, puzzled as to where this was leading. "I thought that one was empty. Solberg canceled, didn't he?"

"I went to the veranda," I said, gaining momentum. I glanced around the listeners again. "And when I looked out there was no one there, but there was blood on the glass safety barrier."

"Good Lord," Lars said. He was openly grinning now, not even trying to hide his disbelief. "It's like something out of a novel." Was he deliberately trying to undermine my account, throw me off-balance? Or was this just his normal manner? I couldn't tell. "Go on," he said, with something close to sarcasm. "I'm on tenterhooks to find how this turns out."

"Your security guard let me in," I said, my voice harder now, and speaking fast. "But the cabin was empty. And the blood on the glass had been—"

There was a chink and a splash, and I stopped.

We all turned and looked at Cole, who was holding something over the side of the Jacuzzi. His hand was dripping blood, running down his fingers onto the pale wooden decking.

"I'm okay, I think," he said unsteadily. "I'm sorry, Richard, I don't know how, but I knocked my champagne over and I broke it, trying to save the glass. I don't think there's any glass in the water."

He held out a palmful of bloodstained shards, and Chloe gulped and squeezed her eyes shut.

"Ugh!" Her face was greenish white. "Oh God, Lars . . ."

Richard put down his glass, heaved himself out of the Jacuzzi, his near-naked body steaming in the cold air, and grabbed a white robe from a pile left on the bench. For a moment he said nothing, just looked dispassionately at Cole's hand, streaming blood onto the deck, and glanced at Chloe, who appeared close to fainting. Then he issued a series of orders like a surgeon barking out commands in an operating theater.

"Cole, for God's sake put down that pile of glass. I'll ring for Ulla to get you cleaned up. Lars, take Chloe off to lie down, she's gone white as chalk. Give her a Valium if that's what it takes. Eva has access to the medical supplies. And Miss Blacklock . . ." He turned to me and then paused, seeming to weigh his words very carefully as he belted the robe around himself. "Miss Blacklock, please take a seat in the restaurant, and when I've sorted this mess out, we'll run through what you actually saw and heard."

- CHAPTER 20 -

By the end of the next hour, I could see why Richard Bullmer had got to where he had in life.

He didn't just take me through my story—he grilled me on every single word, pinning me down on times, specifics, winkling out details I thought I didn't even know—like the exact shape of the blood spatter on the glass screen, and the way it was smeared, rather than sprayed, across the surface.

He didn't fill in any gaps with speculation, didn't try to lead me on, or persuade me on details I wasn't sure of. He just sat and fired questions at me between sips of scalding black coffee, his blue eyes very bright: What time? How long? When was that? How loud? What did she look like? As he spoke the slightly mockney overlay to his speech vanished, and the intonation became pure Old Etonian and 100 percent business. He was utterly focused, his attention on my story absolute, and without a trace of emotion in his face.

If someone had been walking along the deck outside and had glanced in the window, they would never have known that I had just told him something that could deal a sucker punch to his business, and revealed the presence of a possible psychopath

on board a small ship. As my story unfolded I was
expecting echoes of Nilsson's distress, or the clannish
denial of the stewardesses, but although I watched
Bullmer's face carefully, I saw neither of those, no
hint of accusation or censure. We might have been
trying to solve a crossword, for all the emotion he
displayed, and I couldn't help being a little impressed
by his stoicism, though it felt strange to be on the
receiving end of it. It had not been pleasant dealing
with Nilsson's skepticism and upset, but it did at least
feel a very human reaction. With Bullmer, I couldn't
tell what he was feeling. Was he furious, or panicked,
and simply hiding it well? Or was he really as cool
and calm as he seemed?

Perhaps, I thought, as he ran me through the conversation I'd had with the girl again, this sangfroid
was simply what it took to have accomplished what
he had—pulling himself up by his bootstraps to a
position dealing with hundreds of jobs and millions
of pounds of investment.

At last we had gone through my account backwards, forwards, and sideways, and I had no more
details to contribute. Bullmer sat for a moment, his
head bowed, his brows knitted, thinking. Then he
looked briefly at the Rolex on his tanned wrist and
spoke.

"Thank you, Miss Blacklock. I think we've got as
far as we can, and I can see the staff will want to start
laying the table for dinner in a moment. I'm sorry,
this has clearly been a very distressing and frightening experience for you. If you'll give me permis-
sion, I'd like to discuss it with Nilsson, and Captain
Larsen, to make sure that everything is being done

that possibly can be, and perhaps we could meet first thing tomorrow to discuss the next steps. In the meantime, I very much hope you will be able to relax enough to enjoy the dinner that's coming and the rest of the evening, in spite of what's happened."

"What will the next step be?" I asked. "I understand we're heading to Trondheim—but is there anywhere closer we could stop? I feel like I should report this to the police as soon as possible."

"It's possible there might be somewhere closer than Trondheim, yes," Bullmer said, getting to his feet. "But we'll be in Trondheim early tomorrow morning, so it might be that it's still the best place to head for. If we stop somewhere in the middle of the night I think our chances of finding an on-duty police station might be slim. But I'll have to speak to the captain to find out what the most appropriate course of action would be. The Norwegian police may not be able to act if the incident took place in British or international waters—it's a question of legal jurisdiction, you understand, not their willingness to investigate. It will all depend."

"And if it did? What if we were in international waters?"

"I believe the boat is registered in the Cayman Islands. I'll have to speak to the captain about how that might affect the situation."

I felt a sinking in my stomach. I'd read accounts of investigations on boats registered to the Bahamas and so on—one solitary policeman dispatched from the island to do a cursory report and get the issue off his desk as quickly as possible—and that, only where there was a clear sign of someone gone missing.

What would happen in this case, where the only evidence that the girl had even existed was long gone?

Still, I felt better for having spoken to Richard Bullmer. At least he seemed to believe me, to take my story seriously, unlike Nilsson.

He held out his hand, taking his leave, and as his piercing blue eyes met mine, he smiled, almost for the first time. It was a curiously asymmetric smile that pulled up one side of his face more than the other, but it suited him, and there was something wryly sympathetic about it.

"There's one other thing you should know," I said abruptly. Bullmer's eyebrows went up, and he dropped his hand.

"Yes?"

"I . . ." I swallowed. I didn't want to say this, but if he was going to speak to Nilsson, it would come out anyway. It would be better coming from me. "I was drinking, the night before . . . before it happened. And I also take antidepressants. I have done so for several years, since I was about twenty-five. I—I had a breakdown. And Nilsson—I think he felt . . ." I swallowed again. Bullmer's eyebrows rose even higher.

"Are you saying that Nilsson threw doubt on your story because you take medication for depression?"

The bluntness of his words made me cringe, but I nodded.

"Not in so many words—but yes. He made a comment about medication not mixing well with alcohol and I think he thought . . ."

Bullmer said nothing, he just regarded me impassively, and I found my words tumbling out, almost as if I were trying to defend Nilsson.

"It's just that I was burgled, before I came on board the ship. There was a man—he came into my flat and attacked me. Nilsson found out about it and I think that he felt, well, not that I'd made it up, but that I . . . might have overreacted."

"I'm deeply ashamed that a member of this boat's staff made you feel that way," Bullmer said. He took my hand, holding it in a viselike grip. "Please believe me, Miss Blacklock, I take your account with the utmost seriousness."

"Thanks," I said, but that one small word didn't do justice to the relief that someone, *someone* finally believed me. And not just someone—Richard Bullmer, the *Aurora*'s owner. If anyone had the power to get this sorted, it was him.

As I walked back to my cabin, I pressed my hands to my eyes, feeling them sting with tiredness, and then I felt in my pocket for my mobile to check the time. Almost five. Where had the time gone?

Automatically I opened up my e-mails and forced a refresh—but there was still no connection and I felt a pang of unease. Surely, *surely* this outage had gone on too long? I should have mentioned it to Bullmer, but it was too late now. He had gone—slipping into one of those unsettling concealed exits behind a screen, presumably to talk to the captain or radio land.

What if Jude had e-mailed? Rung, even, though I doubted we'd be close enough to land yet for a signal. Was he still ignoring me? For a minute I had a sharp flash of his hands on my back, my face against his chest, the feel of his warm T-shirt beneath my cheek, and it hit me with such force that I almost staggered beneath the weight of longing for his presence.

We would be in Trondheim tomorrow, at least. No one could prevent me from accessing the Internet then.

"Lo!" said a voice from behind me, and I turned to see Ben walking along the narrow corridor. He wasn't a big man, but he seemed to fill it entirely, an *Alice in Wonderland* trick of the perspective that made the corridor seem to shrink down to nothing and Ben grow bigger and bigger as he came nearer.

"Ben," I said, trying to make my voice convincingly cheerful.

"How did it go?" He began to walk alongside me towards our cabins. "Did you see Bullmer?"

"Yes . . . I think it went okay. He seemed to believe me, anyway." I didn't say what I had started thinking after Richard left, which was that he had not got as far as he had by showing all the cards in his hand. I'd come out of the meeting feeling confident and appeased, but as I ran back through his words, I realized he hadn't *promised* anything; in fact, he hadn't really said anything that could be quoted out of context as unqualified support for my story. There had been a lot of *if this is true . . .* and *if what you say . . .* nothing very concrete, when you came down to it.

"Great news," Ben said. "Is he diverting the boat?"

"I don't know. He seemed to think it wouldn't make any difference to divert now, that we'd do better to push on to Trondheim and get there as early as possible tomorrow."

We had reached our cabins, and I pulled my room key out of my pocket.

"God, I hope this dinner isn't another eight-course one tonight," I said wearily as I unlocked and opened my door. "I want to get enough sleep to be coherent for the police in Trondheim tomorrow."

"That's still your plan, then?" Ben asked. He leaned his hand on the doorframe, effectively preventing me from either leaving or closing the door, though I assumed it wasn't that calculated.

"Yes. As soon as the boat docks I'm going there."

"Doesn't it depend on what the captain says about the boat's position?"

"Probably. I think Bullmer's speaking to him about it now. But regardless, I want to get this on record with someone official, even if they can't investigate." The sooner my words were down in some official file, the safer I'd feel.

"Fair enough," Ben said easily. "Well, whatever happens tomorrow, you've got a clean slate with the police. Stick to the facts—be clear and unemotional, like you sound like you were with Bullmer. They'll believe you. You've got no reason to lie." He dropped his arm and took a step back. "You know where I am if you need me, yeah?"

"Yeah." I gave him a tired smile and was about to shut the door when he put his hand back on the frame so that I couldn't shut it without trapping his fingers.

"Oh, I nearly forgot," he said casually. "Did you hear about Cole?"

"His hand?" I'd almost forgotten, but it came back to me now with shocking vividness, the slow drip of blood on to the decking, Chloe's greenish face. "Poor guy. Will he need stitches?"

"I don't know, but it's not just that. He managed to knock his camera into the hot tub at the same time—he's beside himself, says he can't understand how he came to leave it so close to the edge."

"You're kidding me."

"Nope. He reckons the lens will be okay, but says the body and the SD card's fucked."

I felt the room shift and move a little, as if everything were going in and out of perspective, and I had a prickling flash of the photo of the girl on the little screen—a photo that was most likely gone forever now.

"Hey," Ben said with a laugh, "no need to look so doom-laden! He'll have insurance, I'm sure. It's just a shame about the shots. He was showing them to us over lunch. He had some great pics, there was a lovely one of you from last night." He stopped and put out a hand to touch my chin. "Are you okay?"

"I'm fine." I jerked my head away from him and then tried to force a convincing smile. "I'm just— I don't think I'd go on a cruise again, it's really not suiting me . . . you know . . . the sea . . . the kind of hemmed-in-ness of it all. I really just want to get to Trondheim now."

My heart was hammering, and I couldn't wait for Ben to get his hand off the door and leave. I needed to get my head together—needed to work this out.

"Do you . . . mind?" I nodded at Ben's hand, still resting on the doorframe, and he gave an easy laugh and straightened up.

"Sure! Sorry, I shouldn't be gabbing. You probably want to dress for dinner . . . right?"

"Right," I said. My voice sounded high and false.

Ben moved his hand, and I closed the door with an apologetic smile.

When he was gone, I slid the dead bolt across and then I slumped down with my back against the wood, drew my knees up to my chest, and rested my forehead on my knees, a picture, stark in front of my closed lids. It was Chloe, reaching out for her glass of champagne, her arm dripping onto Cole's camera on the deck below.

There was no way Cole or anyone else could have knocked that camera in. It wasn't on the rim of the tub. Someone had taken advantage of the kerfuffle surrounding my announcement and the broken glass and had picked it up from the floor and thrown it in. And I had absolutely no way of knowing who that was. It could have happened at any time—even after we'd all left the deck. It could have been almost any of the guests or staff—or even Cole himself.

The room seemed to close around me, stiflingly warm and airless, and I knew I had to get out.

On the veranda the sea mist was still close around the boat, but I took great gulping breaths of the cold air, feeling the freshness fill my lungs, jolting me out of my stupor. I had to *think.* I felt like I had all the pieces of the puzzle in front of me, that I must be able to put them together if I only tried hard enough. If only my head wasn't aching so much.

I leaned over the balcony, just as I had the night before, remembering that moment—the sound of the veranda door sliding stealthily back, the huge smacking splash, shocking in the quiet, and the smear of blood across glass, and suddenly I was absolutely and completely certain that I had *not* imagined it. None of it. Not the mascara. Not the blood. Not the face of the woman in cabin 10. Most of all, I had not imagined her. And for her sake, I could not let this drop. Because I knew what it was like to *be* her—to wake in the night with someone in your room, to feel that utter helpless certainty that something awful was going to happen, with nothing you could do to prevent it.

The September night air felt suddenly cold, very cold, reminding me how far north we were—almost to the Arctic Circle now. I shivered convulsively and, drawing my phone out of my pocket, I checked the reception one more time, holding it up high as if that would somehow magically improve the signal, but there were no bars.

Tomorrow, though. Tomorrow we would be in Trondheim, and no matter what, I was going to get myself off this boat and straight to the nearest police station.

- CHAPTER 21 -

Making myself up for dinner that night, I felt like I was applying war paint—lacquering on, layer by layer, the calm, professional mask that would enable me to get through this.

Part of me, a big part, wanted to go and huddle beneath my duvet—the idea of making small talk with a group of people containing a potential murderer, eating food served by someone who might have killed a woman last night—that thought was terrifying, and utterly surreal.

But another, more stubborn part refused to give in. As I applied mascara borrowed from Chloe in the bathroom mirror, I found myself searching in my reflection for the angry, idealistic girl who'd started her journalism course at uni fifteen years ago, thinking of the dreams I'd had of becoming an investigative reporter and changing the world. Instead, I had fallen into travel writing at *Velocity* to pay the bills and, almost in spite of myself, I'd begun to enjoy it— had even started to relish the perks, and to dream of a role like Rowan's, running my own magazine. And that was fine—I wasn't ashamed of the writer I'd become; like most people, I'd taken work where I could find it and tried to do the best I could in that job. But how could I look that girl in the mirror in the eye, if I didn't have the courage to get out there and investigate a story that was staring me in the face?

I thought of all the women I'd admired reporting from war zones around the world, of people who'd exposed corrupt regimes, gone to prison to protect their sources, risked their lives to get at the truth. I couldn't imagine Martha Gellhorn obeying an instruction to *Stop digging*, or Kate Adie hiding in her hotel room because she was scared of what she might find.

STOP DIGGING. The letters on the mirror were etched in my memory. Now, as I finished my makeup with a swipe of lip gloss, I huffed on the mirror, and wrote in the steam obscuring my reflection one word: *NO.*

Besides, as I shut the bathroom door behind me and put on my evening shoes, a smaller, more selfish part of me was whispering that I was safest in company. No one could harm me in front of a room full of witnesses.

I was just straightening my gown when there was a knock on the door.

"Who is it?" I called.

"It's Karla, Miss Blacklock."

I opened the door. Karla was outside, smiling with that permanent air of slightly anxious surprise.

"Good evening, Miss Blacklock. I just wanted to remind you that dinner is in ten minutes, and drinks are being served in the Lindgren Lounge, whenever you wish to join us."

"Thank you," I said, and then, on impulse as she turned to go, "Karla?"

"Yes?" She turned back, her eyebrows raised so that her round face looked almost alarmed. "Is there something else with which I can help?"

"I—I don't know. It's just . . ." I took a deep breath, trying to think how to phrase it. "When I came and talked to you earlier today in the staff quarters, I felt like . . . I felt like maybe there was something else you could have told me. That perhaps you didn't want to speak in front of Miss Lidman. And I just wanted to say—I'm going into Trondheim tomorrow, to talk to the police about what I saw, and if there's anything—anything at all—that you wanted to say, now would be a really good time to tell me. I could make sure it was anonymous." I thought again of Martha Gellhorn and Kate Adie, of the kind of reporter I'd once wanted to be. "I'm a journalist," I said as convincingly as I could. "You know that. We protect our sources—it's part of the deal."

Karla said nothing, only twisted her fingers together.

"Karla?" I prompted. For a moment I thought that there might be tears in her blue eyes, but she blinked them away.

"I don't . . ." she said, and then muttered something under her breath in her own language.

"It's okay," I said. "You can tell me. I promise it won't go any further. Are you frightened of someone?"

"It is not that," she said miserably. "I am sad because I am sorry for you. Johann is saying that you make it up, that you are . . . what's the word? *Paranoid*, and that you . . . you seek the attention by making up stories. And I don't believe this. I believe you are a good person and that you believe what you say is true. But, Miss Blacklock, we need our jobs. If the police say that something bad happened on this boat, no one will want to travel with us, and it may not be so easy to find another job. I need this money, I have a little boy, Erik, at home with my mother; she needs the money that I send back. And just because perhaps someone let a friend use an empty cabin, that doesn't mean she was killed, you know?"

She turned away.

"Hang on." I put out a hand towards her arm, trying to stop her going. "What are you saying? There *was* a girl in there? Did someone smuggle her in?"

"I am saying nothing." She pulled her arm out of my grip. "I am saying, please, Miss Blacklock, don't make trouble if nothing happened."

And then she ran up the corridor, punched the code into the staff door, and was gone.

On the way up to the Lindgren Lounge, I found myself replaying the conversation in my head, trying to work out what it meant. *Had* she seen someone in the cabin, or suspected someone was there? Or was she just torn between her sympathy for me and her fear of what might happen if what I was saying was true?

Outside the lounge I checked my phone surreptitiously, hoping against hope that we might be close enough to land for a signal, but there was still nothing. As I was putting it away in my evening bag, Camilla Lidman glided up.

"May I take that for you, Miss Blacklock?" She indicated the bag. I shook my head.

"No, thank you." My phone was set to beep when it connected to roaming networks. If a signal did come, I wanted it by my side so I could act immediately.

"Very well. May I offer you a glass of champagne?" She indicated a tray on a small table by the entrance, and I nodded and took a frosted flute. I knew I should keep a clear head for tomorrow, but one glass for Dutch courage couldn't hurt.

"Just to let you know, Miss Blacklock," she said, "that the talk on the northern lights has been canceled tonight."

I looked at her blankly, realizing that I'd forgotten, yet again, to check the itinerary.

"There was to have been a presentation on the northern lights after dinner," she explained, seeing my expression. "A talk from Lord Bullmer accompanied by photographs from Mr. Lederer, but unfortunately, Lord Bullmer has been called away to deal with an emergency and Mr. Lederer has hurt his hand, so it has been rescheduled for tomorrow, after the group returns from Trondheim."

I nodded again and turned to the rest of the room to see who else was missing.

Bullmer and Cole were both absent, as Camilla had said. Chloe was not there, either, and when I asked Lars, he said she was feeling ill and lying down in her room. Anne was present, although she looked pale, and as she raised her glass to her lips, her robe slipped, showing a deep purple bruise on her collarbone. She saw me glance, and look hastily away, and gave a self-conscious laugh.

"I know, it looks terrible, doesn't it? I tripped in the shower, but I bruise so easily now, it looks worse than it is. It's a side effect of the chemotherapy, unfortunately."

As we took our seats at dinner, I saw Ben motion invitingly at the seat next to his, opposite Archer, but I pretended not to see, and instead took the chair closest to where I was standing, next to Owen White. He was giving Tina a long talk on his financial interests and his role at the investment company he worked for.

As I listened, half an ear on their conversation, half an ear on the rest of the table, I realized that the talk had shifted, and he was speaking in a low voice, as if unwilling to be overheard.

". . . quite honestly, no," he was confiding to Tina. "I'm just not one hundred percent convinced that the setup is sustainable—it's such a niche investment area. But I don't imagine Bullmer will have trouble getting interest from elsewhere. And of course he has pretty deep pockets of his own, or rather Anne does, so he can afford to wait for the right person to come on board. It's a shame Solberg wasn't able to come, this is much more his bailiwick."

Tina nodded wisely, and then the conversation passed on to other topics—holiday destinations they had in common, the identity of the neon green cube of jelly that had just appeared on a plate in front of us, flanked by a little pile of something I thought might be seaweed. I let my gaze pass over the room, Archer was saying something to Ben and laughing uproariously. He looked drunk, his bow tie already askew. Anne, at the same table, was talking to Lars. There was no trace of the tears I'd seen earlier that afternoon, but there was something haunted about her expression, and her smile, as she nodded at something Lars was saying, was strained.

"Pondering our hostess?" said a low voice from across the table, and I turned to see Alexander sipping at a glass. "She's quite the enigma, isn't she? Looks so fragile, and yet they say she's the power behind Richard's throne. The iron fist in the silk glove, you could say. I suppose that having that kind of money from the age when most children are still drooling into their cornflakes has a steeling effect on one's character."

"Do you know her well?" I asked. Alexander shook his head.

"Never met her. Richard spends half his life on a plane, but *she* almost never leaves Norway. It's totally alien to me—as you know, I *live* for travel; I can't imagine confining yourself to a petty little country like Norway when the restaurants and capitals of the world await. Never to taste suckling pig at elBulli, or sample the glorious fusion of cultures that is Gaggan in Bangkok! But I suppose it's a reaction against her upbringing—I believe she lost her parents in a plane crash at the age of eight or nine, and spent the rest of her life being shuttled around the boarding schools of Europe by her grandparents. I imagine you might choose to go the other way as an adult."

He picked up his fork, and we were just starting to eat when there was a noise at the door, and I looked up to see Cole walking unsteadily across to the table.

"Mr. Lederer!" A stewardess hurried to take an extra chair from the ones at the side of the room. "Miss Blacklock, might I ask you to just . . ."

I moved my plate and chair slightly and she put a

seat at the head of the table for Cole, who slumped heavily down. His hand was bandaged, and he looked as if he'd been drinking.

"No, I won't have champagne," he said in answer to Hanni gliding up with a tray. "I'll have a Scotch."

Hanni nodded and hurried away, and Cole sat back in his chair and passed a hand over his unshaven face.

"Sorry about your camera," I said cautiously. He scowled, and I saw that he was very drunk already.

"It's a fucking nightmare," he said. "And the worst of it is, it's my own bloody fault. I should have backed it up."

"Are all the shots gone?" I asked. Cole shrugged.

"No idea, but probably, yes. Got a guy back in London who might be able to get some of the data off, but it's showing fuck all when I put it in my computer, it's not even reading the card."

"I'm really sorry," I said. My heart was beating fast. I wasn't sure if this was sensible, but I figured I had nothing to lose now. "Was it just stuff from the voyage? I thought I saw one shot from somewhere else . . . ?"

"Oh, yeah, I was swapping the cards over, it had a few shots from a shoot I did a couple of weeks back at the Magellan."

I knew the Magellan—it was a very exclusive all-male members club in Piccadilly, founded as a meeting place for diplomats and what the club described as "gentlemen travelers." No women were allowed as members, but female guests were permitted, and I had attended functions there once or twice in Rowan's stead.

"Are you a member?" I asked. He gave a snort.

"Not bloody likely. Not my style, even if they'd let me in, which is doubtful. Too crusty for my taste—anywhere that won't let you wear jeans isn't for me. The Frontline is more my cup of tea. Alexander's a member, though. So is Bullmer, I think. You know the drill, you have to be either too posh to function or rich as shit, and fortunately I'm not either."

His last remark fell into a lull in conversation from the rest of the table, the words painfully loud and noticeably slurred in the silence, and I saw a few heads turn, and Anne glance at the steward with a nod that I interpreted as *Get his food over there before the whiskey.*

"What were you doing there, then?" I said, keeping my voice low, as if I could persuade him to moderate his tone by osmosis.

"Pictures for *Harper's.*" His plate arrived and he began spearing foodstuffs at random, shoving the fragile architectural morsels into his mouth seemingly without even tasting them. "Some launch, I think. Can't remember. Christ." He looked down at his hand, the fork awkwardly balanced against the bandage. "This is sodding painful. There's no way I'm trailing round Trondheim cathedral tomorrow, I'm going to the doctor to get this checked out and get some decent painkillers."

After dinner finished, we took our coffee through to the lounge, and I found myself standing next to Owen White, both of us staring out the long window, into the fog. He nodded politely but seemed in no hurry to open the conversation. I tried to think what Rowan would do. Charm him? Or brush him off and go and talk to someone of more immediate use to *Velocity*? Archer, perhaps?

I glanced over my shoulder at Archer and saw that he was very, very drunk and had pinned Hanni into a corner of the room, her back to the window, his broad frame effectively blocking her exit. Hanni was holding a jug of coffee in one hand and was smiling politely but with a trace of wariness. She said something and gestured to the coffeepot, obviously as a way of taking her leave, but he laughed and put one heavy arm around her shoulders in a gesture of avuncular possession that made my flesh creep a little.

Hanni said something else that I didn't catch, and then slipped out from under his grip with what looked like practiced dexterity. For a moment Archer's face looked a mixture of foolishness and fury, but then he seemed to shrug it off and moved across to talk to Ben.

I turned back to Owen White with a sigh, though I was not sure whether it was a sigh of relief for Hanni, or resignation at my own reluctance to deal with unpleasant people, even for the sake of my career.

Owen, by contrast, seemed reassuringly harmless, though I realized, as I looked covertly at his profile in the reflection of the darkened, foggy window, that I had no real idea whether he would be of use to *Velocity* or not. Ben had said he was an investor, but White had kept himself to himself so much this voyage that I had no clear impression of what he actually did. Perhaps he would be the perfect angel investor for the group, if *Velocity*'s owner ever decided to go into some more profitable area. In any case, I had no desire to go across to the other side of the room.

"So, um," I began awkwardly, "I feel slightly like we haven't been properly introduced. My name is Laura Blacklock. I'm a travel journalist."

"Owen White," he said simply, but there was no sense of dismissal in his tone, I got the impression that he was just a man of few words. He held out his hand, and I shook it clumsily with my left, which was holding a petit four, but seemed better than my right, which was holding a hot cup of coffee.

"So what brings you to the *Aurora*, Mr. White?"

"I work for an investment group," he said, and took a long sip of his coffee. "Bullmer was, I think, hoping I'd recommend the *Aurora* as an investment opportunity."

"But . . . from what you were saying to Tina, that won't be the case?" I said cautiously, wondering if it was bad manners to admit overhearing, though I could hardly have helped it. He nodded, not seeming offended.

"That's so. I must admit, it's not really my area, but I was flattered to be asked and too venal to pass up the chance of a free trip. As I was saying to Tina, it's a shame Solberg couldn't make it."

"He was supposed to have cabin ten, wasn't he?" I asked. Owen White nodded. It occurred to me suddenly that I had no real idea of who the missing Solberg was, or why he hadn't come. "Did you—I mean, do you know him? Solberg, I mean?"

"Yes, fairly well. We're in the same area. He's based in Norway, while my head office is back in London, but it's a small world that we operate in. One gets to know all one's competitors. It must be the same in travel journalism, I imagine." He smiled as he popped a petit four in his mouth, and I smiled back, acknowledging the truth of his remark.

"So, if this is more his cup of tea, why didn't he come?" I asked.

Owen White said nothing, and for a moment I wondered if I'd gone too far, been too bold with my questioning, but then he swallowed and I realized he was simply having trouble with his petit four.

"There was a break-in," he said around a mouthful of bits of nut, and swallowed again, trying to clear his mouth. "At his house, I believe. His passport was taken, but I think that was only part of the reason he didn't come—his wife and children were home, from what I understand, and were rather shaken up. And say what you will about Scandinavian businesses . . ." He paused again and swallowed, heroically this time. "They do understand the importance of putting family first. Dear me, I advise you not to try this nougat unless you have very good teeth, I think I may have loosened a filling."

"*Not* the nougat!" I heard over my shoulder, as I was trying to process what I had just heard and piece this revelation together with my own break-in. I turned to see Alexander bearing down on us both. "Owen, *please* tell me you haven't."

"I did." Owen took a gulp of coffee and swilled it around his mouth, wincing slightly. "To my regret."

"The stuff should carry a dental health warning at the *very* least. You"—he pointed at me—"an investigative report is what's needed. *Velocity*'s no-punches-pulled exposé of Richard Bullmer's shady links with the cosmetic dentistry industry. What with that and the other *incident*, I should think future guests of this cruise liner will find it *very* hard to get health insurance, don't you?"

"Other incident?" I said sharply, trying to remember what I'd told Alexander. I was sure I hadn't mentioned the full story of the accident to him. Had Lars related the conversation in the hot tub? "What other incident are you talking about?"

"Why," Alexander said, his eyes opened almost theatrically wide, "Cole's hand. Of course. What were you thinking of?"

After coffee, the group began to break up—Owen disappearing quietly without a good-bye, and Lars taking a loud leave with a joke about Chloe. Bullmer was still nowhere to be seen, nor was Anne.

"Come for a snifter of something in the bar?" Tina said to me as I placed my empty cup on a side table. "Alexander's going to have a tinkle on the baby grand in there."

"I—I'm not sure," I said. I was still pondering what Owen White had told me over coffee about Solberg's break-in. What did it mean? "I might turn in."

"Ben?" Tina purred. He looked at me.

"Lo? Want me to walk you back to your cabin?"

"No need, I'm fine," I said, and turned to go. I was almost at the door when I felt a hand catch at my wrist and turned. It was Ben.

"Hey," he said quietly. "What's going on?"

"Ben." I glanced behind him at the other guests, laughing and chatting obliviously as the stewards cleared up around them. "Let's not do this here. Nothing's going on."

"Then why were you acting so weird all through dinner? You saw me saving you a chair and you deliberately ignored me."

"Nothing's going on." There was a painful pressure in my temples, as if the anger I'd been suppressing all night was taking its toll.

"I don't believe you. Come on, Lo, spit it out."

"You lied to me." It burst out in a furious whisper, before I could consider the wisdom of the accusation. Ben looked taken aback.

"What? No, I didn't!"

"Really?" I hissed. "So you never left the cabin when everyone was playing poker?"

"No!" It was his turn to glance over his shoulder now at the other guests. Tina was looking across at us, and he turned back, lowering his voice. "No, I didn't— Oh, no, wait, I did go and get my wallet. But that wasn't a lie—not really."

"Not a lie? You told me categorically no one left that cabin. And then I find out from Cole not only that you *did* leave, but anyone else could have left, too, while you weren't there."

"But that's different," he muttered. "I left, God, I don't know when, but it was early in the evening. It wasn't round the time you were talking about."

"So why lie about it?"

"It wasn't a lie! I just didn't think. Jesus, Lo—"

But I didn't let him finish. I pulled my wrist out of his grip and hurried away, through the doors and into the corridor, leaving him gaping after me.

I was so busy thinking about Ben that as I rounded

the corner near the upper-deck toilet, I almost
tripped over Anne Bullmer. She was leaning back
against the wall as if steeling herself for something,
although whether to return to the party, or make
her way back to her cabin, I wasn't sure. She looked
extremely tired, her face gray, the shadows around
her eyes darker than ever.

"Oh, I'm so sorry!" I gasped, and then, thinking of
the bruise on her collarbone, "I didn't hurt you, did I?"

She smiled, the fine skin around her mouth crin-
kling, but the expression didn't reach her eyes.

"I'm fine, I'm just very tired. Sometimes . . ." She
swallowed, and her voice cracked for a moment,
something in the cut-glass English accent slipping.
"Sometimes it all just seems too much—d'you know
what I mean? Such a *performance*."

"I do," I said sympathetically.

"If you'll excuse me, I am going to bed," she said,
and I nodded and turned to make my own way back
aft, down the flight of stairs that led to the rear set
of cabins.

I was almost at the door of my suite when I heard an
angry voice from behind me.

"Lo. Lo, wait, you can't make those kind of accusations and walk away."

Shit. Ben. I felt a strong urge to slip inside my
cabin and slam the door, but I made myself turn to
face him, my back against the door.

"I didn't make any accusations. I just said what I'd
been told."

"You pretty much implied you're suspecting me

now! We've known each other more than ten years! Do you realize how that makes me feel—that you could accuse me of lying like that?"

There was genuine hurt in his voice, but I refused to let myself soften. It had been Ben's favorite tactic in arguments, when we were together, to divert the discussion away from whatever was annoying me to the fact that I'd hurt his feelings and was acting irrationally. Time and again I'd ended up apologizing for the fact that *I'd* upset *him*—my own feelings completely ignored, and always, in the process, we'd somehow wound up losing sight of the issue that had provoked the disagreement in the first place. I wasn't falling for it now.

"I'm not making you feel anything," I said, trying to keep my voice even. "I'm stating facts."

"Facts? Don't be ridiculous!"

"Ridiculous?" I folded my arms. "What does that mean?"

"I mean," he said hotly, "that you're acting completely paranoid. You're seeing bogeymen behind every corner! Maybe Nilsson—"

He stopped. I clenched my fist around my delicate evening bag, feeling the solid bulk of my phone beneath the slippery sequins.

"Go on? Maybe Nilsson . . . what?"

"Nothing."

"Maybe Nilsson was right? Maybe I am imagining things?"

"I didn't say that."

"But it was what you were implying, right?"

"I'm just asking you to take a step back and *look* at yourself, Lo. Look at this rationally, I mean."

I forced myself to keep a hold on my temper and smiled.

"I am rational. But I'm very happy to take a step back." And with that, I opened my suite door, stepped inside, and slammed it in his face.

"Lo!" I heard from outside, and a thump on the door. Then a pause. *"Lo."*

I said nothing, just slid the bolt and the chain across. No one was getting through that door without a battering ram. Least of all Ben Howard.

"Lo!" He banged again. "Look, will you just *talk* to me? This is really getting out of hand. Will you at least tell me what you're going to say to the police tomorrow?" He paused, waiting for me to reply. "Are you even listening?"

Ignoring him, I threw my bag on the bed, stripped off my evening gown, and walked into the bathroom, shutting the door and turning on the taps to drown out the sounds from outside. When at last I stepped into the scaldingly hot water and turned off the taps, the only sound I could hear was the gentle hum of the extractor fan. Thank God. He must have given up at last.

I had left my phone in the bedroom, so I wasn't sure what time it was when I climbed out of the bath, but my fingers were waterlogged and wrinkled, and I felt heavy with sleep, but in a good way, quite unlike the nervous, edgy exhaustion of the last day or two. As I cleaned my teeth, dried my hair, and belted the white bathrobe around myself, I thought of the good night's sleep I would have, and the logical, carefully rehearsed story I would give to the police tomorrow.

And then . . . Christ. I felt almost weak with relief thinking about it. Then I would get a bus or a train or whatever bloody transport Trondheim possessed and get myself to the nearest airport and *home*.

When I opened the door to the cabin, I held my breath, half expecting Ben's hammering and shouting to start up again, but there was no sound. I walked cautiously to the door, my feet silent on the thick pale carpet, and, lifting the cover to the spy hole, I looked out into the corridor. There was no one there. At least no one I could make out—in spite of the fisheye lens, I could only see part of the corridor, but unless Ben were lying on the floor beneath my door, he was gone.

I let out a sigh and picked up my abandoned evening bag to check the time on my phone and set the alarm for tomorrow. I wasn't waiting for a call from Karla—I wanted to be up and off the boat as soon as possible.

But my phone wasn't inside.

I turned the bag upside down, shaking it out but knowing it was fruitless—the bag was small and light, and there was no way anything heavier than a postcard could have been concealed inside. It wasn't on the bed. Could it have slipped onto the floor?

I tried to think clearly.

I could have left it at the dinner table—but I hadn't taken it out of my bag, and in any case, I had a clear memory of feeling it inside my evening bag during the argument with Ben. And I would have noticed its weight missing when I threw the bag on the bed.

I checked the bathroom in case I'd taken it in there on autopilot, but it wasn't there, either.

I began to search harder, throwing the duvet onto the floor, pushing the bed to one side—and that's when I saw it.

There was a footprint, a wet footprint, on the white carpet, very close to the veranda door.

I froze.

Could it have been me? Getting out of the bath?

But I knew that was impossible. I'd dried my feet in the bathroom, and I hadn't walked anywhere near that window. I moved closer, touching the cold, damp shape with my fingertips, and I realized this was the print of a shoe. You could see the shape of the heel.

There was only one possibility.

I stood up, slid back the veranda door, and went out onto the balcony. There, I hung out over the rail, looking across to the empty veranda on the left of mine. The white glass privacy screen to either side was very high, and very sheer, but if you were daring and had a head for heights, and didn't mind the possibility of slipping to a watery grave, you could *just* get over it.

I was shivering convulsively, my thin dressing gown no protection from the cold North Sea wind, but there was one more thing I had to try, though I was going to be very sorry and feel very stupid if it turned out I was wrong.

Carefully, I dragged the sliding glass door closed and let it click into position.

Then I tried to pull it back.

It worked—smooth as silk.

I went inside and did the same thing, and then

checked the lock. As I had thought, there was no way of securing the veranda door to prevent someone entering from the outside. It was logical, really, now that I thought about it. The only person who should be on the veranda was an occupant of the room. You couldn't risk someone accidentally locking themselves out there in bad weather, unable to get back inside and raise the alarm, or a child shutting a parent out there in a moment of rebellion, and then being unable to work the lock.

And really—what was there to fear? The veranda faced the sea—there was no possibility of someone accessing it from the outside.

Except there was. If you were very bold, and very stupid.

Now I understood. All the locks and bolts and DO NOT DISTURB signs in the world wouldn't do any good on my cabin door, not when the balcony offered a clear route to anyone with access to the empty room, and enough upper-body strength to pull themselves over.

My room was not safe, and never had been.

Back inside the suite, I got into my jeans and boots, and my favorite hoodie. Then I checked the lock on the cabin door and huddled on the sofa with a cushion hugged to my chest.

There was no possibility of sleep now.

Anyone could have access to the empty suite. And from there, it was just a short climb across the glass divider into mine. The truth was, I could draw the bolt across my cabin door as much as I liked, but any member of the staff could open the empty cabin with their passkey. As for the guests . . .

I thought again of the layout of the cabins. To the right of mine was Archer's, ex-marine, with an upper-body strength that made me wince when I remembered it. And to the left . . . to the left was the empty cabin, and beyond that, curving round the ship to the other side of the corridor, was Ben Howard's.

Ben. Who had deliberately cast doubt on my story with Nilsson.

Ben, who had lied about his alibi.

And he had known about the photos on Cole's camera before I did. His words came back to me as if in a dream: *He was showing them to us over lunch. He had some great pics . . .*

Ben Howard. The one person on board I had thought I could trust.

But I pushed that thought away—focusing on the phone, and the stupidity and daring of coming in to steal it while I was in the bath. He had risked a lot to take it, and the question was why. Why now? But I thought I knew.

The answer was Trondheim. As long as the boat's Internet was down, the perpetrator had nothing to worry about. I couldn't make a call to land without going through Camilla Lidman. But once we started to draw closer to land . . .

I hugged the cushion harder to my chest, and I thought of Trondheim, and Judah, and the police.

All I had to do was make it until dawn.

WHODUNNIT WEB FORUM—
A DISCUSSION PLACE FOR ARMCHAIR DETECTIVES

Please read the forum rules *before* starting a thread, and exercise caution in posting anything potentially prejudicial and/or libelous to live cases. Posts that violate these guidelines will be taken down.

Monday 28 September

iamsherlocked: Hey guys, anyone else been following this Lorna Blacklock case? Looks like theyve found a body.

TheNamesMarpleJaneMarple: I think you'll find it's Laura Blacklock actually. Yes, I've been following it. Really tragic and sadly not that unusual. I read somewhere that more than 160 people have gone missing off cruise ships in the past few years, and almost none of those have been solved.

iamsherlocked: Yeah I think I've heard that too. Saw in the Daily Fail that her ex was on board the ship. Theres a big sobby interview wiv him saying how worried he is. He reckons she got off on her own accord. Is it me or is that a bit suss? Don't they say that a third of women are killed by ex's or partners or something?

TheNamesMarpleJaneMarple: *"a third of women are killed by ex's or partners or something?"* I presume that must be in the case of women who are murdered, a third of them are killed by a partner or ex, not a third of all women! But yes,

that kind of proportion sounds plausible. And of
course there's the boyfriend. Something about his
statement's not quite ringing true, and apparently
he was out of the country at the time . . . hmm . . .
very convenient. Not that hard to get a plane to
Norway, right?

AnonInsider: I'm a regular on WD (although I've
name-changed as I don't want to out myself) and
actually I know something about this case, I'm
a family friend. I don't want to say too much for
fear of making myself identifiable or impinging
on the family's privacy, but I can tell you Judah is
completely devastated about Lo's disappearance,
and I'd be very careful about implying anything
to the contrary or you'll probably find this thread
gets taken down.

TheNamesMarpleJaneMarple: Anon, I'd find your
claims more convincing if you dropped the mask,
and in any case none of what I said above was
libelous. I said I didn't personally find his statement convincing. Show me the libel in that?

AnonInsider: Look, MJM, I'm not interested in
debating this with you, but I do know the family
very well. I was at school with Laura, and I can
tell you, you're barking up the wrong tree. If you
must know, Lo's got serious problems—she's
taken medication for depression for years and
she's always been . . . well, I think unstable would
be the kind way of putting it. I imagine that's the
line the police will be looking at.

iamsherlocked: what suicide you reckon?

AnonInsider: Not really my place to speculate on the police investigation—but yes, that's my reading of it between the lines. If you notice, they're being very careful not to describe it as a murder investigation in the press.

JudahLewis01: A friend told me about this thread and I've registered to post this, and unlike Anon this is my real name. Anon, I have no idea who you are and to be honest you can fuck off. Yes, Lo takes medication (although FYI it's for anxiety, not depression and if you were really a friend of hers you'd know that) but so do literally hundreds of thousands of people, and the idea that that automatically makes her either "unstable" as you put it, or suicidal, is fucking offensive. Yes, I was out of the country. I was in Russia, working. And yes, they've found a body, but it's not been identified as Lo, so at this stage it's still a missing person's investigation, which is why you've not seen any suggestion it's a murder investigation. Can you people remember this is a real person you're talking about and not just your personal episode of *Murder, She Wrote*? I don't know who the admins of this shitshow are, but I'm reporting this thread.

iamsherlocked: *"unlike Anon this is my real name"* not being funny but we've only got you're word for that mate.

MrsRaisin (admin): Hi all, sorry to say we agree with Mr. Lewis, this thread is straying into some rather unpleasant speculation so we'll be deleting it. We obviously don't want to stop you discussing what's in the news, so feel free to take it elsewhere, but please stick to the reported facts.

InspektörWallander: So what about this Norwegian polis scanner blog that is reporting a positiv identification of Laura's body?

MrsRaisin (admin): We are now closing this thread.

PART SIX

- CHAPTER 22 -

I was trapped. I was not certain where, or how, but I had a pretty good idea.

The windowless room was small and stifling, and I lay on the bunk with my eyes shut and my arms wrapped around my head, trying not to give way to the feelings of panic rising up inside me.

I must have replayed the events a thousand times in my head, through the rising fog of fear—hearing, again and again, the knock at the door as I sat on the edge of the sofa, waiting for Trondheim and dawn.

The sound, though not particularly loud, had been shocking as a gunshot in the silent cabin. My head jerked up, the cushion falling from my hands onto the floor, my heart going a mile a minute. Jesus. I found I was holding my breath and I forced myself to exhale, long and slow, and then inhale, counting the seconds.

It came again, not a rough banging, just a *tap tap tap*, then a long pause and a final *tap* as if an afterthought, slightly louder than the rest. At that last *tap*, I scrambled to my feet and made my way, as quietly as I could, to the door.

Cupping my hand over the opening so no telltale

flash of light could betray my presence, I slid the little steel cover of the peephole open. Then when my face was close enough to the glass to shield any gray dawn light from my window, I withdrew my fingers and peered through the fisheye.

I don't know who I was expecting to see. Nilsson, maybe. Ben Howard. I wouldn't even have been surprised to see Bullmer.

But not even for one minute did I imagine the person actually standing outside. *Her.*

It was the woman from cabin 10. The missing girl. Standing outside like nothing had ever happened.

For a minute I just stood there, gasping like I'd been punched in the stomach. She was *alive.* I'd been wrong. Nilsson was right—and I'd been wrong all this time.

And then she turned on her heel and began to walk down the corridor, towards the door to the staff quarters. I had to get to her. I had to get to her before she disappeared behind that locked door.

Slamming back the chain and the bolt, I wrenched open the door.

"Hey!" I shouted. "Hey, you, wait! I need to talk to you!"

She didn't pause, didn't even glance back over her shoulder, and now she was at the door to the lower deck, punching in the code. I didn't stop to think. I just knew that *this time* I wasn't going to let her disappear without a trace. I ran.

She was already through the staff door by the time I was halfway down the corridor, but I caught the edge of the door as it was just closing, pinching my fingers painfully, and then I wrenched it open and flung myself into the gap.

Inside it was darkness, the bulb at the top of the steps burned out. Or taken out, as I later thought.

As the door swung shut behind me, I stopped for a second, trying to get my bearings, see where the top step was. And that's when it happened—a hand grabbing my hair from behind, another twisting my arm behind me, limbs grappling mine in the darkness. There was a short interval of panting, scrabbling terror, my nails in someone's skin, my free hand trying to reach behind me to get a grip on the thin, strong hand laced in my hair—and then the hand pulled harder, twisting my head painfully back, and rammed my head forwards against the locked door. I heard the crack of my skull against the metal doorframe—and nothing.

I came to alone, lying on a bunk with a thin blanket over me. The pain in my head was agonizing, throbbing with a low pulse that made the dim lights in the room warp and shimmer, with a strange halo effect around them. There was a curtain on the wall opposite and with trembling limbs I slithered off the bed and half stumbled, half crawled across the floor towards it. But when I dragged myself upright, using the top bunk for support, and pulled back the thin orange cloth, there was no window there—just a blank wall of creamy plastic, lightly patterned as if in imitation of textured wallpaper.

The walls seemed to close in, the room narrowing

around me, and I felt my breath come faster. *One. Two. Three. Breathe in.*

Shit. I felt the sobs rising up inside me, threatening to choke me from the inside.

Four. Five. Six. Breathe out.

I was trapped. Oh God, oh God, oh God . . .

One. Two. Three. Breathe in.

Propping myself against the wall with one hand, I made my way unsteadily back towards the door, but I knew before I tried it that it was useless. It was locked.

Refusing to think about what that meant, I tried the other door, set into the wall at an angle, but it opened into a minuscule en suite, empty except for a single dead spider curled in the washbasin.

I stumbled back to the first door and tried again, pulling harder this time, straining every muscle, rattling the door in its frame, yanking so hard at the handle that the effort left me panting, stars exploding in my vision as I slumped to the floor. No. No, this was not possible—was I really trapped?

I got to my feet and looked around me for something to lever into the door, but there was nothing, everything in the room was bolted or screwed down, or made of fabric. I tried forcing the handle again, trying not to think about the fact that I was in a windowless cell maybe four foot by six, and well below sea level, a thousand tons of water just inches away behind a skin of steel. But the door didn't move, the only thing that changed was the pain in my head, jabbing with neon intensity until at last I stumbled back to the bunk and crawled onto it, trying not to think about the weight of water pressing in on me, focusing instead on my aching skull. It was pounding now so much that I could feel my pulse in my temples. Oh God, I had been so stupid, running out of that room straight into the trap. . . .

I tried to think. I had to stay calm, had to keep my head above the rising tide of fear. Stay logical. Stay in control. Think. *I had to.* What day was it? It was impossible to tell how much time had passed. My limbs felt stiff, as if I'd been lying in that position on the bunk for a while, but although I was thirsty I wasn't completely parched. If I'd been unconscious for more than a few hours I would have woken up seriously dehydrated. Which meant it was probably still Tuesday, the twenty-second.

In which case . . . Ben knew that I'd been intending to go ashore at Trondheim. He would come looking for me—wouldn't he? He wouldn't let the boat leave without me.

But then I realized that the engine was running and I could feel the rise and fall of waves beneath the hull. Either we hadn't stopped at all, or else we'd already left the port.

Oh God. We were heading out to sea—and everyone would assume I was still in Trondheim. If they looked for me at all, it would be in completely the wrong place.

If only my head didn't hurt and my thoughts didn't keep stumbling over each other . . . if only the walls weren't closing in on me like a coffin, making it hard to breathe, hard to *think.*

Passports. I didn't know how big Trondheim port was, but they must have some kind of customs check, or passport control. And there would be someone from the ship on duty at the gangway, surely, checking passengers in and out. They couldn't risk leaving without someone. Somewhere, there would be a record of the fact that I hadn't left the boat. Someone would realize I was still here.

I had to hang on to that.

But it was hard—hard when the only light was a dim bulb that flickered and dipped every so often, and the air seemed to be running out with every breath. Oh God, it was so hard.

I closed my eyes, shutting out the looming walls and the claustrophobic warping light, and pulled the thin cover over myself. I tried to focus on something. The feel of the flat, limp pillow beneath my cheek. The sound of my own breathing.

But the image I kept coming back to was that of the girl, standing nonchalantly outside my door in the corridor, her hand on her hip, and then the swing of her gait as she walked towards the staff door.

How. *How?*

Had she been hiding on the boat all along? In this room, maybe? But I knew, even without opening my eyes to look around, that no one had been living here. It had no sense of being inhabited, there were no stains on the carpet, no coffee marks on the plastic shelf, no fading scent of food and sweat and human breath. Even that spider curled in the sink spoke of disuse. There was no way that girl, full of snapping life and vivacity, could have been in this room without leaving some impression. Wherever she'd been staying, it wasn't here.

This place felt like a tomb. Maybe it was already mine.

- CHAPTER 23 -

I was not sure when I fell asleep, but I must have, exhausted by the ache in my head and the roar of the ship's motor, because I awoke, to the sound of a click.

I sat up sharply, cracking my scalp against the bunk above, and then fell back, groaning and clutching my head as the blood pounded in my ears, a shrill ringing in the back of my skull.

I lay there, my eyes squeezed tightly shut against the pain, but at last it receded enough for me to roll onto my side and open my eyes again, squinting against the dim fluorescent light.

There was a plate on the floor, and a glass of something—juice, I thought. I picked it up and sniffed it. It looked and smelled like orange juice, but I couldn't bring myself to drink it. Instead, I got painfully to my feet and opened the door to the little en suite, where I emptied the juice down the sink and refilled the glass with water from the tap. The water was warm and stale, but I was so thirsty now that I would have drunk worse. I gulped down the glass, refilled, and began to sip the next more slowly as I made my way back from the sink and onto the bunk.

My head ached powerfully, and I wished I had some painkillers, but more than that I felt awful—

shivery and weak, as if I were coming down with the flu. It was probably hunger—it was hours since I'd eaten and my blood sugar must be at rock bottom.

Part of me wanted to lie down and rest my throbbing head, but my stomach growled, and I made myself examine the plate of food that was on the floor. It looked completely normal—meatballs in some kind of sauce, mashed potato and peas, and a bread roll on the side. I knew I should eat—but the same gut revulsion that had made me pour away the juice was kicking in. It just felt so wrong—eating food provided by someone who'd locked me into an underwater dungeon. There could be anything in there. Rat poison. Sleeping pills. *Worse.* And I'd have no choice but to eat it.

Suddenly, the thought of putting even a spoonful of that sauce in my mouth made me feel panicked and ill, and I felt like flushing the whole lot down the loo along with the juice, but even as I half stood, ready to pick up the plate, I realized something, and I sat back down again on slow, shaky legs.

They didn't need to poison me. Why would they? If they wanted to kill me they could just starve me.

I tried to think clearly.

If whoever had brought me here had wanted to kill me, they'd have done it. Right?

Right. They could have hit me again, harder, or put a pillow over my face when I was passed out, or a plastic bag around my neck. And they hadn't. They'd dragged me here at some inconvenience to themselves.

So they didn't want me dead. Not right now, at any rate.

One pea. You couldn't die from one poisoned pea, surely?

I picked it up on the end of a fork, looking at it. It looked completely normal. No trace of any powder. No odd color.

I put it in my mouth and rolled it slowly round, trying to detect any strange taste. There was none.

I swallowed.

Nothing much happened. Not that I'd expected it to—I didn't know much about poison, but I imagined that the ones that killed you within seconds were few and far between, and not easy to obtain.

But something did happen. And that was that I started to feel hungry.

I scooped up a few more peas and ate them, cautiously at first, and then picking up speed as the food made me feel better. I skewered a meatball with my fork. It smelled and tasted completely normal—with that slightly institutional air of food prepared for a large number of people.

At last the plate was empty and I sat and waited for someone to come and collect it.

And waited.

And waited.

Time is very elastic—that's the first thing you realize in a situation without light, without a clock, without any way of measuring the length of one second over the length of another. I tried counting—counting seconds, counting my pulse—but I got to two thousand and something and lost count.

My head ached, but it was the weak shiveriness in

my limbs that worried me more. At first I thought it was low blood sugar, and then, after I'd eaten, I started to worry that perhaps there *had* been something in the food, but now I began to count back, to try to work out when the last time was that I'd taken my pills.

I remembered popping one out of the packet right after seeing Nilsson on Monday morning. But I hadn't actually taken it. Something—some stupid need to prove that I *wasn't* chemically dependent on these innocent little white dots—had stopped me. Instead, I'd left it on the countertop, not quite able to bring myself to down it, not quite wanting to throw it away.

I hadn't been intending to stop. Just to show . . . I don't know what. That I was in charge I guess. A little, pointless "fuck you" to Nilsson.

But then the argument with Ben had driven it from my mind. I'd gone off to the spa without taking it, and then the episode with the shower . . .

That made it . . . I couldn't quite work it out. At least forty-eight hours since I'd had a dose. Maybe more like sixty hours. The thought was uncomfortable. Actually, more than uncomfortable. It was terrifying.

I had my first panic attack when I was . . . I don't know. Thirteen maybe? Fourteen? I was a teenager. It came . . . and went, leaving me frightened and freaked-out, but I never told anyone. It seemed like something only a weirdo would get. Everyone else walked through life without shaking and finding themselves unable to breathe, right?

For a while it was okay. I did my GCSEs. Started my A levels. It was around then that things started to get really shaky. The panic attacks came back. First, one. Then a couple. After a while, it seemed like coping with anxiety had become a full-time business, and the walls began to close around me.

I saw a therapist, several in fact. There was the "talking cure" person my mum picked out of the phone book, a serious-faced woman with glasses and long hair who wanted me to reveal some dark secret that would be the key to unlocking all this, except I didn't have one. For a while I thought about making one up—just to see if it would make me feel better. But my mum got annoyed with her (and with her bills) before I could come up with a really good story.

There was the hip young community support leader, with his group of young girls who ran the gamut of problems, from anorexia to self-harm. And finally there was Barry, the cognitive behavioral therapist that my GP provided, who taught me to breathe, and count, and left me with a lifelong allergy to balding men with soft, supportive tenor voices.

None of them worked for me, though. Or none of them worked completely. But I kept it together enough to get through my exams, and then I went away to university and I felt a bit better, and it seemed like maybe all that—that *stuff*—was something I'd grow out of, like *NSYNC, and cherry lip gloss. That I'd leave behind, in my old bedroom at my parents' house, along with all my other childhood baggage. Uni was pretty great. When I left, with my shiny new degree, I felt ready to take on the world. I met Ben, and I got a job at *Velocity* and my own place in London, and everything seemed to be falling into place.

And that was when I fell apart.

I tried to come off the pills once. I was at a good place in my life, I was over Ben (oh my God, I was *so* over Ben). My GP lowered the dose to twenty milligrams a day, then ten, and then, since I was coping pretty well, to ten milligrams every other day, and finally I stopped.

I lasted two months before I cracked, and by that time I had lost thirty pounds and was in danger of losing my job at *Velocity*, although they didn't know why I'd stopped coming into the office. At last, Lissie called my mum, and she marched me back to the GP, who shrugged and said that maybe it was withdrawal, and maybe it just wasn't the right time for me to come off. He put me back on forty milligrams a day—my original dose—and I felt better almost within days. We agreed to try again another time— and somehow that time never came.

Now was not the right time. Not here. Not shut in a steel box six feet below sea level.

I tried to remember how long it had taken last time—how long it had been before I started to feel really, *really* shitty. It hadn't been that long, from what I could recall. Four days? Maybe less.

In fact I could feel the panic begin to prickle over my skin in little cold electric shocks.

You'll die here.

No one will know.

Oh God. Oh God oh God oh God oh God oh—

There was a sound at the door and I stopped. Stopped everything—stopped breathing, thinking, panicking—I sat, frozen, my back against the bunk. Should I pounce? Attack?

The door handle began to turn.

My heart was pounding in my throat. I stood up and backed away against the far wall. I knew I should fight—but I couldn't, not without knowing who was coming through that door.

Pictures flashed through my head. Nilsson. The chef in his latex gloves. The girl in the Pink Floyd T-shirt, a knife in her hand.

I swallowed.

And then a hand snaked through the gap and grabbed the plate, quick as blinking, and the door slammed shut. The light went out, plunging the cabin into inky blackness so thick I could taste it.

Fuck.

There was nothing I could do. I lay there in the impenetrable darkness for what felt like hours but might have been days, or minutes, drifting in and out of consciousness, hoping each time I opened my eyes to see *something*, even just a thin line of light in the corridor, something that would prove I was really here, that I really existed and wasn't just lost in some hell of my own imagining.

At last I must have fallen properly asleep, for I awoke with a jump, and my heart thumping and fluttering erratically in my chest. The cabin was still in complete darkness, and I lay there, shaking and sweating, holding on to the bunk like a life raft as I clawed my way back from the most horrible dream I could remember in a long time.

In the dream, the girl in the Pink Floyd T-shirt was in my cabin. It was dark, but somehow in the darkness I could . . . not exactly see her, but sense her. I just knew that she was there, standing in the middle of the cabin, and I couldn't move, the darkness pressing me down, like a living thing, squatting on my chest. She came closer, and closer, until she was standing just inches away, the T-shirt skimming the tops of her long, slim thighs.

She smiled, and then with one sinuous movement she pulled off the shirt. Beneath it she was skinny as a whippet, all ribs and collarbone and jutting pelvis, her elbow joints wider than her forearms, her wrists knobbly as a child's. She looked down at herself, and then she pulled off her bra, slow as a striptease, except there was nothing erotic about it, nothing sexy about her small, shallow breasts and the hollow of her stomach.

But as I lay on the bunk, panting, paralyzed with fear, she didn't stop there. She kept stripping. Her knickers slipped from her narrow hips to form a puddle at her feet. And then her hair, yanking it out by the roots. Then she pulled off her eyebrows, first one, and then the other, and her lips. She let her nose drop to her feet. She drew out her fingernails, one by one, slowly, like a woman loosening her evening gloves, and let them fall with a slight clatter to the floor, followed by her teeth, *click . . . click . . . click*, one after another. And finally—and most horribly—she began to peel away her skin, as if she were stepping out of a tight-fitting evening dress, until she was just a bloody streak, muscle and bone and sinew, like a skinned rabbit.

She went down on all fours and began to crawl towards me, her lipless mouth spread wide in a horrible parody of a smile.

Closer and closer she crawled, until at last, though I backed away, I came up against the rear wall of the bunk and could retreat no farther.

I felt my breath whimper in my throat. I tried to speak, but I was dumb. I tried to move, but I was frozen with fear.

She opened her mouth, and I knew that she was about to speak—but then she reached inside, and pulled out her own tongue.

I awoke, gasping and crawling with the horror of it, the blackness like a clenched fist around me.

I wanted to scream. The panic built inside me like a volcano, pressing up through the layers of closed throat and clenched teeth. And then I thought, in a kind of delirium—if I scream, what's the worst that can happen? Someone might hear? Let them hear. Let them hear, and maybe they'll come and get me.

So I let it out, the scream that had been rising up inside me, growing and swelling and pressing to get out.

And I screamed and I screamed and I screamed.

I don't know how long I screamed for, how long I lay there, shaking, my fists curled around the thin, limp pillow, my nails digging into the bare mattress beneath.

I only know that at last it was quiet in the little cabin, except for the low roar of the engine, and my own breath, rasping in a throat scoured raw and hoarse.

No one had come.

No one had banged on the door to ask what was going on, or threatened to kill me unless I shut up. No one had done anything. I might as well have been in outer space, screaming into a soundless vacuum.

My hands were trembling, and I could not get the girl from my dream out of my head, the idea of her raw, moist form crawling towards me, clutching, *needing*.

What had I done? Oh God, why had I done this, kept pushing, kept refusing to shut up. I had *made* myself a target, by my refusal to be silenced about what happened in that cabin. And yet . . . and yet what *had* happened?

I lay there, my hands pressed to my eyes in the suffocating darkness, trying to make sense of it. The girl was alive—whatever I had heard, whatever I *thought* I had seen, it wasn't murder. Had she been on the ship all along?

She must have. We hadn't stopped. We hadn't even got near enough to land to see it. But who was she, and why was she hiding on the ship?

I tried to ignore my aching head, to think logically. Was she a member of the crew? She had access to the staff door, after all. But then I remembered Nilsson punching in the code, me standing behind him as he did. He'd made no effort to shield the keypad. If I'd wanted to, it would have been child's play to note down the numbers as he entered them. And after that, once you were below decks, there were not many further locked doors.

She'd had access to the empty cabin, though—and that *did* require a passkey, either a guest one, programmed to that door specifically, or a staff one that opened all the cabin doors. I thought of the cleaners I'd seen in their little hutches below decks, their scared faces looking out at me before the door swung shut. How much would one of them sell a passkey for? A hundred kroner? A thousand? They wouldn't even need to sell it—I was certain there were places you could get key cards copied. They would just have had to loan it out for an hour or two, no questions asked. I thought of Karla—she had practically *told* me that it went on, that someone might have lent the cabin to a friend.

But it didn't have to be that. The passkey could have been stolen, for all I knew, or bought off the Internet—I had no idea how those electronic locks worked. There might have been no one else involved at all.

Was it possible that all this time I had been looking for an accomplice—a perpetrator among the crew or passengers—and they'd been innocent all along? I thought of the accusations I'd hurled at Ben, the suspicions I'd had of Cole, of Nilsson, of everyone, and I felt sick.

But the fact that this girl existed and was alive, that didn't automatically rule out someone else's involvement. The more I thought about it, the more I was sure that *someone* had been helping her above decks—someone had written that message on the spa wall, had tipped Cole's camera into the hot tub, had stolen my phone. They couldn't *all* have been her. Someone would have seen and recognized the

girl I had been shouting about for two days if she'd
been wandering around the ship.

Ugh, this was making my head hurt. Why? That
was the question I couldn't answer. Why go to such
lengths to hide on board the ship, to stop me from
asking questions? If the girl had died, the cover-up
made sense. But she was alive and well. It must be
who she was that was important. Someone's wife?
Someone's daughter? Lover? Someone trying to get
out of the country with no questions asked?

I thought of Cole and his ex-wife, Archer and his
mysterious "Jess." I thought of the way the photograph had disappeared from the camera.

None of it made sense.

I rolled over, feeling the weight of the darkness all
around. Wherever we were, it was very deep beneath
the ship, I was sure of that now. The engine was loud,
much louder than on the passenger deck, louder
even than I remembered it being on the staff deck. I
was somewhere else, on an engine deck, perhaps, far
below the waterline, deep in the hull.

At that thought, I felt again the horror begin to
creep over me, the tons and tons of water weighing
on my head and shoulders, pressing against the hull,
the air in the cabin circulating, circulating, and me
here suffocating in my own panic. . . .

My legs shaking, I climbed cautiously off the bunk
and made my way slowly across the floor, my arms
stretched out in front of me, cringing from what
might be in here with me in the absolute darkness.
My imagination conjured up horrors from my childhood nightmares—giant spiderwebs across my face,
men with clutching arms, even the girl herself, lid-

less, lipless, tongueless. But another part of me knew that there was no one here but myself—that I would have been able to hear, smell, *sense* another human being in such a confined space.

After a few moments of cautious inching, my fingers encountered the door, and I felt my way across it. The first thing I tried was the handle, but it was still locked—I hadn't expected anything else. I felt for a spy hole, but there was none, or none that I could find on the blank expanse of plastic. I didn't remember seeing one earlier, anyway. What I did remember, and what I felt for next, was the flat beige light switch to the left of the door. My fingers found it in the darkness, and I pressed it, my heart beating hard in my chest.

Nothing happened.

I flicked it back, but without hope this time, because I knew what they'd done. There must be some kind of override in the passage outside, some sort of master switch or fuse. The door was already shut when the light went out, and in any case, in any cabin I'd been in before there was always some kind of security light— you were never in *complete* darkness, even when the lights were turned out. This was something else—this was an utter, total darkness that could only come from the electricity being completely cut.

I crawled back to the bunk and beneath the covers, my muscles shaking with a mixture of panic and that sick flu-like feeling I'd had before. My head felt filled with a spreading blankness, as if the dark of the cabin had seeped inside my skull and was filtering through my synapses, deadening and muffling everything apart from the panic that was building in my gut.

Oh God. Don't. Don't give way, not now.

I couldn't. I *wouldn't*. I wouldn't let her win.

The anger that flooded over me suddenly was something that I could hang on to, something concrete in the silent blackness of this little box. That bitch. What a traitor. So much for the fucking sisterhood. I had fought for her, put my credibility on the line, endured Nilsson's doubt and Ben's probing—and all for what? So that she could betray me, bash my head into a steel frame post, and lock me into this fucking coffin.

Whatever the plot was—she was in on it.

She had definitely been the person who had ambushed me in the corridor. And the more I thought about it, the more I was sure that the hand that had come snaking in to snatch my food tray was hers, too, a skinny, lithe, strong hand. A hand that could scratch and slap and smack a person's head against the wall.

There must be *some* reason for all this—no one would go through this elaborate charade for nothing. Had she been faking her own death? Had I been *meant* to see what happened? But if so, why go to such lengths to pretend she was never there? Why clear the cabin, wipe away the blood, destroy the mascara, and deliberately discredit everything about my account of that night?

No. She hadn't wanted to be seen. Something had happened in that cabin, and whatever it was, I was not supposed to have witnessed it.

I lay there, cudgeling my battered brain to try to work it out, but the more I tried to ram the bits of information together, the more it felt like a jigsaw with too many pieces to fit the frame.

I tried to think through the possibilities that would mesh with the scream and the blood and the cover-up. A fight? A blow to the nose, a yell of pain, a gush of blood as the person ran to the veranda to try to bleed into the sea, leaving that smear on the glass . . . no deaths. And if the girl was some kind of stowaway, that could explain why they had covered it up—moved her to a different location, cleaned away the blood.

But other parts of the picture didn't fit. If the fight had been unintended and unpremeditated, how had they cleared the cabin so fast? I had seen the girl in situ earlier that day, the room behind her cluttered with clothes and belongings. If the fight had been unplanned, there was no way they could have stripped and cleaned that suite in the few minutes it had taken me to ring Nilsson.

No—whatever had happened in there had been *planned*. They had cleared it beforehand, meticulously cleaned it. And I was beginning to suspect it was not chance that it was number ten that had been empty. No, one cabin had been left empty deliberately, and it *had* to be ten. Palmgren was the very last one on the ship. Its veranda was not overlooked, and there were no other cabins to see something floating past, disappearing in the foam of the ship's wake.

Someone *had* died. I was sure of it. Just not that girl. But then who?

I tossed and turned in the darkness, listening for any sounds above the roar of the engine and trying to answer the questions churning uneasily inside. My brain felt fogged and thick, but I kept coming back to that question. Who? *Who had died?*

- CHAPTER 24 -

When I woke next it was to the same metallic click I'd heard before, and the lights flickered on. They strobed for a moment, the warming hum of the low-energy bulbs audible above the engine sound and mingling with the whining in my ears. I jumped up, my heart going a mile a minute, knocking over something on the floor beside the bed as I gazed wildly around.

I had missed my chance.

God *damn* it, I had missed my chance again.

I *had* to find out what was going on here, what they intended to do with me, why they were keeping me shut up here. How long had I been here? Was it daytime now? Or was this just the time that it suited the girl—or whoever my captor was—to turn the electricity back on?

I tried to count back. I had been hit in the early hours of Tuesday morning. At the very least it was Wednesday morning now, possibly later. It felt as if I'd been here longer than twenty-four hours—much longer.

I went to the bathroom to splash water on my face. It was as I was drying myself that a wave of vertigo washed over me, making my head reel and the whole room shift and shudder. I had the sudden sensation of falling, and I put out my hand to steady myself against the doorframe, shutting my eyes against the sensation of plummeting very far and very fast into black water.

At last the sensation receded, and I made my way back to the bunk, where I sat and put my head between my knees, feeling my skin shiver with cold and hot. *Had* the ship moved? It was hard to know what was dizziness and what was the movement of the waves, so far down beneath the decks. The movement of the ship felt very different down here—not so much a rhythmic rise and fall, but a sluggish roll that mingled with the constant roar of the engine to give a strange, hypnotic feeling.

There was a tray beside the bed, with a Danish pastry and a bowl of slopped muesli. That must have been what I knocked when I jumped up out of sleep. I picked it up and forced myself to take a spoonful. I wasn't hungry, but I'd eaten nothing but a few meatballs since Monday night. If I were going to get out of here, I would need to fight, and to fight, I needed to eat.

What I really wanted, though, was not food. It was my pills. I *wanted* them, with a fierce, physical longing that I remembered from the last time I tried to stop taking them. Only this time I knew that things wouldn't get better without them, as I had kept telling myself last time. They were going to get worse.

If you're around to see it, said a nasty little voice in my head. The muesli stuck in my throat, and suddenly I couldn't swallow.

I longed for the girl from the cabin to come back.

A vivid, luxuriantly violent image flashed across my brain: me, grabbing her hair the way she'd grabbed mine, smashing her cheekbone against the sharp metal edge of the bunk, watching the blood flow, the way it would smell sharp and raw in the confined, airless cabin. I remembered again the blood on the veranda, the way it had smeared across the glass, and I wished with a powerful, vicious longing that it *had* been hers.

I hate you, I thought. I swallowed against the pain in my throat, forcing the soggy half-chewed muesli down. I took another spoonful, my fingers shaking as I conveyed it to my mouth. *I hate you so much. I hope you* do *drown.* The muesli felt like cement, choking me as I tried to swallow it, but I forced it down again and again, until the bowl was half empty.

I did not know if I could do this, but I had to try.

I picked up the tray, the thin melamine tray, and I smacked it on the metal edge of the bunk. It bounced back and I only just flinched out of the way in time. I had a sudden, sharp flashback to the burglary—to the door smacking into my cheekbone, and I had to shut my eyes for a moment and steady myself on the bunk.

I didn't try that again. Instead, I leaned the tray on the metal edge and put my knee on the nearest side, and all my weight on my hands on the far edge. Then I pushed down. The tray did nothing at first, and I pressed harder. Then it snapped in half with a noise like a gunshot, sending me sprawling onto the bed. But I had what I'd been aiming for—two pieces of plastic, not quite razor-sharp, but each with an edge formidable enough to do some damage.

I picked up each piece, weighing them in my hand

for the best way to hold them, and then, holding the one that felt like the most intimidating weapon, I walked across to the door and crouched against the wall next to the frame.

And I waited.

It seemed to last for hours, that day. Once or twice I felt my eyes sliding shut, my body trying to shut down amid the exhausting flood of adrenaline and fear, but I jerked them back open. *Stay with it, Lo!*

I began to count. Not from panic this time but just to keep myself awake. One. Two. Three. Four. When I got to a thousand I changed and began to count in French. *Un. Deux. Trois. . . .* Then in twos. I played games in my own head—fizz-buzz, that children's game where you say "fizz" for every five or multiple of five, and "buzz" for every seven.

One. Two. Three. Four. Fizz. (My hands were shaking.) Six. Buzz. Eight. Nine. Ten— No wait, that should have been fizz.

I shook my head impatiently, rubbed my aching arms, and started again. One. Two. . . .

And then I heard it—a noise in the corridor. A door slamming. I caught my breath.

They were coming closer. My heart began to race. The pit of my stomach clenched.

A key in the lock . . .

And then the door cracked cautiously open and I pounced.

Her.

She saw me leap towards the gap and tried to close it, but I was too quick for her. I thrust my arm in

the gap, and it slammed onto my forearm—hard. I
screamed with pain, but the door bounced back, and
I was able to wedge half my body into the gap, stabbing at her grappling arm with the jagged edge of
the broken tray, but instead of falling backwards as
I'd anticipated, she rushed forwards into the room,
thumping me back against the plastic wall, the tray
cutting painfully into my arm. I pulled myself up,
blood dripping down the back of my hand, but she
was faster. She lunged at the door, locked it, and then
stood with her back to it, the key clenched in her fist.

"Let me go." It came out like the growl of an animal—not quite human. She shook her head. Her
back was to the door, and she had my blood on her
face, and she was scared, but kind of exhilarated, too,
I could see it in her eyes. She had the upper hand,
and she knew it.

"I'll kill you," I said. I meant it. I held up the tray,
stained with my own blood. "I'll cut your throat."

"You couldn't kill me," she said, and her voice was
just as I remembered it, with a kind of scornful defiance behind her words. "Look at you, you can barely
stand up, you poor bitch."

"Why?" I said, and there was a note in my voice
that sounded like a whining little child. "Why are you
doing this?"

"Because you *made* us," she hissed, suddenly furious. "You wouldn't stop digging, would you? No matter how much I tried to warn you off. If you'd just
kept your mouth shut about what you saw in that
bloody cabin—"

"What did I see?" I said, but she shook her head,
her lip curling.

"God, you must think I'm even dumber than I look. Do you actually *want* to die?"

I shook my head.

"Good. What do you want, then?"

"I want to get out of here," I said. I sat down on the bunk abruptly, not sure if my legs would hold me much longer.

She shook her head once more, vehemently this time, and I saw that flicker of fear in her eyes again.

"He'd never let me."

He? The word sent a prickle through me, the first concrete evidence that someone upstairs had been helping her. Who was *he*? But I didn't dare ask, not now. There was something more important I needed first.

"My pills, then. Let me have my pills."

She looked at me appraisingly.

"The ones you had by the sink? I might be able to do that. Why d'you want them?"

"They're antidepressants," I said bitterly. "They have— You shouldn't withdraw from them too fast."

"Oh . . ." There was sudden comprehension on her face. "That's why you look so bad. I couldn't work it out. I thought I'd hit your head too hard. Okay. I can do that. But you have to promise me something in return."

"What?"

"No more trying to attack me. These are for good behavior, right?"

"All right."

She straightened, picked up the plate and bowl, and held out her hand for the shards of tray. I hesitated for a moment and then handed them over.

"I'm going to unlock the door now," she said. "But don't do anything stupid. There's another door outside this one, operated by a code. You won't get very far. So no silly buggers, all right?"

"All right," I said reluctantly.

After she'd gone I sat on the bench staring into space, thinking about what she'd said.

He.

She *did* have an accomplice on board. And that one word meant I could rule out Tina, Chloe, Anne, and two-thirds of the staff.

Who was *he*? I ticked them off in my head.

Nilsson.

Bullmer.

Cole.

Ben.

And Archer.

In the less-likely column I put Owen White, Alexander, and the crew and stewards.

My mind circled the possibilities, but the one factor I kept coming back to was the spa and the *STOP DIGGING* message. There was only one man who had been down there, one man who could have written that sign. Ben.

I had to stop focusing on motives. *Why* was an unsolvable question that I just didn't have enough information to answer.

But the *how*—there were very few people on board with the opportunity to write that note. There was one functional entrance into the spa, and Ben was the only male who I was certain had used it.

So many things made sense. His quickness to undermine my story to Nilsson. The fact that he—

alone of everyone on board—had tried to get into my cabin on that last night, and knew that I was locked in the bathroom, making it possible to steal my phone.

The fact that his cabin was on the other side of the empty one, yet he'd heard nothing and seen nothing.

The fact that he'd lied about his alibi, playing poker.

And the fact that he had tried so hard to stop me from pushing on with the investigation.

The clicking of the puzzle pieces into place should have given me satisfaction, but they didn't. Because what use were answers to me down here? I needed to get out.

- CHAPTER 25 -

I was lying on my side, staring at the cream melamine wall when the knock came.

"Come in," I said dully, and then almost laughed at myself for the stupidity of social niceties in a situation like this. What did it matter if I said "Come in" when they would do as they liked regardless?

"It's me," said the voice outside the door. "No more shit with the trays, okay? Or this'll be the last pill you get off me, right?"

"Okay," I said. I was trying not to sound too eager, but I sat up, pulling the thin blanket around myself. I hadn't used the shower since I got here and I smelled of sweat and fear.

The door cracked open cautiously, and the girl pushed a tray of food through the bottom with her foot and then slipped through the gap, locking it behind herself.

"Here you go," she said. She held out her hand, and on the palm was a single white tablet.

"One?" I said incredulously.

"One. Maybe I can bring you a couple more tomorrow, if you behave."

I had just given her the best blackmail weapon ever. But I nodded and took the pill from her palm.

From her pocket she pulled a book—one of mine, in fact, from my room. *The Bell Jar.* Not what I'd have chosen under the circumstances, but it was better than nothing, I guessed.

"I thought you might like something to read, you might be going a bit nuts with nothing to do." Her eyes strayed to the pill, and then she added, "No offense."

"Thanks," I said. She turned to go and I said, "Wait."

"Yeah?"

"I—" Suddenly I wasn't sure how to ask what I wanted to ask. I clenched my hand around the pill in my palm. Shit. "What—what's going to happen to me?"

Her face changed at that, something guarded came over her expression, like a curtain falling across a window.

"That's not up to me."

"Who is it up to? Ben?"

She gave a derisory snort at that.

"Enjoy."

As she turned to leave, she caught sight of herself in the little mirror on the back of the en suite door.

"Fuck, I've got blood on my face. Why didn't you say? If he knows you attacked me . . ." She went into the little toilet to splash and wipe her face.

But it wasn't just the blood she wiped away. When she came out, I froze. With that one simple act, I realized who she was.

In wiping away the blood she had wiped both her eyebrows clean off, leaving a smooth, skull-like forehead that was instantly, unbearably recognizable.

The woman in cabin 10 was Anne Bullmer.

- CHAPTER 26 -

I was too stunned to say anything. I just sat there, openmouthed with shock.

The girl looked from me, back to her reflection in the en suite mirror, and realized what she'd done. An expression of annoyance crossed her face for a moment, but then she seemed to shrug it off and stalked out of the room, letting the door swing shut behind her. I heard a key scrape in a lock, and then another door bang farther away.

Anne Bullmer.

Anne Bullmer?

It seemed impossible that she could be the same gaunt, gray, prematurely aged woman I'd seen and spoken to. And yet—her face was unmistakable. The same dark eyes. The same high, jutting cheekbones. The only thing I couldn't understand was how I'd missed it before.

If I hadn't seen her, midtransformation, I would never have believed how much her hair and the delicately penciled eyebrows changed her face. Without them she looked oddly featureless and smooth. It was impossible not to think of death and illness when you looked at that bone-pale sweep of skin, and the scarf tied tight around her skull only emphasized that fragility—painfully underscoring the lines of her neck and the shape of the bones beneath.

But her sleek black brows and the vibrant mass of dark hair changed all that beyond recognition. With it she became young, healthy, *alive*.

I realized, when I'd spoken to Anne Bullmer before, I had been so mesmerized by the trappings of her illness that I'd never really looked at the woman beneath. I had tried *not* to look in fact. I had just seen the distinctive, draping clothes, the missing eyebrows, the distractingly smooth skull beneath those delicate scarves . . .

The hair must be a wig—I had no doubt about that. There was no room under those thin silk scarves Anne wore for those thick dark tresses.

But was she sick? Well? Dying? Faking? It didn't make sense.

I tried to think back to what Ben had told me—four years of chemo and radiotherapy. Could you really fake that, even with private doctors in your pay and enough money to enable you to hop from one health system to another every few months? Maybe.

At least this explained one thing—how she had got on board, and what had happened to her after that splash in the night. She'd simply pulled off her wig, put on her scarf, and resumed her life as Anne Bullmer. It also explained how she had access to every part of the ship—to the passkeys and the staff areas, and this secret locked vault down in the belly of the boat. When your husband was the owner, nothing was out of bounds, presumably.

But the thing that puzzled me most was *why*? Why dress up in a wig and a Pink Floyd T-shirt and spend the afternoon hanging out in an empty cabin? What was she doing there? And if it was so secret, why answer the door at all?

As the last question ran through my head, I had a sudden flash of myself knocking on the door—one, two, three . . . pause, and another bang, and the way the door had been snatched open as if someone had been waiting for that final knock. It was an odd knock, idiosyncratic. The kind of knock you might use if you were arranging a code. Was it possible I had, completely accidentally, stumbled on a pre-arranged signal for the woman in the cabin—Anne Bullmer—to open the door?

If only. If only I'd just knocked twice like any normal person—or even once. I would never have known she was there, never have put myself in this position where I had to be locked up—silenced . . .

Silenced. It was an uncomfortable thought, and the word stuck in my head, reverberating there like an echo.

I had to be silenced. But silenced for how long? Locked up here until . . . what? Some prearranged deadline had passed?

Or silenced . . . permanently?

Supper was white fish in a sort of cream sauce, with boiled potatoes. It was cold, congealing around the edges, but I was hungry. Before I ate I looked at the pill in my hand, wondering what to do. It was half my normal dose. I could take the whole pill now, or I could split it, and start building up a reserve in case . . . but in case what? I could hardly escape, and if Anne decided to stop dispensing the pills, I would run out long before she took pity on me.

In the end, I gulped down the whole thing, reasoning that I had a deficit to make up. I could start biting them in half tomorrow, if it seemed important. I felt better almost immediately, though I knew, logically, that it couldn't be the pills. They didn't absorb that fast, and the effect took a while to build up in my system. Whatever I was experiencing was completely placebo-based. At this point, though, I didn't care. I would take what I could get.

Then I started picking at the lukewarm supper. As I sat on the bunk, chewing the tepid, gluey potato slowly, in an effort to make it less unappealing, I tried to rearrange the pieces of the puzzle I had assembled so painstakingly inside my head.

I knew now what that derisive snort meant when I had said *Who is it up to? Ben?*

Poor Ben. I felt a rush of guilt that I had been so quick to judge him, and then another rush, this time of anger. I'd been so focused on Anne's chance mention of a male accomplice that it had never occurred to me that Anne herself might have been the one to run quickly down the spa stairs while her varnish was supposed to be drying and scrawl those words. Stupid, *stupid* Lo.

But stupid Ben, too. If he hadn't spent so many years belittling my feelings and if he hadn't been so eager to spill the beans to Nilsson, instead of supporting my story, then I might not have been so quick to jump to conclusions.

I knew now who *he* was. It must be Richard Bullmer. He owned the boat. And of all the men on the ship, I could imagine him planning and carrying out a murder better than anyone else. Certainly better than fat, fussy Alexander or the lumbering, bear-like Nilsson.

Except that no murder had taken place. Why did I have to keep reminding myself of that fact? Why was it so hard to grasp?

Because you're here, I thought. Because whatever you saw—whatever happened in that cabin—it was important enough that they would lock you up here and prevent you from going to see the police at Trondheim. What had happened? It must be something so high-stakes that they simply couldn't afford to let me talk about it. Was it smuggling? Were they throwing something overboard to an accomplice?

It'll be you next, you stupid bitch, said the voice inside my head, and an image of myself falling through deep water shot through me, like an electric shock deep in my skull.

I winced and gritted my teeth, forcing myself to swallow another glutinous mouthful of potato. The ship heaved, and nausea swilled around in the pit of my stomach.

What *was* going to happen to me? There were only two possibilities—they were going to let me go at some point. Or they were going to kill me. And somehow, the first one didn't seem very likely anymore. I knew so much. I knew about Anne. I knew she wasn't nearly as ill as she pretended. And they could not afford for me to get out and tell my story—a story of kidnap, imprisonment, and bodily harm—though would anyone believe me?

I touched my fingers to my cheek, where the blood was still caked from where she'd whacked me into the doorframe. I felt suddenly gross—dirty and sweaty and blood-smeared. Anne—judging by her previous timings—wouldn't be back for hours.

There wasn't much I could do to improve my lot, stuck in this two-meter coffin. But at least I could keep myself clean.

The jet was nothing like the one in my suite upstairs. Even turned up full it was a tepid trickle, but I stood underneath it for so long I felt my fingers wrinkle into mush. The clotted blood on my hand dissolved into the water and I shut my eyes and felt the warmth pour through me, seeping into my muscles.

When I climbed out I felt better, more like myself, washed clean of some of the fear and violence that had marked the last few days. It was putting my clothes back on that made me really realize how far I'd sunk. They stank—not to put too fine a point on it—and were stained with blood and sweat.

I lay down on the bunk and shut my eyes, listening to the steady thrum of the engine and wondering where we were. It was Wednesday night—or maybe even Thursday morning now. From what I could remember we had only a little over twenty-four hours of this trip left. And then what? When the boat got into Bergen on Friday morning, the other passengers would leave and with them would go my last hope of someone realizing what had happened.

For twenty-four hours I was probably safe. But

after that . . . Oh God, but I couldn't think about that.

I pressed my hands into my eyes, listened to the blood roaring in my head. What should I do? What *could* I do?

If Anne was telling the truth, hurting her wouldn't achieve anything. There was another locked door the other side of this one, and very likely other codes on the exits. For a minute I wondered if I got out into the corridor, could I find and smash a fire alarm before Anne caught up with me? But it seemed like too long a shot. From what I'd seen of Anne's strength and quickness, I was unlikely to get that far.

No. My best chance was simple—I had to get Anne on my side.

But how? What did I actually know about her?

I tried to think about what I knew about Anne Bullmer—her fantastic wealth, her lonely upbringing, trailing around the boarding schools of Europe. It was no wonder it had taken me so long to make the connection. The rake-thin, sad-eyed woman in her gray silk wraps and designer headscarves—yes, somehow that fit with what I'd been told. But I could not make one word of what Ben had said connect with the girl in the Pink Floyd T-shirt, with her mocking dark eyes and cheap mascara. It was like there were two Annes. Same height, same weight, but that was where the similarity ended.

And then . . . something clicked.

Two Annes.

Two women.

The gray silk robe that matched her eyes . . .

I opened my eyes and swung my legs over the side of the bunk, groaning with my own stupidity. Of course—of *course*. If I hadn't been half-dead with fear and panic and the pain in my head, I would have seen it. How could I not have thought of it?

Of course there were two Annes.

Anne Bullmer was dead—had been since the night we left England.

The girl in the Pink Floyd T-shirt was very much alive, and had been impersonating her ever since.

Same height, same weight, same broad cheekbones—it was only the eyes that didn't match, and they had taken a calculated risk that no one would remember the features of a woman they'd barely met. No one on board knew Anne before the trip. Richard had even told Cole not to take any photographs of her, for Christ's sake! Now I understood why. It wasn't to protect a woman self-conscious about her appearance. It was so there would be no compromising photographs for his wife's friends and family to puzzle over afterwards.

I shut my eyes, my fingers gripping my hair so hard that it hurt, tugging painfully on my scalp, trying to work out what must have happened.

Richard Bullmer—it must have been him—had smuggled the woman in cabin 10 on board somehow. She was in that cabin before the rest of us ever came on the ship.

The day we set sail she had been waiting for the word, for instruction from Richard, to clear her cabin and get ready. I thought back to what I'd seen over her shoulder—a silk robe strewn across the bed, makeup,

Veet in the bathroom—*waxing strips*. Christ—how could I have been so stupid? She had been shaving and ripping off her body hair, ready to impersonate a woman with cancer. But instead of Richard with his prearranged knock, *I* had come along, inadvertently given the signal, and she'd seen me instead.

What the hell must she have thought? I replayed again the fright and irritation in her face as she'd tried to shut the door and I'd stopped her. She'd been desperate to get rid of me but trying to act as unsuspiciously as possible. Far better that I just remembered a strange woman lending a mascara than started telling tales of a fellow guest slamming the door in my face.

And it had nearly worked. It had *so* nearly worked.

Did she tell Richard when he came? I couldn't be sure, but I thought not. He had seemed so normal at that first night's dinner—the perfect host. And besides, it was her blunder, and he didn't look like the kind of man you'd want to confess a mistake to. More likely she just crossed her fingers and hoped to get away with it.

Then she had packed her things, cleared the room, and waited.

After drinks that first night, Anne, somehow, had been taken to cabin 10. Was she alive, lured there by some cock-and-bull story? Or was she already dead?

Either way, it didn't really matter, because the end result was the same. While Richard was back in Lars's cabin, establishing his alibi with an uninterrupted poker game, the woman in cabin 10 had bundled the real Anne overboard and hoped that the body would never be found.

And they would have got away with it, if I—frightened and traumatized from the burglary—hadn't heard the splash and jumped to a conclusion that was so wrong, it was almost completely right.

So who was she? Who was this girl who had hit me, and fed me, and locked me up here like an animal?

I had no idea. But I knew one thing—she was my best hope of getting out of here alive.

- CHAPTER 27 -

All that night I lay awake, trying to work out what I should do. Judah and my parents would not be expecting me home until Friday and would have no reason to suspect anything was wrong until then. But the other passengers must know that I hadn't returned to the ship. Would they have raised the alarm? Or had Bullmer given them some story to explain my disappearance—unavoidably detained in Trondheim, perhaps? Decided to return home unexpectedly?

I wasn't sure. I tried to think who might be concerned enough to ask questions. I had little hope of Cole, Chloe, or most of the others making a fuss. They didn't know me. They had no contact details for any of my family. They would very likely accept whatever Bullmer told them.

Ben, then? He knew me well, enough to know that an early-morning flit to Trondheim without a word wasn't in character. But I wasn't sure. Under normal circumstances I was fairly certain he'd have contacted Judah or my parents with his concerns, but the way I had left things with him wasn't exactly normal circumstances. I had all but accused him of being complicit in a murder, and aside from his justifiable anger, he probably wouldn't be surprised at my disappearing off the ship without a word of good-bye.

Out of all the guests, Tina seemed like my best bet, and I was crossing my fingers that she would contact Rowan when I failed to return. But it seemed very slim odds to hang my life on.

No. I had to take matters into my own hands.

By the time morning came I hadn't slept, but I knew what I had to do, and when the knock came, I was ready.

"Come in," I said. The door cracked open, and the girl put her head cautiously around the doorframe. She saw me sitting quietly on the bed, washed and clean, holding the book in my lap. "Hey," I said.

She put down the tray of food on the floor. She was dressed as Anne this time, wearing a headscarf, her eyebrows not penciled in, but she didn't move like Anne, she moved like the girl I'd seen before, dumping the tray down impatiently and straightening up with none of the meditative grace she'd shown when impersonating Richard's wife.

"Hey yourself," she said, and her voice was different, too—the crystalline consonants elided and blurred. "You finished with that?" She nodded at the book.

"Yes, can you swap it for another one?"

"Yeah, I guess. What do you want?"

"I don't mind. Anything. You choose."

"Okay." She held out her hand for *The Bell Jar* and I handed it over, and then steeled myself for what I had to do next.

"I'm sorry," I said awkwardly. "About the tray."

She gave a smile at that, a flash of straight white teeth, a glint of mischief in her dark eyes.

"That's all right. I don't blame you; I'd have done the same. You've got a rubber one this time, though. Fool me once, and all that."

I looked down at the breakfast lying on the floor. It was true. The brittle melamine tray was gone, replaced by one made of thicker, grippy plastic, like the kind you serve drinks on in bars.

"I can't complain, I guess." I forced a smile. "I earned it."

"Your pill's on the saucer. Remember—good behavior, yeah?"

I nodded, and she turned to leave. I gulped. I had to stop her, say something. *Anything* that might prevent me from being condemned to another day and night here alone.

"What's your name?" I said desperately.

She turned back, her face suspicious.

"What?"

"I know you're not Anne. I remembered, about the eyes. On the first night Anne had gray eyes. You don't. Other than that it's very convincing. You're a really good actress, you know."

Her face went completely blank and for a minute I thought that she was going to slam out of the room and leave me here for another twelve hours. I felt like a fisherman, reeling in a huge fish on a delicate line, my muscles tense with the effort but trying not to jerk or show the strain.

"If I've got it wrong—" I began cautiously.

"Shut up," she said, fierce as a lioness. Her face was

completely transformed, savage with anger, her dark eyes full of rancor and distrust.

"I'm sorry," I said humbly. "I didn't . . . Look, does it matter? I'm not going anywhere. Who would I tell?"

"Fuck," she said bitterly. "You're digging your grave, do you get that?"

I nodded. But I had known that for a few days now—whatever the girl tried to tell herself—whatever *I* tried to tell myself—there was only one way I was leaving this room.

"I don't think Richard will let me leave," I said. "You know that, right? So name or no name, it doesn't really matter."

Her face, beneath the expensive headscarf, was white. When she spoke her voice was bitter.

"You fucked it all up. Why couldn't you leave well enough alone?"

"I was trying to help!" I said. I didn't mean it to sound the way it came out, but in the little room it sounded frighteningly loud. I swallowed, and spoke more quietly. "I was trying to help *you*, don't you get that?"

"Why?" she said. It was half a question, half a cry of frustration. "Why? You barely knew me—why did you have to keep digging?"

"Because I knew what it was like to be you! I know—I know what it's like to wake up in the night, afraid for your life."

"But that's not me," she snarled. She stalked across the little cabin. Close up I could see that her eyebrows had just the faintest brush of regrowth. "It *was never me*."

"It will be, though," I said, holding her gaze so she couldn't look away. I couldn't afford to release her from the knowledge of what she was doing. "When Richard's got Anne's money—what do you think his next move will be? Making himself safe."

"Shut up! You have no idea what you're talking about. He's a good man. He's in love with me."

I stood up, level with her. Our eyes were locked, our faces just inches apart in the tiny space.

"That's bullshit and you know it," I said. My hands were shaking. If this went wrong she might lock the door and never come back, but I had to make her face up to the reality of the situation—both for my sake and hers. If she walked away now, we were very likely both dead. "If he was in love with you he wouldn't be beating you up and forcing you to dress up as his dead wife. What do you *think* this charade is all about? Being with you? It's not about you. If it was, he'd have got a divorce and walked off into the sunset with you—but she'd have taken her money with her. She was heir to a billion-pound dynasty. Those kinds of people don't risk marriage without a prenup."

"Shut up!" She put her hands over her ears, shaking her head. "You don't know what you're talking about. Neither of us wanted to be in this situation!"

"Really? You think it's coincidence he fell in love with someone who bears a startling resemblance to Anne? He planned this from the beginning. You're just a means to an end."

"You know nothing about it," the girl snarled. She turned away from me, walked to where the window would have been if I had one, and back. There was nothing of Anne's weary serenity in her expression now—it was naked fear and fury.

"All the money, without the controlling wife—I think he had that carrot waved in front of his nose by Anne's illness, and suddenly found he liked the idea: a future without Anne, but with the money. And when the doctors gave her the all clear, he didn't want to let go of it—is that right? And then he saw you—and a plan started to form. Where did he pick you up—a bar? No, wait." I remembered the photo on Cole's camera. "It was at his club, right?"

"You know nothing about it!" the girl shouted. "NOTHING!"

And before I could say anything else, she turned on her heel, unlocked the door with a trembling hand, and slammed out of the room, *The Bell Jar* still clutched beneath her arm. The door banged shut behind her, and I heard her key scraping shakily in the lock. Then farther away another bang, and then it was still.

I sat back on the bunk. Had I made her doubt Richard enough to put her trust in me? Or was she going upstairs right now to tell him this whole conversation? There was only one way to find out, and that was by waiting.

But as the hours slipped away and she didn't come back, I started to wonder how long that wait would be.

And when she didn't reappear with supper, and hunger began to claw at my stomach, I began to suspect I'd made a horrible mistake.

- CHAPTER 28 -

It's terrifying how long the hours can feel when you have no clock, no means of telling the time, and no way of knowing if anyone will come for you.

I lay for a long time, staring at the bunk above me, running over the conversation in my head and trying to work out if I'd just made the worst mistake of my life.

I'd gambled on establishing some kind of bond with the girl, forcing her to face up to what she was doing—and it was starting to look like I'd failed.

The hours dragged on and still no one came. My hunger grew more and more distracting. I wished I hadn't given her back the book, there was nothing in the cabin I could distract myself with. I began to think about solitary confinement—how prisoners went slowly crazy, heard voices, begged for release.

At least the girl had left the electricity on, although I wasn't sure it was an act of mercy—she had been so furious when she left the room she'd probably have switched it off just to punish me. More likely she'd just forgotten. But that small fact—the idea that I could choose my environment even in such a minor way—helped.

I showered again and licked the dried croissant jam off the plate. I lay on the bed and shut my eyes, and tried to remember things—the layout of the house I grew up in. The plot of *Little Women*. The color of Jude's—

But no. I pushed that away. I couldn't think of Judah. Not here. It would break me.

In the end—more as a way of taking charge of the situation than because I really thought it would help—I turned out the light and lay, staring into the blackness, trying to sleep.

I'm not sure if I did sleep. I dozed, I guess. Hours passed, or seemed to. No one came, but at some point in the long darkness, I was jerked awake and sat up, my pulse spiking, trying to fathom what was different. A noise? A presence in the dark?

My heart was thumping as I slipped out of bed and felt my way by touch to the door, but when I flicked on the light nothing was different. The cabin was empty. The tiny en suite as bare as ever. I held my breath, listening, but there were no footsteps in the corridor outside, no voices or movements. Not a sound disturbed the quiet.

And then I realized. The quiet. *That* was what had woken me. The engine had stopped.

I tried to count the days on my fingers, and although I couldn't be sure, I was fairly certain it must now be Friday the twenty-fifth. And that meant that the ship had arrived at its last port, Bergen, where we were due to disembark and catch planes back to London. The passengers would be leaving.

And then I'd be alone.

The thought brought panic rushing through my

veins. I don't know why—maybe it was the idea that they were so close—sleeping, most likely, just a few feet above my head and yet there was nothing, *nothing* I could do to make them hear. And soon they would pack their cases and leave, and I would be alone in a boat-shaped coffin.

The thought was too much to bear. Without thinking, I grabbed the bowl that had held yesterday's breakfast and banged it against the ceiling as hard as I could.

"Help!" I screamed. "Can anyone hear me? I'm trapped, please, please help!"

I stopped, panting, listening, hoping desperately that with the sound of the engine no longer masking my cries, someone might hear.

There was no answering thump, no muffled shout filtering back through the floors. But I heard a sound. It was a metallic grinding, as if something was scraping the outside of the hull.

Had someone heard? I held my breath, trying to still my thumping heart, beating so loud it threatened to drown out the faint sounds from outside the ship. Was someone coming?

The grinding came again. . . . I felt the ship's side shudder, and I realized suddenly what it was. The gangway was being lowered. The passengers were disembarking.

"Help me!" I screamed, and I banged again, only now I was noticing the way the plastic ceiling deadened and absorbed the sound.

"Help me! It's me, Lo. I'm here! I'm on the boat!"

No answer, just the breath tearing in my throat, my blood in my ears.

"Anyone? Please! Please help!"

I put my hands to the wall, feeling the thumps against the gangway being transmitted down through the hull and into my hands. The impact of goods trolleys . . . and luggage . . . and departing feet.

I could feel all this. But I could not hear it. I was deep below the water—and they were up above, where any faint vibrations that I could make with my plastic bowl would be drowned out by the sound of the wind and the screech of the gulls and the voices of their fellow passengers.

I let the bowl fall from my hands to the floor, where it bounced and rolled across the thin carpet, and then I dropped to the bed, and I crouched there, my arms wrapped around my head, my head pressed into my knees, and I began to weep, great choking tears of fear and desperation.

I had been afraid before. I'd been scared half out of my wits.

But I had never despaired, and it was despair that I was feeling now.

As I knelt on the thin, sagging mattress, sobbing into my knees, pictures passed through my head: Judah reading the paper, my mother doing the crossword, her tongue between her teeth—my father, mowing the lawn on a Sunday, humming tunelessly. I would have given anything to see one of them in this room, just for a moment, just to tell them I was alive and loving them.

But all I could think of was them waiting for my return. And their despair as I didn't arrive. And finally the endless sentence of waiting, waiting without hope, for someone who would never come.

From: Judah Lewis
To: Judah Lewis, Pamela Crew and Alan Blacklock
BCC: [38 recipients]
Sent: Tuesday, 29 September
Subject: Lo—an update

Dear All,

I'm very sorry to be sending this news in an e-mail, but I'm sure you'll understand that these last few days have been very difficult and we've had trouble responding to everyone's concern and enquiries.

Up until now we didn't really have anything concrete to share, and this has resulted in a lot of hurtful speculation on social media. However, we have now received some news. Unfortunately, it's not what we were hoping for, and Lo's parents, Pam and Alan, have asked me to send this update to her close friends and immediate family on behalf of them as well as myself, as some details seem to have been leaked to the press already, and we didn't want anyone to find this out from the Internet.

There is no easy way to say this—early this morning Scotland Yard asked me to identify some photographs they received from the Norwegian police team handling the case. They were photographs of clothes, and the garments are Lo's. I recognized them immediately. The boots in particular are vintage and very distinctive, and unmistakably hers.

We are obviously in pieces at this discovery, but we are holding on and waiting to find out what the police can tell us—this is all we know at present as the body is still in Norway and the Norwegian police have not shared any information on when we may be able to see it. In the meantime we would please ask you to use your discretion in talking to the media—if you have anything to add to the investigation, I can give you the names of the officers at Scotland Yard handling the case at the UK end. We also have a family liaison officer who is helping us deal with media enquiries, but some of the stories that are running are upsetting and untrue and we'd like to ask you all for your help in respecting Lo's privacy.

We are just devastated at this turn of events and trying to come to terms with what it means, so please bear with us, and know that we'll update you as soon as we can.

Judah

PART SEVEN

- CHAPTER 29 -

She didn't come.

The girl didn't come.

The hours ticked past, blurring into one another, and I knew that somewhere on the other side of the metal coffin of the hull people were talking and laughing and eating and drinking, while I lay here unable to do anything except breathe, and count down the seconds, minute by minute, hour by hour. Somewhere outside the sun was rising and falling, the waves were lifting and rocking the hull, and life went on, while I sank into the darkness.

I thought of Anne's body again, floating through the depths of the sea, and I thought with bitterness that she was lucky—at least it had been quick. One moment of suspicion, one blow to the head—and that was it. I was beginning to fear that, for me, there would be no such mercy.

I lay on the bed, hugging my knees to my chest, and I tried not to think about my hunger, about the pains that were gnawing in the pit of my stomach. My last meal had been breakfast on Thursday and I thought at the least it must be late Friday now. I had a raging headache and stomach cramps, and when I stood to use the toilet I felt weak and light-headed.

The nasty little voice in the back of my head spoke, needling. *What do you think it's like to starve to death? Think it's a peaceful way to go?*

I shut my eyes. *One. Two. Three. Breathe in.*

It takes a long time. It'd be quicker if you could manage not to drink. . . .

An image came into my mind—myself, thin and white and cold, curled beneath the threadbare orange blanket.

"I choose not to think about these images," I muttered. "I choose to think about . . ." And then I stopped. What? *What?* None of Barry's tutorials had focused on what happy images to choose when you were being held prisoner by a murderer. Was I supposed to think about my mum? About Judah? About everything I loved and held dear and was about to lose?

"Insert happy image here, you little fucker," I whispered, but the place I was inserting it probably wasn't the one Barry had in mind.

And then I heard a sound in the corridor.

I leaped upright, and the blood rushed from my head so that I almost fell, and only just managed to lower myself to the bunk before my legs buckled beneath me.

Was it her? Or Bullmer?

Oh shit.

I knew I was breathing too fast, I could feel my heart speeding up and the tingling in my muscles, and then my vision began to fragment into little scraps of black and red—

And then everything went black.

·   ·   ·

"Fuck, fuck, fuck . . ."

One word, over and over, being whispered in a panicked, tearful monotone from somewhere close.

"Oh Jesus, just wake up, will you?"

"Wh—" I managed. The girl gave a kind of teary gasp of relief.

"Shit! Are you okay? You gave me such a scare!"

I opened my eyes, saw her worried face looming over mine. There was a smell of food in the air and my stomach groaned painfully.

"I'm sorry," she said rapidly, helping me to sit up against the steel bunk edge, with a cushion behind my back. I could smell alcohol on her breath, schnapps, or maybe vodka. "I didn't mean to leave you so long, I just . . ."

"S'the day?" I croaked.

"What?"

"Wh . . . what day is it?"

"Saturday. Saturday the twenty-sixth. It's late, nearly midnight. I've brought you some dinner."

She held out a piece of fruit and I snatched it, feeling almost sick with hunger, and tore into it, barely even noticing that it was a pear until the taste exploded in my mouth, almost unbearable in its intensity.

Saturday—nearly Sunday. No wonder I felt so awful. No wonder the hours had seemed to stretch out forever. No wonder my stomach was even now cramping and griping as I gulped down the pear in huge, wolfish chunks. I had been locked up here without food or contact for . . . I tried to do the maths. Thursday morning to Saturday evening. Forty-eight . . . sixty . . .

sixty-something hours? Was that really right? My brain hurt. My stomach hurt. *Everything* hurt.

My stomach shifted and cramped again.

"Oh God." I tried to scramble to my feet, my legs weak and shaky. "I think I'm going to be sick."

I stumbled to the tiny en suite, anxiously shadowed by the girl, who put out a hand to steady me as I elbowed my way through the narrow doorway, and then fell to my knees and vomited sourly into the blue-stained pan of the toilet. The girl seemed to feel my wretchedness for she said, almost timidly, "I can get you another one, if you want. But there's some kind of potato thing as well. That might be better for your stomach. The cook called it pittypanny or something. I can't remember."

I didn't reply, just knelt over the bowl, bracing myself for the next heave, but it seemed to be gone, and at last I wiped my mouth and then stood slowly, pulling myself up by the handrail and testing the strength in my legs. Then I walked unsteadily back to the bunk. The cubes of fried potato looked and smelled divine. I picked up a fork and ate, more slowly this time, trying not to gulp the food. The girl watched me as I ate.

"I'm sorry," she said again. "I shouldn't have punished you like that."

I swallowed a mouthful of the tepid, salty potato pieces, feeling the caramelized skin crunch between my back teeth.

"What's your name?" I said at last.

She chewed her lip, looked away, and then sighed.

"I probably shouldn't tell you, but what does it matter? Carrie."

"Carrie." I took another mouthful, rolling the word around as I chewed. "Hi, Carrie."

"Hi," she said, but there was no warmth or life in her voice. She watched me eat for a moment longer and then scooted slowly back across the floor of the cabin and slumped against the opposite wall.

We sat in silence for a while, me eating methodically, trying to pace myself, she watching me. Then she gave a small exclamation, felt in her pocket, and pulled something out.

"I nearly forgot. Here you go." It was a pill, wrapped in a scrap of tissue. I took it, almost wanting to laugh with relief. It seemed pathetically hopeful, the idea that this tiny little white dot could make me feel better about my situation. And yet . . .

"Thanks," I said. I put it on the back of my tongue, took a gulp of the juice on the tray, and swallowed it.

At last the plate was empty, and I realized, as I scraped up the last of the potato, Carrie still watching me from across the room, that it was the first time she had waited while I ate. The thought made me bold enough to try something, maybe something stupid, but the words came out before I could stop them.

"What's going to happen to me?"

She said nothing, only levered herself to her feet, shaking her head slowly and dusting down her cream silk trousers. She was painfully thin, and I wondered, briefly, whether that was all part of the part for impersonating Anne or whether she was naturally that skinny.

"Is he—" I swallowed. I was pushing my luck, but I had to know. "Is he going to kill me?"

She still didn't answer, just picked up the tray and made for the door, but as she turned to pull it shut behind her, I saw there was a tear, welling up, about to spill. She paused for a second, the door almost shut, and I thought for a minute that she was about to say something. But instead, she just shook her head again, sending the tear tracing across her cheek, and then she wiped it away, almost angrily, and the door slammed shut behind her.

After she had gone I stood, holding on to the bunk, steadying myself, and then I saw it, on the floor, another book. This one my copy of *Winnie-the-Pooh*.

Pooh has always been my comfort read, my go-to book in times of stress. It's a book from the time before I started getting afraid, when there were no threats that were not Heffalumps, and I, like Christopher Robin, could conquer the world.

I had almost not packed it. But at the last moment, when I was shoving clothes and shoes into my case, I had seen it there, resting on my night table, and I'd put it in as a kind of protective charm against the stresses of the trip.

For the rest of the night I lay on the bunk with the book open on the pillow beside me, running my fingers over the worn dust cover, but I knew the words by heart, too well perhaps, and somehow they failed to exert their familiar magic. Instead, I found myself running over the conversation with Carrie again and again, and thinking about what lay in wait for me.

There were only two ways I was getting out of here—one was alive and the other was dead, and

I knew which way I wanted it to be. In which case my choice was simple: to leave with Carrie's help, or without.

A few days ago, a few hours ago, I would have said unhesitatingly that my only real option was without—after all, she had beaten me, imprisoned me, starved me, even. But after tonight, I wasn't so sure. Her hands as she helped me to sit, the way she had waited as I ate, watching every mouthful, her face full of sadness . . . her eyes as she turned to leave . . . I didn't think she was a killer, not by choice, anyway. And something had happened these last few days that had made her realize that. I thought of the long, nightmarish wait for her to come, the way the hours had ticked past so slowly for me, my hunger growing and growing inexorably. But now, for the first time, I thought that perhaps the hours had been as slow and torturous for her, too, and perhaps she, too, had come face-to-face with something she was not ready for. She must have imagined me down here, growing weaker and weaker, clawing at the door. Until at last her resolve broke and she ran down with a stolen plate of lukewarm food.

What must she have thought when she opened the door and found me slumped on the floor—that she had come too late? That I had collapsed, maybe from hunger, maybe from sheer exhaustion? And suddenly perhaps she knew—that she couldn't live with another death, not one that she'd caused.

She hadn't wanted me to die, I was utterly certain of that. And I doubted if she could kill me, not if I kept reminding her of the fact that I was here because of her, because I had fought for her and tried to help her.

Bullmer on the other hand . . . Bullmer, who had lived through his wife's chemo, counting her money and planning her death, only to be cheated out of it at the eleventh hour . . .

Yes. Bullmer, I could imagine all too clearly, would kill. And he probably wouldn't lose a single hour of sleep over it.

Where was he? Had he left the ship, establishing an alibi while Carrie starved me to death? I wasn't sure. He had taken good care to isolate himself far away from Anne's death; I couldn't imagine he would allow himself to be implicated in mine.

As I was pondering this, I heard the slow grinding roar of the ship's engine start up. It hummed for a while, and then I felt the whole boat rock and shift, and I knew that we were moving again, out of Bergen harbor, the darkness swallowing the ship as we sailed out into the North Sea.

CHAPTER 30

The engine had stopped again when I woke up, but I could feel the shifting mass of water all around us. I wondered where we were—in the fjords, perhaps. I imagined the walls of dark rock rising up all around us, framing a narrow slip of bleached sky above, and sinking down below into the deep blue sea. I knew that some of the fjords could be more than a kilometer deep—unimaginably deep and cold. A body sunk into those kinds of depths might very easily never be found.

I was just wondering what time it was when there was a knock at the door, and Carrie appeared with a tray of muesli and a mug of coffee.

"I'm sorry it's not more," she said as she put the tray down. "Now that the passengers and crew have all left, it's got harder to take food without making the cook suspicious."

"The crew have left?" The words dismayed me, though I couldn't quite put my finger on why.

"Not all of them," Carrie said. "The captain's still here, along with some of his people. But all the passenger-facing staff have gone into Bergen with Richard for some kind of team-building-review thing."

Richard. So Bullmer wasn't on the boat. Maybe

that explained Carrie's change in attitude. With Bullmer gone . . .

I began to eat the muesli, slowly, and as before she sat and watched me, her eyes sad beneath their savagely epilated brows.

"You didn't pluck your eyelashes?" I said between mouthfuls. She shook her head.

"No, I couldn't quite bring myself. My eyelashes are a bit skimpy without mascara anyway, but I thought if anyone noticed, I'd claim they were false."

"Who—"

I stopped. I'd been going to say "Who killed her?" but suddenly I couldn't bring myself to voice that question. I was too scared that it might be Carrie. And anyway, my best hope was in persuading her that she *wasn't* a killer, not reminding her that she'd done it once and could do it again.

"What?" she asked.

"I . . . What did you say, to my relatives, I mean? And the other passengers? Do they think I'm in Trondheim?"

"Yes. I put my wig back on and left the boat with your passport. I picked a time when the stewards were all preparing breakfast and it was a member of the sailing crew on duty at the gangway—lucky you didn't go on the tour of the bridge, you didn't meet any of them. And lucky we've both got dark hair. I don't know what I would have done if you were a blonde— I don't have a blond wig. And then I rejoined the boat as Anne, and hoped they wouldn't notice that Anne got on but had never actually got off."

Lucky. It wasn't the word I'd have chosen. So the paper trail was complete—a record of me leaving the boat and never returning. No wonder no police had turned up to search the vessel.

"What was the plan?" I said quietly. "If I hadn't seen you? What was supposed to happen?"

"I would still have got off at Trondheim," she said bitterly. "But this time as Anne. And then I'd have put my wig on, changed my clothes, drawn on my eyebrows, and disappeared into the crowd as just another anonymous backpacker. The trail would have ended in Trondheim—an unstable woman, facing death, disappearing without a trace . . . And then, when everything had died down, Richard and I were going to 'meet,' fall in love, publicly this time—do it all over again for the cameras."

"Why did you *do* it, Carrie?" I asked despairingly, and then bit my tongue. Now wasn't the time to antagonize her. I needed to get her on my side and I wasn't going to do that by making her feel accused. But I couldn't hold it in anymore. "I just don't understand."

"Nor do I, sometimes." She put her hands over her face. "It wasn't supposed to *be* like this."

"So tell me," I said. I put my hand out, almost timidly, and let it rest on her knee, and she flinched as though she was expecting to be struck. I realized how frightened she was—how much of that vicious energy had come from terror, not hate.

"Carrie?" I prodded. She looked away and spoke towards the orange curtain, as if she couldn't face me.

"We met at the Magellan," she said. "I was a waitress there while I was trying to make it as an actress. And he—he just swept me off my feet, I suppose. It was like something out of *Fifty Shades*, penniless me, and him, falling in love, showing me this life I'd never dreamed of. . . ."

She stopped, swallowed.

"I knew he was married, of course—he was completely honest about that. So we could never see each other in public, and I couldn't tell anyone about him. Their marriage had been over almost before it started—she was horribly cold and controlling, and they lived separate lives, her in Norway and him in London. He hasn't had an easy life, you know—his mother left when he was a baby, and his father died when he was barely out of school. It seemed so unfair that Anne, the person who should have loved him most of all, couldn't even bear to be with him! But she was dying, and he couldn't bring himself to divorce a woman with just months to live—it seemed too cruel, and he kept talking about afterwards, when she died, when we'd be together . . ." Her voice trailed off, and for a minute I thought that was it, she was going to get up and go, but she started speaking again, the words coming faster now, as if she was unable to stop herself.

"One night he had this idea—he said that I should dress up as his wife and go to the theater, so that we could be out in public together. He gave me one of her kimonos, and I watched a film of her talking, so I knew how to carry myself and how to act, and I hid my hair under a swimming cap, with one of her scarves on top. And we pulled it off—we sat in a box, just the two of us, and drank champagne and, oh, it was amazing. Like a game, fooling everyone.

"We did it once or twice more, only when Anne was passing through London, so people wouldn't be suspicious, and then a few months later he had this idea—it seemed crazy at first, but he's like that, you know? Nothing is impossible—he truly makes you believe that. He said that he had a press trip coming up, that Anne was due to be there for the first night, but that she was getting off the boat late that night and going home to Norway. And he said, what if I stayed on and pretended to be her? He could smuggle me on board, and we could be a *real* couple—together, in public, for a whole week. He promised me I could pull it off, he said that no one on board had actually met her, and he would make sure no one photographed me so there wouldn't be any chance of getting caught afterwards. The boat was stopping in Bergen at the end of the trip, so people would just assume Anne had stayed on for a few extra days, and then I could change into my own clothes on the last day and go home as me. He arranged for one of the other guests not to turn up so there was an empty cabin and he said the only thing—" She stopped. "The only thing was, I'd have to cut my hair, to be convincing. But it seemed . . . it seemed worth it. To be with him."

She swallowed, and when she spoke again, it was more slowly.

"On the first night I was just getting into my clothes as Anne, when Richard came to the cabin. He was beside himself. He said that Anne had found out about the affair and had gone mad, lashing out at him. He'd pushed her away to try to protect himself, and she had stumbled and hit her head on the coffee table. When he tried to revive her he—he found—" She faltered, but carried on. "He found she was dead.

"He didn't know what to do—he said that if there was a police investigation, my presence on board would come out and no one would believe his version of the fight. He said that both of us would be prosecuted, him as a murderer, me as an accessory to a premeditated plot. He said it would come out—the fact that I'd been dressing up as Anne. He said that Cole had a photograph of me in Anne's clothes. He persuaded me—" She stopped again, emotion choking her voice. "He persuaded me the only thing to do was to tip Anne's body overboard and carry on with the plan. If she went missing in Bergen, nothing could be traced back to us. But it wasn't *supposed* to happen like this!"

Objections crowded to the tip of my tongue, screaming to be unleashed. How could Anne have got off the boat on the first night when we weren't due to arrive in Norway until the following day? And how could she get off without her passport, without the crew knowing that she'd left? It didn't make sense— the only explanation was that Richard had never been intending for Anne to walk down that gangplank of her own volition, and Carrie must know that herself. She wasn't stupid. But I'd seen this kind of willful blindness before, women who insisted their boyfriends weren't cheating in the face of all the evidence, people working for horrendous employers who'd persuaded themselves they were just following orders and doing what was necessary. There seemed to be no limit to the capacity of people to believe what they wanted to see, and if Carrie had argued herself into accepting Richard's twisted version of the facts in the face of all logic, she wasn't likely to listen to me.

Instead, I took a deep breath, pushed back the

protests clamoring in my head, and asked the question that everything hinged on.

"What's going to happen to me?"

"Fuck!" Carrie stood up, raking her hands across her head so that the headscarf slipped, showing the shaven scalp beneath. "I don't *know*. Stop asking me, please."

"He's going to kill me, Carrie." He was going to kill us both, I was fairly sure of that now, but I wasn't sure if she was ready to hear that. "Please, *please*, you can get us both out of here, you know you can. I'll give evidence—I'll say that you saved me, that—"

"First"—she broke in, face hard—"I'd never betray him. I *love* him. You don't seem to get that. And second, even if I went along with you, I'd end up on a murder charge."

"But if you testified against him—"

"No." She cut me off. "No. That's not going to happen. I love him. And he loves me. I know he does."

She turned away, towards the door, and I knew that it was now or never, that I had to *try* to make her see the truth of what she was involved in, even if she walked away and I ended up starving to death down here in my metal coffin.

"He's going to kill you, Carrie," I spoke to the back of her head as she reached the door. "You know that, right? He's going to kill me, and then kill you. This is your last chance."

"I love him," she said. There was a crack in her voice.

"So much that you helped him kill his wife?"

"I didn't kill her!" she shouted, the anguished cry painfully loud in the cramped space. She stood with her back to me, her hand on the door handle, and her whole narrow body shook, like a child racked by sobs. "She was already dead—at least, that's what he said. He left her body in the cabin in a suitcase, and I wheeled it to cabin ten when you were all at dinner. All I had to do was throw the whole thing over the side while he was playing poker. But . . ."

She stopped, turned back round, slumped to the ground, her head bowed to her knees.

"But what?"

"But the case was incredibly heavy. I think he'd weighted it with something, and I banged it against the doorframe getting it into the suite. The lid sprang open and that's when"—she gave a sob—"oh God, I don't know anymore! Her face—it was all bloody, but just for a second—I—I thought her eyelids fluttered."

"Jesus." I went cold with horror. "You mean—you didn't throw her over alive, did you?"

"I don't know." She buried her face in her hands. Her voice was cracked, high and reedy, with a tremor like someone on the verge of hysteria. "I screamed—I couldn't help it. But I touched the blood on her face, and it was *cold*. If she'd been alive, the blood would have been warm, wouldn't it? I thought perhaps I'd just imagined it, or it was some kind of involuntary movement—they say that happens, don't they? In morgues and stuff. I didn't know what to do—I just shut the case! But I can't have fastened it properly, because when I threw it over the side, the catch burst open and I saw her face—her face in the water— Oh God!"

She stopped, her breath coming fast and choking, but just as I was trying to grapple with the horror of what she might have done, think of what I could possibly say in reply to her confession, she spoke.

"I haven't been able to sleep, ever since, you know? Every night I lie there, thinking about her, thinking about how she could have been alive."

She looked up at me, and for the first time I saw her feelings naked in her eyes—the guilt and fear she'd been trying so desperately to hide ever since that first night.

"This isn't what was supposed to happen," she said brokenly. "She was supposed to die at home, in her own bed—and I—and I—"

"You don't have to do this." I spoke urgently. "Whatever happened with Anne's death, you can stop this now. Can you really live with killing me? One death on your conscience has driven you half-crazy, Carrie. Don't make it two—I'm begging you—for both of us. *Please*, let me go. I won't say anything, I swear. I'll— I'll tell Judah I got off in Trondheim and must have blacked out. No one would believe me anyway! They didn't believe me when I said a body went over the side—why would this be any different?"

I knew why: because of DNA. Fingerprints. Dental records. The traces of Anne's blood that must remain on the glass screen and somewhere in Richard's cabin.

But I didn't say any of that, and Carrie didn't seem to have thought of it. Her panic seemed to have been excised along with her tumbling, spewed-out confession, and her breathing had slowed. Now, her face, as she stared at me, was tearstained but calm, and oddly beautiful now that her hysteria had passed.

"Carrie?" I said timidly, hardly daring to hope.

"I'll think about it," she said. She got to her knees, picked up the tray, and turned for the door. As she did, her foot knocked against the copy of *Winnie-the-Pooh*, and she looked down. Something in her face changed, and she picked it up, riffling the pages with her free hand.

"I loved that book as a kid," she said. I nodded.

"Me too. I must have read it a hundred times. That bit at the end, with the ring of trees . . . it always makes me sob."

"My mum used to call me Tigger," she said. "She used to say, you're like Tigger, you are, no matter how hard you fall, you always bounce back." She gave a shaky laugh and then tossed the book onto the foot of the bunk, making an obvious effort to snap back to practicalities. "Listen, I might not be able to bring you supper tonight. The cook's getting suspicious. I'll do my best, but if I can't, then I'll bring you something extra for breakfast, okay?"

"Okay," I said, and then, moved by some impulse, "thank you."

I thought about it after she left—the stupidity of thanking a woman who was keeping you captive, buying your compliance by withholding food and drugs. Was I developing Stockholm syndrome?

Maybe. Although if I was, she had a considerably more advanced case than I did. Maybe that was closer to the truth—we weren't captor and captive, but two animals in different compartments of the same cage. Hers was just slightly larger.

That day passed agonizingly slowly. After Carrie had left I paced the room, trying to ignore my growing hunger, and my growing fear of what would happen if Carrie didn't face up to the reality of Richard's plan.

I was absolutely certain that he had never intended Carrie to live much beyond establishing Anne's departure at Bergen. When I shut my eyes, pictures rippled in front of them—Anne's face, glassy-eyed with terror as Carrie let the suitcase fall. Carrie, walking innocently along some alleyway in Norway, a figure coming up behind her.

And now me. . . .

To distract myself I thought about home and Jude, until the pages of *Winnie-the-Pooh* blurred in front of me, and the familiar well-worn phrases dissolved into a flood of tears that left me too exhausted to do anything but lie there.

I was just beginning to lose hope of supper, and conclude that Carrie hadn't been able to get any food after all, when there was a sound from the outer door and the noise of rushed footsteps in the corridor outside. I was expecting her to knock, but instead I heard the key in the lock and she flung the door open. It was obvious as soon as she came into the room that she wasn't carrying any food, but all that went out of my head when I saw her panicked expression.

"He's coming," she burst out.

"What?"

"Richard. He's coming back tonight—it was supposed to be tomorrow, but I just got a message, he's coming back tonight."

Tuesday, 29 September

TELEGRAPH WEBSITE

BREAKING NEWS: Second body found in search for missing Briton Laura Blacklock.

PART EIGHT

- CHAPTER 31 -

"He—he's coming back?" My mouth was dry. "What does that mean?"

"What do you think it means? We've got to get you off the boat. They're docking to pick up Richard in about thirty minutes. After that . . ."

She didn't have to say anymore. I swallowed, my tongue sticky against the roof of my mouth.

"I— How . . . ?"

She pulled something out of her pocket and held it up, and for a moment I didn't understand. It was a passport, but not mine: hers.

"It's the only way." She pulled off the headscarf, revealing her shaven head beneath, bristly with regrowth, and then began to strip.

"What are you *doing*?"

"You're going to walk off this boat as Anne and get on a plane as me. Understand?"

"What? You're crazy. Come with me!"

"I can't. How the fuck am I going to explain this to the crew? Here's my friend who's been hiding out in the hold?"

"Tell them! Tell them the truth!"

She shook her head. She was down to her underwear

now, shivering in spite of the fuggy heat of the stale air in the cabin.

"And say what? Hi, I'm a total stranger, the woman you think I am got pushed off the boat? No. I have no idea if I can trust any of them. At best he's their employer. At worst . . ."

"So what then?" I was half hysterical. "You'll stay here and let him kill you, too?"

"No. I've got a plan. Just stop arguing and take my clothes." She held them out, a bundle of silks that felt featherlight in my hands when I took them. Her skinniness was shocking, her bones practically poking through her skin, but I couldn't look away. "Now give me yours."

"What?" I looked down at myself, at the stained, sweaty jeans and the T-shirt and hoodie I'd been wearing for almost a week now. "These?"

"Yes. Hurry *up*!" Her voice was edgy. "What size are your feet?"

"Six," I said, my voice muffled as I stripped off my T-shirt.

"Good. Mine, too." She pushed the espadrilles she was wearing towards me and I kicked off my boots and began to peel off my jeans. We were both down to our underwear now, me awkwardly trying to cover myself, she completely focused as she began to pull on my discarded clothes. I pulled the silk tunic over my head, feeling the expensive fabric whisper cool against my skin. She pulled an elastic band off her wrist and handed it silently across.

"What's this for?"

"Pulling back your hair. It's not ideal. You'll have to be *very* careful with the headscarf, but it's the best

I can do. We don't have time to shave your head, and in any case, if you're going to skip the country under my passport, it's probably better that you have real hair for passport control. We don't want to give them a reason to look twice at the photo."

"I don't understand. Why can't I just go as me? The police must be looking for me, surely?"

"For starters, Richard has your passport. And he has a lot of friends around here—not just in business, he knows people high up in the Norwegian police force as well. We have to get you far away from him before he puts two and two together. Get out. Get away from the coast. Cross the border into Sweden. And when you do get on a plane, don't fly to London. He'll be expecting that. Go via somewhere else— Paris, maybe."

"You're being ridiculous," I said, but her alarm had infected me. I shoved my feet into the espadrilles, and the passport into the pocket of the kimono. Carrie was zipping up my vintage leather boots. I felt a faint pang of regret—those boots were the single most expensive piece of clothing I owned. It had taken me weeks, and a fair amount of encouragement from Judah, to pluck up the courage to shell out for them. But the boots felt like a small sacrifice in exchange—potentially—for my life.

At last we were almost fully dressed—just the headscarf lay on the bunk between us.

"Sit," Carrie said brusquely, and I sat on the edge of the bunk while she stood beside me and swathed the beautiful printed scarf around my head. It was green and gold, blazoned with a pattern of intertwined ropes and anchors, and I had a sudden, distracting flash of Anne—the real Anne—floating down into the blue-green depths, her white limbs tangling in the detritus of a thousand wrecks, caught forever.

"There you go," Carrie said at last. She slid in a couple of pins, holding the edge of the scarf in place, and then looked at me critically, up and down. "It's not perfect—you're not thin enough—but you'll pass in poor light. Thank God I've not met most of the sailing crew."

She looked at her watch and then said, "Right. Last thing. Hit me."

"What?" Her words made no sense. Hit her with what?

"Hit me. Hit my head against the bunk."

"What?" I was starting to sound like an echo—but I couldn't help it. "Are you crazy? I'm not going to hit you!"

"*Hit me*," she said furiously. "Don't you get it? This has to be convincing. This is my only chance of Richard believing I wasn't in on it. It has to look like you attacked me, overpowered me. *Hit me*."

I took a deep breath and slapped her on the cheek. Her head whipped back, but it wasn't hard enough, I could tell it wasn't, even as she looked sourly round at me, rubbing her cheek.

"Oh, for Christ's sake. Do I have to do everything?"

She took a deep breath, and then, before I realized quite what she was about to do, she smacked her head into the side of the bunk.

I screamed. I couldn't help it. Blood started welling from the shallow cut the metal edge had made, dripping down her—my—white T-shirt and puddling on the floor. She staggered back, gasping in pain and holding her hands to her skull.

"*Jesus!*" she whimpered. "Fucking hell, that hurt. Oh God." She fell to her knees, her breath coming short and sharp, and for a second I thought she was about to faint.

"Carrie!" I said in panic, dropping to my knees beside her. "Carrie, are you—"

"Don't kneel in it, you stupid bitch!" she screamed, pushing my hand away. "Do you want to ruin everything? You can't have blood on your clothes! What the hell would the crew say? Oh Christ, oh God, why won't it stop bleeding?"

I got awkwardly to my feet, half tripping on the trailing kimono, and for a moment I just stood there, trembling. Then I came to my senses and ran to the bathroom to get a thick wad of tissue.

"Here you go." My voice shook. She looked up, ruefully, and then took the tissue and pressed it to the cut. Then she sank back onto the bunk, her face gray.

"Wh-what should I do?" I asked. "Can I help you?"

"No. The only thing that can help me is if Richard believes you beat me up so badly I couldn't have stopped you. Hopefully this'll do the job. Now get out," she said hoarsely. "Before he comes back and this is all for nothing."

"Carrie, I— What can I do?"

"Two things," she said, her teeth gritted against the pain. "First, give me twenty-four hours before you go to the police. Okay?"

I nodded. It wasn't what I'd meant, but I felt I couldn't refuse her that, at least.

"Second, *get the fuck out.*" She groaned. Her face was now so white that I was frightened, but there was a fierce determination in her expression. "You tried to help me, didn't you? That's what got you in this mess. Now this is the only thing I can do to help you. So don't make it a waste of my time. Get the fuck out!"

"Thank you," I croaked. She didn't say anything, just waved a hand towards the corridor. As I got to the door, she spoke.

"The key to the suite's in your pocket. You'll find about five thousand kroner in a purse on the dressing table. It's a mixture of Norwegian, Danish, and Swedish, but there's nearly five hundred pounds' worth, I think. Take the whole thing—it's got credit cards and ID. I don't know the PIN for the cards—they're not mine, they're Anne's, but you might find somewhere that'll let you sign. You'll have to ask someone to lower the gangway so you can get off the boat—unless they've already got it out for Richard. Tell them that he just phoned and you're going to meet him en route."

"Okay," I whispered.

"Change your clothes, and get away from the port as soon as you can. That's it." She shut her eyes and lay back. The chunk of paper pressed to her temple was already soaked with red. "Oh, and lock me in when you go."

"Lock you in? Are you sure?"

"Yes, I'm sure. It has to be convincing."

"But what if he doesn't come and find you?"

"He will." Her voice was flat. "It's the first thing he'll do if he finds me missing. He'll come and check on you."

"Okay . . ." I said reluctantly. "Wh-what's the PIN for the door?"

"The door?" She opened tired eyes. "What door?"

"You said there was a second locked door outside this one. With a PIN panel."

"I lied," she said wearily. "There's no door. I just said that so you wouldn't jump me. Just keep climbing."

"I— Thank you, Carrie."

"Don't thank me." Her eyes were closed again. "Just pull this off—for both of us. And don't look back."

"Okay." I moved towards her, I don't know why— to hug her, maybe. But her chest was spattered with fresh blood, with more coming from the wound at her temple. And she was right—bloodstains on my gown wouldn't help anyone, least of all her.

It was the hardest thing I'd ever done—turning my back on a woman who looked like she was bleeding to death, all because of me. But I knew what I had to do--for both of us.

"Good-bye, Carrie," I said. She didn't answer. I fled.

The corridor outside was narrow and hot as hell, even hotter than the stuffy little cabin I had left. There was a heavy clasp across the door, drilled roughly into the plastic, and a thick padlock with a key sticking out of it. I snapped it across, swallowing against the guilt that was constricting my throat, and then hesitated, my fingers over the key. Should I take it? I left it. I didn't want Carrie to spend a moment longer in there than she had to.

The cabin door was at one end of the drab beige

corridor. At the other was a door marked NO ENTRY—
AUTHORIZED CREW ONLY and then, past that, a flight
of stairs. I took one stricken look back at the locked
cabin door, behind which Carrie lay bleeding, and
then I ran for the stairs and began to climb.

Up and up I climbed, my heart beating in my
chest, my legs shaky with disuse. Up the service
stairs, drably carpeted and edged with metal. I felt
my hand slip with sweat on the plastic banister, and
in my mind's eye I saw the dazzling glare of the Great
Staircase, the glint of crystal, the feel of the polished
mahogany rail beneath my fingers, smooth as silk. I
felt a laugh bubble up inside me, as irrational as the
time I giggled through my grandmother's funeral, my
fear and fright turning to a kind of hysteria.

I shook my head and pushed on, up the next flight,
past doors marked MAINTENANCE and STAFF ONLY.

I kept climbing, until I reached a huge steel door
with a bar on the inside, like a fire escape. I stood for
a moment, panting from the long climb, feeling the
cold sweat pooling at the base of my spine. What was
on the other side?

Behind me lay Carrie, curled on the bunk in that
airless coffin of a room. My stomach turned, and I
forced myself to put that picture out of my mind and
focus, coldly and deliberately, on the steps that lay
ahead. I had to get out—and then as soon as I was
safe I could . . . but what? Call the police, in defiance
of Carrie's request?

As I stood there, my hand on the door, I had a
searing flashback to that night in my flat—to cowering inside my own bedroom, too scared to open
the door and confront whatever—whoever—was on

the other side. Perhaps it would have been better if I'd kicked down the locked door, burst out and confronted him, even if it meant being beaten bloody. I could be in the hospital right now, recovering, Judah at my side, not trapped in this waking nightmare.

Well, the door wasn't locked now.

I shoved my hand against the release and pushed it open.

- CHAPTER 32 -

The light. It hit me like a slap, leaving me blinking and dizzy, gaping at the rainbow prisms of a thousand Swarovski crystals. The service door led directly out onto the Great Staircase, where the chandelier blazed, day and night, a giant "fuck you!" to economy and restraint and global warming, not to mention good taste.

I steadied myself on the polished wooden handrail and looked left and right. There was a mirror at the turning point of the stairs, throwing back the reflected glare of the chandelier, multiplying the dancing light again and again, and as I turned I caught sight of myself in it and for a moment I did a double take, my heart leaping into my throat—for there in the glass was Anne, her head swathed in gold and green, her eyes hunted and bruised.

I looked like what I was—a fugitive. I forced myself to stand up straighter, and walk slowly, in spite of wanting to scurry like a terrified rat.

Hurry, hurry, hurry, snarled the voice in the back of my head. *Bullmer's coming. Get a move on!* But I kept my pace slow and steady, remembering Anne's—Carrie's—stately walk, the way she measured each pace like someone conserving their strength. I was heading towards the front of the ship, where cabin 1 was, and in my pocket my fingers closed over the cabin key, feeling its reassuring hardness under my sweaty fingers.

And then I came to a dead end, stairs leading up to the restaurant, no way through into the prow. *Fuck*. I had taken a wrong turn.

I turned back, trying to remember the route I had taken when I went to see Anne—Carrie—that night before Trondheim. God, was it really only last week? It felt like an age, a different life. Wait—it was supposed to be right at the library, not left. Wasn't it?

Hurry, for God's sake, hurry!

But I kept my pace steady, kept my head up, trying not to look back, not to imagine the hands snatching at my flowing silk robes, dragging me back down below. I turned right, then left, then past a storeroom. This looked right. I was sure I remembered the photograph of the glacier.

Another turn—and another dead end, with stairs leading up to the sundeck. I wanted to sob. Where were the fucking *signs*? Were people supposed to find cabins by telepathy? Or was the Nobel Suite deliberately hidden away so that the hoi polloi couldn't bother the VIPs?

I bent over, my hands on my knees, feeling my muscles trembling beneath the silk, and I breathed slowly, trying to make myself believe I could do this. I would not be still wandering the halls, sobbing, when Richard came up the gangplank.

Breathe in. . . . One. . . . Two. . . . Barry's soothing voice in my head gave me a surge of anger, enough to propel me upright, set me walking again. Stick it, Barry. Stick your positive thinking somewhere painful.

I was back at the library, and I tried again, this time turning left at the storeroom. And suddenly I was there. The door to the cabin was ahead of me.

I felt in my pocket for the key, feeling the adrenaline zipping up and down every neuron in my body. What if Richard was already back?

Don't be the loser cowering behind the door again, Lo. You can do this.

I shoved the key in the door and opened it, faster than fast, ready to drop and run if there was someone in the room.

But there was not. It was empty, the doors to the bathroom and adjoining bedroom standing wide.

My legs gave way, and I sank to my knees on the thick carpet, something very close to sobs rising in my throat. But I wasn't home and dry. I wasn't even halfway there. Purse. Purse, money, coat, and then off this horrible boat forever.

I closed the door behind me, stripped the kimono off, hurrying now that there was no one to see my feverish movements, and in my bra and knickers searched through Anne's drawers. The first trousers I tried were jeans, and impossibly tight, I couldn't get them halfway up my thighs, but I found a pair of Lycra sports leggings I could get into, and an anonymous black top. Then I put the kimono back on over the top, belted it tight, and adjusted the headscarf in the mirror where it had slipped.

I wished I could wear dark glasses, but glancing out the window I saw it was pitch-black—and the clock on Anne's bedside table said quarter past eleven. Oh God, Richard would be back any minute.

I pushed my feet back into Carrie's espadrilles, and then looked around for the purse she had described. There was nothing on the immaculately polished dressing table, but I opened a couple of the drawers at random, wondering if the maid might have put it away for safekeeping. The first drawer was empty. The second I tried had a clump of patterned headscarves, and I was about to close it again, when I noticed there seemed to be something beneath the pile of soft silks, a hard, flat shape among the gossamer-thin wraps. I pushed them aside—and my breath caught in my throat.

Nestled beneath was a handgun. I had never seen one in real life before, and I froze, half expecting it to go off without even being touched, questions clamoring at the back of my skull. Should I take it? Was it loaded? Was it *real*? Stupid question—I doubted anyone would bother to keep a replica handgun in their cabin.

As for whether I should take it . . . I tried to imagine myself pointing a gun at someone, and failed. No, I couldn't take it. Not least because I had no idea how to use it and was more likely to shoot myself than anyone else, but more because I *had* to get the police to believe and trust me, and turning up to a station with a stolen, loaded gun in my pocket was the best way to ensure I was locked up, not listened to.

Half reluctantly, I pulled the scarves back over the gun, shut the drawer, and resumed looking for the purse.

I found it at last in the third drawer down, a brown leather wallet, rather worn, laid carefully on top of a file of papers. Inside were half a dozen credit cards and a wad of bills—I didn't have time to count them, but they looked like easily the five thousand kroner Carrie had mentioned, maybe more. I slid it into the pocket of the leggings, beneath the kimono, and then took one last look round the room, ready to leave. Everything was as I'd found it, except for the purse. It was time to go.

I took a deep breath, readying myself, and then opened the door. And as I did so, I heard voices in the corridor. For a minute I wavered, wondering whether to brazen it out. But then one of the voices said, with a touch of flirtation, "Of course, sir, anything I can do to ensure your satisfaction. . . ."

I didn't wait to hear any more. I shut the door with a stealthy click, dimmed the lights, and stood in the darkness with my back to the solid wood, my heart going a mile a minute. My fingers were cold and prickly, and my legs felt weak, but it was my heart—my heart, racing crazily out of control, a panicked stampede of a beat—that threatened to overwhelm me. Fuck fuck fuck, I couldn't have a panic attack now!

Breathe, Laura. One. . . . Two. . . .

Shut the fuck up! I had no idea whether the scream was inside my head, but somehow, with a huge effort, I managed to peel myself away from the door and stumble to the veranda. The door slid open, and I was outside, the cold of the September night shocking against skin that hadn't felt fresh air for days.

I stood for a moment, my back to the glass, feeling my pulse in my temples and my throat, and my heart banging against my ribs, and then I took a deep breath and edged to one side, to where the veranda curved around the corner of the boat. I was out of sight of the window now, my back to the cold steel hull of the boat, but I saw the flash of light as the door to the corridor opened, and then the lamps in the cabin itself blazed on, illuminating the glass wall of the veranda. *Don't come out; don't come out,* I prayed, as I cowered in the corner of the veranda, waiting for the click and slide of the glass. But nothing happened.

I could see the reflection of the room in the glass barrier. The image was cut in half where the glass ended at rib height, and the reflection was jumbled with ghosts thrown up by the double and triple layers of glass. But I could see a man in the room, moving around. The dark silhouette of his shape moved off in the direction of the bathroom and I heard the noise of taps and the flush of a toilet, then the television came on, its blue-white flicker instantly recognizable in the glass. Above its sound, I heard the noise of a phone call, and Anne's name, and I held my breath. Was he asking about Carrie's whereabouts? How long before he went looking?

The phone call seemed to end, or at least he stopped talking, and I saw his shape move again as he threw himself onto the white expanse of the bed, a dark sprawl across its bright rectangle.

I waited, growing colder now, shifting from foot to foot to try to keep myself even a little warm, but not daring to move too much for fear he would see the movement reflected back at him from the same barrier I was using to spy on him. The night was unbelievably beautiful, and for the first time since I had come out here, I looked around.

We were deep inside one of the fjords, the rocky sides of the valley rising up all around us, the waters beneath black and still and unfathomably dark and deep. Far across the fjord I could see the lights of small settlements, and the lanterns of boats moored out on the still waters, but the overriding thing was the stars—clear and white and almost unbearably lovely. I thought of Carrie, down below, trapped and bleeding like an animal in a snare. . . . Please, dear God, let her be found. I couldn't bear it if something happened to her. I would be responsible for locking her down there, leaving her to her crazy plan.

I waited, shivering helplessly now, for Richard to fall asleep. But he did not. At least he dimmed the lights slightly, but the television continued to blast away, the flickering images turning the room shades of blue and green, with sudden cuts to black. I shifted my weight again, pushing my chilly hands beneath my arms. What if he fell asleep in front of the TV? Would I know? But even if he did fall asleep, properly and deeply, I was not sure if I could summon up the courage to enter the room with a murderer, tiptoe through it while his sleeping form lay there just inches away.

What was the alternative, then? Wait until he went in search of Carrie?

And then I heard something, something that made my heart seem to stop, and then stutter back to life, twice as fast. The boat's engine was starting up.

Panic washed over me like a cold sea wave and I tried to think—we weren't moving yet. There was a chance the gangway was still down. I would have heard it being raised. I remembered from when we set out from Hull that the engine had hummed and thrummed for a good long time before we actually departed. But it was a ticking clock. How long did I have? Half an hour? A quarter? Perhaps less, given there were no passengers on board, no reason to hang about.

I stood there, frozen in agonized indecision. Should I make a run for it? Was Richard asleep? I couldn't tell from the reflection in the balcony barrier—it was too blurred and indistinct.

Craning my head and moving as stealthily as I dared, I peered around the edge of the veranda door and into the silent room—but just as I did, he shifted and reached for a glass, and I whipped my head back, my heart thumping.

Fuck. It must be one a.m. Why wasn't he asleep? Was he waiting for Carrie? But I had to get off the ship. I *had* to.

I thought of the veranda windows, how they could be opened from the outside, how someone very brave—or very stupid—might scale the high glass wall between the verandas and gain entry to an empty cabin. Once inside I could just let myself out of cabin 2 and then make a break for the gangway. I didn't care what story I had to spin when I got there. Somehow I would get off this boat, if not for me, then for Anne, and Carrie. No—fuck it.

For *me.*

I was getting off this boat for me—because I had done nothing to deserve this apart from being in the wrong place at the wrong time, and I was damned if Bullmer was going to add me to the list of women he had screwed over.

I looked down at myself, at the flowing, slippery lines of the kimono, impossible to climb in, and I untied the belt and shrugged off the soft silk. It fell to the floor with barely a whisper, and I picked it up, balled up the fabric as tight as I could, and then tossed it over the privacy screen, where it landed with a soft, barely perceptible *flump*.

Then I looked up at the glass screen, towering above me, and swallowed.

I was never going to be able to climb the privacy screen itself, that was clear. At least not without some serious equipment and/or a ladder. But the barrier over the sea—that I probably could climb. It was rib height, and I was flexible enough to get one leg up and over and pull myself to sit astride it, and from there I could use the privacy screen to stand up.

There was just one problem. It was over the sea.

I'm not phobic about water—at least, I never used to be. But as I looked over the edge at the dark waves, sucking hungrily at the ship's prow, I felt my stomach shift and roll in a way not unlike seasickness.

Shit. Was I really going to do this? Apparently, yes.

I wiped my sweaty palms on the back of the Lycra leggings and took a deep breath. It wouldn't be easy—I wasn't fooling myself. But it *was* possible. Carrie had done it, after all, to get into my cabin. If she could do it, so could I.

I flexed my fingers, and then very slowly I hooked one leg up onto the glass overlooking the sea, and using all the strength in my weak caged-hen muscles, I pulled myself up so I was sitting astride the wall of glass. To the left of me was the cabin, its curtains pulled back, the veranda doors framing me in full view for anyone who turned their head to see. To my right was a sheer drop to the waters of the fjord below—I had no idea how far, but from this angle it looked like the equivalent of a two- or three-story house. I was not sure which side was more frightening—I just had to hope that my movements didn't attract Richard's attention. I swallowed and gripped the slippery glass with my legs, trying to get my courage up for the next step. I hadn't done the hard bit yet. That was coming.

Shaking with fear and exertion, I got one foot up in front of me, and I gripped the edge of the frosted privacy screen and hauled myself to standing. Now, all I had to do was edge my body weight out, round the seaward side of the privacy glass, and swing myself to safety on the other side.

All. Yeah. Right.

I took a deep breath, feeling my cold, sweaty fingers slip on the glass. There was no bloody *purchase.* Every other part of this boat was pimped up, couldn't they have spared a little bling for the privacy glass? Just a few rhinestones, some fancy etching, *something* to give my fingers an edge to hang on to?

I put one foot out, edging it round the high wall of glass . . . and I instantly knew the espadrilles had been a mistake.

I had left them on, thinking that something to protect my feet and give me extra purchase on the glass would be no bad thing, but as my weight swung out over the water, I felt the sole of my supporting foot slip against the sharp edge.

I gasped, and my fingers tightened desperately on the glass in front of me. If sheer willpower could have held me steady, I would have made it. I felt one nail break, then two—and then the glass seemed to be pulled out from between my scrabbling hands with a suddenness that left me unable to do anything—even scream.

I felt the wind against my cheek for a brief, terrifying instant, my hair flapping in the darkness, my hands still clutching at the air—I was falling, falling backwards towards the fathomless waters of the fjord.

I hit the blackness of the sea with a sound like a gunshot, a fierce, smacking blow that knocked all the breath from my lungs.

I felt the air bubbling from my lungs as I plummeted through the stone-cold chill, I felt the icy water strike through to my bones, and as I plunged deeper into fathomless black, I felt a silky current rise from far below me, grip my feet, and pull.

- CHAPTER 33 -

I didn't scream. I didn't have time. I was twenty, thirty, forty feet down in icy black water before I had time to draw a breath.

I don't remember what I felt as I fell—only the bone-cracking smack as I hit the sea, and the paralyzing cold of the water. But I do remember the gut-churning panic as the current seized me, deep, deep below.

Kick, I told my legs, feeling the breath sob in my throat. And I kicked. In the black and the cold, I kicked, first because I didn't want to die, and then as the black cold began to grip, because there was nothing else I could do, because my lungs were screaming and I knew that if I didn't break the surface soon, I would be dead.

The current pulled and tugged at my legs with slippery fingers, trying to drag me deep into the darkness of the fjord, and I kicked and kicked with increasing desperation and despair. In the dark, with the swirling currents of the fjord all around, it was almost impossible to tell which way was up. What if I was driving myself further into the depths? And yet, I didn't dare stop. The instinct to survive was too strong. *You're dying!* shouted a voice in the back of my head. And my legs had no other response except to kick, and kick, and kick.

I shut my eyes against the salt sting, and against my closed lids lights began to spark and shimmer, terrifyingly close to the shards of light and dark that fragmented my vision when I had a panic attack. But amazingly, unbelievably, when I opened my eyes again, I could see something. A pale, luminous shimmer of the moonlight on water.

For a second I almost didn't believe it, but it was coming closer . . . and closer, and the tug of the current on my body was loosening, and then I broke the surface with a breath that sounded closer to a scream, water streaming down my face, coughing and sobbing, and coughing again.

I was very close to the hull of the ship, close enough to feel the throb of the engines like a pulse through the water, and I knew that I had to start swimming. Not just because it was totally possible to die of hypothermia in really not-very-cold seas, but more urgently because if the ship started moving while I was this close, nothing short of divine intervention would save me, and I'd had bad luck enough these past few days to make me think that if there was a God up there, he didn't like me very much.

Shivering, I trod water and tried to get my bearings. I had surfaced at the front of the boat, and I could see the string of lights at the quayside and what I thought might be the dark shape of a ladder, although my streaming eyes made it hard to be sure.

It was hard to make my body obey; I was shaking so convulsively that I could barely control my limbs, but I forced my arms and legs to start moving, and

gradually I began to swim towards the lights, coughing against the waves that slapped my face, feeling
the chill of the water striking through to my bones,
forcing myself to breathe slowly and deeply, though
every part of my body wanted to gasp and pant at the
physical assault of the cold. Something soft and yet
solid bumped against my face as I swam, and I shuddered, but it was more with cold than revulsion. I
could worry about dead rats and decaying fish when
I got to shore. Right now, the only thing I cared about
was surviving.

I could not have fallen in more than twenty or
thirty yards from the quay, but now it seemed to
be much farther. I swam and swam, and at times I
could swear the lights of the shore were getting farther away, and other times they seemed almost close
enough to grasp—but at last I felt the rusted iron
of the ladder bang against my numb fingers, and I
was climbing and slipping and slipping and climbing
up the ladder, trying not to shiver loose my grip as I
hauled my wet and shuddering bones up the rungs.

At the edge of the quay I collapsed onto the concrete, gasping and coughing and shaking, and then I
got to my hands and knees and looked up, first at the
Aurora and then towards the little town in front of me.

It wasn't Bergen. I had no idea where we were, but
it was a small town, barely even a village, and this
late at night there was not a soul about. The smatter-
ing of cafés and bars that lined the quayside were all
closed. There were a few lights in shop windows, but
the only establishment I could see that looked as if I
might stand a chance of finding someone to open the
door was a hotel overlooking the quay.

Trembling, I got to my feet, lurched over the low chain that fenced off the sheer drop to the sea, and half walked, half staggered across the quayside towards the hotel. The *Aurora*'s engine had picked up a notch, and there was an urgency to it now. As I crossed the seemingly endless concrete apron of the quay, it rose again in pitch, and there was the sound of sloshing water, and as I glanced fearfully behind me, I saw the boat begin to pull slowly away, its prow pointing out into the fjord, its motors grinding and thrumming as it inched slowly away from the shore.

I looked quickly away, filled with a kind of superstition, as if just turning to look at the boat could attract the attention of the people on board.

As I reached the steps up to the hotel door, the sound of the engine picked up, and I felt my legs give way as I banged, banged, banged on the door. I heard a voice saying "Please, please, oh please somebody come . . ." And then the door opened and the light and warmth flooded out, and I felt myself helped upright and over the threshold to safety.

Some half hour later I was huddled in a wicker armchair, wrapped in a synthetic red blanket, in the dimly lit, glassed-in terrace overlooking the bay. I had a cup of coffee in my hands, but I was too tired to drink it, and I could hear voices in the background, speaking in . . . Norwegian, I supposed it must be. I was overwhelmingly tired. I felt as if I hadn't slept properly in days—which perhaps I hadn't, and my chin kept nodding onto my chest and then jerking back up as I remembered where

I was, and what I'd escaped from. Had it been real, that nightmare of the beautiful boat, with its coffin-like cell, far beneath the waves? Or was this all one long hallucination?

I was half dozing and half watching the still black lights of the bay, the *Aurora* a distant speck far up the fjord, moving west, when I heard a voice over my shoulder.

"Miss?"

I looked up. It was a man wearing a slightly skewed name tag reading ERIK FOSSUM—GENERAL MANAGER. He looked as if he had been dragged from his bed, his hair rumpled and his shirt buttons awry, and he passed a hand over an unshaven chin as he sat down in the armchair opposite me.

"Hello," I said, wearily. I'd gone through my story with the man at the desk—at least as much of it as I thought safe to give, and as much as his English would permit. He was obviously the night porter, and he looked and sounded more Spanish or Turkish than Norwegian, although his Norwegian seemed to be better than his English, which was fine when it came to stock phrases about checking in and opening hours, but not up to a garbled tale of mixed identity and police.

I had seen him showing the only ID I had with me—Anne's—to the manager, and heard his low, guarded tones, and heard my own name repeated several times.

Now the man sitting opposite me folded his fingers and smiled, slightly nervously.

"Miss—Black Lock, is that right?" He pronounced it as two words. I nodded.

"I don't completely understand—my night manager tried to explain—how do you have Anne Bullmer's credit cards? We know Anne and Richard well; they stay here sometimes. Are you a friend?"

I put my hands over my face, as if I could press back the tiredness that was threatening to overwhelm me.

"I—it's a really long story. Please, can I use your phone? I have to contact the police."

I had made up my mind as I hung, dripping and exhausted, over the polished check-in desk. In spite of my promise to Carrie, this was my only chance to save her. I didn't for one second believe that Richard would let her live. She knew too much, had screwed too much up. And without the headscarf I had no chance of passing myself off as Anne, and without Carrie's passport I had no chance of posing as Carrie, and both were lost somewhere in the bay, fathoms down. Only Anne's purse had survived, miraculously still in the pocket of the Lycra stretch pants as I crawled up the ladder, out of the water.

"Of course," Erik said sympathetically. "Would you like me to phone them? They may not have an English speaker on duty at this time of night. I must warn you, we don't have a police station in the town, the nearest one is a few hours away in the next . . . what's the word. The next valley. It will probably be tomorrow before someone can come out."

"Please tell them it's urgent, though," I said wearily. "The sooner, the better. I can pay for a bed. I have money."

"Let's not worry about that," he said with a smile. "Can I get you another drink?"

"No. No, thanks. Just please tell them to come *soon*. Someone's life could be in danger."

I let my head rest, heavy on my hand, my eyelids almost closing as he went back to the front desk, and I heard the sound of a phone receiver being lifted, and the *beep-beep-beep-beep . . . beep-beep-beep* of a number being dialed. It sounded like a long one. Maybe the Norwegian number for 999 was different? Or perhaps he was calling the local station.

It rang. Someone at the other end picked up and there was a brief exchange. Through the haze of exhaustion I heard Erik saying something in Norwegian out of which I could only pick the word *hotel . . .* then a pause and then another burst of Norwegian. Then I heard my own name, given twice, and then Anne's.

"*Ja, din kone, Anne,*" Erik said, as if the person on the other end had not heard correctly, or had not believed what he'd heard. Then more in Norwegian, and then a laugh, and finally. "*Takk, farvel, Richard.*"

My head jerked up from my supporting hand, and every part of me went suddenly cold and still.

I looked out to the ships in the bay, to the *Aurora*, its lights disappearing in the far, far distance. And . . . was it my imagination? It looked as if the ship had stopped.

I sat for a moment longer, watching its lights, trying to measure them against the landmarks of the bay, and at last I was almost sure. The *Aurora* was no longer moving west up the fjord. It was turning around. It was coming back.

Erik had hung up, and was dialing another number now.

"*Politiet, takk*," he said as someone answered.

For a moment I couldn't move, frozen with the realization of what I'd done. I hadn't believed Carrie's assertions about Richard's web of influence, not really. I'd dismissed them as the paranoia of a woman too beaten down to believe in the possibility of escape. But now . . . now those fears seemed all too real.

I set the coffee cup gently down on the table, let the red blanket fall to the floor, and, very quietly, I opened the terrace door and slipped outside, into the night.

- CHAPTER 34 -

I ran, up through the winding streets of the little town, my breath tearing in my chest, stones cutting into my bare feet and making me wince with pain. The streets petered out, and the streetlights began to disappear, but I ran on in the dark and the cold, stumbling through invisible puddles and over wet grass and graveled paths, until my feet grew too numb for me to even feel the cuts and the stones.

Even then I kept going—desperate to put as many miles as possible between myself and Richard Bullmer. I knew that I could not keep this up, that at some point I was going to have to give in—but my only hope was to keep going as long as possible, until I found myself some kind of shelter.

Finally, I could not run anymore. I let myself drop back to a kind of gasping, limping jog, and then as the lights of the village grew smaller in the distance, I slowed to a walk, a painful, stumbling walk, along a winding dark road that twisted into the darkness, climbing up the side of the fjord. Every few hundred yards I looked back over my shoulder, down into the valley, to the shrinking speckle of lights of the little portside town, and to the dark slick of the fjord waters, where the lights of the *Aurora* were coming closer. They were unmistakable now. I could see the ship clearly, and I could see, too, light beginning to tinge the sky above me.

Dawn must be coming already—God, what day did that make it? Monday?

But something seemed wrong, and after a few minutes I realized what it was. The lights were not to the east but to the north. What I could see was not dawn but the eerie green and gold streaks of the northern lights.

The realization made me laugh—a bitter, mirthless choke that sounded shockingly loud in the still night air. What was it Richard had said? Everyone should see the northern lights before they died. Well, now I had. But it just didn't seem that important anymore.

I had stopped for a moment, watching the shifting glory of the aurora borealis, but now at the thought of Richard I began walking again. With each step, I remembered Carrie's frantic exhortations to get running and get out—her hysterical assertions about the reach of Richard's influence.

It didn't seem so hysterical now.

If *only* I had believed her—I should never have shown Anne's ID at the hotel, or trusted Erik with even the few details I'd given him. But I just hadn't quite believed that anyone, however wealthy, could have the kind of reach Carrie believed. Now I realized I was wrong.

I groaned, at my own stupidity, at the cold that was striking through my thin, damp clothes. Most of all at the fact that I'd left the wallet on the desk. Stupid, stupid, stupid. That was five thousand wet, soggy, but still usable kroner, and I'd left them there for Richard as a little golden hello when he turned up at the hotel. What was I going to do? I had no ID, nowhere to sleep, no means of buying so much as a bar of chocolate, let alone a train ticket. My best hope was finding a police station, but how? Where? And did I dare tell them the truth when I got there?

I was just considering this when I heard the roar of an engine behind me and turned to see a car coming round the bend, frighteningly fast, clearly not expecting anyone to be out here at this time of night.

I scrambled for the verge, lost my footing, and fell, sliding down a length of scree that left me bloodied and scraped, my leggings in tatters, and came to a halt with a splash in a pebbly ditch that seemed to be some kind of stream or drainage channel down to the fjord below. The car itself had screeched to a halt on the road some five or six feet above me, the head-lamps pointing out into the valley, and the smoke from the exhaust billowing red in the rear lights.

I heard the crunch of feet on the road above. Richard? One of his men? I *had* to get away.

I tried to stand on my ankle, felt it give, and then tried again, more carefully this time, but the pain made me give a sob.

At the sound, a figure, lit from behind so that I could see his shape only in silhouette, peered over the edge of the road, and a voice said something in Norwegian. I shook my head. My hands were trembling.

"I d-don't speak Norwegian." I tried to keep the sob out of my voice. "Do you sp-speak English?"

"Yes, I speak English," the man said in a heavily accented voice. "Give me your hand. I will help you out."

I hesitated, but there was no way I could get out of the ditch without help, and if the man really intended to hurt me he could just as easily climb down here and attack me in the shelter of the ditch. Better to get out, where I could at least run if I had to.

The lights of the car shone in my eyes, blinding me, and I put my hand up, shielding them against the glare, but all I could see was a dark shape, and a halo of blond hair beneath some kind of cap. It wasn't Richard, at least, that I was sure of.

"Give me your hand," the man said again, with a touch of impatience this time. "Are you hurt?"

"No, I'm n-not hurt," I said. "At least, my ankle hurts, but I don't think it's broken."

"Put the leg there." He pointed at a rock about a foot out of the ditch, "and I will pull you up."

I nodded, and with a feeling that I might be doing something very stupid, I set my good foot to the rock and leaned upward with my right hand.

I felt the man grab hold of my wrist, his grip immensely strong, and with a grunt he began to pull, bracing himself against a rock at the edge of the ditch. The muscles and sinews in my arm were screaming in protest, and when I tried to put my weight on my bad foot, I cried out, but at last, with a painful, scrambling rush, I was up and out of the ditch, and standing trembling on the edge of the verge.

"What are you doing out here?" the man said. I couldn't see his face, but there was concern in his voice. "Are you lost? Have you had an accident? This road leads directly up the mountain, It's no place for a tourist."

I was trying to think of how to answer, when I realized two things.

The first was that he was carrying something in a holster at his hip, the shape of it silhouetted against the car lights. And the second was that the car itself was a police car. As I stood there, frozen, trying to think what to say, I heard the crackle of a radio pierce the night.

"I—" I managed.

The policeman took a step forward, tipping his cap so that he could see me more clearly, and frowned.

"What is your name, Miss?"

"I—" I said, and then stopped.

There was another crackle from his radio and he held up a finger.

"One moment, please." He put his hand to his hip, and I saw that what I had taken for a gun was actually a police radio in a holster, hanging next to a pair of handcuffs. He spoke briefly into the receiver and then climbed into the driver's side of the car and began a longer conversation on the car radio.

"*Ja*," I heard, and then a burst of conversation I didn't understand. Then he looked up at me through the windscreen, and his eyes met mine, his gaze puzzled. "*Ja*," he said again, "*det er riktig*. Laura Blacklock."

Everything seemed to slow down, and I knew with a cold certainty that it was now, or not at all. If I ran now, I might be making a mistake. But if I didn't, I might not live to find out, and I could not afford to take that risk.

I hesitated for just one second more, and then I saw the policeman replace the radio receiver and reach for something in his glove compartment.

I had no idea what to do. But I had not believed Carrie before, and it had nearly cost me everything.

Screwing my courage for the pain I knew was coming, I began to run—not up the road as before but down, cross-country, scrambling headlong down the vertiginous side of the fjord.

- CHAPTER 35 -

It was growing light when I realized that I could go no farther, that my muscles, exhausted beyond endurance, just simply would not obey me. I was no longer walking, I was stumbling as if I were drunk, my knees buckling when I tried to climb over a fallen tree stump.

I had to stop. If I didn't, I would fall where I stood, so deep in the Norwegian countryside that my body might never be found.

I needed shelter, but I had left the road a long time back, and there were no houses to be seen. I had no phone. No money. I didn't even know what time it was, although it must be close to dawn.

A sob rose in my dry throat, but just at that moment, I saw something loom from between the sparse trees—a long, low shape. Not a house—but some kind of barn, perhaps?

The sight gave my legs a last shot of energy, and I staggered out from between the trees, across a dirt track, through a gate in a wire fence. It *was* a barn— although the name seemed almost too grand for the shack that lay in front of me, with its rickety wooden walls and corrugated iron roof.

Two shaggy little horses turned their heads curiously as I trudged past, and then one of them returned to drinking from what I saw, with a leap of my heart, was a trough of water, its surface pink and gold in the soft dawn light.

I staggered to the trough, falling on my knees in the short grass beside it, and cupping the water in my hands I drank great gulps of it down. It was rainwater, and it tasted of mud and dirt and rust from the metal trough, but I didn't care. I was too thirsty to think about anything except slaking my parched throat.

When I'd drunk as much as I could, I straightened up and looked around me. The shed door was shut, but as I put my hand to the latch, it swung open and I went cautiously through, shutting the door behind me.

Inside there was hay—bales and bales of it—some tubs that I thought might be feed or supplements, and, hanging on the wall on pegs, a couple of horse blankets.

Slowly, drunk with weariness, I pulled the first one down and laid it over the deepest pile of hay—not even thinking about rats or fleas, or even Richard's men. There was surely no way they could find me here, and I had got to the stage where I almost didn't care—if they would just let me rest, they could take me away.

Then I lay down on the makeshift bed and drew the other blanket over the top of me.

And then I slept.

"*Hallo?*" The voice in my head spoke again, painfully loud, and I opened my eyes to a blinding light, and a face gazing into mine. An elderly man with a full white beard and a strong resemblance to Captain Birdseye was peering at me with rheumy hazel eyes, and a mix of surprise and concern.

I blinked and scrambled backwards, my heart thudding painfully, and then tried to get to my feet, but my ankle gave a wrench of pain and I stumbled. The man took my arm, saying something in Norwegian, but without thinking I jerked it savagely out of his grip, and fell back onto the floor of the barn.

For a few minutes we just looked at each other, him taking in my scrapes and cuts, me looking at his lined face and the dog barking and circling behind him.

"*Kom*," he said at last, getting painfully to his knees and holding out his hand with cautious calm, as if I were a wounded animal that might snap at any provocation, and not a human at all. The dog barked again, hysterically this time, and the man shouted something over his shoulder that was clearly *quiet, you!* or something to that effect.

"Who—" I licked dry lips and tried again. "Who are you? Where am I?"

"Konrad Horst," the man said, pointing at himself. He pulled out his wallet and flicked through until he found a photo of an elderly lady with rosy cheeks and a bun of white hair, cuddling two blond-haired little boys.

"*Min kone*," he said, enunciating slowly. And then, pointing to the children, something that sounded like "*Vorry bon-bon*."

Then he pointed out of the barn door at an extremely elderly Volvo standing outside.

"*Bilen min*," he said, and again, "*Kom*."

I didn't know what to do. There *was* something reassuring about the photos of his wife and grand-children—but even rapists and killers had grandkids, right? On the other hand, maybe he was just a nice old man. Maybe his wife would speak English. At the very least they'd likely have a phone.

I looked down at my ankle. I didn't have much choice. It had swollen to twice its usual size, and I wasn't sure I could even hobble as far as the car, let alone make it to an airport.

Captain Birdseye held out his arm and made a little gesture.

"Pleese?" he rumbled interrogatively, as if giving me a choice. But it was an illusion. I had no choice.

I let him help me to my feet, and I got into the car.

It was only as we drove that I realized quite how far I had run the night before. You couldn't even see the fjord from this wooded fold of the hillside, and the Volvo must have jolted down several miles of rutted track before we reached the semblance of a road.

We were turning onto the tarmac when I noticed something in the little well beneath the radio—a mobile phone. It was very, very ancient, but it was a phone.

I put out my hand, hardly able to breathe.

"May I?"

Captain Birdseye looked across, and then grinned. He put the phone in my lap but then tapped the screen, saying something in Norwegian. As soon as I looked at the phone, I realized what he was saying. There was no reception at all.

"*Vente,*" he said loudly and clearly, and then slowly, in what sounded like heavily accented English, "Wait."

I held the phone in my lap, watching the screen with a lump in my throat as the trees flashed past. But something didn't make sense. The date on the phone showed the twenty-ninth of September. Either I was miscounting, or I had lost a day.

"This," I pointed at the date on the phone. "Today, is it really the twenty-ninth?"

Captain Birdseye glanced at the screen and then nodded.

"*Ja, tjueniende.* Toos-day," he said, enunciating the word very slowly, but he didn't need to. The pronunciation was close enough to the English for me to be in no doubt about what he was saying. Tuesday. Today was *Tuesday.* I had been asleep in that little hut for a full day and a night.

I was just computing that, and trying not to think about how worried Judah and my parents must be, when we turned into the driveway of a neat little blue-painted house, and something flickered in the corner of the phone's screen—a single bar of reception.

"Please?" I held it up, my heart suddenly beating so hard in my throat that the words felt choked and strange in my mouth. "Can I call my family in England?"

Konrad Horst said something in Norwegian that I didn't understand, but he was nodding, and so, with fingers that shook so hard I could hardly find the right keys, I pressed +44 and dialed the number of Judah's mobile phone.

- CHAPTER 36 -

We said nothing for the longest time, either of us. We just stood in the middle of the airport like two fools, holding each other, Judah touching my face and my hair and the bruises on my cheek like he truly couldn't believe it was me. I suppose I was probably doing the same to him, I can't remember.

All I could think was *I'm home. I'm home. I'm home.*

"I can't believe it," Judah kept saying. "You're okay."

And then the tears started, and I began to cry into the harsh scratchy wool of his jacket, and he didn't say anything at all, just held me like he'd never let me go.

At first I hadn't wanted the Horsts to call the police, but I couldn't make them understand that, and after I'd spoken to Judah and he had promised to call Scotland Yard with my story—a story so improbable that I almost didn't believe it myself—I began to accept that not even Richard Bullmer could buy his way out of this one.

When the police arrived, they took me to a health center first, to get treatment for my cut feet and wrenched ankle and to have my medication represcribed. It seemed to take forever, but at last the doctors pronounced me fit enough to leave, and the next thing I knew, I was being driven to a police station up the valley, where an official from the British Embassy in Oslo was waiting.

Again and again I found myself reciting the story of Anne, and Richard and Carrie, and each time it sounded more and more implausible to my own ears.

"You have to help her," I kept saying. "Carrie—you have to go after the boat."

The official and the police officer exchanged a look, and the policeman said something in Norwegian. I knew, suddenly, that whatever it was they were holding back, it was not good news.

"What?" I asked. "What is it? What's wrong?"

"The police have found two bodies," the embassy official said at last, his voice awkward and formal. "The first in the early hours of Monday morning, dredged up by a fishing boat, the second later on Monday, recovered by police divers."

I put my head in my hands, grinding my fingers into my eyes, watching the pressure build and bloom as flames and sparks on the insides of my lids. I drew a deep breath.

"Tell me." I looked up. "I have to know."

"The body recovered by divers was a man," the embassy official said slowly. "He had been shot through the temple, the police believe it may have been a self-inflicted wound. He had no ID on him, but they are presuming it to be the body of Richard Bullmer. He was reported missing from the *Aurora* by the crew."

"And . . ." I swallowed. "And the other?"

"The other was a woman, very slim, with shorn hair. The police will have to conduct a postmortem, but the preliminary findings are that she was drowned. Miss Blacklock?" He looked around, nervously, as if unsure what to do. "Are you all right, Miss Blacklock? Can someone get her a tissue, please? Please don't cry, Miss Blacklock, you're all right now."

But I couldn't speak. And the worst of it was that he was right, I *was* all right, but Carrie was not.

It should have been a comfort that Bullmer had killed himself, but I couldn't find any. I just sat there, crying into the tissue they gave me, and thinking of Carrie and everything she'd done to me and for me. Whatever the rights and wrongs, she had paid with her life. I hadn't been fast enough to save her.

- CHAPTER 37 -

The taxi from the airport took us back to Judah's. We didn't discuss it, exactly, but somehow I couldn't face my basement flat. I'd had enough of being shut up in lightless rooms, and Judah seemed to realize that.

In his living room he tucked me up on the couch with a blanket, as if I were a small child, or someone recovering from an illness, and he kissed me very gently on my forehead, like I might break.

"I can't believe you're home," he said again. "When they showed me your boots in that photo . . ."

His eyes welled up, and I felt my own throat scratch with tears.

"She took them," I said croakily. "So I could pretend to be her. She—"

But I couldn't finish.

Judah held me for a long time, and then when he could speak he swallowed and said, "You—you've got a lot of messages, you know. People have been calling me because your voice mail got full. I've been writing them down."

He felt in his pocket, and handed me a list, and I scanned down it. Most of them were names I would have expected . . . Lissie . . . Rowan . . . Emma . . . Jenn . . . One or two were a surprise.

Tina West said one, in Judah's handwriting. *Very relieved you're safe. No need to call back.*

Chloe Yansen (I assumed that was Judah's phonetic spelling of Jenssen.) *Hopes you're okay. Please call if there is anything she or Lars can do.*

Ben Howard. No message.

"God, Ben." I felt a stab of guilt. "I'm surprised he's speaking to me. I more or less accused him of being behind all this. Did he really call?"

"That's not the half of it," Judah said, and I saw him wipe his eyes surreptitiously on his T-shirt. "He was the one who raised the alarm. He called me from Bergen trying to find out if you'd made it home okay, and when I said I hadn't heard from you since Sunday, he told me to call the UK police and tell them it was a matter of urgency. He said he'd been raising hell since Trondheim and no one on the crew would listen to him."

"Don't make me feel worse." I put my hands over my face.

"Hey, he's still a self-important little shit," Judah said. He gave me his endearing smile, and I saw with a pang that his tooth had re-rooted. "And he did give a pretty crappy interview to the *Mail*, which made it sound like you two had barely just broken up."

"Okay," I said, with a slightly shaky laugh. "That makes me feel a bit better about accusing him of murder."

"Look, do you want a cup of tea?"

I nodded, and he got up and made his way to the kitchen. I took a handful of tissues out of a box on the coffee table and wiped my eyes, then picked up the remote control and turned on the television, trying for some semblance of normality.

I was just scrolling through the channels, looking for something reassuring and familiar—a *Friends* rerun, maybe, or *How I Met Your Mother*—when I stopped dead, my heart in my mouth.

My eyes were fixed on the television screen—at the man staring out at me.

It was Bullmer.

His eyes were locked onto mine, his mouth quirked in that asymmetric smile, and for a second I thought I might be hallucinating. I drew a breath, ready to scream for Judah, ask him if he could see the face staring out of the screen at me like a nightmare—but then the screen cut back to a newsreader, and I realized what was happening. It was a report of Bullmer's death.

"... breaking news of the death of British businessman and peer Lord Richard Bullmer. Lord Bullmer, who was the majority shareholder in the troubled Northern Lights Group, has been found dead after being reported missing just hours earlier from his luxury yacht the *Aurora* off the coast of Norway."

The screen cut again, this time to Richard standing on a podium as he gave some kind of address.

His lips were moving, but his speech was muted, so that the newsreader could carry on narrating the story over the top of the images, and as the camera zoomed in on his face, I found myself turning down the volume, leaving the couch and kneeling in front of the TV, my face just inches from his.

When the talk came to an end, Richard bowed, and the camera went close up on his face, and he looked

straight out of the screen and gave me his character-
istic little wink—so that my stomach turned, and my
skin crawled.

I picked up the remote with shaking hands, ready
to exorcise him from my life once and for all, when the
camera panned, and I saw a woman seated in the front
row, smiling and applauding, and I paused, my finger
hovering over the off button. She was extraordinarily
beautiful, with a long river of dark gold hair and broad
cheekbones, and for a moment I couldn't think where
I had seen her before. And then . . . I realized.

She was Anne. Anne as she had been before Richard was through with her, young and beautiful and
alive.

As she applauded, she seemed suddenly to realize
that the cameras were on her, and her eyes flickered
towards the lens, and I saw something there, although
whether it was my imagination or not, it was hard to
tell. It seemed to me that there was something sad in
her expression, something a little trapped and afraid.
But then she smiled more broadly and put her chin
up, and I saw that this was a woman who would never
capitulate, never give way, a woman who would fight
to the last.

Then the picture changed and we were back in the
newsroom, and I turned off the screen and went back
to the couch. I drew the blanket over me and turned
my face to the wall, listening to Judah making tea in
the next room . . . thinking.

The clock on Judah's bedside table showed gone
midnight. We were lying together, his chest molding

to my spine, his arm around me, holding me close, as if he didn't trust me not to disappear in the night.

I had waited until I thought he was asleep before I let myself cry, but when a particularly big sob shook my ribs, he spoke, soft and low against my ear.

"Are you okay?"

"I thought you were asleep." My voice came out cracked and hoarse with tears.

"Are you crying?"

I wanted to deny it, but my throat had closed up and I couldn't speak, and anyway, I'd had enough of lies and pretending.

I nodded, and he put his hand up, feeling the wetness on my cheeks.

"Oh, honey." I heard the movement of his throat as he swallowed. "It'll be . . . you don't have to . . ."

He stopped, unable to continue.

"I can't stop thinking about her," I said against the ache in my throat. It was easier not looking at him, speaking to the quiet darkness and the slivers of moonlight across the floor. "I can't accept it; it's all wrong."

"Because he killed himself?" Judah asked.

"Not just that. Anne. And . . . and Carrie."

Judah said nothing, but I knew what he was thinking.

"Say it," I said bitterly. He sighed, and I felt his chest rise and fall against my spine, his breath warm against my cheek.

"I probably shouldn't say this, but I can't help but feel . . . glad."

I twisted round under the sheets to look at him, and he held up a hand.

"I know, I know it's wrong, but what she did to you . . . honestly, if it had been up to me, I wouldn't have dredged her out. I'd have left her there for the fishes. It's probably a good thing it wasn't my decision."

I felt anger rise up inside me, anger on behalf of Carrie, beaten and bullied and lied to.

"She died because of me," I said. "She didn't have to let me go."

"Bullshit. You were only there because of her. She didn't have to kill a woman and lock you up."

"You don't know that. You don't know what goes on in other people's relationships."

I thought of Carrie's terror, of the bruises on her body, of her belief that she would never escape Richard. She had been right. Judah said nothing, and I could not see his expression in the dark, but I felt his silent disagreement.

"What," I demanded, "you don't believe me? You don't think people can be sucked into doing something out of fear, or inability to see any other way out?"

"No, it's not that," Judah said slowly. "I believe that. But I still think, in spite of it all, we're responsible for our own actions. We all get scared. But you can't tell me that you'd do that to another person, no matter how tough things seemed—lock them up like that, imprison them—no matter how scared you were."

"I don't know," I said. I thought of Carrie, of how brave she had been, and how fragile. I thought of the masks she wore to hide the terror and loneliness inside. I thought of the bruise on her collarbone, and the fear in her eyes. I thought of how she had given up everything for me.

"Listen." I sat up and wrapped the sheet around me. "That job you were talking about, before I left. The one in New York. Did you turn it down?"

"Yes, I mean, well, no . . . I'm going to. I haven't called them yet. After you went missing, it kind of slipped my mind. Why?" Judah's voice was suddenly uneasy.

"Because I don't think you should. I think you should take it."

"*What?*" He sat up, too, and a shaft of moonlight fell across his face, showing me an expression full of shock, anger. For a minute he didn't seem to know what to say, then the words came pouring out. "What the *hell*? Why? Where has this come from?"

"Well, this is a chance in a lifetime, right? It's the post you've always wanted." I twisted the sheet around my fingers, cutting off the blood until they went numb and cold. "And let's face it, there's nothing holding you here, is there?"

"Nothing holding me here?" I heard him swallow, saw his fists clench and unclench against the white sheets. "I have *everything* holding me here, at least I thought I did. I—am—are you breaking up with me?"

"What?" Now it was my turn for shock. I shook my head and took his hands, rubbing my fingers across the sinews and the bones of his knuckles, hands that I knew by heart. *Fuck.* "Jude, no. Not in a million years. I'm saying—I'm trying to ask . . . Let's go. Together."

"But—but *Velocity*—your job. Rowan's maternity cover. This is your big chance. I can't screw that up for you."

"It's not my big chance." I sighed. I slid down

beneath the sheets, still holding Judah's hands in mine. "I realized that when I was on the boat. I've spent, what, nearly ten years working at *Velocity*, while Ben and everyone else took risks, went on to bigger and better stuff, and I didn't. I was too scared. And I felt like I owed *Velocity* for standing by me when things were bad. But Rowan's never going to leave—she'll be back in six months, maybe less, and I've got nowhere to go. And the truth is, even if I did pull myself up the ladder, it's not what I want anymore. I never wanted it—I realized that on board the boat. God knows I had enough time to think about it."

"What do you mean? It's—ever since we met, it's all you've talked about."

"I think I lost sight of what I wanted. I don't want to end up like Tina and Alexander, traveling from country to country and only seeing five-star hotels and Michelin restaurants. Yes, Rowan's been to half the luxury resorts in the Caribbean, but in return she spends her life reporting the stories that people like Bullmer want her to tell, and I don't want that, not anymore. I want to write about the things people *don't* want you to know. And if I'm going to start pulling my way up from the bottom again, well, I can freelance from anywhere. You know that."

A thought came to me, and I let out a shaky, involuntary laugh.

"I could write a book! *My Floating Prison: True-Life Hell on the Seven Seas*."

"Lo." Judah took my hands, his eyes wide and dark in the moonlight, and painfully beseeching. "Lo, stop, stop joking. Are you serious about this?"

I took a deep breath. Then I nodded.

"I've never been more serious in my life."

Afterwards, Judah lay in my arms, his head in the crook of my shoulder in a way that I knew would give me a cramp eventually, but I couldn't bear to pull away.

"Are you awake?" I whispered. He didn't answer for a moment, and I thought that he had fallen asleep, in that way he had of slipping out of consciousness between one breath and the next, but then he stirred, and spoke.

"Just."

"I can't sleep."

"Shh . . ." He rolled over in my arms, touching my face. "It's okay, it's all over."

"It's not that . . . it's . . ."

"Are you still thinking about her?"

I nodded in the darkness, and he sighed.

"When you saw her body," I started, but he shook his head.

"I didn't."

"What do you mean? I thought the police sent you photographs to identify?"

"It wasn't a body—I wish it *had* been, if I'd seen it was Carrie's corpse, not yours, I wouldn't have spent two days in hell, thinking you were dead. It was just clothes. Photographs of clothes."

"Why did they do that?" It seemed an odd decision—why ask Judah to identify the clothes, and not the body?

I felt Judah's shoulders lift in the darkness in a shrug.

"I don't know. At the time I assumed it was because the body was too bashed up, but I spoke to the FLO in charge of the case after you called—I wanted to find out how the hell they could have got it so wrong—and she spoke to the Norwegians and seemed to think it was because the clothes were found separately."

Huh. I lay there, trying to puzzle it out. Had Carrie kicked off the boots and hoodie to try and swim for it, in a desperate attempt to get away from Bullmer?

I was almost afraid to go to sleep, expecting to be haunted by Carrie's reproachful face, but when I finally closed my eyes it was Bullmer's face that rose up in front of me, laughing, his black hair riffled by the wind as he tumbled down, down from the deck of the *Aurora*.

I opened my eyes, my heart thumping, trying to remember that he was gone—that I was safe, that Judah was lying in my arms and the whole nightmare was over and done with.

But it wasn't. Because I just didn't believe what had happened.

It wasn't just Carrie's death that I couldn't accept—it was Bullmer's. Not because I thought he should have lived, but because his death, out of all of it, just didn't make *sense*. Carrie's suicide I could have believed, but not his. Try as I might, I couldn't imagine that man, with his cold, fierce determination, giving up. He had fought so hard, played his cards with such cold daring. Would he really throw in his hand, just like that? It didn't seem possible.

But it was. And I had to accept that. He was gone. I shut my eyes again, pushing his specter away from me, and I curled my body around Judah's, and I thought, very deliberately, about the future, about New York, and about the leap of faith I was about to make.

For a moment I saw a sharp, flashing image imprinted on the darkness of my closed lids: myself poised on the very edge of a high, high place, balancing on a rail, the dark waves below.

But I had no fear. I had fallen before, and I'd survived.

STANDARD

Thursday, 26 November
MYSTERY WOMAN IN AURORA DROWNING IDENTIFIED

Almost two months after the shocking discovery of two bodies at sea, one of them British businessman and peer Richard Bullmer, Norwegian police have today released a statement announcing the identity of the body dredged up by fishermen in the North Sea to be that of his wife, Anne Bullmer, heiress to the billion-pound Lyngstad fortune.

The body of Lord Bullmer was found several hundred miles away by police divers searching the coastal waters near Bergen, in Norway, after the peer was reported missing from his boat, the exclusive boutique cruise liner the *Aurora*.

NOT SUICIDE

The English-language statement confirms the previous announcement by Norwegian police that the cause of Lady Bullmer's death was drowning, while Lord Bullmer's death was due to a gunshot wound to the temple. However, the document contradicts earlier reports of **Lord Bullmer's suicide, stating simply that the injury was "not self-inflicted," according to the findings of the local pathologist.**

The discovery of a gun, recovered along-side Lord Bullmer's body and wrapped in clothing belonging to missing British journalist Laura Blacklock, led to initial allegations that his death was connected to her disappearance some days before.

Miss Blacklock was later found alive and well in Norway, but her parents have called for a police inquiry after they were left for several days believing that the body had been identified as that of their missing daughter. Scotland Yard stressed that the body had never at any stage been identified as Miss Blacklock, but admitted that the finding of Miss Blacklock's clothes had been "poorly communicated" to the family. They blamed the failings on "cross-force communication issues" with the Norwegian police handling the case, and have said that they are in private contact with the Blacklock family over the incident.

In answer to the *Standard*'s inquiry, a Norwegian police spokesperson stated that although they have interviewed Miss Blacklock in connection with the case, they are not considering the Briton as a suspect in either death, and that their investigations are continuing.

BANKING LIVE CHAT

6 DECEMBER, 4:15
Hi, welcome to our online customer
services live chat.
You are speaking with Ajesh from
online personal banking.
How can I help you today,
Miss Blacklock?

> Hi, I'm e-mailing because
> I've received an odd credit
> to my account.
> I wanted to check if you had
> any info on the sender.
> Thanks. Lo.

Hi, Miss Blacklock, sure, I can
look into that.
Is it okay if I call you Laura?

> Yep, that's fine.

What is the transaction you are
concerned about, Laura?

> It's the one two days ago,
> dated 4 Dec., for 40,000
> Swiss francs.

Let me check that for you.
I have your details here—is it
the transaction with the reference
"Tiggers bounce"?

> Yes, that's correct.

I have checked the sort code,
it's a Swiss bank account based

*in Bern I'm sorry to say I do not
have any information on the identity
of the bank account holder. It is a
numbered account.
Does the reference convey anything?*

It's fine, thanks. No worries.
I'm pretty sure it's from a friend,
I just wanted to check.
Thanks for looking into it.

*You're welcome. Is there
anything else I can help you
with today, Laura?*

No, that's fine. Thanks.
And good-bye.

ACKNOWLEDGMENTS

Many thanks to all the people who have helped me along the road with *The Woman in Cabin 10*. Writing is an odd, solitary pursuit, but publishing is most definitely a team sport, and I am very grateful to have such dedicated, funny, and downright nice people involved with my book at Scout in the United States and Harvill in the United Kingdom.

First thanks must go to the two Alisons, Alison Hennessey and Alison Callahan, for being tactful, insightful, and fearless editors, and generally proving that three brains are most definitely better than one.

Also at Scout Press, I must thank Nina Cordes, Meagan Harris, Jen Bergstrom, Liz Psaltis, Melanie Mitzman, Carolyn Reidy, Louise Burke, Wendy Sheanin, Erica Nelson, Jennifer Robinson, and everyone else at Simon & Schuster who has helped to bring *The Woman in Cabin 10* to the public—you make me very proud to be a Scout author.

My agent, Eve White, and her team always have my back, and I am always astounded by and grateful for the generosity of the brilliant community of crime writers, online and off.

My friends and family know how much I love them, so I won't repeat it here—but I do!

Turn the page for a sneak peek
at Ruth Ware's third novel

THE LYING GAME

Available now.

*T*he Reach is wide and quiet this morning, the pale blue sky streaked with pink mackerel-belly clouds, the shallow sea barely rippling in the slight breeze, and so the sound of the dog barking breaks into the calm like gunshots, setting flocks of gulls crying and wheeling in the air.

Plovers and terns explode up as the dog bounds joyously down the river bank, scampering down the runnelled side, where the earth turns from spiky grassy dunes to reed-specked mud, where the water wavers between salt and fresh.

In the distance the Tide Mill stands sentinel, black and battered against the cool calm of the morning sky, the only man-made structure in a landscape slowly crumbling back into the sea.

"Bob!" The woman's voice rings out above the volley of barks as she pants to catch up. "Bob, you rascal. Drop it. Drop it, I say. What've you found?"

As she draws closer, the dog tugs again at the object protruding from the mud, trying to pull it free.

"Bob, you filthy brute, you're covered. Let it go. Oh God, it's not another dead sheep, is it?"

It's the last heroic yank that sends the dog staggering back along the shore, something in its jaw. Triumphant, he scrambles up the bank to lay the object at the feet of his owner.

And as she stands, looking dumbstruck, the dog panting at her feet, the silence returns to the bay like a tide coming in.

RULE ONE

TELL A LIE

The sound is just an ordinary text alert, a quiet *beep beep* in the night that does not wake Owen, and would not have woken me except that I was already awake, lying there, staring into the darkness, the baby at my breast snuffling, not quite feeding, not quite unlatching.

I lie there for a moment thinking about the text, wondering who it could be. Who'd be texting at this hour? None of my friends would be awake . . . unless it's Milly gone into labor already . . . God, it can't be Milly, can it? I'd promised to take Noah if Milly's parents couldn't get up from Devon in time to look after him, but I never really thought . . .

I can't quite reach the phone from where I'm lying, and at last I unlatch Freya with a finger in the corner of her mouth, and rock her gently onto her back, milk-sated, her eyes rolling back in her head like someone stoned. I watch her for a moment, my palm resting lightly on her firm little body, feeling the thrum of her heart in the birdcage of her chest as she settles, and then I turn to check my phone, my own heart quickening slightly like a faint echo of my daughter's.

As I tap in my pin, squinting slightly at the brightness of the screen, I tell myself to stop being silly—it's four weeks until Milly's due, it's probably just a spam text, *Have you considered claiming a refund for your payment protection insurance*?

But, when I get the phone unlocked, it's not Milly. And the text is only three words.

I need you.

It is 3:30 a.m., and I am very, very awake, pacing the cold kitchen floor, biting at my fingernails to try to quell the longing for a cigarette. I haven't touched one for nearly ten years, but the need for one ambushes me at odd moments of stress and fear.

I need you.

I don't need to ask what it means—because I know, just as I know who sent it, even though it's from a number I don't recognize.

Kate.

Kate Atagon.

Just the sound of her name brings her back to me, like a vivid rush—the smell of her soap, the freckles across the bridge of her nose, cinnamon against olive. Kate. Fatima. Thea. And me.

I close my eyes and picture them all, the phone still warm in my pocket, waiting for the texts to come through.

Fatima will be lying asleep beside Ali, curled into his spine. Her reply will come around 6:00 a.m., when she gets up to make breakfast for Nadia and Samir and get them ready for school.

Thea—Thea is harder to picture. If she's working nights she'll be in the casino, where phones are forbidden to staff and shut up in lockers until their shifts are finished. She'll roll off shift at eight in the morning, perhaps? Then she'll have a drink with the other girls, and then she'll reply, wired up with a successful night dealing with punters, collating chips, watching for card sharps and professional gamblers.

And Kate. Kate must be awake—she sent the text,

after all. She'll be sitting at her dad's worktable—hers now, I suppose—in the window overlooking the Reach, with the waters turning pale gray in the pre-dawn light, reflecting the clouds and the dark hulk of the Tide Mill. She will be smoking, as she always did. Her eyes will be on the tides, the endlessly shifting, eddying tides, on the view that never changes and yet is never the same from one moment to the next—just like Kate herself.

Her long hair will be drawn back from her face, showing her fine bones, and the lines that thirty-two years of wind and sea have etched at the corners of her eyes. Her fingers will be stained with oil paint, ground into the cuticles, deep beneath the nails, and her eyes will be at their darkest slate blue, deep and unfathomable. She will be waiting for our replies. But she knows what we'll say—what we've always said, whenever we got that text, those three words.

I'm coming.
I'm coming.
I'm coming.

"I'm coming!" I shout it up the stairs, as Owen calls something down above Freya's sleepy squawking cries.

When I get up to the bedroom he's holding her, pacing back and forth, his face still pink and crumpled from the pillow.

"Sorry," he says, stifling a yawn. "I tried to calm her down but she wasn't having any of it. You know what she's like when she's hungry."

I crawl onto the bed and scoot backwards into the pillows until I'm sitting against the headboard, and Owen hands me a red-faced, indignant Freya, who takes one affronted look up at me and then lunges for my breast with a little grunt of satisfaction.

All is quiet, except for her greedy suckling. Owen yawns again, ruffles his hair, and looks at the clock, and then begins pulling on his underwear.

"Are you getting up?" I ask in surprise. He nods.

"I might as well. No point in going back to sleep when I've got to get up at seven anyway. Bloody Mondays."

I look at the clock. Six a.m. It's later than I thought. I must have been pacing the kitchen for longer than I realized.

"What were you doing up, anyway?" he asks. "Did the bin lorry wake you?"

I shake my head.

"No, I just couldn't sleep."

A lie. I'd almost forgotten how they feel on my tongue, slick and sickening. I feel the hard, warm bump of my phone in my dressing gown pocket. I'm waiting for it to vibrate.

"Fair enough." He suppresses another yawn and buttons up his shirt. "Want a coffee, if I put one on?"

"Yeah, sure," I say. Then, just as he's leaving the room, "Owen—"

But he's already gone and he doesn't hear me.

Ten minutes later he comes back with the coffee, and this time I've had time to practice my lines, work out what I'm going to say, and the semi-casual way I'm going to say it. Still I swallow and lick my lips, dry-mouthed with nerves.

"Owen, I got a text from Kate yesterday."

"Kate from work?" He puts the coffee down with a little bump, it slops slightly and I use the sleeve of my dressing gown to mop the puddle, protecting my book, giving me time to reply.

"No, Kate Atagon. You know, I went to school with her?"

"Oh, *that* Kate. The one who brought her dog to that wedding we went to?"

"That's right. Shadow."

I think of him. Shadow—a white German shepherd with a black muzzle and soot-speckled back. I think of the way he stands in the doorway, growls at strangers, rolls his snowy belly up to those he loves.

"So . . . ?" Owen prods, and I realize I've stopped talking, lost my thread.

"Oh, right. So she's invited me to come and stay, and I thought I might go."

"Sounds like a nice idea. When would you go?"

"Like . . . now. She's invited me now."

"And Freya?"

"I'd take her."

Of course, I nearly add, but I don't. Freya has never taken a bottle, in spite of a lot of trying on my part, and Owen's. The one night I went out for a party, she screamed solidly from 7:30 p.m. to 11:58, when I burst through the doors of the flat to snatch her out of Owen's limp, exhausted arms.

There's another silence. Freya leans her head back, watching me with a small frown, and then gives a quiet belch and returns to the serious business of getting fed. I can see thoughts flitting across Owen's face . . . That he'll miss us . . . That he'll have the bed all to himself . . . Lie-ins . . .

"I could get on with decorating the nursery," he says at last. I nod, although this is the continuation of a long discussion between the two of us—Owen would like the bedroom, and me, back to himself and thinks that Freya will be going into her own room imminently, when she turns six months. I . . . don't. Which is partly why I've not found the time to clear the guest room of all our clutter and repaint it in baby-friendly colors.

"Sure," I say.

"Well, go for it, I reckon," Owen says at last. He turns away and begins sorting through his ties. "Do you want the car?" he asks over his shoulder.

"No, it's fine. I'll take the train. Kate will pick me up from the station."

"Are you sure? You won't want to be lugging all Freya's stuff on the train, will you? Is this straight?"

"What?" For a minute I'm not sure what he's on about, and then I realize—the tie. "Oh, yes, it's straight. No, honestly, I'm happy to take the train. It'll be easier; I can feed Freya if she wakes up. I'll just put all her stuff in the bottom of the pram." He doesn't respond, and I realize he's already running through the day ahead, ticking things off a mental checklist just as I used to do a few months ago—only it feels like a different life. "Okay, well, look, I might leave today if that's all right with you."

"Today?" He scoops his change off the chest of drawers and puts it in his pocket, and then comes over to kiss me good-bye on the top of my head. "What's the hurry?"

"No hurry," I lie. I feel my cheeks flush. I hate lying. It used to be fun—until I didn't have a choice. I don't think about it much now, perhaps because I've been doing it for so long, but it's always there, in the background, like a tooth that always aches and suddenly twinges with pain.

Most of all, though, I hate lying to Owen. Somehow I always managed to keep him out of the web, and now he's being drawn in. I think of Kate's text, sitting there on my phone, and it feels as if poison is leaching out of it, into the room—threatening to spoil everything.

"It's just Kate's between projects, so it's a good time for her and . . . well, I'll be back at work in a few months, so it just feels like now's as good a time as any."

"Okay," he says, bemused but not suspicious. "Well, I guess I'd better give you a proper good-bye kiss then."

He kisses me, properly, deeply, making me remember why I love him, why I hate deceiving him. Then he pulls away and kisses Freya. She swivels her eyes sideways to regard him suspiciously, pausing in her feed for a moment, and then she resumes sucking with the single-minded determination that I love about her.

"Love you, too, little vampire," Owen says affectionately. Then, to me, "How long is the journey?"

"Four hours, maybe? Depends how the connections go."

"Okay, well, have a great time, and text me when you get there. How long do you think you'll stay?"

"A few days?" I hazard. "I'll be back before the weekend." Another lie. I don't know. I have no idea. As long as Kate needs me. "I'll see when I get there."

"Okay," he says again. "Love you."

"I love you, too." And at last, that's something I can tell the truth about.

I can remember to the day, almost to the hour and minute, the first time I met Kate. It was September. I was catching the train to Salten, an early one, so that I could arrive at the school in time for lunch.

"Excuse me!" I called nervously up the station platform, my voice reedy with anxiety. The girl ahead of me turned around. She was very tall and extremely beautiful, with a long, slightly haughty face like a Modigliani painting. Her waist-length black hair had been bleached gold at the tips, fading into the black, and her jeans were ripped across the thighs.

"Yes?"

"Excuse me, is this the train for Salten?" I panted.

She looked me up and down, and I could feel her appraising me, taking in my Salten House uniform, the navy-blue skirt, stiff with newness, and the pristine blazer I had taken off its hanger for the first time that morning.

"I don't know," she said at last, turning to a girl behind her. "Kate, is this the Salten train?"

"Don't be a dick, Thee," the girl said. Her husky voice sounded too old for her—I didn't think she could be more than sixteen or seventeen. She had light brown hair cut very short, framing her face, and when she smiled at me, the nutmeg freckles across her nose crinkled. "Yes, this is the Salten train. Make sure you get into the right half, though; it divides at Hampton's Lee."

Then they turned, and were halfway up the platform before it occurred to me, I hadn't asked which was the right half.

I looked up at the announcement board.

"Use front seven carriages for stations to Salten," read the display, but what did *front* mean? Front as in the closest to the ticket barrier, or front as in the direction of travel when the train left the station?

There were no officials around to ask, but the clock above my head showed only moments to spare, and in the end I got onto the farther end, where the two other girls had headed for, and dragged my heavy trunk after me into the carriage.

It was a compartment, just six seats, and all were empty. Almost as soon as I had slammed the door the guard's whistle sounded, and, with a horrible feeling that I might be in the wrong part of the train completely, I sat down, feeling the scratchy wool of the train seat harsh against my legs.

With a clank and a screech of metal on metal, the train drew out of the dark cavern of the station, the sun flooding the compartment with a suddenness that blinded me. I put my head back on the seat, closing my eyes against the glare, and as we picked up speed I found myself imagining what would happen if I didn't turn up in Salten, where the house-mistress would be awaiting me. What if I were swept off to Brighton or Canterbury or somewhere else completely, or worse—what if I ended up split down the middle when the train divided, living two lives, each diverging from the other all the time, growing further and further apart from the me I should have become.

"Hello," said a voice, and my eyes snapped open. "I see you made the train."

It was the tall girl from the platform, the one the other had called Thee. She was standing in the doorway to my compartment, leaning against the wooden frame, twirling an unlit cigarette between her fingers.

"Yes," I said, a little resentful that she and her friend had not waited to explain which end to get. "At least, I hope so. This is the right end for Salten, isn't it?"

"It is," the girl said laconically. She looked me up and down again, tapped her unlit cigarette against the doorframe, and then said, with an air of someone about to confer a favor, "Look, don't think I'm being a bitch, but I just wanted to let you know, people don't wear their uniforms on the train."

"What?"

"They change into them at Hampton's Lee. It's . . . I don't know. It's just a thing. I thought I'd tell you. Only first-years and new girls wear them for the whole journey. It kind of makes you stand out."

"So . . . you're at Salten House, too?"

"Yup. For my sins."

"Thea got expelled," a voice said from behind her, and I saw that the other girl, the short-haired one, was standing in the corridor, balancing two cups of tea. "From three other schools. Salten's her last-chance saloon. Nowhere else would take her."

"At least I'm not a charity case," Thea said, but I could tell from the way she said it that the two were friends, and this goading banter was part of their act. "Kate's father is the art master," she told me. "So a free place for his daughter is all part of the deal."

"No chance of Thea qualifying for charity," Kate said. *Silver spoon*, she mouthed over the top of her teas, and winked. I tried not to smile.

She and Thea shared a look and I felt some wordless question and answer pass between them, and then Thea spoke.

"What's your name?"

"Isa," I said.

"Well, Isa. Why don't you come and join me and Kate?" She raised one eyebrow. "We've got a compartment of our own just up the corridor."

I took a deep breath and, with the feeling that I was about to step off a very high diving board, I gave a short nod. As I picked up my case and followed Thea's retreating back, I had no idea that that one simple action had changed my life forever.

Want more?

The Lying Game is in stores now.

THE
WOMAN
IN
CABIN
10

RUTH WARE

A Reading Group Guide

TOPICS AND QUESTIONS
FOR DISCUSSION

1. What's the effect of having Lo's e-mails and various news reports interspersed throughout Lo's narration? In what ways do they help you better understand what's happening aboard the *Aurora*?

2. When Lo first enters the ship, she says, "I had a sudden disorienting image of the *Aurora* as a ship imprisoned in a bottle—tiny, perfect, isolated, and unreal" (p. 41). In what ways does this

statement foreshadow the events that take place on the ship? Describe the *Aurora*. In what ways do you think life on the ship may seem unreal? Discuss the book's title. Why do you think Ware chose it? Did the title influence your reading of the novel? If so, how?

3. Who is Carrie? Did you like her? Why or why not? Describe her relationship with Lo. In what ways, if any, are the two women alike? How do Lo's feelings about Carrie change as Lo gets to know her? Did your opinion of Carrie change as you read?

4. Lo questions Alexander about eating fugu during dinner aboard the *Aurora*, and he tells her that the fact it is poisonous is "what *makes* the experience" (p. 85). What does Alexander mean by his statement? Lo seems dubious about the appeal of it. Does Lo strike you as someone who takes risks? Were you surprised by any of her risky actions aboard the *Aurora*? Which ones, if any?

5. After Lo's flat is burglarized, she calls *Velocity*'s assistant features editor, Jenn, and tells her about it. Lo says, "I told her what happened, making it sound funnier and more farcical than it really had been" (p. 14). Why do you think Lo underplays the break-in? How might this make her feel more in control? Have you ever underplayed an event of significance in your life?

6. When Lo panics on one of her first nights aboard the *Aurora*, she says, "I imagined burying my face in Judah's shoulder and for a second I nearly burst into tears, but I clenched my teeth and swallowed them back down. Judah was not the answer to all

this" (p. 55–56). Why is Lo so resistant to accepting help from Judah? Do you think that she's right to be reticent? Describe their relationship. Do Lo and Judah support each other?

7. When Nilsson challenges Lo's claim that she's seen something happen in the cabin next to hers, she tells him, "Yes, someone broke into my flat. It has *nothing to do with what I saw*" (p. 162). Did you believe her? Did you think that the break-in made Lo more jumpy and distrustful? Give some examples to support your opinion.

8. When Lo first speaks to Richard Bullmer, she notices that he gives her "a little wink" (p. 90). What is the effect of this gesture? What were your initial impressions of Bullmer? Did you like him, or were you suspicious of him? After a prolonged conversation with Bullmer, Lo says, "I could see why [he] had got to where he had in life" (p. 222). Describe his manner. What does Lo think accounts for his success?

9. Archer tells Lo that self-defense is "not about size, even a girl like you can overpower a man if you get the leverage right" (p. 83). Is Lo able to do so? What kind of leverage does she have? What different kinds of power and leverage do the people on the *Aurora* use when dealing with each other? How did you react?

10. Judah tells Lo that "I still think, in spite of it all, we're responsible for our own actions" (p. 384). Do you agree? In what scenes did you think the deception and violence that occurred were justified? In what scenes did you think they were not justified?

11. When Lo sees the staff quarters on the *Aurora*, she says, "the rooms were no worse than plenty of cross-channel ferries I'd traveled on. . . . But it was the graphic illustration of the gap between the haves and have-nots that was upsetting" (p. 129). Contrast the guest quarters to those of the crew. Why does Lo find the discrepancy so unsettling? Much of the crew seemed unwilling to speak to Lo. Do you think this was caused by the "gap between the haves and have-nots"? Or some other reason?

12. Lo tells Judah, "You don't know what goes on in other people's relationships" (p. 384). Describe the relationships in *The Woman in Cabin 10*. Did you find any particularly surprising? Which ones, and why?

13. Bullmer tells Lo, "Why wait? . . . One thing I've learned in business—now almost always *is* the right time" (p. 218). Do you agree with his philosophy? In what ways has this attitude led to Bullmer's success? Does this attitude present any problems aboard the *Aurora*? Do you think Lo shares the same life philosophy as Bullmer? How would you describe Lo's philosophy on life?

14. Describe Lo's relationship with Ben. She tells him "[e]verything I hadn't told Jude. What it had been like . . . that I was vulnerable in a way I'd never thought I was before that night" (p. 94). Why does Lo share all this information with Ben rather than Jude? Did you think that Ben had Lo's best interests at heart? Why or why not? Were you surprised to learn of their history?

ENHANCE YOUR BOOK CLUB

1. Ware's debut novel, *In a Dark, Dark Wood*, received rave reviews when it was first published and was named a best book of the year by NPR and Shelf Awareness. Read *In a Dark, Dark Wood* with your book club, then compare and contrast the two books. In what ways are they similar? How has Ware's writing style evolved since she published her debut novel?

2. Richard Bullmer tells his guests, "The aurora borealis is something that everyone should see before they die" (p. 73). Look at pictures of the northern lights with your book club. Do you find them as breathtaking as Richard Bullmer does? Would you travel to see the northern lights as the guests of the *Aurora* plan on doing?

3. Lo says, "*Pooh* has always been my comfort read, my go-to book in times of stress" (p. 320). Why might *Pooh* bring Lo comfort? Do you have any "comfort reads"? Share them with your book club, and describe what you find so comforting about the books.

ABOUT THE AUTHOR

© Ollie Grove

Ruth Ware grew up in Sussex, on the south coast of England. After graduating from Manchester University, she moved to Paris before settling in North London. She has worked as a waitress, a bookseller, a teacher of English as a foreign language and a press officer, and is the internationally bestselling author of *In a Dark, Dark Wood*, *The Woman in Cabin 10*, and *The Lying Game*. She is married with two small children. Visit her at **www.ruthware.com**.

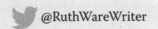 @RuthWareWriter